MW01532649

WORTH

OF

LUCK

K.A. Ashcomb

Glorious Mishaps Series

Liquid Hare Publishing

WORTH OF LUCK

Contact me:
k.a.ashcomb@gmail.com
Follow my blog:
https://ashcombka.com

Cover Design by K.A. Ashcomb
Contact: http://soldevia.cl
Edited by Silvia Curry
Contact: https://www.silviasreading.webs.com

To Henri
For his support, his advice, and his sense of humor, which never failed.

ACKNOWLEDGMENTS

A special thanking are needed for those who helped me to complete this book. Writing *Worth of Luck* and publishing it wouldn't have been possible without their support. Foremost, thank you for my husband, Henri, who carried me through the tough times and never let me give up, who is always pushing me to be the best version of myself. Special thanks to my friend Emma, who said I have a gift for storytelling. Thank you for Juho who beta read my book and pointed out its weaknesses. Thank you for Sol Devia who created an amazing cover which entraps me. Thank you for my editor, Silvia Curry, making my text better. And thank you for my family who for some incomprehensible reason believes in me.

Worth of Luck

CHAPTER ONE
In the Sewers

I
t has always been highly debated amongst the gods who masters the destinies of men. Of course, most of them thought they did, but then again, the silly buggers did things they weren't supposed to do and thus, the whole debate began. Uncontrollable masses were not something the gods wanted, as such things would be disastrous for them. Who knew if people would, at some point, decide altogether they didn't need their superiors to show the way and went and did things the way they wanted. That was not how it should go. So, the gods watched, nudging here and there, pushing and pulling.

They were always there.

* * *

A mouse's head lay on a smooth stone altar. The head's flesh had long since rotted away, and now its empty eye sockets peered into the darkness. Candles placed around the head made it look ominous whenever the flames cast their light the right way. *If you were into such ambiance.* For any careless glancer, it was just a skull, which had met the ultimate decider: entropy or a cat. Beyond the altar came the sounds of rustling fabric and people arguing. The noises pierced the head's ear sockets, disturbing its slumber. It would rather be at the usual place, inside a velvet cloth bag, seeing into the future and the past, yet never being in the presence. The skull knew what was to come, and that was people getting killed for lousy reasons, like greed, vanity, and for the ultimate mystery to the mouse's head, boredom.

The sound emanated from a small group of nine people.

The skull knew one amongst them would die. Of course, all of them were eventually going to meet the reaper, but that would come a lot later. The death, or this silly ritual or anything really, had nothing to do with it. The head was just happy to still have a working mind and the ability to hop around the world to witness reality unfolding. Not that it cared for reality much—there was something horribly wrong with existence. It was like this ultimate test, and in the end, you get to find out it was all for nothing and you didn't do enough.

"The goat's head will work, trust me," a hooded fellow said. He wore a thick, crow-black robe. They always did, the skull had noticed.

"Are you sure? It didn't work last Friday, and we already trusted you more than once," another fellow said, dressed in a similar robe. He was hopping from one foot to another, staying agile for the upcoming ritual.

"Yeah, but that was last Friday. Now there's a full moon and everything. It will work," the first one said.

"If you say so. Now put the goat's head on the altar," a third hooded fellow said, wrinkling his nose.

The first fellow walked to the milk-white altar. He took the mouse's head between his thumb and index finger and looked behind him, and from under his hood came a sigh of contempt.

The mouse's head didn't mind the whole thing being picked up. The skull was just a conduit for its presence, and there was no attachment. Really, truly, there wasn't. Still, if it could speak, it would have asked if the fellow might scratch the itch it had at the back of its skull for a decade, if it was no bother.

"I don't know what you thought bringing a mouse's head with you," the first one said, looking at a smaller man standing in the back row. The first one knew full well the smaller man had brought the head—it was just his style to bring something so disgusting.

The smaller man said with a quiet voice, "It brings me luck. The last year has been nothing but marvelous for me. I'm getting married and all that. I wanted to share my fortune." With all the confidence he could muster, he tried to stare down the hooded fellow at the altar, but failed.

The mouse's head wanted to hide from its keeper, but again, things got very murky at the spirit level. Less so, if it happened to live at Necropolis, where the dead roamed the street, but the mouse's head didn't. So, here it was, stuck with whatever this was suppose to be.

"Ha, lies. A mouse's head can't bring luck. It has to be a goat's head; everyone knows that," the first one said. He had a knack for letting his disgust be known.

The smaller man straightened to his full height. "Then you don't mind if I take it back," he said with a hint of defiance.

The fellow at the altar snorted.

The others let out a sheepish laugh as he dropped the mouse's head.

The hooded fellow dove to catch the skull before it hit the sewer floor. He sighed with relief as the lucky head smacked into his open palm.

The midnight ritual continued after the embarrassing incident, and no one mentioned the mouse's head again. They moved around the goat's head at first clockwise, then counterclockwise, waving their hands and chanting nonsense words meant to bring the assembled people luck. The mouse's head slumbered inside its keeper's pocket, sensing the rhythm of their movements and hearing their words echoing through the sewers. But it wasn't fully there. It also was at the cosmic level, feeling the tides to change. It sniffed a lot of blood and a lot more corpses to come. It was that time of the cycle again... People had to die for the thrones.

Next to the chanting assemblage, the kingdom's filth oozed through the sewer canal, occasionally gurgling when it digested something odd or too big for its own good. If you looked at the sludge closely, you might see discarded treasures, along with body parts and other useless things people throw away. It was a good thing the altar next to the canal was the only thing illuminated. The sewer's gurgling and other noises were enough to get on the chanters' nerves. They tried to drown the noise by saying their words louder and without pause, though it was a futile effort.

Of course, they had the option of moving the altar somewhere else, but the waste in the other sewers wasn't that much quieter. That sludge had as much to say as the river flowing next to them this night. Right now, the sludge was trying to point out there was a jeweled crown floating past them, and whoever fielded it owned the kingdom. It was unsure which kingdom, but a kingdom nonetheless.

The secret society continued chanting vigorously.

Soon their chant ended; their pleas had been sent to the gods. All of them wanted just little luck toward them, or either they didn't survive in the Kingdom of Leporidae Lop, where your life depended on the luck you could score.

Tonight was the secret society's best night so far. No one could remember the time when as many of them had attended. After tonight's performance, their luck was bound to change. The other secret society groups,[1] with their disgusting habits, would fall from the gods' graces. Tonight's intense chant would guarantee that. If you asked the first hooded fellow— who talked the most in their so-called egalitarian society—the goat's head changed everything. If tonight's ritual failed to get any attention from the gods, it would be because of the

---

[1] Which the city was riddled with.

incident with the mouse's head, not the other way around. The only thing to fix that gaffe was to pray for forgiveness for soiling such a sacred act.

The first hooded fellow did just that. He said a silent prayer to ensure everything had been done the right way. Also, it was always a good thing to end the chant with his voice being the last thing heard, just to be sure.

"Good night," the first hooded fellow said.

"And to you, too," the meek man who had brought the mouse's head said, his voice sounding hoarse.

"Good night," the others repeated.

It was the end of their Thursday practice. They all hurried home from the altar room, hidden in the kingdom's sewer system.

The mouse's head safely slumbered inside its master's pocket, feeling lucky it had never been born as a human. Their lives seemed a whole lot more complicated and moronic for its liking.

* * *

"Sewers, sewers," the first hooded fellow, Edbert Pollock, muttered to himself as he climbed the slimly stairs to get back to the nightly air of Leporidae Lop. *Never again*, he thought. But still, of all the secret society's members, he attended the most and knew he would come back. He had never trusted the power of the word 'never.' It was a slippery fellow, making one take back their words more than once.

Edbert would swallow his pride over and over again for luck's sake, as he'd done many times before, climbing up and down the slime-coated stairs. Yet, as always, he now swore this to be the last time, hoping the next time they would meet at an abandoned manor or under the royal palace of White Cuniculus, which would mean the secret society had made the big time. He kept dreaming their society would rise from the sewers to their rightful place on the kingdom's social ladder—but so did all the other secret societies in the city with their luck rituals. Such was the game he and other Leporidae lops played.

The only way to make it in the kingdom was through luck, and the most efficient way to get luck was through the secret society meetings. There's strength in numbers when it comes to milking the gods. And you needed gods for luck, since charms did work—only for the small stuff, like finding a penny or two. And while a penny bought you your bread, it didn't give an entire future.

"Holy Lop," Edbert groaned as his hand ached for squeezing the metallic stairs for the seven-hundred and forty-second time. The two-hundred and nineteenth time had almost sent Edbert spiraling into madness. He had sworn never to come back, pray to the gods, and carry the wretched goat's head with him anywhere. Edbert had failed on every count, even with swearing off not swearing.

Every Thursday he let the stairs try to murder him, his old body no longer what it used to be, and the stairs being their usual self—slippery bastards; the prominent goat's head traveling with him. Edbert stubbornly clung to the belief the goat's head worked. The same head had worked for his father and his grandfather before him, so surely, it would work for him and his miserable group. Or else. Edbert couldn't even think about the 'or else' bit.

Bringing a mouse's head to the meeting had been utter rubbish. Mice can't be lucky. Their whole essence told a tale of vermin. They were not a creature for kings, and least of all, for gods.

He needed the gods on his side.

Edbert finally got out in the night air. He was the first to climb up. He took his spot in the darkened corner to watch everyone else hurry home, avoiding being seen by the others. Everyone committed to the secrecy part in their little society, and for Edbert, the society part annoyed him the most. He hated people and their mistakes. If only he could worship, bribe, or extort the gods to do his bidding alone, everything would be perfect. But no, gods wanted masses, and now everything wrong in life existed because Josh, Carrol, Mary, Mike, or someone else didn't do their part right.

Of course, he knew who attended. It had taken him two months to discern all the secret society members' identities, so none of them could call Edbert Pollock a fool. Josh was the meek man with a passion for the mouse's head. How dare he call the mouse's head lucky.

Edbert sneered. *Being a clerk at the public library wasn't lucky.*

Water dripped from a nearby building's rooftop, spattering the top of Edbert's velvet hood. The water almost washed away the rotten smell of waste he had grown accustomed to, but still, the stench coming from his robes made him turn up his nose.

At the back of his mind, the doubting Edbert woke up. He deemed this night's ritual to be fruitless, like usual. He blamed Josh's naïve optimism for driving away his chance for salvation. Josh must irritate the gods as much as he did him. Or it was the stupid name they called themselves, the Order of Regulators, that repelled the gods away.

Edbert pushed the sewer grate into place when he thought no one was there. The grate clattered as it slid in, sealing the sewers off from unwanted visitors.

But he wasn't alone. Somewhere beyond his vision, even past the mouse's head radar, sat a girl on a rooftop, watching Edbert. She tilted her head, unsure what to make of the old man. A meeting by chance or her destiny, the girl wasn't sure. Neither was Edbert, who had no clue he was being observed. He was too focused on thinking that whoever had come up with their society's name was nuts. It had to be the mouse head boy; Edbert wouldn't put it past him. But Josh hadn't attended the meetings when the order had been first established, nor, for that matter, had he. Before the Order of Regulators, Edbert had belonged to a group called the Cadetblue Dot Order—an even unluckier group than his new society.

Edbert forced a smile to his lips. He had no choice. And he could always keep blaming Josh for everything else that went wrong. He had to be guilty of something, a little fellow like that.

Then there was Mary. Her quest to get luck to breed cats to her specific want made Edbert shutter. She spoke only about creating the ultimate cat breed, which none could resist. Edbert had always been scared of cats, and animals altogether. And if Mary succeeded, it would be an end to him. Okay, he was in his eighties, so it might not be such a shame, yet he wasn't ready to throw in the towel, not yet. He had still years ahead of him—if his father's and grandfather's age was any indication.

Edbert turned around to head home. Next to him, on the quiet streets of Leporidae Lop, the tall residential buildings rose with their beige walls and huge windows, flowerpots resting on their sills. He had time to watch at the darkened windows and ponder the lives being lived behind them as his painful hip made his movements slow. His hip had stopped working properly forty years ago, and it had gradually gotten worse since. He massaged the hip to make it functional for a while longer until he got to home.

Once he was farther away, Edbert took off his hood, again thinking he was alone. But there, in the rainy air, someone followed him, watching his every move. The girl wasn't the only one. The gods had stirred; they saw him and what he desired. Damned if they were not going to deliver.

Edbert's body ached as the rain fell harder. His ash-white hair, which he kept trimmed short, got wet from the drizzle. He smoothed his hair with his spotted, wrinkled hand and looked around, having his back hair crept up. Edbert had piercing blue eyes, and they almost made the grumpy old man charming enough to fool others into thinking there was a kind heart underneath his shabby exterior, but there wasn't. There had never been time to grow a kind heart or opportunity to make it better. Just history, the lousy kind.

But there was no one to observe him. The streets were clearly empty—as they should be past midnight. This time of night was special in Leporidae Lop. Proper ceremonies were held at midnight as it was the only time when the gods listened.

They were peculiar that way. Sometimes Edbert thought the gods were completely bonkers, though he would never say that aloud. Without the gods, he wouldn't survive in the kingdom for even a week.

People whispered that the most powerful figures in Leporidae Lop had personal relationships with the gods. That they came down from the heavens or crawled up from the ground to give their luck to the special ones. Edbert wanted that, his own personal god. With one, life was a smooth ride into happiness, and in his case, becoming a distinguishable figure in the kingdom he loved.

Edbert's grandfather had once been in a god's favor. They had given him a start with his livelihood and made sure he flourished—hence the building Edbert now stepped into, three blocks from the sewer grate; a building where he'd lived all his life.

The door creaked shut behind him.

The building was old. The structure's rough stones leaned against its timber frames, which leaned against the stones. The force they put on each other kept the place standing, but soon another force might make the building collapse. The kingdom's Palace Housing Committee wanted to tear Edbert's home down, or so they'd threatened him. Edbert had received dozens of seizure orders, but thus far, he had been able to fight off the ridiculous claims. If luck didn't intervene soon, he might not be able to continue defending his shop, being an old man and all. He would fail his legacy.

The committee claimed his shop made the kingdom ugly and jeopardized the safety of its customers. Edbert snorted. The building had served his grandfather and father well, and he lived here, for Holy Lop's sake. It should suit the rest of the snobby kingdom. He would fight against the palace, even if it took him to an early grave.

What made Edbert angrier was he'd served the committee members well. He'd helped them educate themselves so they could get to their esteemed positions, and now they dared to repay him by demolishing his bookshop and home. Edbert shook his fist at no one in particular—maybe at life and the universe in general; and everyone knew those two deserved all they got. But shaking his fist didn't do a lot of good; all it did was make his arthritis flare up.

Edbert dropped the goat's head, clutched his right hand, and wailed in pain.

He cursed the pain.

The bookshop was his whole life. How dare they take it away from him?

The goat's head had to work.

He picked the head up and placed it on his work desk. He sat down and massaged his hand.

His work desk, where he repaired old books, doubled as the shop's counter. The desk had bowed under the weight of all the books he'd placed upon it, and one of the table legs had collapsed. Now a thick leather-bound tome kept the desk steady. On its back, in faded golden letters, was the title: *The Practical Way to Make Your Business Work*. The book had helped hold up the desk ever since Edbert had taken over the business from his father. The book would continue to prop the table up until the world ended, or the shop was demolished. Both very good possibilities as the gods were hungry again. And Edbert was just the perfect tool for what was to come.

Edbert sighed and opened a huge volume lying open on the table. Every page of *The Pantheon of Gods* was worn out. He flipped through the tome yet again, in hopes of finding a solution to his problems. There had to be a god for him who could help.

CHAPTER TWO
Hairy Feet

The next morning, in the sewers beneath the royal palace of White Cuniculus, the god of luck scratched its stomach. Then it moved to lick its white feet, going over every inch of them. Then its right foot slowly lifted behind its gray ear and began to hit the spot again and again. The god finally let out a huge sigh as an itch melted away.

Now the god could concentrate on getting out of the gloomy iron cage it was trapped in. To tell the truth, the god wasn't an 'it'—the god of luck was gender neutral, or at least, it was so for mere mortals. The god knew its sex, but wretched if it would tell that to the dumb humans. They seemed to be oddly curious about things, like what's in your pants.

Anyway, yes, it's essential to be able to separate gods from each other, but that has nothing to do with their sex. With their names, yes, but sex, no. Names are important, especially on those rare occasions when a god is trying to murder you during their bouts of drunken boredom. Luckily, that only happens once in every millennium, but during those moments, it's extremely important to curse with the right name, so as not to enrage another god in the process. One might think to add the word 'innocent' before the 'god' part, but that would be a mistake. Gods aren't innocent, not even close.

Of all the gods in the world, only one god symbolizes luck with such strength that it overshadows all the others, and that's the rabbit god of luck, whose feet are famously fateful. They can alter the course of the entire universe, your life, or a football match without a second thought.

All in all, the luckiest of all gods had gotten itself trapped inside an iron cage. One might mistakenly think gods can't be trapped, but that's an absurd notion. There's always a way, and a stack of sweet, juicy carrots had done the trick for the rabbit. Instead of enjoying itself in a local pub, dressed as a human and drinking a carrot cocktail,[2] the rabbit was now stuck inside a circular cage with iron bars that curved at the top, forming a hoop to hold the cage together. The cage reminded the god of a birdcage, but the rabbit refused to chirp.

The cage's bars stood inches apart, keeping the god in, while leaving enough room for its feet to stick out. That's the way its life seemed to work. It and its mind held nothing against the infamous feet.

Usually, the rabbit could easily walk through objects, but the iron in the cage was made with it especially in mind.

The rabbit god of luck sat back in the middle of the cage to meditate on what the future might bring. Usually, it brought a wrinkled old woman in a foul mood—and this time wasn't any different.

A clicking sound disturbed the god's meditation. The rabbit opened one of its black eyes and watched as the woman descended into the sewer.

The rabbit shut its eyes and went back to meditating.

Click, clack, clack, click, clack, clack, the woman's shoes echoed, pouncing off the walls and arriving at the rabbit's ears. It shook its pink nose and rubbed its right front paw on its huge, velutinous ear. It rubbed its ear again to reassure itself to be able to face her.

---

[2] Its invention.

Click, clack, clack... the echo of her shoes went on in the damp sewer.

The rabbit wanted to shiver but used its godly powers not to... or more simply put, it chose not to.

The rabbit god of luck opened its eyes and watched the horrible woman—whose youthful beauty had long-since vanished—approach its cage. Her lovely face had become a lined mask which could scare armies away, and did so on special occasions. Everyone in the kingdom, and far outside it, knew not to mess with her, as the ramifications were beyond nightmarish. Not even the god of luck dared to contradict the woman, despite being able to trick the hearts of men.

Sometimes the god tried to stand up to her when it was in the right kind of mood—it was still a god and all that—but the act never amounted to anything. A mere smile from the woman's tight, light red lips drove strong men and women insane, and a scold from her could kill anyone on the spot... or so they said.

It would be a mistake to think the woman as a queen or a wicked witch—those positions were too low for her. She was more powerful than the evil found in storybooks. She was the guardian of the kingdom's chest or, in modern terms, the prime minister of Leporidae Lop.

The prime minister was tall and slender, looking like a woman who had run marathon after marathon for the better part of her life. Her short black hair curled behind her ears, and a dash of dark gray had snuck into her front hair, which was kept in place with a plain bobby pin. The touch of gray made her look distinguished. However, the thin glasses framing her face took that away, and she looked more headstrong than anything else.

The god of luck shuddered as she came closer. The lines on her face were stern and the twinkle in her eyes meant something bad would happen. Its stomach twisted into a tight knot. To gain peace, the rabbit reverted back to meditating, which was an impossible task to do in the face of inevitable doom.

The prime minister stopped next to the cage.

The god tried not to let its body show any sign of weakness.

The woman held her hands behind her back, making the rabbit wait for its prize, which it knew would come. Its ears vibrated in the same way as a cat's tail does when a can of tuna was opened. The rest of the rabbit tensed with anticipation.

If the god of luck had a weaker mind, it would launch against the bars, but no, the rabbit sat there, scratching its gray side with white spots instead.

The prime minister produced a carrot from behind her back and dangled it in the air, making the rabbit's eyes twitch.

The battle of wills went on for a while, and she finally had to yield. "Come on," she said. "I know you want it."

The rabbit's body moved an inch without asking permission.

"Come on," she said again, and the smile stayed on her lips.

The rabbit's perfect pink nose shook.

Soon after, its whole body ached. The carrot's sweet smell was too strong. Slowly, it stuck its gray foot through the bars, wanting to squeak, but that didn't seem right being a god and all that. The rabbit held its mouth shut and let the woman pet its foot.

The rabbit's toes convulsed from her touch. In a different situation, the god of luck would have enjoyed the light petting, but her stroking only reminded it how the mighty can fall.

The god watched the prime minister to ride the ecstatic tingling sensation flowing from its paw into her hand, and from there, to the rest of her body. All the luck in the world poured into the woman. What she would do with it was not the rabbit god of luck's problem. Humans were good at making their existence unnecessarily complicated. The god had never understood the whole purpose of kingdoms, prime ministers, and governance all together. Carrots were real, and so was a flowery meadow or a roaring sea. Kingdoms were dreams built upon shared stories. But the humans seemed to like telling stories and making them real, so who was it to deny their ways?

The woman let go of its foot. There was only a slight sparkle of luck left inside the god. It would generate and this would happen again. It needed to get out, and soon.

* * *

As luck from the rabbit poured into Prime Minister Harriet Stowe, she hummed with a loud, purring voice. She hadn't meant to, but every time she did this, her body succumbed to the weirdness the pure luck made her feel. The luck moving inside her would ensure her victory over all the little matters running the kingdom made her battle with. Currently, it was the frizzled bookshop owner who kept defying her.

Harriet Stowe rarely had obstacles in life, at least, not for years. She had been running this racket as long as most could remember. Acquiring the rabbit god of luck had made sure that the little hiccups were gone. Of course, she had been playing the game of luck even before trapping the god—so it was done—but having a personal access made everything a whole lot easier. Before that, and presently, she relied on the fact that most of the population feared her, including the king and queen. So, you could say everyone in Leporidae Lop obeyed her to their fullest. In a sense, the bookshop owner's defiance made life more exciting. For now, she had tried to tackle him with committees and other legal routes, but those clearly weren't working. The man had luck on his side, and to battle luck, you needed luck. So it went; meaning she had to crush the man for the sake of the kingdom.

Harriet let go of the rabbit's soft foot.

The god watched her with its huge watery eyes when it took its foot back into the cage. Harriet tossed in the carrot and watched as the rabbit jumped at it. The god devoured the carrot with a mixture of snorting, licking, and rubbing against it. She turned her head away, leaving the rest of the carrots just outside the cage.

She hurried off, though hurrying might be the wrong word

to describe her flight.

Harriet moved away more slowly than she liked to. A slight misstep might dislocate her bony knees, and even now, they crackled as she walked. Years hadn't been kind to her. Of course, she could always ask luck to fix her knees, but for as long as she could remember, she'd put the kingdom's matters first.

In the background, the rabbit ate. Harriet was sure she heard a chirp in there somewhere. As she got to the door, a sigh of relief swept through her. Harriet carefully locked the door open behind her and collapsed against it, having escaped back to the palace.

Harriet actually liked the sewers more than the palace—they were simpler. The former kings and queens had overly decorated the palace with golden vines and rabbits. And someone had thought it was a good idea to hang paintings of the old rulers and aristocrats on every wall; their eyes seemed to follow her everywhere she went. But that was how palaces were; they came with the necessary pompousness, and with huge rugs, which took at least ten servants to clean.

It wasn't the sewer that made her nervous or the rabbit's disconcerting eating manners. Harriet just didn't care for the methods she had to resort to.

She straightened her back, smoothed her black high neckline dress, and walked away, slipping the sewer key against her chest. The palace staff and clerks hurried away at the sight of her—some even squealed and weren't ashamed to do so.

Harriet had gotten used to the sound. And she wasn't ashamed of making others squirm in front of her. It was the price to be paid for a perfectly running kingdom. Not that anything could be ever perfect, but at least she could strive to manifest the closest harmony one could achieve.

Harriet walked to her office on the second floor of the palace. She tried not to wince as she took the stairs and as her knees crackled from every step she took. She followed the line of golden flowers painted on the railings to the one corridor the king and queen had left plain, where she held her audiences. Already a huge endless line squirmed, waiting for her. Scared and impatient citizens were there to have an audience with her, waiting to be guided with their mundane problems. Others might hate the constant decision-making and putting into other people's business, but Harriet thrived on it. To her, it was power in its best and purest form. She was part of the kingdom. Of course, she handled the public, legal, and monetary affairs of the Leporidae Lop, but she saw those tasks as the icing on the cake. It was the people who made the kingdom, not the rules and laws.

The crowd stiffened as she passed them. She heard their murmurs and whispers. There were a lot of words used to describe her, so many that she'd forgotten some. Dragon lady was the one she liked the most, but that wasn't what they used of her the most. It was the ones which rhymed with witch, and all the other flattering words women get called. She didn't mind the name calling; it meant she did something right. She had always believed in what her mother had said to her and her little sister when they were young. 'You can't make a cake without breaking the eggs.' Such a silly saying, truly. But when it came to politics, it was one that she was reminded of constantly. Something old always broke when something new was created.

And Harriet couldn't deny she wasn't made to rule. It made her so happy to tell everyone how to live their lives and see they did as she told them. The kingdom was proof that her tactics worked. There was no society on the whole continent that functioned better than Leporidae Lop.

She walked past the line and stepped into her office, which wasn't much bigger than a broom closet. Her desk barely fit, and the two chairs for the audience seekers made it impossible to turn around or walk without bumping into something. The four bookcases circling the room took up the rest of the space, but they were necessary, as they were filled from top to bottom with law books, kingdom documents, and other essential papers Harriet used daily. The only unnecessary items in the room were the two chairs, and she insisted on them being there. They made the audience seekers more at ease with her. Most of the time, they were so nervous, they could not get their words out. More often than not, the comfort of sitting down and squeezing their hands against the chairs' manchettes made them stammer out the basic outlines of their troubles. They always said enough for Harriet to piece together what to do.

The small room also had its advantages when it came to minor things, like assassination attempts, angry mobs with pitchforks, and draught. There simply wasn't room to form a mob or even get angry enough to swing a blade. There was room to get claustrophobic, but that was not one of Harriet's concerns. She was more afraid of the draught, the silent killer of the elderly. But the closed space stayed warm, so warm it pampered Harriet's weak knees.

She sat behind her desk, smiling a huge smile, and ordered the first audience seeker to come in. A perfect start for a perfect day.

Before a young man with thick brown hair and coarse hands sat down and opened his mouth, she had already solved his problem. "Rent your fields for now and collect money from them until you can stand on your own two feet. After you have settled your loans and got the smaller patch of your farm working, then you can get the fields back and expand. You can't keep borrowing and hoping the bad situation takes a turn for the best," she said.

The young man opened and shut his mouth without making any noise. As Harriet hurried him out, he let out a shriek of relief.

Harriet said nothing and smiled. They thought what she did was magic, and she let them think that. It was better for her reputation than the thought she had eyes and ears everywhere.

Time and again, the audience seekers came to her with their simple problems with easy, predictable solutions. On rare occasions, she had to strain her brain, but only when the interests of different people clashed, and seldom cutting them in half solved anything. But in the end, she always fixed their issues, not always to the subject's liking, which, actually, was quite seldom. People tend to think they are in control of their own lives and the decisions they make, but Harriet begged to differ.

She was.

The squirming line went home at the end of the day, but they would be back tomorrow. The prime minister stretched her hands over her head, making her scapula snap. A pressure she'd felt since morning was gone, and she groaned.

"You out there, come here," she said.

Her new assistant rushed in. *They never seemed to last*, she thought. People never did; and for a short moment, she got stuck inside her memories, seeing the face of her late husband. She pushed such useless thoughts away and met the assistant's gaze.

The assistant smelled of spices and cinnamon rolls, and he looked scared to death. He wore the black palace uniform and almost looked presentable. He tried to hold his posture high, but a slight tremble in his hands betrayed his uneasiness.

"Take the papers and file them," she said.

"Yes, sir," he said and hurried to the records Harriet kept of all her audiences. The assistant relaxed.

"Why haven't you come in earlier and filed the papers after every audience?" she asked.

The boy's tremble came back. "I'm sorry, ma'am… I mean, sir—"

"Ma'am is fine," Harriet said and smiled.

"This is my first day; I didn't know what you wanted of me."

"I see. Why didn't you come and ask?"

"I didn't want to bother you, ma'am."

"So, you have sat outside the office, twiddling your thumbs instead? No, don't answer," she said, lifting her hand. "From now on, come and take the files as soon as I'm finished with an audience. And occasionally pop your head in to see if I need anything: food, coffee…"

"Yes, ma'am."

"It's a start. If you can manage that, we can see what else you can do. If our new working relationship goes well, you can call me Harriet, but until then, ma'am or prime minister will do."

"Ma'am," he said, nodding.

He took the papers and left her alone.

He wouldn't last. Those nerves of his would get the better of him. She gave him a week. If he lasted longer than that, she'd misjudged him, but she doubted that. Harriet turned her attention back to the political issues stacked on her table, which took her the rest of the night.

When she finished the last file, she ordered the assistant to come in. "After filing these, go home to get some sleep. I want you here at sunrise."

The poor boy wouldn't get any sleep tonight, but he had to learn. In their line of work, days were long and rest was for the dead and forgotten.

Harriet yawned and remembered the issue which she should have solved today. She cursed. How on earth had the bookshop owner slipped her mind?

Harriet snorted, opened the bottom drawer to take out a bundle of carrots, and walked out.

CHAPTER THREE
The Gods Are Peculiar Folk

utside the royal palace of White Cuniculus, the kingdom of Leporidae Lop opened up. It had come a long way from the farming days. Now the streets were packed full of people, businesses, theaters, coffee shops, and the rest people could think of, forcing the kingdom to expand outward to make room for its ever-growing population.

The palace stood in the heart of Leporidae Lop, and it had been so two hundred years now. The king's great-great-great-great-grandfather had conquered the land underneath the building. He'd sailed there overseas and fell in love with the lofty, green fields, perfect for herding cows and sheep, and growing wheat and carrots, bringing with him his gods and customs of luck. Before that, the old lands knew just the whispers of the sea and the sky with their nature gods. Now those gods were gone, hiding underneath the land as the other ones stirred. The ones with names, the ones whose thirst could never be satisfied, just like their flock.

"How interesting," one of the named ones said aloud and laughed.

"You can't help but marvel at humans and their ways,"

another one said.

The pleas humans sent to their gods bombarded the new ones' consciousness sharply after midnight and continued for about an hour or so. The most tenacious luck seekers extended their chant with an additional hour. It didn't help, as the gods instantly ignored them, as the extended words were like a guest who had stayed past their welcome. If you asked the gods, humans were a pester and should be obliterated. But there was the small, tiny, annoying, little thing that prevented them from flooding the plains and scorching the earth—they needed humans and their constant chatter. As long as humans saw the gods as the source of prosperity, and as long as they believed in them, they continued to exist. Simple as that. That didn't mean the gods had to succumb to be their slaves. No.

The key to granting wishes was a subtle balance between what to give and what not to give, and most importantly, who to give luck to. The game was played on a neighborhood level. It was enough to grant a wish for a few to make sure the rest kept believing in their jealous rage and continued refining their performance. Undoubtedly, the mistakes they made in their rituals were the reason ensuring their neighbors' better horse, wife, and a miraculous cure for baldness.

For the gods, the resulting bickering and resentment was a great source of amusement, along with the foolish acts humans willingly put themselves through to get what their hearts' desired. Still, wish-granting, as a whole, was an important business and couldn't be taken too lightly.

The gods tuned in to listen as the chatter poured in. They made complex calculations to balance the right mood with their own chanters. If they could schedule this so only one worshiper prayed at a time, it would be a lot easier task to do; but then sorting out the wishes would take up their whole time. An hour daily was better than constantly listening to humans' petty problems. And if mistakes were made, it wasn't really the infallible gods' fault; surely, the chanter must have done something wrong.

"What do they need all those things for?" one of the gods

asked.

"Who knows? Just give them what they ask, and they are happy and will come back for more."

"Are you sure?"

"Sure as anyone can be. They seem to have an insatiable need for something, anything they can get their tiny little hands on."

"All right, here goes the third muted mother-in-law for tonight. Why do they keep insisting on that?"

"Who knows? Next time answer the mother-in-law's prayers. That will show them."

But nothing is ever free, or so they say. Even the smallest gratitude can be bent and twisted in the right, devious hands into lifelong debt. And gods weren't in this for the goodness of their hearts.[3] You could say when the time was right—and soon it was—they would come to collect, refusing to forget the tiniest favor given—and they do add on when you have a mind that likes to tally up the score.[4]

* * *

Elsewhere, right in the middle of Leporidae Lop, cobblestones clicked under a cart's wheels, waking up the whole neighborhood. As the cart moved on, people went to their frozen windows to yell curses. The cold morning air forced them back inside.

In spite of the air, one elderly lady tried to scream unspeakable things. By the time she opened her mouth for a third time, the cold air leapt into her throat and made all the words stick. She staggered back inside the cozy, warm room and fainted on the floor. Her unuttered curses escaped through

---

[3] Not these gods who saw playing games with the destinies of men as a great amusement.

[4] The eternal build-in scorecard installed in the head to ensure fairness in the name of the whole lot's survival, yet never being that fair or life-saving.

her open, drooling mouth, causing havoc and distrust for the rest of the household. In return, she was only found at suppertime, and by then, she was a goner. One of her relatives found joy in her death and did a happy dance because the spiteful old hag would now be silent once and for all.

In the distance, the click of the cart's wheels continued. The elderly lady never left the noise behind, not even in her afterlife. The sound kept haunting her over and again. Because the old hag was a resilient woman, who'd endured a bad marriage, the loss of a child, and a world full of ignorant buffoons who insisted on calling themselves her relatives, she turned the noise into an obscene song to cheer up her otherwise gloomy afterlife.

Despite the old lady's misery, the cart moving through the modern kingdom of Leporidae Lop—the only civilized place in the world, or so its residents thought—had a purpose and a good one, if you asked the rider. But no one ever did. People were too busy enjoying the good life of experiencing operas, theaters, bakeries with fancy cakes, and most of all the marvelous architecture spiced with spite and superiority, letting the reversed side of urban life being buried under the false pretenses of friendliness and cheap fashion.

The fat man riding the cart didn't notice the angry shouts he received. He whistled a joyful, broken tune, which came out of his small mouth. The tune made his round face beam with happiness and calm. There was an intelligent glint in his deep, dark brown eyes.

He watched as the sun rose behind the buildings. The rays hitting the frosted cobblestones, sparkling like diamonds made the fat man smile.

He continued riding, jollily and ignorantly, deeper into the kingdom crammed with homes, shops, and alehouses that the streets barely fitted in there. His whistling wrought more havoc on the weary inhabitants, for whom this forsaken hour wasn't even close to being morning. Only the less fortunate knew this time of day existed at all. None thought his happy tune was the bliss it truly was.

Soon the fat man found a green spot—the only one in four blocks. He hopped off the cart, acting maybe a bit too agile for a man his size. The jolly fellow could move as smooth and silent as a tiger if he wanted to. But the fat man wasn't jolly because of his size; he was jolly because why shouldn't he be? Life was wonderful, full of new experiences and small furry creatures to marvel at. Even the dark vultures circling around the future didn't matter because the future happened at the next moment, and for now, the picture-perfect cold, sunny morning won.

He sat under an aspen tree and closed his eyes, leaving the wooden cart and an old horse unsupervised. Neither of them minded to be left alone to their own devices. Least of all the plain, lifeless, non-magical cart, as not an ounce of thought could be found within its wooden frame.

Another thing could be said about the brown horse with a dash of gray on its sides. The horse always stayed near the man as he had apples, carrots, and other vegetables tucked under his sleeve. Instantly, a huge green apple appeared in the fat man's hand out of nowhere. The man had his eyes closed, yet there the hand and the apple were, just in the horse's reach.

The horse snatched the apple and let out a short, happy neigh.

The horse had noticed a magical aura surrounded the man. He made people and animals around him feel happy. It was a fact of life, surrendering any need to poke holes into the fabric of reality by trying to understand why. He made life that much better for those who dared to venture close enough and yield into his happy roundness.

The horse watched as a man in a blue uniform approached them. A man who humans might call "well-formed," but he looked puny to the horse. He interrupted the fat man's slumber by poking him with his nightstick. Instead of angry words rising to the fat man's lips, he gave the constable his best smile The horse didn't know if the fat man could ever get angry. The horse reasoned he most likely saw nothing in the world worthy of anger. It had to be so, or else he was completely bonkers, and the horse was sure that couldn't be.

The constable looked at the fat man's smile with a baffled expression. "No sleeping on public property. And your horse is eating the grass."

The fat man smiled. "Horses eat grass, that's what they do."

"No, bu—" the constable began to say, but he stopped mid-sentence when he noticed the man had shut his eyes and begun snoring.

The constable's left eyelid twitched. He almost poked the man with his nightstick again, but thought better of it. Altogether, it was better if he left the park singing a tune. A more sensible thing to do than try to bring order where there was no need for order.

Another constable waited for him outside the park. The first constable shook his head to warn the other one, who was taller but not as bulky, not to protest.

The fat man opened his left eye and smiled. Then he continued snoring, and the horse continued nibbling the grass as it saved its appetite for the next apple to come.

CHAPTER FOUR
What All the Luck Can Buy

ll the next day, the brown, worn-out door to Edbert's shop constantly swung open and shut. The door creaked after every tenth customer, getting on everyone's nerves.

It was Edbert's lucky day. Everyone in Leporidae Lop wanted to see the man who dared to defy Prime Minister Stowe. Somehow, word had spread like butter on hot toast, but not to Edbert's ears. He thought luck drove people in his shop, and he was the happiest he'd ever been. Never before in his life had he seen as many customers at the same time, not even when he was a child and his grandfather had managed the shop. What made the day even more unusual was the shop was visited by citizens who would not darken any bookshop's door, let alone his. Today his life would change, and his shop would continue its existence; the attacks against it would cease as surely the kingdom's bureaucrats would see his shop was profitable and made the kingdom a much better place. He didn't need to be ashamed anymore.

Edbert counted the people coming into his shop and made notes in a small leather-bound notebook. His hand worked tirelessly, and at least a few times, he recounted those he had already added. His contentment was short-lived, however, because at the end of the day, Edbert was astonished by how little money he'd earned after such a busy day with only a few extra coins. Edbert collapsed into his cushioned chair and cursed. *The cheap bastards*, he thought. People happily spent their money on beer and useless junk rather than invest it in a sensible thing like a book.

It was cruel to get his hopes up this way and then dash them as soon as his shop door closed. Edbert leaned against the desk to write in a ledger the amount he'd earned today, totaling the meager amount in beautiful, precise cursive. He moved his fingers down the profit and expenditure columns with a desperate heart. His earnings kept declining every day. He closed the book and thought the world was becoming a dreadful, soulless place where books didn't matter.

All this meant was that a week from now, he had to go back to the sewers and crawl on his knees to pray for more luck. And a week after that, there might not be a shop left.

Edbert pushed himself up and moved around the shop floor, getting things ready for tomorrow. He knew every inch of the place. The dark bookshelves, the yellow armchair at the corner, the storage at the back, everything here was as it had been when his father had died.

He'd lived in this same house all his life. For a year, he'd tried to live in the university's dormitory, but such life wasn't for him. He'd done everything in his power to get his degree in literature and be done with the place.

Edbert swept the board floor, straightened a book or two on the shelves, and blew out the beeswax candles.

A gentle knock startled him.

Edbert squinted and scratched his head.

Someone knocked again.

"Hmm," he said, searching for anything to use as a weapon. In a bookshop, there are lots of things one can use to hurt others. For example, scissors, hot tea, even any pen would suffice. And it's well known what's the mightiest of them all, and that's a nice cup of tea accompanied with a friendly chat.

Edbert, however, chose a heavy green book with a golden finish as his weapon. The book was too heavy to swing, but it was better than nothing.

He opened the door to peer outside. Two men stood in the cold, late autumn night. They lifted their top hats and nodded.

"Good evening. May we come in?" a man asked, his breath swirling from his lips.

"Sure," Edbert said, letting the gentlemen step inside. If the men had been common riffraff, he would have used his big book of words to drive them away.

He scuffled back to the broken desk, dropped the book onto it, causing a loud *thud*, and said, "What do you want?" The gentlemen clearly weren't here for alms.

One of them, the taller one, coughed and nudged the shorter one.

"Thank you for letting us in. May I ask, do you happen to know who we are?" the shorter fellow asked.

Edbert shook his head, despite having a clear idea who the two men standing in his dimly lit shop were. One of their fathers had refused his father's request for expanding the shop next door.

"My name is Udolf Huxley, and my friend here is Norville Upwood," the shorter fellow said, as if the names should say everything important. To Edbert's sadness, they did. The two men combined owned half the kingdom. Udolf Huxley owned the postal service, a few local markets, and was head of the Business Owners' Assembly, as had his father. He was a short and thin man, except when it came to his soft round belly. He had a bad posture and narrow eyes.

The quieter fellow, Norville Upwood, was the owner of a fabric factory and dozens of sheep farms. He held his back straight and his muscles bulged under his suit. He was in his fifties, with dark brown hair and a pleasant, smiling face.

"The bookshop is closed. Come back tomorrow, and I can help you acquire any book you might need," Edbert said, even though he knew Huxley and Upwood weren't there for his books. He lacked time and patience for them tonight; his nerves were in tatters, and he was in a foul mood. The last part didn't really differ from any other day, but it worked as a perfect excuse.

Huxley's lips curled into a condescending smile.

"Gods, no," Upwood let slip.

"We are here for a different matter. A proposal which might interest you... a lot," Huxley said, giving Upwood a disapproving glance.

Edbert grunted.

"You see, you have become quite a folk-hero overnight. Suddenly, everyone is talking about this amazing bookshop owner who defies Harriet Stowe. We had to see you for ourselves," Huxley said.

Edbert swallowed. His expression turned blank, and he braced himself against the desk.

For a split second, he felt he might faint. There was only one sensible thing to do if offending the great Harriet Stowe, and that was to flee the kingdom. Merely the thought made Edbert's knees wobble and his heart skip a beat. "I... I better close for tonight. Better if you come back tomorrow," he said.

"Don't be silly," Huxley said. "Let me finish. We are here to offer you our help. You see, the whole of Leporidae Lop has waited a long time for a brave man to save us, and we think that man is you."

Edbert quivered. He was sure 'brave man' and his name didn't belong in the same sentence, let alone near his vicinity.

"With our help, you'll get to keep the place and become a legend," Huxley said, giving Edbert an encouraging smile.

Edbert doubted that. Only a suicidal and ignorant numbskull went up against Harriet Stowe. Her absolute power was a fact of life. Edbert had heard rumors about people going missing, especially those Harriet disapproved of, and he wasn't going to be one of those people.

"You better leave now," he said.

"Don't dismiss us so easily. It's a legitimate suggestion. We want you to run opposite Harriet Stowe in the next election," Huxley said.

Edbert's mouth hung open, then he closed it. The men were joking at his expense; they had to be. "Eh, the prime minister's position?" he asked.

"Yes."

"But… but Miss Stowe has always run unopposed."

Actually, Harriet wasn't a Miss, but no one seemed to remember that. It had been a long time since Harriet was married—her husband had died when she was barely twenty years old. Back then, there had been rumors of murder.

"An even better reason for you to run," Huxley said.

"I think you have come to the wrong place. I'm merely a bookshop owner. And this folk-hero thing doesn't sound right."

"Don't be silly. You are the man we want. Don't you think it's time for a change? Time for a man to sit in the seat of power?" Huxley asked.

Edbert let the thought sink in. Not even in his wildest dreams would he have dared to take the office from Harriet Stowe, but that might be possible if the two richest men in the kingdom backed him up. This might be the chance he had been praying for—an opportunity, not a disaster like he thought. There was much he could do with the power. But then there was Harriet Stowe.

"How do you suppose we go around doing it?" he asked.

"That's easy." Huxley smiled a sharp smile that revealed all his teeth, then nudged Upwood, urging him to go on.

"The first thing we do is take your heroism to the next level before announcing our intentions. Of course, in addition, we'll consult the gods and get their approval. But all in all, you come to our circles, we take care of you, and that's that. You'll be a strong candidate against Harriet Stowe," Norville Upwood said and habitually glanced behind.

"Yes, listen to Norville. Him backing you up is a guaranteed win. He can make even a mouse think a snake is a viable candidate," Huxley said.

"Eh," Edbert said.

Huxley moved by his side, tying his arms around Edbert's

shoulder and turning him to see the bookshop in all its glory and decade. "Think of what your newly found reputation can do. Think of how coming to our circles makes a difference. Think of how you can make the kingdom a better place, how your bookshop and the knowledge it hides inside it can alter everything."

Edbert could feel his caution fly out the chimney. The chimney, which was blocked by a dead mouse, though not the same mouse who'd voted for the snake. This had been a mouse with more sense but with a lousy sense of orientation.

Edbert envisioned what he would do when in power. First thing he would do would make buying books once a year obligatory. Oh crit, why not make it once a week? It was all for the good of humanity.

He smiled. The more he thought about it, replacing Harriet Stowe was a good thing. She was against books, and no such person should be in power. What next? She would insist on burning the books. The mere thought made Edbert shake from anger.

"What do you say? Shall we raise a glass for the occasion?" Huxley asked.

"What an excellent idea, and I have just the bottle stashed away," Edbert replied.

"Yes, excellent." Huxley looked at the shabby old man and winced.

Edbert's worn-out coat was patched in so many spots the original fabric had gone missing. His trousers were a tad better, but they wouldn't do for a prime minister. The grossest thing about Edbert Pollock was his ear hair, which stuck out from his spotted ears. That needed to go. But Edbert's blue eyes almost made up for that.

Edbert saw Huxley looking at him. He patted his coat pockets and disappeared into his living quarters, mumbling on his way out. He rummaged through a cupboard for a bottle of whiskey, which his father had left there. He himself didn't touch the ghastly stuff; however, the whiskey should be good for his guests. The expensive stuff.

Edbert found the bottle stashed behind a piece of stale bread and a turnip.

He took the bottle and came back to the shop floor, where the two nervous men waited for him. It was his turn to be smug. The place could get spooky at nighttime. His dead father and grandfather haunted the place. Luckily, it stopped there, since his grandfather's father had died a long way from the shop and haunted a hill or a swamp somewhere. He was an evil man, if there were any. His grandfather and father were creepy, but harmless.

Edbert poured three glasses of whiskey and said, "To our success."

Huxley and Upwood lifted their glasses and toasted, but they took a sip only after they had wiped the glass clean with their sleeves when Edbert wasn't looking.

"To new beginnings," Huxley and Upwood said.

"To us," Edbert said.

* * *

Harriet climbed the sewer stairs for the second time today. Luck tingled inside her. She needed it to work its magic while the kingdom slept, and she retired to her private quarters for tonight. She couldn't do anything for now. However, luck would make sure she could pick up where she'd left today and have the ties of the future be favorable towards her.

As she walked through the palace, the staff and the royalty kept ducking behind vases and statues, hoping she didn't see them. She did see them; she just chose to ignore them. She wanted to speak with them as much as they did with her. The whole business of communication was ever so necessary; it was just that one had to be careful with whom to share one's thoughts. After the age of three, humans invented lying, letting themselves experiment with the words they let out. The scholars were yet to decide if the whole business of lying was a way for personal gain or just a byproduct of a bored mind creating bizarre realities. Either way, you could argue it had to aid survival somehow. And while it was so, it made social situations a whole lot more complicated.

Harriet's private quarters had four huge rooms, two of which were empty, and the rest only minimally furnished. She had little use for them, not even for sleep. She stole her rest throughout the day by taking little naps here and there, and she spent most of her time inside that little broom closet of hers.

One of the furnished rooms was another audience chamber. In that, she had two simple wooden chairs, no paintings, no rugs, and nothing else. She was minimalist to her core. The chairs she had chosen were uncomfortable, and the visitors, mostly the king and his queen, thought they were selected to give Harriet an upper hand in negotiations. They couldn't be farther from the truth. The true explanation was Harriet's lack of interest. She disliked wasting money and time—though her visitors' discomfort came as a welcomed bonus. People were too pampered, if you asked her.

Harriet headed to her bedroom, which contained a low bed, a red, Oriental rug, a blue and white porcelain washing bowl with flowers on it over a wooden table, and a waste bowl. That was all of it, except for the huge pile of legal and private surveillance documents next to her bed.

She glanced towards the mattress, which stood there looking alluring, but Harriet ignored the bed. The last time she'd slept a full night's sleep was in her fifties, and now in her mid-nineties, it felt like sleep happened to others. It was as well. She had things to do. She had always believed in keeping oneself busy. If you did, you could almost forget your own mortality.

Harriet opened the window over the table with the washing bowl, pursed her lips, and made a loud whistle.

A reddish-brown messenger bird with a dash of white and gray on its wings flew onto the windowsill.

"Find me Sigourney Perri," she said.

Harriet watched the bird fly away. It swirled over the courtyard and made a drastic turn, then flew over the place and the window.

Harriet closed the window and turned to walk to the pile of documents and rummaged through it, looking if there was any information about Edbert Pollock. She needed a find a way to make the bookshop owner see eye to eye with her, or else she would have to force the man's arm. Harriet preferred cooperation, as it often yielded better results.

Sigourney would find out something she could use to negotiate with the man. Harriet couldn't function without Sigourney Perri. The girl was the source of all the tiny bits of essential information she used to run the kingdom. All the thorough surveillance documents lying next to Harriet's bed were written by her.

Harriet lifted the document she had on Edbert's father, but there was no file on the man himself. As she turned around, Sigourney stood there beside her, staring. The girl had the annoying skill of creeping in without making a noise. Harriet was sure not even a single floorboard had made a sound.

She pursed her lips and said, "You came fast."

Sigourney shrugged. All her moss-green clothes were wrinkled, and her straw-colored hair was a mess. She was a short girl who looked calm, but Harriet was sure a storm brewed inside the mild-tempered teacup. There was something nervous about Sigourney, which made Harriet uneasy.

"I was... in the neighborhood," Sigourney said after it became clear Harriet wanted more than a gesture.

Harriet raised an eyebrow and said, "Lucky for me."

Sigourney gave Harriet a dispassionate smile, but her demeanor said she was in a hurry to get away. So she better hurry with whatever she had to say, or the girl would flee.

"I need you to find everything about Edbert Pollock—" Harriet began to say, but she paused to look through the papers. "You can find his a—"

"I know where he lives," Sigourney said.

Harriet raised an eyebrow, which seemed to ask, "How?"

Such a gesture usually caused sheer panic in other people, but not in Sigourney. She stood there looking at Harriet, without an expression on her face. Harriet was unaccustomed to the lack of fear. Parents in Leporidae Lop practiced naming girl-children 'Harriet' in the hope of transferring some of her... shall we put it nicely, determination; and everyone feared the day all the Harriets grew old enough to run around wreaking havoc. Yet, Sigourney knew Harriet's reputation, along with everything else, and she didn't even blink.

"Do you need anything else?" Sigourney asked, shifting her weight from one foot to another, having said more than she usually did.

She was always in a hurry, making it impossible for Harriet to fish out any additional information about her. Whenever she asked anything personal from the girl, she evaded the question or, more often, fled so fast Harriet could hear the wind gushing.

"That's all. There must be more than meets the eye," Harriet said more to herself than to Sigourney. "No one..." Harriet turned her attention back to her papers to glance at the estimates of Edbert's income the place's housing committee had drawn, but when she lifted her head, Sigourney had disappeared.

Harriet shook her head and went on reading the other documents that couldn't wait.[5]

---

[5] The documents saw the matter differently. It was always humans that eagerly rushed to fondle them. They were perfectly fine laying there and doing nothing.

CHAPTER FIVE
All the Monsters in the Dark

Sigourney Perri closed the window behind her as silently as she could. She stood there at the edge of the small windowsill, looking down at the several-feet-high drop to the ground. While she'd felt terror inside that room, having to talk to another human being, here, she was in full control. Whatnot, she kept replaying her previous encounter over and over again in her head. All the tiny mistakes she'd done with Harriet caused the doubt goblins to parade around her stomach, banging their pots and pans together. The night air of Leporidae Lop, which almost was calm in the wee hours, couldn't drive away the goblins. She pressed her moccasins against the stone sill and looked over the city. She could barely see the stars from the gray clouds, but there was a faint twinkle here and there.

Sigourney began climbing down the place wall, leaving behind all the incomprehensible thoughts she'd had for having been in Harriet Stowe's private quarters. On the ground, she slipped silently behind the palace guard station at the opening before the palace walls. They stood there smoking their pipes, unable to see her, even if they'd tried. Such was Sigourney's talent. No one ever saw her, even if she stood right there in front of them.

Sigourney left the stone yard behind her with flowerpots around the lit lamps, keeping the darkness away. She passed the new shopping district with their fancy buildings and signs, telling her what to buy. Sigourney had always been fascinated by shop windows, especially the one's belonging to apothecaries. The little drawers and bottles held so many secrets inside them that she felt elated just by standing with her nose pressed against the windows.

Edbert's bookshop wasn't anywhere near the new shopping district—it was hidden where the old center had been, forgotten. But Sigourney liked the walk since it made the goblins fade away. She made to Edbert's front door, feeling more like herself, meaning she could concentrate on the task at hand and forget she as a person existed.

Sigourney knelt in front of the door and tilted her head. The door had the standard number eight metal lock, which she could easily lock-pick open. She opened her tool set, wiggled a narrow blade inside the lock, and there came a loud *click*. Sigourney carefully opened the door, not to make a sound, and slipped inside, stepping on a loose floorboard, which gave a loud *creak*.

Sigourney grimaced and wished she didn't exist at all. She slowly shut the door behind her and stepped farther in, this time balancing her feet more carefully. But she had already made a mistake. There came a commotion beyond the shop floor and soon, Edbert Pollock rushed in, holding a poker high.

"Come out or you will get it from the poker!" the man shouted, waving his chosen weapon once more, just to be sure.

Sigourney did nothing. She just stood there in plain view.

The man waved the poker again and then she saw as he winced. Edbert let the poker drop and he squeezed his right hand.

"Come out and I won't hit you." Edbert pushed past the pain and lifted the poker from the floor into the air again.

Sigourney felt bad for him, but she couldn't reveal herself, not even with the line like that.

Sigourney watched as Edbert searched for her in agony, limping from one room to another. He walked past her several times without seeing her. Sigourney could hide in plain sight. She merged into the background, making it difficult, but not impossible, for others to see her. If they knew to look for her, they might detect a glimpse, but only if they really knew what they were searching for.

The first time she hid in plain sight was when she'd turned five. She was trying to stay away from her older brother, who liked to test reality with her. One time he'd wanted to know what would happen when a hand was dunked inside an anthill—and Sigourney could attest nothing good came out of it—and that was the most harmless way her brother observed the world around him. He wasn't exactly a bad person. Sigourney never thought that. It was just that he had... he was like her. Not all parts there.

On the day of her fifth birthday, Levi, her brother, had stormed into the common room, shouting her name. He sounded agitated, and right away, she knew he would finally kill her. She didn't have enough time to dash under the bench, so she stood there in the middle of the room, frozen to her position, fearing for her life, and he'd walked straight past her. He went around the house like Edbert did now, without seeing her.

Thereafter, Sigourney could just stay hidden in plain sight. It annoyed the misery out of her brother.

Only later in life did she understand she didn't turn invisible—at least, not in the traditional sense, as all the stories went. She affected others' minds instead by persuading them to believe she wasn't there. It was kind of sad skill to possess. But even now, she rejoiced it for keeping her out of harm's way, despite knowing it had made her become secluded. So badly that even a slightly uncomfortable moment triggered it. All of which had made her socially awkward, nervous, and mute. Well, not exactly mute, but more like voluntarily silent.

To top it all, she hated herself and what she did. She felt

extremely sorry for Edbert, who must be frightened to death. An old man like him might have a heart attack at any moment, and it would be her fault. She let out a nervous, suppressed laugh. Edbert shot a glance in her direction, looking straight through her. Sigourney shifted her weight to ease the pressure bottling up inside her. Again, the floorboard groaned, but Edbert didn't pay any attention. He walked out of the shop, searching for her.

But what else could she do? Yes, gathering information for Harriet neared her sense of wrong. Actually, her work had hopped onto the side of cookies and doom a long time ago, but she did her work because she thought Harriet was her friend. If she wasn't her friend, that meant Sigourney was all alone in the world.

And she didn't want that.

Sigourney scratched her head. Everything itched when she tried not to think about her past and the loneliness she felt daily.

Soon, Edbert came back to the shop floor from his private quarters, but then, unable to find her, he headed upstairs and went back to bed. Sigourney stood there in place until she heard a quiet snore coming from Edbert's bedroom. After that, she dared to search the place for any useful information Harriet could use against the man.

There wasn't much to find out. He was just a plain man, who loved books and nothing but books—based on the fact that it was the only thing he spent his money on. Otherwise, Edbert Pollock liked to be stingy. The only other thing he bought with his personal money was food. No new fedoras, no hats, or a more chipper attitude. It was clear from his faded clothes, precise ledgers, and the musty shop that everything was second-hand and passed on to him. All she saw was an old, miserable man whom Harriet should leave alone.

Upstairs, inside a closet, she found a happy and deranged garden gnome with a red hat and a belly full of enough gold for Edbert to retire to some remote village and live a peaceful life. Why he was still here baffled Sigourney. Maybe he liked to torture himself and others with this fading bookshop. Maybe this was all he had ever wanted out of life.

Sigourney wondered more often than not why people did what they did, but she never got the answer. But from what she gathered for Harriet, she surely made them dance to her will, so somewhere in their actions must be reason and logic. Otherwise, it was just madness and randomness, and Sigourney refused to believe life could be about that. She, like many other people, was afraid of the small step it took to lose one's mind.

Sigourney let the gold be, walked back downstairs, and went over Edbert's desk. He clearly kept everything important to him there. On the disheveled desk lay his ledgers and *The Pantheon of Gods*. It was the only other book which had seen good use. She glanced through it. The man had circled gods and deities, scribed notes about their usefulness, and ranked them from best to worse.

Sigourney bit her lip. She didn't care about gods. The only god she believed in was an omnipotent god who existed only on Wednesdays. That was enough god for her, and it was debatable if the god would be the same god on the next Wednesday; and it wasn't blasphemy to question the function of gods as it was Friday, and her god didn't exist at all.

The night slipped away from her, and she woke from her own thoughts as Edbert made noises upstairs, startling her. Sigourney put the ledgers and *The Pantheon of Gods* back in their rightful places and left the building, feeling too tired to observe him all day, and doubtful she would find anything useful, anyway. Why on earth did Harriet send her here, inside the old bookshop full of antiquated books no one wants to buy?

But it wasn't her duty to question what Harriet wanted. She hadn't found anything useful to give to her and she couldn't disappoint her. She had to get someone to continue watching Edbert. Someone who didn't ask questions and someone who she could reveal herself.

Sigourney knew just the right fellow for the job.

She slowly opened the front door. The floorboard underneath it still creaked, making all the hairs on her back stand up. She waited for a moment to see if Edbert hurried down, but the man made no noise. Sigourney closed the door after her and hurried to find Lars. He was the right, cheap man she needed. She was sure Lars would be sleeping behind his favorite pub—he always was.

Sigourney hopped on from one foot to another, gathering momentum. Whenever she ran, it felt like she was flying, and for that short moment, she was more than she was. And the best part of it was no one ever saw her.

Sigourney's moccasins barely touched the ground as she sprinted from Edbert's shop to the shopping district. From there, she had to run three more blocks to Lars's pub. Sigourney turned at the corner of Odd Mona, a pub but not Lars's pub. His would be at the pub at the end of the lane, The Red Wishbone. When Sigourney got there, she wished she could go running and never to stop. She stopped and walked to the pub's backyard.

Like she'd expected, Lars slept in the untidy backyard, snoring loudly. Annoying all the neighborhood's cats, rats, and other creatures, which saw loud noises as horror coming from the darkest dimension there can be. Sigourney sympathized with them.

She gently pushed Lars with her foot, pressing her hands against her ears. He groaned and pulled a bit of cardboard over him. The man smelled like yesterday's booze and looked sweaty and puffy. He was drunk, as always. A sight ever so familiar from her childhood.

"It's me. Wake up." Sigourney bit her lip. When the man made no move, she had to add more words. It was a painful process to come up with the right phrase to say. She didn't know what word to use, when to use it, and how to use it. After careful consideration, she said, "Money?"

The word snapped the man to attention. He groaned when he tried to get up, but he fell face-first on top of the cardboard bed. Sigourney helped him up and waited for him to sober up enough to perceive there was a world out there beyond his lulled existence.

Lars had ginger hair, a split lip, and dull eyes, which looked as if someone had shut off something important inside him. He was much taller than Sigourney and of average build. He was a sad man, but there was no one else she could go for help. All the interacting with Lars had already strained her socially, and she didn't know anyone else, for that matter. Also, Lars met the criteria of what she needed him for. He wasn't a bright fellow, a rich fellow, or a great fellow, but he could follow people unnoticed due to being so plain that everyone thought nothing of him, which didn't help his alcoholism. Mostly Lars followed people for those who thought their husbands cheated on them, and most times he lied to the ladies on behalf of their husbands for even bigger paydays. Occasionally, Lars did the job and reported the truth. On those occasions, his dead mother had visited her alcoholic son to remind him that the dead were always watching. Alcohol helped him forget that, hence his constant drinking.

"Go watch Edbert Pollock," she said.

"Pollock?" Lars asked. "Isn't he the man who dares to fight against the Dragon Lady? What about him?"

Sigourney tilted her head. She'd missed something.

"Crit. I hope Pollock isn't in trouble. He's a good man," Lars said, wiping puke off the side of his mouth.

"No, just follow him," she said.

"Sure," Lars said, knowing Sigourney well. He staggered toward the bookshop. He understood the language of money, and Sigourney had a habit of paying well. One might even say she had a habit of paying royally.

As soon as the man vanished, Sigourney trotted back to the palace, which was on the other side of the inner kingdom, cursing her own ignorance.

Already people were queued up at the palace to see Harriet. They looked ill-matched against the glamour of the palace, with lavish decor and ornamental moldings, with their plain clothes, clutching their hats.

Sigourney climbed up, using the window ledges and drainpipes. She wasn't going to see Harriet. Not yet. She headed to her small shack nestled on the palace rooftop. She'd built it there by herself without Harriet's consent. But what Harriet didn't know couldn't harm her, and Sigourney got to her faster, which she was sure sanctified her actions.

The rent-free shack was small and draughty, but it was hers and she liked it. Sigourney had already lined her home with royal fabrics emblazoned with Leporidae Lop's insignia on them for the upcoming winter. She opened the shack's door and quickly snuggled beneath the stack of blankets she had also borrowed from the palace. Sigourney melted between them. Before dreamland took her, she kept repeating her nightly mantra, "I'm not a monster."

CHAPTER SIX

They Are All Here to See You

A loud knock awakened Edbert on Saturday morning. He was sure that before the knock sounded, his front door had opened and closed without his knowledge. But mornings were generally groggy for him, and separating what was real and what wasn't was almost impossible. The last night had been extremely bad for him— he'd had his usual delusions. After the whiskey and after Huxley and Norville had left, the thought of becoming the prime minister of Leporidae Lop had made his nerves so tattered that he had been sure there was an intruder in his shop. But there hadn't been anyone there. When he'd gotten back to bed, he'd tossed and turned all night, dreaming about the Dragon Lady's assassins getting him. And in one of his dreams, Harriet walked him, naked, in front of the whole of Leporidae Lop to make him a laughingstock of the entire kingdom. He could still hear the laughter in his ears.

Maybe he should say no.

In the background, he heard the familiar *tsk-tsk* sound his father made as he sucked his teeth. Back when he had been younger, the sound had made the hair on the back of his neck stand up, but now, it only made disappointment goblins march inside his stomach. Those same ones Sigourney experienced ever so often.

Edbert refused to let his dead father control his life.

The loud knock sounded again.

Edbert pushed himself up and wished the morning away. He would happily spend the day in bed reading a book. He dressed in his light blue morning robe and walked down the stairs with slow, careful steps to see who violated his peace by making such a racket. He found a short postman waiting for him. The man stared at Edbert with awe. in spite of him parading in his morning robe and pajamas. He gave Edbert a huge, bright blue postal sack, which almost tipped the man over. When he regained his balance, he hurried away.

"What? Hey, wait!" Edbert yelled after him.

The postman came back and groveled in front of Edbert, nervously smiling and averting his gaze at every turn. The man had overly large ears and nose for his head, and his too big blue hat with a black rim made his ears and nose pop out even more.

"What's going on?" Edbert groaned.

The man's odd behavior, glazed eyes, general nervousness, and inability to speak made him ready to attack the scrawny man.

"I-it's all f-for you," the postman said, finding the front door fascinating.

"This has to be a mistake," Edbert let out and pushed the neck of the sack back to the postman.

The man took a step away from the door. "In all honesty, it's for you. The whole post office has been sorting your letters all morning."

Edbert frowned. "Are you sure?"

The postman nodded.

"Then why are you standing there? Are you waiting for me to pay you?"

The postman half-ran away, nearly colliding into Udolf Huxley, who was making his way down the street past the unusual crowd that had started to gather. They kept staring at

Edbert.

Edbert tightened his robe and watched Huxley approach the shop.

"Top of the morning," Huxley said.

"Good morning," Edbert said, looking past Huxley at the crowd.

"What's up with all the people this morning? Everyone is suddenly turning immorally nosy," Edbert complained as he looked at the fleeing postman and the people staring back at him.

"You'll get used to it." Huxley laughed and slapped Edbert's back, almost tipping him over the postal sack.

"Let me help you with that," Huxley said, ignoring the fact he almost maimed the old man.

Edbert's heart pounded heavily against his chest, and Huxley's musky shaving lotion made him gasp for breath.

He let Huxley take the heavy sack. Ten years ago, Edbert's pride wouldn't have allowed such a gesture, but now, pride, in general, was reserved for the young and fools, and he couldn't afford to be either of those. He scuffed after the younger man, who'd dropped the sack near Edbert's work desk and began opening his mail.

Edbert stopped in his tracks and coughed.

"Oh, I'm sorry, a bad habit of mine." Huxley grinned as he noticed the old man looking at him.

"It's fine. You didn't mean it. All fine," Edbert muttered. "All fine." He wanted to be sure not to have offended the younger man.

"That's quite an amount of post to have. Do you always receive as many letters?" Huxley kept that grin on his face.

Edbert didn't like it a bit, nor did he care for the bulging postal sack. He would rather toss it out and let the street kids have their way with it. The ones who always hung around the corner of his shop, hassling money out of poor unsuspecting visitors.

"No." Edbert shook his head.

"Then, by all means, do read them." Huxley smiled and

backed away to sit on the mustard-colored armchair pushed into the corner near the bookshelves Edbert's father had made. When Huxley sat, a cloud of dust puffed out and a few not-so-welcome guests scurried off. Huxley took a book to read, but he kept glancing over at Edbert, who muttered and occasionally moaned as he read the letters.

After Edbert had read a few, a pattern started to emerge. There were five kinds of letters. The first kind asked him for help with Harriet Stowe, and they arrived in white envelopes. The second kind asked him to attend parties and also came in white envelopes. The third wanted to tell him how much they admired him, and came in white envelopes, just like he expected. The fourth kind, which he only received a few, asked him to join their cult, again going with the safe option of white envelopes. Those letters excited him the most. Then there was the fifth kind, which proposed marriage to him. They arrived in pink envelopes and smelled strongly of something unsuitable, like insect repellent. Those he quickly put back and tried to forget but never could, especially those with graphic details and... drawings.

While he read, the crowd outside grew bigger. The sounds behind the front door grew louder with every minute that went past the opening time. Then came the loud knocks, startling Edbert from his slumber. He stuffed the interesting letters into his desk drawer, and he put the rest back into the sack. He hurried upstairs as fast as he could to get dressed and open the shop, which was surprisingly fast for a man of his age.[6] When he was ready, Edbert was almost flattened by the crowd rushing through his front door. It wasn't like yesterday's spectacle. They wanted more than to peer at him. Every single one of the customers wanted alone time with Edbert. They instantly began shouting their questions at him, making Edbert's feet freeze while the rest of the body wanted to flee. Huxley rushed to his rescue, arranging himself between the

---

[6] Something to do with wasting time.

crowd and Edbert, and when he'd secured enough breathing room, he said, "Form an orderly line and we can start." He sounded as if he knew everyone was coming.

Huxley made Edbert sit behind his desk and turned him into a sideshow freak. He encouraged, or more like forced, Edbert to answer all the visitors' bizarre questions. If that wasn't bad enough, the tacky answers, which Huxley prompted him to say, left a bad, sugary taste in Edbert's mouth. Every time he used his own words, Huxley corrected him, or shook his head, or did something else to make Edbert feel insecure and out of place inside his own shop.

Edbert moaned and groaned at every opportunity he got.

"It's you, it's really you?!" a woman gushed. She was next in line after a man with a sore throat and unpaid bills had left.

Edbert gave her an awkward smile. "Yes."

In the background, Huxley shook his head.

Edbert frowned.

"How can I help?" he asked the old woman.

Huxley shook his head again.

Edbert wanted to stand up and demand Huxley to take his place if nothing he did was good enough. But he couldn't, and the woman babbled on about a problem she had with her chickens They didn't provide enough fresh eggs for the madam she served, or something else absurd. While she spoke, she fiddled with her lace apron and locked her eyes with him. "What should I do?" she asked.

"I don't k——" he began, but once again, Huxley shook his head, and this time, it was short and angry.

"Are your chickens healthy?" he asked, looking over at Huxley.

He nodded, but twirled his hand for Edbert to hurry.

"Oh, yes. I take good care of them. Feed them quality food and speak to them every day. They are perfect little birdies, my chickens."

"Then, I——" he said before he saw Huxley's face. How did Huxley suppose he should answer? It was more honest if he said he knew nothing about chickens—and to be honest, he lacked any interest in knowing more about the vermin-covered birds. Fish was the only sort of meat he consented to eat, and you could argue it wasn't meat at all. It was more like a concentration of algae, water crickets, and your common earthworm—and the latter was more like a spice before the hook, line, and sinker.

The murmurs from the back of the queue made his heart feel heavy and his palms sweat. The woman continued babbling, reciting the chickens' names. "Lazy, Rosa, Audrey, Sofia, Mary..."

Huxley looked at Edbert under his eyebrows.

"How long have you had the chickens?" he asked, prolonging the conversation in spite of it all, giving himself time to think and, to be honest, rebel against Huxley a little. Who was the young man to think he could boss him around like that?

"Oh, I have had them since forever. How old is my granddaughter now? I took them before her birth. Oh, I say fifteen or sixteen years."

"They are quite old; maybe you should get younger chickens?" He didn't have a clue how long chickens lived, but fifteen or sixteen years sounded a lot for a bird.

"Oh, you are right, but—" she said, but Huxley interrupted her and guided her outside.

Edbert felt relieved. Did becoming the prime minister mean this? Chickens, cows, and mad ladies?

When everyone left, and the shop was empty, save for Huxley, Edbert's head swirled. He did his ledgers to get back to the reality, but reality was too harsh. He hadn't sold a single book.

"Unacceptable!" He slammed the ledger shut.

"What's unacceptable?" Huxley asked, looking up from the book he'd tried to read the whole day, not getting past the first ten pages.

"I haven't sold a single book!"

"Don't worry about it," Huxley said, closing his.

"Don't!? Don't!? It's my livelihood; of course, I worry.

Things can't keep going on this way. The huge crowds are scaring away the customers. This isn't a library."

"Here." Huxley stood up, walked over to Edbert, and dropped a bag full of coins into his hand. "I'll buy this book. You can keep the change."

"I can't," Edbert said in protest, but Huxley silenced him with a meaningful shrug.

Edbert gritted his teeth. A proper man earned their own keep, period. *The Modern Warfare* book, which Huxley held in his hands, had found a rightful owner, but still, taking alms was beneath Edbert.

He sank into his chair, picked up his pen, and noted in his ledger the book and the amount paid. Then he yawned.

"Day isn't over yet. We need to see more people. I think a pub round would do us good," Huxley said.

Before either man said anything, someone knocked on the front door.

Edbert massaged blood to his hips before he got up and opened the door.

"Evening," Upwood said. The open door let in the cold, wet air, making Edbert's bones ache.

When Edbert closed the door behind Upwood, it rammed against something and wouldn't shut. Edbert tried again with stronger force.

The door closed, making a loud *bang*. He glared at the door. Everything was getting impudent all of a sudden.

Upwood's whole body stiffened, startled by the loud noise. "How's everyone this fine evening?" Upwood asked, managing to sound unusually cheerful.

"We were just talking about a pub round. A marvelous idea, eh?" Huxley said, watching Edbert like a hawk.

Edbert got back to his chair and sank into it. He didn't want to go to a pub, let alone a round of them. Bed with a good book sounded better.

Another knock at the front door startled them all. Edbert shuffled to the door and thought it would be easier if he removed the door entirely. Huxley and Upwood peered over his shoulder as he yanked the door open.

A man in a palace uniform handed over a letter. He left so fast that Edbert hadn't time to register what was going on.

He opened the letter, and after reading the first two lines, his mind shut down, his body went limp, and he fainted.

* * *

Harriet Stowe woke up on Saturday morning as her head jerked. She refused to believe she'd fallen asleep after Sigourney had left. She took her silver pocket watch, opened it, and grimaced. Harriet got up, straightened her wrinkled dress, and put a few misplaced curls in their rightful places. Not a good start, but so it had gone.

Harriet washed her face, welcoming the fresh water against her skin. She lingered to repeat the process just a few minutes longer to steal that one moment to call her own. After that, she was there to serve the people and the people alone. When that moment almost went too long, she stopped herself and hurried out to meet the crowds queuing at her office.

The wicked never rest, she thought.[7]

On Sunday, she would go back to handling the state's affairs and babysitting the king and his queen—the two multidimensional-fools making her life miserable. Consulting was the only break she got from them. The freedom she enjoyed every Friday and Saturday was the highlight of her week.

Harriet stepped into the corridor, heading to her office. She saw the master of the household chatting with a staff member. "Morning," she said to the tall man and the cleaning lady as she passed them.

The cleaning lady curtsied and rushed off.

"Ma'am," the master of the household said, and nodded.

Two of them disliked each other—the animosity came

---

[7] Unsure whether she meant herself or the public.

down to money and status. Harriet had stepped onto the man's toes too many times for them to see eye to eye or be more than civil. They'd started working at the palace at the same time, Harriet as a widow seeking justice for her husband and him a lackey.

The man looked at her like he'd swallowed something sour and poisonous. "Fine weather we have today," the man said.

"And what a blessing it is," she said.

"Yes."

"Good day," she said.

"To you, too."

She walked past him. Sometimes she wondered how she'd ended up here. Not as the prime minister—that path she knew by heart. Thinking about her dead husband wasn't a past she wanted to visit too often. No, she meant being disliked and hated. The venom in the master of the household's gestures said it all. There was no one left in the world who knew Harriet behind the title. Oh well, Harriet shook off such thoughts. They had no time and place in her daily schedule.

Harriet headed to her office, where she found her assistant already behind his desk. He looked tired, dozing off at least three times while Harriet walked up to his desk.

"Good morning," she said, grunting approvingly.

"Morning... ma'am," he said.

Harriet gave him a sympathetic smile. "It seems we have our work cut out for us today," she said, nodding towards the line outside her office.

The assistant smiled weakly. "Yes."

The boy might last, Harriet thought and gave herself permission to become familiar with him. He was a narrow man, a bit short if you asked Harriet. There was an intelligent and compassionate way about him, though the system would beat that out of him if Harriet didn't protect the boy. Who knew, they might even get along.

"Did you sleep all right?" she asked.

The boy stuttered, groping for words to reply.

She smiled. "Don't worry, today won't stretch so far into

the night."

The boy smiled back awkwardly. His wrinkled uniform could use some ironing, and Harriet made a note of that. She would ask one of the maids to look into the matter. He should get a room from the palace as well. She would arrange that later today.

She nodded at the boy and walked into the office, which hadn't gotten miraculously bigger overnight. The office's size showed her and everyone else how much the king appreciated her. Still, the public came and did as she told them to. The king's ingratitude seemed to bring no harm, and you might say his attitude towards her even helped her reputation, which was so skewed, she didn't see a point in keeping up with what they said about her anymore. They thought she'd killed the last prime minister to get to her position. At first, she'd tried to correct that mistaken impression, but she had to give up that battle. Nevertheless, she hadn't killed anyone. Her husband had been a trusted advisor to the king before his sudden death. After his death, the court had tried to push her out, but she'd continued to advance her husband's causes, and little by little, she'd gained a foothold for herself and finally achieved the post of prime minister. Nothing had scared or swayed her since her husband's death.

Harriet sat behind her desk and shouted to let the first person in for today. After consulting with five people, the corridor outside fell unnaturally silent. Usually, it sounded as if a carnival was visiting the otherwise forgotten corridor.

"Next," Harriet yelled.

None came.

She was met with silence.

She waited a second or two longer, which turned to thirty seconds, and then she shouted, "Next!"

The assistant's looked in and he shook his head. "There's no 'next,' ma'am. Everyone has gone."

"What?!"

The assistant's face turned red.

"Is there some special event today?" she asked.

The boy shrunk a couple of inches under Harriet's stern gaze. "No, at least, not to my knowledge," he replied.

"Then where's everybody?"

"They have gone to s—"

"Spit it out," Harriet snapped.

"To the bookshop," he whispered.

"The bookshop?" Harriet asked.

"You know, the new guy."

Harriet frowned. "Edbert Pollock?"

The assistant answered unnaturally bravely under Harriet's frown, "Yes, him. Everyone wants to meet the man who defies the prime minister and have his advice."

Harriet composed herself. "Thank you. You can file the audiences we had today and then come back to see if I need anything else. You may go."

The assistant hesitated and stood in place, but he moved when Harriet looked at him with impatience. When the boy was gone, Harriet unleashed her fury. She squeezed her desk and counted to ten to calm down before she did something she might regret. If she had any magical powers, the palace would have exploded by now. Thankfully, she lacked in that department, but not for a second did it hinder her. If she needed to blow the building up, she could do it anytime she wanted. For now, the palace got to stay.

There had to be something else going than just Mr. Pollock's obstinate stance over relocating his bookshop. Thus far, she'd sent official letters to the man, but clearly, it was time to find out what his true aims were.

Harriet summoned Sigourney. She opened the window, letting out her pigeon and, once again, the bird turned around and swooped over the palace.

The small woman again appeared unnaturally fast, and she looked as if she came straight from bed. Her hair was a mess, and her eyes were half closed, just like last time.

Harriet crossed her arms and tapped them with her forefingers. When she noticed what she was doing, she released her arms next to her. "What did you learn about Mr.

Pollock?"

"Nothing much, yet." Sigourney rubbed her eyes.

"Then why aren't you watching him?" Harriet asked.

Sigourney shrugged.

"There has to be something you are leaving out," Harriet said with a tight voice. Today, Sigourney's special quirks were getting to her. She usually ignored them, but now her inability to speak was a hindrance.

Sigourney twisted her hands nervously.

"All right, write it down."

Sigourney's awkwardness made interacting with her an ordeal, but Harriet put up with her and tried to be nice about her personality because somehow, the woman got information no one should be able to. She handed her a piece of paper and the pen she used to sign off her orders.

Sigourney took them and wrote: *He's what he seems to be. Though Lars seemed to like him and was worried about his safety when it came to you, and the gods are his passion.*

"A normal bookshop owner? That can't be. Dig deeper, and fast. You have missed something," Harriet said, then muttered something inaudible about Lars.

Sigourney nodded and disappeared as soon as Harriet looked at her note again. Harriet crumpled the note and tossed it aside.

She took another sheet of paper from her desk and began to write. Time to call the man's bluff and have a private audience with him. That normally scared them straight. Harriet closed the letter she'd written with her crest hanging on her neck and put it on the desk to wait until she formed a solid plan to get Edbert finally off her to-do list. There were other, more important matters needing her full attention. The kingdom couldn't crumble because of one bookshop and its keeper.

CHAPTER SEVEN
Changing the Fabric of Leporidae Lop

here are two things which govern Leporidae Lop, and those are luck and advice. Upon careful examination, luck might seem too whimsical to be trusted, but not in Leporidae Lop. The kingdom's citizens knew how to harness luck to their fullest advantage. Those who had been lucky generations ago were lucky now. They kept their formula a secret, passing along the information only when on their deathbeds, and only if they felt gracious.

The great examples of wealthy, lucky families in the kingdom were the Huxleys and Upwoods. They didn't seem to run out of luck—not even when others tried their best, and do believe others did their best. What was outrageous was the Huxleys and Upwoods didn't seem to use luck. They seemed to hoard their luck and kept going. Many reasoned if you had luck, then you should spend it, thus putting it back into circulation for everyone's benefit. But no. Occasionally one of them, Upwood, would use his influence to gain more sheep. Sheep were nice, but they hardly made the kingdom for the better. And what was with his passion with them, anyway?

In general, luck was a zero-sum game. If one had good fortune, someone else didn't. Like with money, there's only a tight amount of luck in the world; but unlike money, people can't go around printing luck when they want to. The only other way to balance the little amount of luck floating around in the world was to take advice from those luckier or wiser. For a long time, the only one qualified to give advice in Leporidae Lop had been Harriet Stowe. But Edbert Pollock changed that. His defiance caused ripples in the fabric of their existence. Not huge ripples, not meaningful ripples, but ripples enough to change the entire continent for the worst. Just to be accurate, the ripples didn't happen because Edbert gave bad advice, but because, when the power dynamic changed amongst the elite, there's always a nasty consequence for the little guy.

And the gods didn't care. They were quite happy with the little guy getting the short straw as long as blood flowed and their name kept being mentioned. Also, the gods liked games. Games meant there was a set of rules to be broken and there was a winner. So what if kingdoms were crumbled and lives were crushed? Moves had to be made.

So it went. And thusly, in the darkness, a group chanted— not the Order of Regulators, not the Cadetblue Dot Order, but a different group, a family one. Their complex words sounded rhythmical and precise. Forty candles cast light, pushing back the room's gloom, freeing the chanters from the horrors the dark brought. In the outskirts of their circle, the dead chattered. As the bright candlelight made the sound of the deceased bearable, a faint sound of relief spread amongst the chanters.

The dead wailed again, causing more terror. It would be nice if they could stay away, at least on a special night like this, when any misplaced word, noise, or movement was fatal.

The ominous ritual continued in an abandoned mansion. This ritual had been done there for generations, as it was demanded from the chanters. They knelt and waved they hands, singing words for luck. Most would even lick the floor if that would guarantee years' worth of luck. If even one of them would have tried, it would have instantly given them luck delivered to their front steps with a big red bow on it. But the chanters mistakenly thought their superiors liked them to have some dignity, but that was far from the truth. You couldn't have dignity when you were nothing.

Ten years ago, the mansion had pulsed with life. It was the center for the Upwood family. Back then, the mansion had been furnished from top to bottom with rare, overseas fashion, but when they left, they'd taken everything with them. Now only the stone altar stood in the middle of the room. The dead were forced to live alone there, which was their own darn fault. Norville had taken his family away as the burden of their dead relatives and their constant advice made him neurotic and unable to function, making him release his stress via the weirdest hobbies there could be—involving costumes, woods, and animals.

Norville did appreciate good advice as much as the next fellow, but advice about which side of the bed to get up on, how a real man held his spoon, or which shoe to put on first was far from useful. To cap it all, the dead didn't agree on anything, always arguing amongst themselves.

"No, that's not the way to do it," Aunt Margaret would say.

"Yes, it is. You can't wear black socks on Thursday," Uncle George would say.

"Could you hurry up? My feet are getting cold, and I just want to be done with the matter," Norville would say, and they would ignore him. If he went and put on the socks anyway, all their fury was turned on him and he wouldn't hear the end of it for days.

As things got worse day by day, he simply left. That had shut the dead up. It had never crossed their minds he could just up and leave like that.

Now a deaf caretaker looked after the house. She never complained about anything and never passed on the messages written on the walls. The woman was bit daft but really nice.

The ritualistic chant grew stronger as it hit the altar in the middle of the room like a tidal wave. The chants echoed through the altar to the gods, who had already rolled the dice for tonight and for the other nights to come.

Tonight's ritual was Norville's obligatory ritual. If he didn't do it once a week, his brother would get the family fortune—a cruel clause left by his father to his heritage. Upwood sometimes entertained the thought of letting his brother have it all, but then he remembered his responsibilities to his wife and children and never went through his inclination. Passing on the burden to his son bothered him to a greater extent, but so it was done in their family. If he left the fortune to his daughter—whose strength would keep the family going, unlike her easy-going kid brother—the dead would retaliate since no girl would ever run their family. In order to stop that, Petula Upwood, his daughter, studied to be necromancer overseas on another continent, in a city called Necropolis. That would shut their relatives up once and for all, and maybe give the dead the peace they badly needed. Luckily, he still had his other daughter with him.

Norville laid a drawn picture of Edbert in the middle of the candles and their chant grew stronger. After they'd sent their wishes to the gods, silence filled the room. The ritual was done.

A woman put her hands on his tight shoulders and asked, "Will this fix everything?" Her strawberry-colored hair came out of her hood, and the faint scent of clovers was intoxicating.

Norville nodded and took off his black velvet hood. "The gods have heard our pleas for Edbert Pollock. The rest is out of our hands," he said and took his wife into his arms. After so many years together, their touch was still soft and warm, and the love they had for each other was there between them. There, in the silence, they both knew what the other thought. *Edbert Pollock would either save or ruin them.*

"I have to go, they are waiting for me at the shop," he said.

"Be careful," she said and kissed him.

* * *

Sigourney left Harriet alone in her office. Like the rest, she knew little about Harriet and a lot about the rumors. Her head was heavy from the disappointment she'd caused her. Unlike Norville Upwood, Sigourney couldn't ask the gods to pardon her; she had to deal with her mistake herself. Sigourney swallowed her tears and hurried back to the bookshop to prevent losing Harriet's friendship.

Sigourney picked up speed and ran faster back to the shop. The distance from the palace felt like an eternity, even when she took the shortest route. She had to run past the garden and the baking district, then make a turn at the Hunt's Library and go through an entire aristocratic neighborhood[8] to arrive where the shops were. When she got to Edbert's bookshop, Lars stood in a queue leading inside the building. She panted a little and watched the spectacle—the buzz around Edbert. People bumped into her as she stood there on the street, her head swirling as she tried to piece together what was happening. More and more people came, and they pushed past her to join the line. Even the police officers had come to watch people going in and out of the shop. Sigourney had to confess the bookshop owner had a strange allure she'd missed.

This shouldn't be happening, Sigourney thought. Edbert lacked the usual charisma needed to draw this much attention. There had to be something odd going on. She had to talk to Lars. She approached the man carefully, trying to stay hidden from the other people.

"Why did you critting do that? I lost my spot! If I don't get to meet him…" Lars said as she tugged his sleeve and pulled him out of the queue.

"So?" Sigourney asked, knowing using too many words welcomed mistakes, and she hated mistakes. Mistakes were a reminder that you weren't good enough; that you didn't deserve a spot on the merry-go-round.

Lars held his words back—he always did—having seen Sigourney flee and take her money with her too many times.

---

[8] A place which made her uncomfortable. It was bad enough trying to interact with the common folk. The extra layer of nob confused her.

"At first it was quiet, then this nob man went in and soon after, people started to wait to see Mr. Pollock."

Sigourney looked at Lars and waited. It was the silence; it always got to them. People felt compelled to fill the void or the discomfort would swallow them as whole and spit them out in an unrecognizable form. And no one wanted that. But it didn't win favors, either. Silence made people stay away—something Sigourney could attest to.

"How should I know who he is? That's all I know," Lars said, half lying and half ignoring what he had seen. There was no mistaking who Huxley was, but then again, Lars wasn't exactly sober and not exactly paying too much attention to anything other than the queue. It had to be important; why else would people stand in line.

Sigourney let him get back to it, giving Lars more coins from her pocket than he deserved. Just enough to satisfy her conscience.

While they'd chatted, the streets had gotten fuller, if that was even possible. The kingdom's vendors had arrived to hassle money out of the people with their trinkets, bagels, and pretzels. Then, as the rumor of the whole thing had spread across the kingdom, more came to gawk at the show in hopes of something, anything to happen to make it worth their while. The atmosphere was ecstatic; nothing the world had seen before, nothing Sigourney had seen before. The sight terrified her. She wasn't the only one who found this the end of sanity, but those who thought thusly kept their mouth shut. It was bad enough to think differently, but even worse to let everyone know that.

Sigourney pushed through the crowd, stepping aside, slipping through, and taking pirouettes not to collide with anyone. Getting into the shop turned out to be the tricky part. The doorway was packed full, and people fought to keep their place by using elbows and other illegal weapons. If a god had appeared in the middle of the crowd, even he, her, or it wouldn't get ahead in the line. Not without a guaranteed miracle and a bucketful of gold, and even then, it was doubtful the god would get the people's attention. People had to get in as other people wanted to get in, and they wanted to get in because you had to get in.

All that left Sigourney one choice. She crawled in between people's legs. A few of them kicked her, and she winced, but she kept her mouth shut, not letting out even a peep. To Sigourney's misery, the space inside the shop was even more scarce—the air was stuffy and stagnant, making it hard for her to breathe. She tried to take deep breaths in, but her lungs were full of sand. Those who had already met Edbert didn't leave willingly. They lingered in hopes of another opportunity to speak with him.

All this made Sigourney feel like someone was setting off tiny explosions all over and around her. She blinked and her heartbeat got faster. She searched for an escape route. She found several, but couldn't take any of them, making her want to scream. She forced herself to stay calm. Sigourney bit her lips and looked around, ignoring the distracting smells of perfume, sweat, and smoke, the constant murmurs, chatter, and laughing, and the stares. The only space which people stayed clear of was next to a nob man… Udolf Huxley. She should have guessed he would be here. If there was one man who hated Harriet Stowe and had making the prime minister's life miserable on his agenda, it was Huxley.

Sigourney fixed her attention to the man and everything else turned unimportant. Her breathing slowed.

Huxley and Sigourney had met before. She had even worked for him back in her early days in Leporidae Lop—a very dark period in her life she didn't want to revisit, not even in her memories.

Huxley was a man without a conscience, a man who saw granny as a good source of dried meat to sell. A man to stay away from.

It all made sense now. He was here to shake the core of Leporidae Lop like a bully shakes a small schoolboy for his lunch money. This had nothing to do with Edbert, but everything to do with hatred and creed and arrogance. All things Sigourney understood.

She sat on the floor next to the man and watched as Huxley coached Mister Pollock, wagging his head or fingers when Edbert did something daft, which happened more than once. Actually, it seemed to be a constant occurrence. Sigourney took pleasure seeing a continuous frown on Huxley's face. Poor Mister Pollock, though. He would continue his miserable existence from now, letting a vampire, or more like a goblin, latch onto him. He should had been more careful. Sigourney bet Huxley would suck the life out of Edbert before the week's end. She had seen it happen. The only one who could stop that was Harriet. Sigourney had to tell her, but not yet. She had to wait to see what all this meant.

Huxley being behind it all made things a lot simpler. Getting rid of a selfish man like Huxley was easy compared to getting rid of a mystery man like Pollock. Still, Huxley was cunning and ruthless, and should never be taken too lightly. Sigourney was happy she didn't have to think of a way out of this. She only had to observe and report back.

After hours passed, Huxley ordered food from outside—a huge sandwich tucked with odd meat, lettuce, and pickles. Sigourney's stomach grumbled. She stole pieces from the sandwich every time the man left it unguarded, causing great discomfort to Huxley and leaving a smile on her face. A payback for all the critty jobs he made her do, which still haunted her. She could still see the faces of all the people whose lives they'd ruined. A few of them were still alive, and on holidays, she did her best to ease their discomfort. But money and kind words only went so far.

Not her problem; she had just done her work, she reminded herself. But she didn't believe what she said. If people went around thinking that way, it was no wonder the world was in the shitter.

Sigourney shifted her weight, but not out of mental discomfort, which was a constant occurrence in her life. She'd learned to live with it. No, it was about sitting at a bad angle, putting strain on her back and legs. She needed to walk around, but there was no space. She continued watching Edbert, shifting from one buttock to another. Edbert did fair better. He leaned on his hand and let out a sigh, or more liked wheezed without a stop. Every time he showed signs he would drive people out of the shop, Huxley shook his head.

What Huxley did to Edbert was cruel. Sigourney hated nothing more than cruelty toward anybody or anything. She had seen her fair share. She would have to convince Harriet that Edbert wasn't her enemy; that she needed to help the poor man, even if the man didn't want her help. His need for their aid was more evident at the end of the day. Edbert went over his ledgers, and Sigourney saw how painful it was for him. In his ledgers was the proof how much he loved and cared for the shop. She quite understood why now that the place was empty. There was this reassuring clarity, calm, and kindness that seemed to be woven into the wooden frames of the shop. It felt like a home. She could picture Edbert playing with his toy soldiers next to the counter while his father sold books. She could hear him reading to Edbert, sitting on the floor side-by-side at the children's section with all the engraved bunnies and ducks between the pages.

All so wonderful, all taken away by the present and by the knock on the front door, alarming all three of them. Sigourney followed Edbert to the door, jumping at the opportunity for fresh air. To her surprise, Norville Upwood stood outside. She never thought a decent man like Norville would associate with a man like Huxley. She had never seen them interact publicly. But then she remembered that somewhere in her reports, she had written Huxley and Upwood had grown up together; that they'd went to school together. She had their score cards somewhere hidden in her surveillance documents. Yet, somehow, she'd let that slip from her mind.

She balanced there between the doorway and the shop, not knowing if to go back in or to report back to Harriet. This was information she needed right away. But if she stayed, she might discern how Huxley would use Edbert as a weapon against Harriet. Sigourney scratched her head and the door slammed on her. She pushed back but let go. There was no use fighting and cause an alarm. It was better anyway if she went back to tell Harriet everything, so she could stop the attack on her before it even began.

She hurried back to the palace in the dead of night.

CHAPTER EIGHT
A Stack of Carrots

Harriet collapsed into her chair after the assistant hurried to give her invitation to Edbert Pollock. She'd come up with a way to make Edbert do her bidding, and if he said no, he would look foolish and petty in the eyes of the public. The way she solved the problem made her proud, if she said so herself.

Good, another thing off her worry list. She moved on to tackle the royal family's budget. It was a gruesome task, always ending up with animosity between her and them as the king, queen, and the master of the household saw new clothes and trinkets as necessities, and she didn't. Unfortunately, they were right to some extent, but Harriet would never admit that aloud. Altogether, the budget was a task she willingly would leave for later, but as her nature prohibited postponing anything, she took their proposals and went through them like a sledgehammer.

After the first empty words were put there to butter her up, she began to strike out their boisterous claims for money. No sensible person would agree with them, least of all a person with her humble upbringing. She and her sister grew up with nothing. She'd married well beyond her class, and her sister...

well, she was a teacher. When the queen's expenditures were in order the way she saw they should be, she inscribed her name under the line of approval. She still winced. The money could be spent somewhere sorely needed. The royal family had come with the kingdom, and there was no getting rid of them. And to Harriet's wonderment, people seemed to like the whole concept of royalty. Not only because they could stitch the royal family's faces on their handkerchiefs and sell them to foreigners, but also because it seemed to elevate the kingdom in their mind. Anyone could make a democracy, but kings and queens didn't come around that often.

Harriet leaned back. The king's allowance was next, but she mistakenly glanced toward the kingdom's general budget, and for a while, she entertained the thought of handling the truly important matters. At least sense and challenge lay in there. She often spent her days thinking of ways to make Leporidae Lop a perfect and dignified society. Nevertheless, even when she'd managed the kingdom for decades, it lacked something. Something which she could almost grasp, but not quite. So the only solution was to tighten her monitoring and advising to make everything strive towards perfection. The easiest solution to all her problems and making the kingdom the best it could be was to remove the difficult variable out of the equation, and that was humans. But without them, a country wouldn't be a country or a society a society. The people had to stay.

When the last paper of the royal family's budget was signed, she read through her formal to-do list and yawned.

Next, she had to go over the Ferrum issue. Their neighbor kingdom had raised the price of iron ore so high, it made fair trading Leporidae Lop's livestock, food, fabrics, and other commodities impossible. Leporidae Lop's progression demanded ore, not only as a building material, but also as a basic material for all the new apparatuses the Department of Modern Lop Appliances came up with. Those apparatuses would revolutionize the world, or so they said, though she hadn't seen any evidence of that. She'd seen many lost fingers but not a changed world. But they promised it was about to come, hinting that even luck and gods would have to yield under the new science. That would be a day.

There was even now a proposal on her desk, asking for money and permission to install rails on the ground to be used by monsters called locomotives. Who needed such foolish things? Horses were perfectly fine. Anything faster was unnatural. And there was no reason to leave Leporidae Lop. Yet, Harriet knew, at some point, she would have to allocate the money for the contraption. There was no stopping change; she'd learned as much by now. Change had a habit of sneaking around the corner and throwing a punch if you tried.

The problem with Ferrum had to be dealt with and soon. But it was a task which needed a personal chat with their prime minister. Before that, she had to study the market values of all the products in question, not only locally but also continent-wide. In addition, she had to go over Ferrum's economic situation to have leverage in the negotiations. Still, she knew it wouldn't be enough to secure a better deal for Leporidae Lop. Ore was valuable, so she needed something extra for the negotiations and for the other proposal the kingdom's bankers had given her. It was something to do with a new way of doing bookkeeping. Something about turning loans into assets and assets into loans. Harriet grunted. When it came to bankers, she had to win without compromises. If you gave them robe enough, they would not only hang you, they would hang themselves and the whole nation in their pursuit of profit. And as always, what she needed to solve any of her problems was locked inside the sewers.

She badly needed to get a boost of luck. Using such a cheap trick made her angry. Taking care of the kingdom's wealth and health should be about statesmanship, not about a hairy foot.

A loose wisp of hair dropped to her cheek when she leaned to get the carrots; she put it back behind her ear, opened a bobby pin, and secured the strand between the pin's teeth.

Worshiping luck had changed from a blessing to a nuisance. At first, luck worship gave Leporidae Lop a head start by assuring they stayed alive with good weather and healthy livestock, making the kingdom the center of the known world. But luck had come with a heavy price, centuries later. Luck governed the citizens' happiness to such an extent that pursuing luck to gain happiness left them unhappy. It had become a vicious cycle, a cycle she had to stay ahead of, and that meant she had to rub the rabbit's foot daily—and at worst, several times a day. In addition, her private source of luck added a heavy amount to the kingdom's budget. Carrots weren't cheap, not with a creature of the rabbit's size.

Altogether, luck had become a huge industry in Leporidae Lop. There were trinket sellers, luck brokers, luck tellers, luck exchangers, and so on. One could buy a whole year's worth of luck with a price, a price that kept changing daily and hourly, thus the need for brokers and other bloodsuckers.

What would happen when the luckiest kingdom in the world exhausted all the luck there was? For now, Harriet dared not to think about when that day might come. The gods continued favoring their kingdom, and she had to work with that premise.

Sometimes Harriet's sneaky thoughts came up with ways to get rid of the gods and their influence. Locomotives were the first step. The rest she kept close to her heart, never daring to say them aloud for fear of being smited. Nevertheless, she had a plan worked out if ever an opportunity presented itself. Of course, she already had defied the gods once by trapping the rabbit, but she refused to get too cocky about it.

Harriet took the carrots out of the desk drawer and laid them on the table. She had to write her name under the rest of the orders for today before she was done, and the rest she had to leave for tomorrow.

Harriet put the papers back in their places and stood. Time to see the bloody rabbit and give into the system she'd helped to create.

She headed to the sewers. The palace was quiet at this time of night, but not empty. The only ones she encountered were the night guards, who pretended they didn't see her—and she did likewise. When she got to the sewers, the atmosphere felt wrong. The door to the sewers was unlocked. She stepped in, shutting the door behind her. As she made her way down the stone steps, the echoes from her shoes sounded different. Also, the rabbit's fast, heavy breathing was missing. The closer she got to the god's cage, the emptier it looked, and she couldn't deny it any longer.

The cage was bare, and the god was missing.

Harriet rushed to the cage. Its bars laid scattered all over the ground. The bars had been pulled out of the frame. The forger had promised her no one could be able to do that. The only one who could interact with the cage was her, and she was darn sure she hadn't let the god of luck out. She crouched to touch the broken bars, which felt warm against her skin, but as soon as her fingers brushed against them, they crumbled. Steel shouldn't do that, either, especially since the cage was forged from the finest iron there was. Harriet quickly pulled her hand away. She watched the broken bars and the symbols on them, which glowed in a faint, purple light. Harriet grimaced.

The floor was still warm. The rabbit had been here a moment ago. It couldn't be too far away. She had to get the god back or the kingdom would slide into chaos. Who knew what her enemies would use the rabbit for? Even if the god had gotten away on its own, this would be catastrophic.

Harriet pushed herself up, letting out a low, "Crit." Feeling the movement in her stiff knees, she didn't get farther than that. A noise, a liturgy, rang out behind her. She stood as fast as she could and swirled around, only to see the cage become whole again. Harriet took long, quick steps toward the closing gap, but she was too slow and her knees gave in. She fell forward against the forming bars. The carved spells in the iron activated as her hands hit them, electrocuting her with such a force that she flew in an arc onto the cage floor, causing her to hit her head and lose consciousness. The carrots scattered all around her, forming a perfect circle.

There came a quiet sniff beyond the cage, and an even quieter, 'Sorry.'

* * *

You could say that Edbert was having as bad of a time as Harriet. He would end up unconscious as well, but in a wholly different way—the more usual route. When Edbert had recovered from the initial shock of receiving the invitation from the Dragon Lady herself, Huxley had forced him to do the pub rounds. Now, his words slurred out, "I can't go see her." He and the others knew the visit was a suicide mission, and he wasn't that willing to die on the behalf of his new acquaintances.

"I can't go see her," Edbert said again, as none gave him the sympathetic answer he craved. This time, his tongue tasted funny, and it moved like it swam in pudding. He had never been this drunk before. The ale kept coming, and he was told a refusal might alienate his new friends and make the Dragon Lady eat him whole. His doom had been a fruity drink, which had stopped his tongue from working altogether.

"No, no… I won't go," he slurred.

"Don't worry about it. Her reign is over and you, my good fellow, will be our next prime minister," Huxley said, sounding sober and alert. He took a sip from his drink, which wasn't even close to being ale.

Don't worry, ha, Edbert thought. It was easy for the man to say that. He wasn't the one going to be skinned alive and made a laughingstock of the whole kingdom. Edbert took a huge gulp from his pint to kill his last functioning brain cells. It worked, and they happily shut down. He stared into emptiness and breathed heavily.

A drunk man staggered toward them and splashed his beer all over the table and Edbert's clothes. Huxley moved like a cat under the shower of beer and got to keep his dignity. For a fraction of a second, his pleasant mask crumbled, revealing murder in his eyes. The man took no notice of him; he only had eyes for the spaced-out Edbert.

The drunk man fought to get his words out. If he could, his words would have come out like this: "You are a helluva guy for going against the prime minister. Good luck, and you are my hero." But due to the beer he'd splashed earlier, and all the others before that, his words came like this: "Yur hell guuy, mmm heeero…" Neither man understood the other, but that didn't matter, because the message was the same Edbert had received all night. Everyone loved him, the matter of the bookshop symbolized their own struggles against the evil bitch, and every single one of them wanted him to succeed.

Earlier, Edbert had panicked for every encouraging word, but now his brain hummed a tune which wouldn't be invented for years to come. When the music was finally revealed to the world, it was called 'elevator music.'.

Edbert liked the newly found sense of calm and serenity. He was finally starting to understand why people spent their money on ale rather than books. There was something to be said for this warm, lighter-than-air feeling inside him, despite all the dragons in the world.

The next morning, Edbert woke up in his sweat-soaked bed with no idea how he'd gotten there. Edbert patted himself and was relieved to find he still wore yesterday's clothes. His relief quickly ended when a headache pierced his skull. The headache sounded a lot like heavy metal or techno, depending how he tilted his head. He kept his head straight in hopes whatever the sound was, it would stay away and the elevator music would come back. In the meantime, he tried to piece together what had happened last night. Impossible, especially as loud *clangs* echoed from downstairs. Edbert knew he should get up and prevent someone from robbing his priced books and private collection, but he just laid there, unable to move. His dead father and grandfather would never let him forget this day. It was as well. He would never forgive himself. A quick death would make up for everything.

To his luck, he didn't have to kill himself. Huxley poked his head in through the bedroom door. "Morning… Good gods, you look awful." Huxley grinned at Edbert. "You, my dear fellow, don't hold your liquor well. But never mind. We'll beat that out of you. Anyway, when you are ready, I made you eggs.

They are waiting for you at the kitchen."

"I can't," Edbert said, holding his stomach, ready to play a round of the fun game called 'What I ate last night.'

Huxley paid no attention to him or the sickening expression on his face. "Okay," he groaned. "Suit yourself. You are missing a lot. They were the best I have ever made." They weren't; they were burned and soggy at the same time, but in Huxley's eyes, they were a five-star gourmet breakfast. You could say Huxley was good at deceiving himself. Not out of delicate ego. No. It was for the fact that if he believed in his words, then others would, too. His mind registered that automatically, and for a good reason. To the horror and failings of humanity, it actually worked that way. People were more positive and cooperative toward you if you behaved overly positive toward yourself and future rewards. They even gave more money to you because of that, even over those who had more secure predictions and returns. Hope is a funny thing.

Huxley shrugged as Edbert didn't jump at the opportunity. It was the bookshop owner's loss. "I leave you to it. I have a few errands to run. Be ready at midday, I'll come and get you." Huxley left without an answer.

Edbert laid there for longer than he should. He ignored the knocks coming from downstairs, knowing well he should have already opened the shop. But even holding his head above the pillow made his head sway. So, after an hour with great effort, he dragged his feet on the carpet next to his bed. He tried to follow his morning ritual, which he had done exactly the same way and at the same time for as long as he could remember. But he had already missed the one most important item on the list, and that was to read his ten pages before getting up. Earlier, if he'd missed even one item on his ritual, he'd panick and had to repeat everything in the right order, even in the middle of the day. But now, the whole morning ritual seemed the most unimportant thing in the world. He just needed to survive this day, then he could do his nightly ritual, and everything would be fine again. Except, he was sure he didn't even get to do his nightly ritual after Harriet got to him. Maybe there would be peace and quiet in the forgotten dungeons where the Prime Minster sent those who disagreed with her. Hopefully.

After washing up and cleaning himself mildly presentable, Edbert opened the bookshop, and once again, the shop filled with curious Sunday-spectators. At midday, Huxley arrived and drove out all the people, which didn't matter since not a single one of them had bought anything. They had come to gawk at him, and he had gawked back at them, daring any of them to speak. None did.

His head felt worse.

Edbert couldn't help but wonder how he, Edbert Pollock, had become the symbol for resistance and freedom? It had to be a mistake. They had to be looking for someone else. He was sure that someone else always stood behind him in the shadows being better at everything.

It didn't matter. Huxley hurried Edbert out of the bookshop after several wardrobe changes. His clothes didn't seem to make the man happy. Some even horrified the man, and he had thrown out good clothes without asking Edbert's permission. Edbert would get them back when Huxley wasn't looking. Outside the shop, Upwood waited for them in his carriage. They crammed into it and drove to the palace, where a crowd already awaited them.

Edbert didn't want to know who had summoned the people here at the gawk at him. He just stared at the crowed, listening to their yells of, "Edbert, Edbert."

Even the reporters had come to witness the historical event of his humiliation. *Poor old me*, Edbert thought. He watched as they scribbled on their pads, immortalizing what was about to come.

Edbert searched for Harriet and her icy stare, but he saw only the king and his queen at the palace steps. The king wasn't very tall. He wore high heeled shoes, and his soft round belly was covered with a red velvet cloak lined with stoat fur. His queen wasn't much to look at, either. She had a potato nose on her petite face, which was rimmed with honey-colored hair. They looked comical, but Edbert guessed that was what royalty should look like. He had never actually seen them in person. The whole concept of royalty was just there. It was good to have around, like any old custom, but there was no reason to pay too much attention to it.

The carriage came to a halt, and Huxley and Upwood guided Edbert out. As soon as he emerged from the door, a cheer rang out. Edbert tried to get back in to escape the horror, but Huxley blocked his way. He pushed Edbert toward the royal family, almost tripping him over his own feet, which preferred to stay right where they were.

"It's all right, they are waiting for you," Upwood said.

The fact gave Edbert more courage than Huxley's pushing, but still not enough to make him want to go anywhere. Yet he complied. There was no other choice.

The crowd continued cheering with every step he took. They cheered as he groaned while climbing the palace steps. They cheered as he arrived in front of the royal family. Edbert's knees were ready to give out. He pushed them straight and looked past the king to see if Harriet stood behind him, but she was nowhere to be seen. But even when she was missing, he felt her murderous gaze on him.

Huxley hit Edbert's side, making Edbert notice the king was waiting for him to do something. Even the crowd held their breath and waited. Edbert frowned and then realized what was expected. He turned red.

Edbert gave the royal couple a deep bow.

The king turned to address the crowd, satisfied the right protocol had been done, "It has come to my attention we have another candidate for the prime minister's position this year..."

The crowd cheered.

"Harriet Stowe..."

The crowd fell silent.

"What did he say?" someone asked.

"I don't know. Harriet something..." another someone

said.

The king cleared his throat. "The position for the prime minister is open for an early election, and those who want to apply should do so by the end of next week. Edbert Pollock is the first one to register for the race, and if Edbert Pollock will run unopposed, he will automatically be appointed to the position—"

Edbert was sure he hadn't registered for anything.

The crowd cheered over the rest of the king's speech.

Edbert was dumbfounded. He looked over his shoulder, waiting to see Harriet standing there, scowling at him; to tell him this was just a joke at his expense and now he would be sent directly to jail without passing go and collecting his two hundred bucks. But no, he was mistaken.

The king's speech ended the public part of the nomination. Huxley and Upwood escorted the dumbfounded Edbert as he followed the king and his queen inside the palace.

"Where's the prime minister?" Edbert whispered to the two men as they walked behind the royal couple.

"Who cares," Huxley said. "Now please, shut up and just do what's told."

Edbert swallowed his, "I do," and did as he was told.

CHAPTER NINE
Not as Planned

Sigourney ran straight back to Harriet's office after leaving Edbert's shop. The words, the truth, everything wanted to come out as she hopped from shadow to shadow. She had been hopping from shadow to shadow a lot more now than a couple of days ago,. Not that she was complaining, being in motion kept any unwanted thoughts away. Her feet moved faster when they got to the palace. She strode up the stairs and headed to Harriet's office. Once she was there, she found an empty room. She ran to Harriet's private quarters, but she was absent from there as well. She searched them twice, looking for the woman, even in her wardrobe. But there was no secret door to a lair or other dimensions, just Harriet's black governess dresses. Odd, she thought. Harriet was always at the palace. Sigourney shut the wardrobe's door and went to Harriet's audience chamber in her private rooms.

Sigourney sat on one of the wooden chairs to wait.

She settled herself so she was able to see the entry. She watched the door, following its golden vine trimming. The pale blue door became more familiar than any door should. But she had to keep watch of it.

At some point, she must have fallen asleep, because her muscles jerked, waking her up. The sun shined straight into Sigourney's eyes from an open window. She rubbed her eyes and stretched .

Sigourney listened to the quiet whispers seeping through the walls into the audience chamber. They grew louder every second she sat there.

Sigourney rubbed her eyes again and stood. She followed her yesterday's steps, but Harriet was still missing. The prime minister's office looked miserable without her, as did her private quarters. Even the space under Harriet's bed looked extra haunting, and not for a second because of the normal, depressed bogeyman living under there.

Sigourney bit her lip. She was sure if she didn't, it would start to quaver and then the tears would follow, and she didn't like tears. In her opinion, they were a broken social alarm system, she had no use for. But that didn't matter now, because something was wrong. Harriet wouldn't abandon her or Leporidae Lop like this. She should already be bossing around the two multidimensional fools as the prime minister called the king and queen—or so she had heard Harriet to mutter. Sometimes she followed Harriet around as she went on with her daily business, but in the shadows, of course. But only on those days when she needed to be close to someone to drive away the scary, monstrous words inside her head. If there was ever a scarier dungeon than her head space, then she knew she'd arrived to atone all the mistakes she'd done. But until then, nothing compared to what her mind could do. Not even being trapped by a giant, house-sized spider with red cross on its back and enough eyes to share with the blind and foul.

She would find out whatever had happened to Harriet and bring her back.

She just didn't know where to start. But it didn't matter. The universe had thought to provide her a clue. Or more like her personal god did, who loaned their wisdom and guidance for her to survive the forsaken Sunday. It was impossible to tell if the god did it in advance or afterward, being only able to exist on Wednesdays, but nevertheless, they did poke Sigourney in the right direction with a growing murmurs coming from the place courtyard. Okay, it all might have been a coincidence, but that didn't stop the god from taking credit of it. Not for a second.

Sigourney heard murmurs as was intended. She rushed to the windows, tearing through layers of curtains, knowing in her heart that they had finally decided to lynch Harriet.

There, in the yard, stood the biggest crowd of people Sigourney had ever seen. The mere sight made her shiver and want to hide under the bed with the bogeyman. She searched for the gallows and Harriet, but she saw neither out in the palace yard.

Sigourney drew the window just enough to have room to climb down. She took hold of the little tiles and the joints they formed in the wall. She gripped harder where the edges were nothing but small crimps. Sigourney had done this all her life—climbing on and off things—and her movements where like a flow of water. She was soft and relaxed, and for that fleeting moment, there was nothing but the next move. But that was short-lived, especially when she saw what was happening. Edbert was entering the race to become the next prime minister, and Harriet was still nowhere to be seen. Huxley was there, so was Upwood, and not to mention the king and his queen. There was no doubt in Sigourney's mind that they had done something to Harriet. Even a blind person would see that. And that was just what the crowd whispered. Some in bewilderment, but most with content that the witch was finally gone.

Stupid, stupid, stupid, she screamed at herself. Not being there. Having not warned Harriet sooner. It was all her fault. She had let the Prime Minster down, and now she was gone and dead. Sigourney's whole body shook. She clutched her hands to keep herself hidden and to keep herself from crumbling. Sigourney concentrated on watching the spectacle unfold. The cheers died down when Edbert and his new friends headed back into the palace without inviting the public to the after-party. People murmured as they walked back to their homes, feeling somewhat disappointed.

Sigourney followed Edbert and the others in, who spoke of trivialities. They did this bizarre social dance where they all fawned over Edbert, even the king and queen, but in every opportunity given, when Edbert wasn't quite up to the social standards, they put him down, showing him his place. At the royal audience chamber, they spoke nothing but how the society would be organized once Edbert became the next prime minister. How the silly audiences Harriet held had to stop. How some laws about taxation and private ownership had to be altered, how truly the business owners should become advisers to both Edbert and the royal family, how Edbert should bring back fiat currency, freeing the citizens to speculate with the future to create grander projects. What the projects were was irrelevant, as long as resources were moved around. Even an environmental catastrophe would suffice, because it meant equipment to clean it up and manpower to do it, meaning money went around and around, and made more money, especially with a wonderful thing called inventive accounting. But mostly, Edbert would have to strike out any laws about sacrifices and luck rituals and how often and when they should be held. Luck should be free to use whenever and wherever.

Edbert listened to the demands mutely, and when he finally spoke, he asked, "I was wondering where Miss Stowe is? Shouldn't she be here with us?"

The king smiled at Huxley, who smiled at the king, and Upwood gave them all an awkward smile. No one paid any attention to the queen, who sat there with a pleasant smile on her lips—the same one she always wore of a wax doll. Most likely not from her own free will.

"My good fellow, when luck does what it's suppose to do, we don't question its ways. We cease the moment and run with it." That was the only answer he got. That was the only thing what was spoken. Edbert had killed the mood.

The three men were ushered out soon after. The agitated

royal couple left through a secret panel and the three men walked out like commoners the way they had come in, through the golden doors.

Sigourney followed Edbert and his companions around the whole day, waiting for a slip of tongue or anything else, but all they did was campaign for votes. At first, at a public park giving speeches. Edbert stammered out his words, but the crowds cheered for him, anyway. Then they fraternized with the commoners at a pub, or shall we say, several pubs, which really could be thought of as one and the same, for they had identical decor, almost identical clientele, and the same sole purpose. The only exception was their passionate fan base, who thought the other pubs were lame.

After the third pub and Edbert's sixth beer, his words became slurred. "Your support means so much," he said to no one particular. He had been saying that for twenty minutes straight, occasionally dozing off. Sigourney was the only one paying any attention to him. Unlike Edbert, Upwood and Huxley poured their drinks away. They whispered in secrecy about something Sigourney couldn't quite hear.

Edbert took the last deadly sip from a pint full of foam and passed out, banging his head on the table. Everyone in the pub cheered. The public loved the drunk man.[9]

Upwood and Huxley took the man home.

Sigourney followed them, still hoping they might know where Harriet was, but she'd started to grow ever more doubtful that the men had anything to do with Harriet's disappearance, at least not directly. Not the way they acted. But there was nothing else she could do, so she hopped into Upwood's carriage, and sat between Huxley and Upwood on a purple velvet cushion.

Before the carriage even took off, the two men's closeness made her uncomfortable. She moved to sit next to the foul-smelling Edbert and immediately felt a lot better, despite the

---

[9] The sober man was entirely a different matter.

snoring and drool leaking on the man's right shoulder.

"This is going great. They love him," Upwood said.

Huxley grunted. "Even when he looks like that." He swept dust off his jacket and looked down his nose at Edbert.

"He's a common man to them; you wouldn't get even a fraction of his popularity," Upwood said, clearly hitting the mark.

Huxley winced.

He sulked the rest of the journey back to Edbert's place. Before the carriage stopped, he said, "Politics shouldn't be about popularity; it should be about the most convincing argument or about power. Not about who's the prettiest or who has a way with the people. That's what's wrong with the world; the most competent person won't win. Look at him. Is this a man you want to run our kingdom?"

"Have you changed your mind, then?" Upwood asked, turning from watching out of the window to face Huxley.

"No, I haven't changed my mind. It's not about that. There's no other choice than him. We made sure of that. But it's still wrong. You know as much as I do that even when my mother home-schooled me and all of you rest, it was never about who understood the topic or knew what to make of it. It was about who was the richest kid or who had a set of hair that swayed others, or you know. It shouldn't be him getting the seat from Harriet. It should be me, but it won't be." Huxley sighed.

"You were the richest kid," Upwood said, half whispering.

"What did that matter? I still got my ass handed to me," Huxley spat.

"Not when I was around," Upwood said.

"Forget what I said." Huxley opened the door when they arrived at Edbert's shop.

The driver helped them to carry the drooling Edbert to his bed, leaving him there. Sigourney was forced to decide who to follow. She chose Huxley, which was a huge mistake. He went straight home, where his mistress waited for him naked… and perfect. The mistress's long, chestnut-brown hair covered her breasts. But the woman's nakedness didn't bother Sigourney; it was what happened next which made her want to end her life. The sight of Huxley, naked, tainted her soul in a way nothing else could. A king without his clothes on is a man like any other, and in Huxley's case, like a wrinkled old goblin.

Sigourney fled through an open window. She couldn't force herself to watch them. She doubted she would find Harriet between Huxley's sheets, anyway. If that was the case, it would be the end of the world as she knew it.

Altogether, the day hadn't made her any wiser. Dirty and defiled, yes, but not wise. Sigourney had no clue what she should do next—Harriet had always told her what to do. This was the first time she was let loose on her own, and it made her feel lousy.

* * *

The rabbit god of luck snuck out of the palace after its release. It had fooled its liberators to take Harriet instead. It was a god, after all. It suppressed the sneaking thought that they had been after Harriet instead of it in the beginning, and there was something hugely wrong with such course of events. But it was foolish to question a perfect escape, since it would be like inviting Calamity—and she wasn't a nice sister at all, always pulling its tail. Anyway, the fresh air felt amazing against its fur. The air felt like freedom. It stood there in its full nakedness, not looking anything like a goblin. It had been sure it would die in the damp sewer, but human nature perplexed it with its deeds. Humans constantly defied their original meaning. The silly buggers thought they were independent and free, despite being made to be the gods' playthings. But it seemed humans had decided otherwise. Good for them, but bad for it and its kind. Not that the rabbit god of luck cared much for the other gods. Their bloody sports didn't amuse it at all.

The rabbit hopped down on the alleyway behind the palace, looking for shadows to hide in. No human should see it in its true form, especially now, when its powers had been mostly drained by the wicked woman with her constant foot grinding. The rest of its energy had gone to its liberators. Eventually, the powers would return, but until then, the rabbit would be vulnerable and in great need of a hiding place.

Its paws smacked against the cobblestones. The rabbit noticed it had already hopped down the same alleyway twice. *Odd*, it thought and twitched its nose. Being held captive for a long time seemed to have affected its movement abilities. Its muscles were weak and sore. The rabbit put more weight on its left foot to correct a tendency to go to the right, but it only made matters worse. Now it went around and around in the different direction down the same alleyway.

It moved on for a few more hops and paused to catch its breath. The rabbit patted its arms, trying to find a slight tingle of power to use to get away from there, but only a residual spark was left. That spark was still enough to get it off the street. It jumped high and landed on the palace rooftop—the same palace named after it. The rabbit didn't appreciate the irony.

At least it was off the street where any human might trap it again and use it for their amusement, not to mention the fact that some nasty god might come along and trap it for its evil plans. All the more reason why it liked to stay away from the gods and their plans for humans.

The rooftop was a safer bet.

The rabbit twitched its nose. A fresh breeze brought a smell of tiles, plaster, pigeons, and a residual smell of desperation, but no sign of any humans. *Good*, it thought. The only downside to being up high was the late autumn wind wanted to burrow into its bones. Winds and their murderous sprees.

It would die without its powers in the cold night if it didn't find shelter soon. As soon as it had a tiny part of its powers back, it had to get out of Leporidae Lop or the cold would be the least of its worries. It was that time of the cycle, when they came back. And it shouldn't be even near Leporidae Lop for its own good. Plus, the cage wouldn't hold Harriet for long.

The rabbit waited for luck to work its magic, to find it a

place to hide, but nothing happened. The rabbit continued waiting. How could the rest of the world live like this, without the constant guidance and cooperation from the universe? Usually, things just happened to it. An old woman should be there to give the rabbit god shelter, food, a hot bath, and a nice foot rub.

It swayed from one foot to another, back and forth, still waiting for that old woman. One of them, it or the universe, had to yield, but both were as stubborn as the other when it came to getting their way. The universe could wait longer, however.

The wind picked up speed, making a shiver go up the rabbit's spine.

CHAPTER TEN
Missing Harriet Stowe

arriet woke up in the pitch-dark cage, her head hurting and feeling disorientated. The cage slightly rocked from side to side, and the motion made her feel sicker. She tried to stand after lying there for a while, but the cage swayed violently, and she lost her balance. She waited for a little longer, feeling the rhythm of the cage before daring to stand again, listening to the voices coming from outside. There were at least two people there, who chatted jovially. That was all she could piece together. A thick fabric covered the cage all around her. She wanted to shout at them to shut up, but she needed to hear them. There was this tang to their speech, and they sounded like anyone in Leporidae Lop. Yet, it was not enough to tell her who they were or had they sought her audience. They spoke about trivialities—the weather, what they had eaten last, what the horses were doing, and about the desert sand. Nothing much to give her a leg to stand on. It was as well.

Harriet steadied herself and got to her feet. She straightened her back and smoothed the wrinkles in her governess dress. She'd gathered her dignity and wrapped her head around the situation. Situation that called for her not to panic. She had seen a lot worse. She had been at the mercy of someone else before, and there would come a time she would be again. The whole human condition was fragile, especially as the social part was integral to the whole surviving thing. And Harriet had survived Leporidae Lop's court all these years, so this would be a cake walk.

Harriet assumed a posture of authority and said, "You there."

The earlier voices fell silent.

"It seems we have arrived in a very tricky situation. I know you are out there. You know I'm here. And we both know that once I get out, there will be a price to pay. And I will get out. You have showed me I'm to be taken alive. So, you can make the wise choice; let me go now and I will spare you," Harriet said. "Or…" She let the threat hang there.

All remained quiet, the kind of silence when somebody tries not to be there, but after a while, she heard the older male. "Not a word. That's how she gets them."

"Let me out of the cage this instant," she said in her sternest voice, which always made others to obey her; the sound like a leather whip hitting against a marble wall.

As always, they had their effect. Her words caused a rattle outside. There was heavy tumbling, accompanied with laborious breathing. For a moment, Harriet thought who'd found her voice compelling would win, but that was not in the cards.

The older man said, "Put this in your ears, now."

"Say something," the younger man said, who sounded squeaky.

"What?" the first fellow asked.

"I can't hear you," the other one replied.

A few more, "I can't hear you," were exchanged before the cage began to move again.

Harriet sat back down in the middle of the cage and let out a long sigh. There was only one other way out now, as she had no help from her fellow humans, nothing new there. She had to find flaws in the cage's design—a design she'd helped create.

It was just that finding defects in one's own logic was almost impossible. Blind spots, biases, and the mere thought that the cage was ironclad made it hard to get around to the solution.

Harriet knew the cage could only be opened from the outside. They were forged with magic and sealed with carved symbols to keep the god in, and now it seemed her, too. She wasn't sure what kind of magic it was, but the engineer she'd found promised nothing would get out without Harriet's approval. She had to say the words installed into the cage to open it and touch the correct symbols in the right order.

Harriet got up and searched for the first opening symbol, which was a little wiggly line with a circle turning into a box around it. But before she even got the first syllable out, and as her fingers brushed the symbol, the cage electrocuted her. Bluish purple sparkles flew around her hand as she drew it back.

It had only been a brush but still, it had given an agonizing, tingling sensation shooting all over her body. She didn't even want to think what it had been like for the rabbit god of luck.

Harriet lowered back to sit on the floor, massaging her hand. She went over the design a few more times, just to be sure, but no luck whatsoever. The cage was unbreakable, no matter how she approached it. For the first time in her life, she needed someone to question her. To say she was wrong, and there was no one around for it. Most Leporidae Lops would have happily lined up to do just that, and more if given an opportunity, but that was never going to happen as Harriet was escorted out of the kingdom.

She sensed in her bones that the cage was leaving her beloved home. They ached. This was the first time she had been out of Leporidae Lop. On some level, she knew that she deserved this. That she should have been more mindful how she led her kingdom. But such thoughts were drowned by anger. She'd dedicated all her life to serve her people and make Leporidae Lop what it was: the center of the continent, prosperous beyond anyone's wishes, luscious and green, and most importantly, alive.[10] She didn't deserve this. She had given everything to make their lives better, and this was how they repaid her. Harriet grimaced. She could let the anger take her, but it would be pointless. With anger, she would succumb to the situation and the wills of others, rather than be the master of her own fate. She had no choice than to collect her strength to what was to come.

Harriet took naps, got up, and went over the cage's design, moving on to thinking how to take control of the situation. She repeated that over and over again, the whole night. Now she watched as the gray wool fabric covering the cage fluttered as a gust of wind caught it. The sun leaked in. Harriet stood and took a step closer to the bars. Soon she heard the two male voices from earlier, one winded and one squeaky. The cage had stopped moving. She wanted to see.

Despite the earlier electrocution, Harriet tried to grab the fluttering fabric. Her hand brushed against the bars, giving her that familiar agonizing tingling sensation along with the bluish-purple sparks. She snatched her hand back. She tried again, but the electric shocks were too painful to bear. Harriet had to wait for the wind to scoop off the fabric. But the fabric only fluttered a little at the foot of the cage. Too little for her to see out. Then someone began to fasten it. Harriet made a dive for that hand, but again, the electric shock stopped her. But this time her effort wasn't completely futile. The man to whom the hand belonged made a high-pitch scream as his hand got fried with Harriet's.

A loud but short argument broke out.

"Let's get going before someone notices us," the older man said, ending the quarrel.

"I still think we should abandon her. We already got paid."

"We can't leave her to be found by some poor bastard. We

---

[10] Kingdoms, cities, countries needed to feel alive. If they didn't, decay had a habit of sneaking into the citizens' minds to gradually erode their sense of joy and humanity. And when those two were gone, apathy and violence followed.

finish this."

"Alright," the other one said with a groan. "But you will pay for the next round."

There came a snort and soon, the cage moved again, accompanied by a short neigh.

Harriet sat down, massaged her electrocuted hand, took a carrot, and began to eat it. Then she plotted a beheading... more like two of them.

* * *

Sigourney's Sunday faded away faster than she liked, and she felt she was farther from finding out what had happened to Harriet than when everything began. Oddly enough, she had a vivid vision of a beheading, though it went away as fast as it had come. She continued walking away from Huxley's place and decided to head to Harriet's office, to find something, anything, maybe a few blood marks, to show she had been really taken and Sigourney hadn't dreamed this all up. No one else seemed to care their prime minister had gone missing; in fact, they seemed extra chipper today.

Sometimes she found this whole bloody luck thing to be a pain in her ass. People accepted everything because they thought luck had made it so—the good and the bad. It was so and you didn't mess with it or else. Sigourney had never figured out what the 'or else' at the end of their sentences meant. But clearly the Leporidae Lops thought if you had sorrows, if you needed something rituals of luck were the only thing accepted as a proper action to mend all the miseries. They had only taken advice from Harriet because of fear and customs, but mostly, they relied on luck to provide or not to provide. And it was your own darn fault if you didn't get the four green houses and one red hotel.

Sigourney made her way back to the palace, avoiding those who were still up at this hour of the night. There wasn't many, but the few who still went about their business were either there because their jobs demanded it or their nights were robbed from them by their tormented thoughts. It was funny how many suffered the latter fate, even in a kingdom where destiny was determined by one ritual, one concept, and your effort on it. It was easy to mistake that in such a place where people slept soundly.

The guards were making their rounds around the palace. Sigourney had always seen the whole effort pointless. She had no trouble in entering and exiting as she pleased—and neither did anyone who meant business. But she had kind of figured out that it was for the show and for those who believed in stories about security and strength. Sigourney hid herself and walked past the guard who thought no one was there and scratched his backside with his truncheon. When he was satisfied, he moved on, and so did Sigourney.

She had only one purpose for tonight. She hoped to find a clue, one thing to lead her in the right direction in search of Harriet as she slipped in through the front door. It wasn't locked. That was another funny thing about security. Once you got it, you started to forget the basics. It was just that Sigourney knew going to the office was hopelessly stupid because she had been there last night, and the office hadn't been exactly cooperative or revealing when it came to Harriet's whereabouts. But she had to hope or else... There wasn't any 'or else' here, at least, not in the way the Leporidae Lops used it.

When she got to the office, she confirmed what she already knew—there was no blood, no Harriet, and no life-altering realizations. She had come to realize she wasn't made for life-altering realizations. Those happened to others; the one's with big houses and bowl of fresh berries every morning. There was only one proper way to get enlightened, or so the social vines kept insisting. And as Sigourney didn't believe in the whole enlightenment thing or have the patience to listen to the social vines, she was doomed from the get-go.

Sigourney searched the room for anything that might give her a better picture of what had happened. She went over Harriet's papers and tried to find hidden doors in the office.

Out of desperation, she even searched through her wastebasket, which happened to be neatly organized and surprisingly boring. She grew restless after every useless discovery. There had to be something here to tell her where Harriet was. This was the woman's sanctuary, after all. But no. All Harriet's secrets were kept close to heart. And Sigourney would be surprised to hear she happened to carry most of them with her. She just didn't know. She just had to get enlightened enough to put two and two together.

Sigourney sat there on the floor, smoothing out all the papers she'd found. They were just your typical documentation of the day-to-day matters. Not that there didn't lie great secrets, there did. The fundamentals of life. It was just that they weren't exactly revealing material when it came to kidnappings or murders. Or actually, there was one minor detail, which might lead Sigourney to the right direction. It was an invoice for a cartload of carrots, but she dismissed the items and barely saw the amount ordered. Even if she had, it was highly unlikely she would have leaped to the right conclusion—at least, not without a very imaginative mind and habit of fantasizing the impossible.

Not that it mattered. Her investigation was disturbed by a heavy panting and faint squeal from the doorway. Sigourney flickered out of view and back to be seen, then on and off again, unable to control her talent as she blinked, staring at Harriet's assistant having a bewildered expression on his face. One of those kinds which you weren't sure if the other was angry, afraid, or having a bad case of constipation. And the thing is, the key to social success was being able to read other people's emotions moderately good enough. And here a mistake might cost Sigourney her life, being in closed space and all, having the boy block the only exit, and the palace being riddled with guards with pointy helmets and weapons. But Sigourney was pretty sure it was anger that she met. Again, the thing was that people too often thought they could recognize the inner state of others based on their reactions and default settings and whatnot. It just didn't work that way. Emotions, thoughts, and all the reasons behind them were a lot more nuanced than people gave them credit for, and highly dependable on the situation and what had come before it and what would come after. But then again, anger was a safe bet in a situation like this.

The boy's hands trembled. "You," he let out. "Get out, get out right away!"

Sigourney kept blinking rapidly, as if her eyes tried to wire a distress signal to get her off from the upcoming awkward social interaction. They failed. She had no control over her reactions, and somehow, the boy made it worst. She had seen him around. There was kindness into him; it was there, in his eyes. Somehow Sigourney felt connection to him, making things worse.

"I'll call the guards if you don't leave right this second," the assistant said. The scrawny boy looked deadly serious at the door; so serious, Sigourney knew she couldn't shrug him off with her usual silence. She had to say something, but what? With people like the assistant there had to be more words. The late night wasn't helping her verbally formulate what she wanted to say. There wasn't actually anything she wanted to say. Maybe just 'please.' Sigourney would prefer if communication between humans had been designed in a simpler way. It would be nice if a smile or frown would suffice, or rubbing against someone's leg like the cats did. So simple, yet so effective.

"Huh?" she asked, still sitting on the floor, clutching the last paper she had been reading like a security blanket.

The boy's anger melted away. He looked more dumbfounded than anything by Sigourney's 'huh' full of meaning. His bewilderment gave Sigourney enough time to open the desk drawers she had left last to search for at least one clue about Harriet's disappearance before she had to hide from the guards and the assistant. The last drawers she opened were filled with carrots from top to bottom.

"Huh," she said again. It was a different kind of 'huh.' There were more nuances to her words than with those who used them willy-nilly. But this time, neither her nor the boy could interpret what the new 'huh' meant. A great detective would have discerned her latest 'huh' contained a hint of bewilderment, desperation, and a strong sense of "you've got to be kidding me." Later, after an hour or so of analyzing, this 'huh' might have revealed new meanings and gained a life of its own, probably driving the detective insane.

The assistant snapped out of being mesmerized by Sigourney's words and her odd behavior. "Leave now or I'll call the guards." His threat sounded repetitive, and a feeble attempt to gain control.

Sigourney searched for words to say, and ended up slowly saying, "Have you seen Harriet Stowe?" It seemed like a good idea.

"Huh?" the boy asked.

"Harriet?"

"She isn't here, and I haven't seen her for a while. Now please go," he said, his words more like a plea than a demand. He looked tired and scared, and not angry at all.

Sigourney stood, having an odd sensation that she had actually been visible throughout the whole conversation. The boy made her act unlike herself, and she didn't like it for a bit.

But it was better to call it a day than make a hopeless effort trying to discern the reason for Harriet's disappearance by studying carrots or hanging here to find out if the boy's threat had been empty or not. She put the carrots back into the drawer. It would be desperate even by her standards to hold the carrots as a clue. She walked past the assistant, who looked suspiciously at her. Sigourney tried to give the boy a pleasant smile, but it came out all wrong, making the boy frown.

This was one of those moments when Sigourney's reasoning that animals were lot better creatures than humans was proved right. Animals were straight from the start, no need for second-guessing. You petted them and they liked you or not. She couldn't pet the assistant... nope, she couldn't.

She drew her hand back because it had jumped the gun and began petting him.

She left, leaving the boy stunned by her behavior. When she was out of sight. She ran and made herself invisible. She turned around the corner and when she was sure the boy hadn't followed her, she opened a window. Any window would do since they all led to the roof, to her sanctuary.

The silver moon and clear starry sky illuminated her way to the top. Her feet slipped a few times off the tiles from sheer tiredness, but her hands held her in place. She squeezed so hard that her knuckles turned white. She knew it was a mistake to waste her strength like that and invite the possibility of falling, but it was the day. All the reasoning had left her. The only thing she wanted was to get under the blankets and melt away, forgetting all about the assistant, Huxley, and everything else.

It was just that the universe was kind of a bastard, and sometimes it and the destinies it spun—especially here, where luck and gods liked to stir things up—didn't exactly give you something you wanted. Most of the time, actually. It was entirely another question if what you wanted was good for you, or if sometimes the most horrendous thing you could think provided you with all you had ever needed. The universe, luck, and especially the gods, or in this case, a god with a horse and a cart, hadn't decided if this was such a moment for Sigourney or not. The jury was still out if she got to be the hero or not, or just another victim of a cosmic joke.

Sigourney instantly knew something was wrong as she got to her shack. Its door was closed the wrong way. When she'd left the shack, the door was tilting more to the right, and now, too much weight was put to the left side boards. The wind couldn't do that; the wind didn't do that. Sigourney and it had an agreement, and they left each other alone.

Sigourney stopped behind the door to listen to the air inside. She heard nothing out of the ordinary—no nervous guardsman, no deranged brothers, or anything else to alarm her.

That alarmed her.

A warm rush of air caressed her face as she carefully

opened the door. The shack never got this warm. The shack was never occupied by any other than her. And now there was a huge lump in her bed under all the covers. Sigourney's mind wanted to turn back and flee, but her body didn't. It knew that Sigourney would never stop. That she would run at the edge of the world, just to end up hating herself for abandoning Harriet and the only place she had ever called home. So her body made an executive decision and rushed to the mound of blankets to make Sigourney tear her way in. As soon as Sigourney's hands touched the top layer, she was kicked off with nasty force. Her fast reflexes made her snap her chin against her chest, then her hands hit the floor hard to soften the fall. The next step would be to jump up to meet the attacker, but she was too slow. A huge dark creature loomed over her. Sigourney readied to sweep out its legs from underneath it, but when she fully saw what stood there, she froze.

A huge rabbit stood, doubled over on its hind legs, staring back at her. One of its ears had a round edge and was dark-colored while the other ear was light pink.

Now she was sure she'd gone mad, and Harriet wasn't really missing.

She let out a long sigh. A sigh she had been holding ever since all this started.

CHAPTER ELEVEN
A Party for Me?

n Monday morning, after another episode of hangovers, headaches, and late openings, Edbert sewed up the tears in his best suit. Huxley had announced in the morning there would be another event they needed to attend in order to secure more votes, but this time, not from the public but from those who really mattered.

Huxley also had made it clear he should appear presentable at the party. Preferably, he should buy an entirely new outfit. Buying new clothes was robbery in Edbert's book. They made them cheap nowadays, and nothing compared to the suits his father and grandfather wore. His father's suit fit perfectly fine. It was stylish and ageless, and most importantly, it was clean and intact—except for maybe a few holes here and there—and free.

In truth, it was moth-eaten, its tastefulness could be vigorously questioned, and the thread to piece it together wasn't exactly free. But Edbert had a knack for giving life to old things.

He stitched the suit with beautiful, fine, and precise stitching, which would make a seamstress proud or envious, depending on how twisted the mind in question was. Patching the suit's holes took the whole day, but it didn't matter. The bookshop was empty. The people's curiosity toward him had simmered down. He welcomed the relief from the constant buzzing, but a nagging voice inside him insisted it was the beginning of the end. But he wasn't exactly sure the end of what.

After dressing up, Edbert went to the kitchen to prepare his lunch. Edbert boiled cabbages, sliced stale bread to thin slices, and set them on a porcelain plate his mother had acquired before running off with the street sweeper. He took his lunch to the shop and ate while waiting for customers to appear, but none came. The whole shop smelled of his wretched lunch, sneaking out the open front door, making anyone think twice before stepping in.

The smell made Huxley gag when he arrived to retrieve Edbert.

"It's time to go," Huxley said, wrinkling his nose when he saw—and, more importantly, smelled—what Edbert wore. At first, it smelled of boiled cabbages, but from underneath that came the smell of mold. "You have got to be kidding me." He looked Edbert from head to toe as he lingered by the open door.

"This won't do at all," Huxley continued after Edbert refused the engage with him. "You'll be laughed out of the party if you go there looking like that. For the Lop's sake, didn't I tell you to buy a new suit? And not to fish out those which I already threw out?"

"This is perfectly fine. It's a fine suit. They don't make them like this nowadays," Edbert protested.

"For a good reason." Huxley sighed. "The shops are already closed…" Huxley eyed him once again from head to toe and shook his head. "You are about the size of my manservant. One of his suits will have to do." Huxley gave him no opening to argue. They rode to his place in the posh district, and Edbert had never been in one of the houses there. He had once taken a stroll down the city and walk the streets and wondered what kind of folk lived in the fancy manors in the middle of the city, but that was as close as he had ever gotten to the place.

Now here he was, being fussed over by Huxley's servants, especially the one whose clothes he was to borrow. The man didn't appear happy about it, but neither he nor Edbert could protest when Huxley had set his mind. The new clothes made Edbert look ridiculous. They itched, felt stiff, and they fitted him illy. The old fabric of his father's suit draped down nicely, but the new suit made him feel like a stick figure. He hated it from the bottom of his heart. He was no dandy and would never be.

When Huxley was satisfied, they left for the dinner party. They arrived late to the shindig, even when it was on the next street from Huxley's place, but none seemed to mind or dared to mind. But Edbert minded, a lot. It was downright rude and scandalous to be late just because of clothes.

Instead of being snapped at, he was introduced to everyone. After the awkward introductions, he was ushered to the luscious dinner table. The cream of the kingdom's society gathered around the table to fawn over him, making Edbert fidget with his jacket's hem.

A big laugh swept the group whenever he answered their questions, which only confused him more. Did they laugh at or with him?

Instead of networking and making backhand deals as Huxley had instructed, he tried to be invisible, which was absurd because only a few days ago, he'd wanted this. But now the jacket hem's rigid and smooth fabric was too alluring to pass up. Edbert slid his fingers along the rim over and over again. Udolf Huxley signaled him to stop for the hundredth time, but Edbert stubbornly spaced out, trying to survive the dinner without making a fool of himself… thus making a fool of himself. He had never figured out that everything came down to poise rather than actual deeds. As long as you were sure what you did was right, the others accepted it, no matter how bizarre it might be. But Edbert wasn't made to be sure of anything—even the amount of silverware on the table baffled him, despite having read countless books about etiquette. He waited to see what fork the banker, George Morgan, took. The man sat next to Edbert, making it easy to follow. He was a thin man with round golden glasses; his hair had turned silver years ago.

The hostess, Morgan's wife, tried to chat with Edbert, but her voice was drowned under everyone's babbling. He tapped his ear and looked away from her round face with demanding piercing eyes.

In the background, Huxley put his right hand's fingers on the bridge of his nose and massaged it, letting out a long sigh.

Morgan's wife repeated her question, but Edbert thought about a book he had read as a child, the one he still owned. The book was securely locked away with the other rare books, and it was about a mouse and a lion and their unnatural friendship. He felt like that mouse releasing the trapped lion. But Leporidae Lop's aristocrats eating, laughing, and enjoying themselves didn't look like any caged animal he'd seen, though they behaved as such. They praised him for his courage, his deeds to liberate the people. They praised him for the change to come.

The hostess dinged her glass and finally got through to him. "So, you own that quaint bookshop we all love so much?"

Edbert gave her an awkward smile. "Yes, I own it," he replied. "Would you like me to find a book for you? Name your subject, and I guarantee I'll find a suitable one."

"Gods, no, I don't touch the ghastly stuff myself," she said.

Edbert's eyes widened. He couldn't help himself. He felt his face get red and hot. He wasn't sure if it was out of anger or embarrassment. Either way he wanted to stand up and march out of the table, but he didn't. He waited for the earth to swallow him whole.

"I mean, I would like to, but I leave such things to my husband. I'm entirely too busy taking care of the household." The woman corrected her posture. She had a somewhat similar expression on her face as Edbert did. But Edbert didn't see that; he was too occupied with his emotions, the words, and the silence around the table. Everyone seemed to hold their breath.

"I have a whole section of books about running a household," he jumped into the only recognizable word in the utterance.

The other women at the table let out a suppressed giggle, making Edbert blush. The men joined in.

Edbert squeezed the hem of his jacket hard.

"I do have to visit that fantastic shop of yours, and you can show me what you have," the hostess said, silencing the women and men alike. "What do you say? Shall we make it an excursion?" she asked, looking around the table, meeting every female eye there was. Eyes Edbert could barely have met the whole evening.

"You should," he said, fiddling his jacket's hem again with such passion, a religion could be organized around it.

From then on, he tried to engage with the aristocrats and join in the conversations rippling around the table, but he failed. He couldn't find anything to say to their chatter about who had been seen at what party and who had bought what thing. He just kept wondering why Upwood was absent, and couldn't figure it out. He was like so many who clumped the rich together with high disregard for how the wealth was made or obtained. While Upwood was a rich man, with his sheep farms and the rest; and while his father had been a rich man, it didn't make him an aristocrat. It made him useful to have him around. Mostly to keep an eye out, not letting him slip too far with his wealth and influence, but make him a friend was out of question. But Edbert saw no difference. He thought Huxley and Upwood were the best of chums.

Edbert felt drained by the end of the party. Huxley slapped him on his back as they walked out to meet the carriage waiting for them. "It went splendidly. Don't you agree?"

"Sure," Edbert replied, but he thought the word 'disastrous' would better describe the party.

What Edbert had pictured in his mind about high society dinner parties was nothing like the party he'd attended. At first, they'd confused him with their elegant words, but at the end of the evening, he understood their words were condescending toward him. The constant need to sustain a pecking order had confused him even more. Weren't they there amongst equals? And the fear and hate... He would rather forget how the men and women in that room saw each other and the rest of humanity. Yet, he feared that he was stuck with them for good. He had given too much for them.

Edbert shuttered from the thought of the looks the Duke and Duchess of River-Bridge had directed at him. They didn't hide their disgust that he was just a bookshop owner. They cared not for the fact that he owned his business and might be their next prime minister. He lacked blue blood, and they would never let that go. Edbert was sure they even had laughed at his clothes. It had been a mistake to come here in a service suit.

Then there was the word 'quaint,' which still rang in his ears, making his blood boil.

"Cheer up man," Huxley said. "We loosened their purse strings."

It was easy for Huxley to be cheerful after robbing his friends, but what had Edbert gained? Nothing but misery.

"Here," Huxley said, dropping a coin purse into Edbert's palm.

"I can't."

"Don't be silly. They gave money to support you. The best way to spend it is to keep you afloat."

It was hard to argue with Huxley and say he didn't need the money. Edbert needed funds. He hadn't sold a single book today, and he hated resorting to his savings. If he couldn't support himself with the books he sold, then it was time to quit.

When Edbert got home, he collapsed behind his desk, dropping the coin purse in front of him. Taking Huxley's money made him feel dirty. For the first time in years, he skipped going over the ledgers and the *Pantheon of Gods*, and climbed upstairs to his bed without opening a book to read and fell asleep. He dreamed nightmarish dreams about a lioness hunting him... more like a pack of them.

CHAPTER TWELVE
In Your Honor

fter three days of traveling, the cage finally stopped. The constant travel had left Harriet nauseated. Whoever took her had offered her food, water, and a bucket to do her business into, but they never let her stretch her legs or showed their faces. Just the essentials arriving under the fabric and that was it. She was treated like a caged lion. The whole business was the most humiliating experience in her life. Still, Harriet made an effort and stood to her full height, which was slightly less than a few days ago. She waited, straightening her black dress as an unruly lock side out of place. She moved the gray hair back behind her ear and dared it to do it again; it didn't.

An annoying thought reminded Harriet of the fact she'd done this to someone else. Then it had seemed like the right thing to do, but now she saw it as the most inhumane act she had ever done. And no words justified it… not without sounding pathetic and ignorant.

Harriet grimaced.

The cage began to rock again, and she lost her balance and fell to the floor, twisting her ankle. She sat there, waiting for the motion to stop. Harriet was sure the cage was lowered off the cart it had been traveling. When she was sure no more surprises would come, she stood back up and put more weight on her right leg, not wanting anyone to notice her injury. She heard the distinctive squeaking of the cart's wheels fading farther away—the noise which had pierced her skull day after day, breaking her mind. Now as the sound subsided, she wanted it back. It was familiar, unlike what was about to come.

Soon, the gray wool fabric lifted off the cage. The bright moonlit sky hurt her eyes. Harriet drew her arms to cover them and noticed how foolish she was being. The starry sky couldn't hurt her. She forced her hands down, ashamed to show any sign of weakness. Harriet blinked several times, and the world became clearer.

A courtyard opened in front of her, surrounded by a deep desert with nothing but sand everywhere she looked. A somewhat ancient palace loomed farther from her, plain but massive. Harriet and the cage were peanuts compared to that place, and she was inside the cage designed for the rabbit. Whoever had built the palace knew how to motivate people.

One man, a boy, and a woman stood a few feet away from her, staring at Harriet with fear and respect. On the outskirts, she saw more people observe and judge her. There had to be at least a hundred men and women, and even more poured out of the palace.

Harriet squinted and made an effort to figure out where she was and what they wanted from her. The visual clues only left her perplexed. This was no place she'd heard of, and these people in front of her were complete strangers.

A cold wind lifted a small sandstorm, hitting against all those standing unprotected under the full moon.

"Get her inside," the woman said, pushing a letter inside her jacket. Her dark brown hair whipped against her hollow cheeks, and she spat out sand from her mouth.

Weak-looking women and men in rags hurried to touch the cage, pushing against the wind. Harriet reached for the nearest man and pulled him against the bars. While Harriet got electrocuted—and the force made her stagger back—it also caused the man to slam against the cage, then fell unconscious to the ground. The rest hurried away from her, dragging the man with them.

Harriet stood there, waiting them come again, and they didn't disappoint her. The ragged people tried again to move Harriet but with the same results. The wind paused and held its breath, watching who would win this fight. It bet on Harriet.

"All right, have it your way," the woman said. Her eyes looked tired, but they observed every move, every pose Harriet took, keenly.

Harriet stood there, giving away no emotion, despite the searing pain the shocks had caused her. Her chest felt heavy, her heart beat wrongly, and the tips of her fingers were numb. She bit her teeth together and steadied her breathing to lower her heartbeat.

"We can talk outside if you want, though I would have rather taken you inside where it's warm and less windy," the woman said. Her hollow cheeks looked even hollower. Harriet could see the shape of her skull. This woman would be the death of her, Harriet was sure of it.

She shook the uncomfortable image off and squinted. Harriet grimaced but nodded to let them move her.

The ragged people lifted the cage, carrying her inside the palace. A place made of plain, yellowish stones with simple decor. A pleasing and welcoming diversion from the ornamental style Harriet had gotten used at Leporidae Lop. It was clear she was far from home.

As the woman promised, the air inside was slightly warmer. She was carried into some sort of audience chamber. The men and women struggled to carry her down the stairs, making the cage sway and forced Harriet to sit down. In the end, they managed to lower her to the floor without any unwanted electrocutions or other damage.

The audience chamber was in the shape of a reversed pyramid. In the past, the room would have easily held hundreds of people, but now, the thin men, women, and their children couldn't even fill half the seats. But there was still plenty of them to cause harm. Harriet was a firm believer in the power of the masses, but she was an even firmer believer in the power she held. She stood and held her ground without shaking. She didn't even wince at the pressure the pose put on her ankle. All of that was irrelevant against what was happening. She couldn't wait to hear an explanation as to why she had been brought here.

Someone had gone to all this trouble, so it had to be done for something important. Something which required her to stay alive; otherwise, she would already be dead. Of course, there was a slight possibility it had been done for surprisingly insignificant reasons, like for her eighty-fifth birthday party, which the Leporidae Lops had seemed to forget. Or this could be their twisted way of showing her respect and getting rid of her at the same time. None of it mattered. None of it was the truth. But who was to say a situation or event had uniform truth. There were too many forces at play in any given moment to find the one single reason for the motion. But here, the truth was that someone had indeed gone to lengths to send her here. But then again, others might have played their parts in the shadows, too. If one was highly accurate, there was more than one—there were three someones who had wished to see Harriet arrive here and set on the events to come, and all done for competing reasons. If she would have known, she would have made sure to rob the victory of all of them, whoever they were.

"Welcome to our humble Palace of the Green Jewel," the hollow-cheeked woman said as soon as everyone in the room had settled. The word 'green' came out like a distant dream.

Harriet looked at the plain woman from head to toe, who withered under her stare. She looked malnourished, but stern. The kind of woman who would do everything in her power to ensure her goals. She'd seen such eyes before, but rarely with the intensity the woman was showing. *Interesting*, Harriet thought.

"To our homeland, to Gainsboro. I don't know if you have ever been here or noticed us. I'm afraid there isn't much to notice as our land is dying and our people are half-dead already. All there is left of us is here in front of you. We seem to wither to nonexistence while your kingdom flourishes." The woman paused, fighting back her tears.

Harriet had to look away, letting her gaze glide around the room. The men, women, and children looked hardened and tired. The sun had scorched their faces, their lips had cracked from thirst, and their clothes were worn out by dust. Small, malnourished children stepped behind their mothers to hide from Harriet's basilisk gaze—one she'd learned to master to best her older sister in arguments. It had worked; it had driven Henrietta to become a bitter and resentful spinster who hadn't even attended Harriet's wedding. There were so many things you end up regretting, never imagining where they might lead. Henrietta's fate and their relationship was one of the biggest Harriet had. Her older sister was her only relative still alive, yet both of them were as alone as having none.

"I'll be frank. Leporidae Lop is the reason we are dying. When we think we have found copper, iron, or fertile land, it disappears, and you miraculously find some. We can't compete with you. We harvest our food by hand, and our days go to surviving. To us, it's like your kingdom has all the luck in the world, while we don't even get scraps. Those times when we get a glimpse of something good and it's taken away instantly, I think we are tormented by nightmarish dreams sent to us because of our past mistakes, but that would be too cruel. ." The woman swallowed her last words.

Harriet had forgotten the outside world didn't have access to Leporidae Lop's luck system and that luck, in general, was in short supply in the rest of the world. She watched their tired and hardened faces and saw for the first time the real downside to using luck irresponsibly. Harriet's mind automatically reasoned she had done it for the sake of her people, but that was a fool's argument, and she knew it. The same argument which she could use to justify tormenting the rabbit.

These people were far from the glorious lifestyles her people in Leporidae Lop had grown accustomed to, and far from the ascetic lifestyle she had chosen for herself.

"We will die within a year as the land is bare and dry and we have done all we can." The tears finally poured down the woman's cheeks—genuine, not done for show. The woman looked deep into Harriet's eyes, something no one had done in ages. In them, Harriet saw the pain she felt and the horrors her people had to endure. There was no mistaking it. Their suffering was real and to some extent, her fault.

Harriet cleared her throat. "What do you want from me?"

"Isn't that obvious?" a bearded man standing next to the woman asked.

"We want your help," a young boy who lurked behind the man said.

The woman swallowed her tears and said, "Yes, you have to help us or we'll die. You are our only chance for life." Her eyes glistened in the dimly lit chamber.

CHAPTER THIRTEEN
Time to Move on

The small shack at the top of royal palace of White Cuniculus filled with warmth, making the uncomfortable silence between the rabbit and Sigourney even worse. They still gazed at each other without saying a single word, both finding the other as odd.

The rabbit rapidly moved its nose up and down while simultaneously folding its ears.

Sigourney kept flickering off and on again.

They continued this for a while as crazy thoughts kept popping into Sigourney's head. She couldn't help but think she'd won her own fluffy plush toy. Yet, at the same time, fear whispered in her ear that a mutant assassin had been sent by Harriet's enemies.

"Are you the usual washerwoman?" the rabbit finally asked, breaking the silence.

Sigourney shook her head. She calculated her odds of... what exactly, she didn't know. One of them had to ask what the crit was going on and not ask silly questions about washerwomen, but Sigourney knew it wasn't going to be her. She continued measuring the rabbit from head to toe and back again. At least she'd stopped flickering out of the view, having heard the giant creature speak almost reassured her this was real in some bizarre way. And then there was the fact that she couldn't help but find the giant bunny to be soft and cute, and on a primal level, she wanted nothing more than to embrace it. Sigourney fought against her insane urges.

"Okay, if you are not her, then I guess it's nice to meet you," the rabbit said, offering its paw. "Are you sure you are not just a different version of her? She's always there for me when I need her."

Sigourney just stared at the paw offered to her.

"I get it, not her then. Do you happen to own the pathetic shed, then?"

Sigourney hesitated. She shifted her gaze from the paw to expecting eyes. She mumbled an inaudible yes, and caved in solely because she needed to touch the rabbit's perfect white-gray fur. She shook the paw, and a little sparkle crackled between them when their hands met. Sigourney missed the sparkle as the paw's soft velvety touch swept her away. She would be happy just holding it for the rest of her life. She prolonged the greeting for an awkwardly long moment. It felt good to feel the warmth of another living being… better than she'd expected. She couldn't remember the last time someone had touched her.

The god of luck had to tug its paw free. It had been a mistake to give it in the first place. Sigourney's eyes shined in a weird light. But there, Sigourney was innocently wondering if she'd made a friend. Still and all, the rabbit's thoughts were more in the line with, "Oh, shit. This is going to end badly."

"I'm sorry I entered your place without permission, but I had no other choice," the rabbit said and massaged its great paw, eying her.

"It's all right." Sigourney gave a weak smile. Being nice to a seven-foot-tall, muscular rabbit seemed like the sane thing to do, and she liked being nice. Also, this felt like something which had to happen to her. That somehow, she'd waited for all her life to be found by a talking animal and befriend it—not that she was that far from the truth. One thing she got wrong, though, was the fact that this was meant to be. You could argue that nothing was meant to be, that things kept changing constantly. Even sneezing might spin you into a new reality without you knowing. Not to mention fluttering wings altering the existence just like that. Or so some scientists proposed when they get their mind all bent with words like chaos.

But this was not the work of brother Chaos. No, this was the same luck, which had been spinning out of control from overuse and different wants competing to harness it just for them. Luck was leaking into places where it shouldn't.

"Then you don't mind if I go back to sleep," the rabbit god of luck said with the audacity only reserved for the gods, and their like.[11] It tilted its head, shook it, and without a response, went back to the bed and snuggled between the blankets. A snore soon filled the little shack—a fake snore, just to be clear.

Sigourney just sat there, watching it and not saying anything. She wasn't sure how to react or why to react. Maybe this was how the universe was supposed to work. Who was she to know the mechanics of it? If you asked her, this felt more sane than the fact that people kept fighting against what happened to them with value judgments, like 'I deserve this or not.' That rarely had anything to do with the outcome or in some cases, with reality. Reality was altogether a silly bugger. It played tricks on the minds of people, not letting anyone truly grasp it, showing only glimpses to one party or another. And the ludicrous thing was, that the communication between those two parties seldom met, especially when things got sticky. So people went on carrying their half as a truth, making more realities they had composed, and birthing more truths and falsehoods, and pleasures and hurts, and so on, until the dinosaurs would roam the planet once more.

Outside the wind picked up, bringing cold air from the north. The howling winds painted Leporidae Lop in a glimmering white frost. The little shack got colder, and

---

[11] Those who thought very highly of themselves.

Sigourney shivered. The rabbit stopped snoring, and soon, a paw appeared under the blanket mound, offering her the topmost blanket. She took it and wrapped it tightly around her. Soon she fell asleep, too tired to be vigilant in the wee hours after having a horrible and bizarre day.

You could speculate what kind of dreams both of them had, but that would be a waste of good speculation. Neither dreamed anything; they were too tired for that. Someone had beaten their bodies to that point where only a complete shutdown could do all the recovering. Not that they didn't dream; it was just they didn't remember any of it.

In the morning, the wind had subsided, and the shack was all warm and nice. Sigourney was already awake, though the rabbit was still snoring loudly. What had seemed like normal last night, or somewhat close to normal, was now utterly wrong in the light of day. The rabbit couldn't exist, and she shouldn't have just let it hog her bed.

The rabbit thought differently. It opened its huge black eyes and yawned. "Morning," it said and stretched its paws toward the ceiling.

"Morning," Sigourney said weakly. This was the first time she'd slept in the same room with someone other than her family member. She'd slept oddly well, yet her thoughts kept insisting this was all wrong.

The rabbit shook its nose and tilted its head. Sigourney was sure it was trying to read her mind.

The rabbit wasn't. It was thinking about carrots, but such is the human mind for you. Always thinking that the other one is highly obsessed with them. Gods weren't. Their thoughts were about their wants and needs more than anything. It was a trick how they kept being gods. As soon as you got worried about the other creatures, you turned into a servant. And the rabbit couldn't have that, not now at least. So it asked, "Could you be a dear and get me a carrot?"

"Please, you have to leave," Sigourney mumbled. She wasn't sure why she'd said that, but it seemed like the right thing to do. One of those kind of rights.

"Sorry, I badly need those carrots, and there's just you. The usual you-know-who is only-the-universe-knows-where and gods only know what lurks outside ready to trap me. You will have to do it. You have no other option." The rabbit snatched its right ear and started to lick it nonchalantly, occasionally glancing at the stunned Sigourney, who was trying to recover from the rabbit's rudeness.

Sigourney tried her best not to cry. Not because heroes shouldn't cry. Not that she knew she could be one—the story was still unwritten. It was just that she couldn't comprehend what to do with herself, what to say, where to put her hands, and most importantly, she'd lost her voice to argue back—a voice she didn't have to begin with. The rabbit's conviction overrode any reason left in her. Right now, the rabbit had the opportunity to insist a white elk danced between them, and Sigourney would readily believe it. Such things happened when someone acted without even a tiny speck of doubt. The rabbit carried with it the capacity to change the course of the future, past, and present, even to get people to mass-hallucinate little green men from outer space, but such statements were too far-fetched. A dancing white elk might be possible—it was on the same page as a giant talking rabbit—but little green men were just plain silly. Then the universe started to work again, and Sigourney blurted out, "But…"

But the laws of time, space, and the universe had shifted fundamentally to another track, and Sigourney stood in front of a vendor's booth in the market, buying carrots. She had no recollection how she had gotten there. Actually, she had. She distinctly remembered agreeing on the third request and leaving to get the carrots more than willingly. All her 'buts' had melted away when the rabbit had used another set of illegal weapons against her: it had made its eyes water and its lower lip quiver. She hadn't found any reasonable words to decline the rabbit's request, or in her case, any words at all—only several "buts" while looking at the rabbit with tormented eyes. So here she was, pushing money into the hands of a vendor with thick eyebrows and tobacco on his lips.

After the buying the carrots, Sigourney climbed back to the palace rooftop, carrying an unnerving feeling inside her that someone was messing with her. When she got to the roof, she stopped to wonder if she really needed a home or a friend or anything at all. It might be better if she skipped town as she'd done with her brother and her family. That had turned out fine. Then again, she'd promised the rabbit she would get the carrots.

She stepped into the shack like a good girl.

Sigourney soon found herself outside, pressing her hands against her ears. She sang a song her grandmother had taught her. It was, fittingly, a song about rabbits, but there was nothing soft and harmonious about the way she sang. When one song ended, she began another one. Even a slight pause made the horrible sounds the rabbit made while devouring its food assault her eardrums.

After ten songs, the rabbit poked its head out. "Thank you."

Sigourney murmured, and half expected to hear the words, "Get me more carrots," but the rabbit said, "Let me reward you for your kindness. Whatever you want, you will have."

A white elk danced between them.

"Name it. Whatever you want will be yours."

When the elk passed, Sigourney knew what to ask. "I want to find the prime minister; I want to find Harriet Stowe."

"Crit," the rabbit said.

* * *

The fat man, Cornelius, who had happily snored in the public park, stood, flexed his stiff body, and looked around. He was bewildered to see a crowd had gathered in the park to gawk at his slumber. The police officer who'd tried to shoo him away stood amongst them, looking flabbergasted. They all stared him with open mouths, eyes wide, and frozen in place. They hadn't expected him to move, just as he hadn't expected them to be there. He had been too occupied with all the events, big and small, swirling around the city, observing and guiding them to take a form not entirely the path his brothers and sisters wanted.

Cornelius blinked.

They blinked.

No white elk appeared, but a fragile snowflake floated between Cornelius and them. The entire world stood still, waiting and watching the tiny flake drop. It was a foolish early snowflake which would melt away as soon as it touched the ground

Cornelius blinked again.

They blinked.

The air smelled of burned candles, lilies, and cloves. Cornelius looked at his feet and then around. He saw a shrine near him and the aspen tree. *Oh, that.*

A huge smile spread across his face.

The crowd relaxed. A general sigh from their part made the snowflake fly to the horse's muzzle. The horse who wasn't white nor elk licked it away. It had been eying the humans for a while, and in its mind, it had been keeping them away from its master. Now it could relax as the fat man woke up.

Cornelius let out a gleeful whistle. The tune never stayed low for too long. When it dipped down, it always came up with a fanfare. He took the horse by its reins and guided it out of the park.

"Hurrah!" rang out in a chorus from the crowd as Cornelius and his horse left.

A young man dashed to the spot where Cornelius had sat and swirled his hands to get the fat man's mojo.

Leporidae Lops were good at noticing gods and their likes. When the others noticed what the young man did, a fight broke out. They tore each other apart to be the first one to sit in the spot Cornelius had vacated. The first one of them to get there would surely have a whole year's worth of luck and, of course, happiness. Mind you, the happiness part was the reason they fought so brutally.

A squirrel hurried down the aspen tree and paused at the

spot where the fat man had been. It moved its head rapidly from side to side, watching the fight. It witnessed a man being tripped onto the ground by a woman and kicked a few times just to make sure he stayed down. The kicker dashed forward, but soon, someone else tackled her. The squirrel hurried from the spot, zigzagging its way through the fighting men and women to another safer tree. It shook its nose and smelled an odd scent in the air.

The last remaining leaves on the aspen tree floated down and caught fire. No one seemed to pay any attention to the burning tree, but the tree did, screaming in agony.

The fat man didn't hear or notice what happened—he had his task ahead—but the horse did, and it neighed and willingly got as far away from the mad humans as possible.

When he was farther away, Cornelius turned the whistle into a melodic hum. It spread from him to others, from ear to ear and mouth to mouth. In a day or two, the song plagued the whole kingdom, but for now, the tune cheered up the otherwise cold and gloomy morning.

With the joyful whistle came a jiggle. Cornelius's steps were a bit too light for his weight and a whole lot too happy for a man of his size. The same jiggle jumped from the man to his horse. Two of them caused snickers behind their backs, snickers Cornelius heard, too. He only nodded when he saw someone laughing from delight. Those who snickered at him out of mockery avoided his gaze.

Cornelius continued jiggling his body. The exercise took his mind off the impending doom, and it was a nice move to do altogether, loosening his whole body. He would have his work cut out for him to stop the upcoming blood bath. The little interferences he'd done would carry out only so far.

CHAPTER FOURTEEN
The Wheels of Fortune

n Tuesday morning, after the embarrassing dinner party, Edbert's life got a lot more complicated. He had been ushered to the prime minister's office, where he now read a thick book which gradually killed his faith in humanity. A kind clerk, or not-so-kind, had brought the book to him the same moment he sat behind his new desk—or Harriet's desk, as he saw it.

"Learn this," the sour clerk had said before he hurried off.

Edbert was now the acting prime minister until either the election or Harriet was found. Huxley had assured him that he had nothing to do with Harriet's disappearance. It was just that such a statement was hard to believe. If it wasn't Huxley, then who? Maybe the woman was teaching him a lesson of some sort. Harriet just couldn't go missing.

Edbert found this whole ordeal bizarre. All this should have been his dream come true, yet the couple of days had ended up chipping away his confidence to such an extent he second-guessed all his actions and thoughts. Even the lines he read in the law book made him think twice in case he misunderstood something. He waited for Harriet to appear behind his shoulder and say, "Ha, I knew you were an imbecile."

127

The more pages he read, the tighter his throat got. Edbert scratched his ear with a loose fountain pen he'd found on the table and ended up turning his ear black.

Reading through *The Laws and Regulations of Leporidae Lop*, by Harriet Stowe, made him wonder, were humans incapable of cooperation or was Harriet simply being pedantic? Page eighty-three handled how to record and conserve official documents. The words left him cold, disorientated, and in desperate need of a match. Along with the book, the accumulating stack of papers on the desk made his heart burn.

The papers kept coming. The assistant kept bringing them in every fifteen minutes. Luckily, the boy was somewhat pleasant to have around. He kept saying things like "You can do it, sir." A day ago, he would have let the boy hear an earful, but now he needed friendly words. Running a kingdom was not an easy business. He had quickly figured out it wasn't about having an opinion about this or that and letting it to be known. He bloody crit had to go try to fix it. How was he to know what solution would lead where? And the laws weren't helping. He just had to think of Huxley and his nob friends and how they wiggled around them, not only with luck, but with a pleasant smile and a knife to the back.

His assistant popped his head in at the same moment Edbert seriously considered throwing the book out and having a tantrum, neither of which he really wanted to do.

The boy asked, "Sir, do you need anything?"

"Tea and biscuits would be fine." Edbert welcomed the distraction the assistant brought. Before the boy went to fetch the food and tea, he asked, "Boy, what's your name?"

"Siarl, Siarl Ellis, sir," he replied.

"Young Ellis, I want my tea boiling hot."

"Yes sir, and Siarl is fine, sir."

"Then call me Edbert, not sir."

Siarl gave him an awkward smile and left, much to Edbert's dislike. He moved on to page eighty-four, which read: *These rules are made to safeguard transparency and prevent civil servants or any other third-party exploiting the system.*

Edbert snorted. What a lie. He slammed the book shut and stared into nothingness, tightly squeezing the thick book. He dozed off, his head dropping to his left side and his mouth hanging open. He got to sleep so long that the first dreams snuck in. He was back at the bookshop and Harriet was behind the counter as the owner. The bookshop looked all wrong. Instead of books, there were rows of papers spilling out everywhere. Edbert backed away as Harriet rose behind the desk.

"Sir! Sir! Sir!" Siarl shook him.

Edbert stared at the assistant, unsure who he was, where he was, and for the matter why he was. But world seemed to make sense as he saw the spilled tea on the table. It had soaked the biscuits through and through. He grunted disapprovingly of the sacrilegious act. The world made sense again. Or not as much as he wanted. There were still the other uncomfortable moving parts he wasn't quite sure how to handle.

"Sir, you have to get up. They are here. I have never seen so many of them."

"Who?"

"The audiences. The whole kingdom is here to see you and it isn't even Friday!"

Edbert flashed back to the bookshop and forced the unpleasant memory away. He seriously lacked stamina for another day like that. The experience still gave him living nightmares But however he might detest the duty, he followed Siarl to the corridor and was proved wrong. The situation was nothing like the bookshop; it was worse. The assistant had been right. The whole kingdom was here.

Holy Lop, he thought.

It was at least twice as much, no three times, or if he truly counted accurately, four times the amount of people he'd met in his shop. Edbert desperately wanted to turn around and flee to the little closet he had been in and lock the door. He couldn't go through with it. It would be madness; he would be here advising them for days to come, and that was not even counting the breaks he would take. And as soon as he'd emerged from Harriet's office, everyone had begun shouting their questions at him. If that wasn't bad enough, Edbert was sure he saw people shoving each other to get to the head of the line.

"My horse…" someone—or more like, several of them— shouted.

"I can't afford…"

"The chickens aren't still…"

Edbert's eyes widened with horror. His knees shuddered, and he was willing to let his sudden rapid heartbeat kill him. Anything was better than this. Edbert wasn't made for people. People had always been the annoying part of owning a bookshop, and this was even worse. He couldn't fathom how Harriet dealt with this day after day, year after year. The lines around his mouth grew tight.

His desperation was somewhat short-lived. Huxley moved through the crowd toward Edbert and his assistant, his self-entitlement carving a path by default. When he arrived next to them, he lifted his hand and said, "Now, now, ladies and gentlemen, let us give our new prime minister time to learn the ropes. What do you say? Come back tomorrow and he will sort out all your concerns." He flashed them a smile. "It isn't like anything bad will happen overnight, will it?"

They obeyed him, much to Edbert's surprise. He wondered why they needed him, since Huxley could do the job better and faster.

Siarl sighed. "Oh sir, I mean Edbert, your tea. I'll get you another one." He disappeared.

Huxley snarled at the assistant, only seeing the boy now. He hurried Edbert back into the tiny office. Huxley glanced over the room, picked up the law book from the table, and said, "Our luck has changed—" He stopped mid-sentence and tossed the book into the wastebasket. "As I was saying, our luck has changed, and we have achieved what we wanted, you to sit in this office." Huxley looked around, measuring the room inch by inch, and sneered. He took one of Harriet's audience chairs and sat on its manchette.

"But our work isn't close to being done yet. The kingdom needs a lot of work to improve, starting from ceasing the useless audiences Harriet used to control us all. There we can move on and elevate our kingdom from the mess it is in now. Think of all the possibilities we have if we use luck in a grander scale. Not just to advance our personal needs. We could harness it to power our kingdom. But we begin our work tomorrow because we celebrate your victory tonight." Huxley smiled

Somewhere in the distance came the sound of coins clinking against each other and sharp laughter, both echoing in Edbert's ears. He looked around but saw nothing. The sounds quickly faded away.

"But—" Edbert said, glancing at the law book in the wastebasket.

"No 'buts.' We meet behind the palace at midnight, and it's not optional," Huxley interrupted Edbert. The man tilted his head and encouraged Edbert to utter his objections. The older man swallowed his words. Again, Edbert was sure he was swimming in deeper waters than he was supposed to. But his mind objected. Surely, if others saw he could do a good job and surely, he'd always had good opinions about how to run the kingdom, then surely he would make a good prime minister. But if he'd examined closer to the notions going inside him, he would find a thing called Peter Principle worming its way into his guts and nestling there. You know, the one proposing people rising to their level of respective incompetence. And like others, Edbert most likely would never admit it aloud that he knew nothing of what he was doing. Not at least, if not given a glorious way to back down. Huxley was sure not to let Edbert escape from his grasp. Before Edbert got any funny ideas in his head, Huxley left.

"But—" Edbert let out for no good reason.

He took the book out of the bin and sat back down. Huxley was beginning to get on his nerves. He wasn't going to let anyone make a fool of him. That was one thing Edbert had detested all his life. The laughter and mockery that had followed him everywhere. Edbert dusted the book off and opened it. No one disturbed him. Only the assistant occasionally kept him fed, but that was all.

At the end of the day, Edbert didn't feel any wiser. He kept thinking that he had been forgotten and abandoned in the little broom closet, and all the papers pilling on his desk were just there to keep him busy and not actually do anything of what Huxley spoke of—shaping the kingdom and making it a better place. It was as well. It was already closing to midnight, and he hadn't even gone to home, let alone open his bookshop. It had stood closed and dark the whole day. Edbert sighed, hearing the quiet rustle of unread, dissatisfied paper. But he had no time to go home, time to keep words being read. He hurried out behind the palace to Huxley's appointment. He nodded to every guard he passed by. They were another thing he fully didn't understand. Their presence made him feel safe, yes, yet left a bad taste in his mouth. Something which tasted like danger and potential catastrophe waiting to happen. It was like the guards' existence welcomed something bad to happen, and if nothing was to happen, then they would surely invent a threat out of boredom and out of not getting to use their pointy weapons. It wasn't that Edbert thought armies and guards weren't needed. It was just that there were individuals amongst them with all sorts of thoughts and wishes. Some sort of mindless controllable army would be better.

Edbert found Huxley waiting for him next to a fence with vines grown perfectly even and symmetrical. Huxley pulled him in through a small opening without saying a word. Behind the fence there were men in dark robes awaiting them.

Huxley offered Edbert a velvet robe, and said, "Put this on. And hurry up. We cannot miss when the moon is at its best."

Edbert glanced up to the sky, holding his breath. The silver moon shone perfectly in the cold night. Edbert's stomach got to all knots and ties. He held his breath. This was it. This was what he had been waiting for all these years. A real ritual. Real power. Real luck. This was what he wanted to do rather than sit in an office reading about laws. Huxley wasn't a complete idiot, after all. Here and now, they would lead the kingdom to victory. Here and now, Edbert had an opportunity to sneak in a wish for his bookshop. It couldn't harm.

He put his robe on and let himself to be escorted through a small opening in the palace wall. It led to a narrow corridor lit by gas lanterns which had a golden finish. Edbert squinted and gasped. Yes, it was getting better every second. This was what a secret society entrance should look like; gold guiding the chanters deeper into the palace, not a sewer grater. Edbert wanted to laugh. It was so beautiful and perfect, and it was only hidden behind a fence.

At the end of the corridor, they emerged into a magnificent cylindrical shaped room. He gasped again, taking in all the details he saw. Everything was perfect, including the beautifully arranged murals on the walls with tiny figures representing the gods and the past leaders of the kingdom. There was the founding father and his boat circled by his men. There were the small rabbits all over the murals—luckiest of all creatures, or so they said. But Edbert had never believed so. He had always thought goats secured prosperity.

Beyond the murals were the golden ornaments which encircled the huge gas lamps, illuminating the elegantly carved altar in the middle of the room. Everything was to Edbert's liking, as it should be. His mind basked in the room's aesthetics. It was perfect.

Huxley guided Edbert to his position.

The ritual began as soon as five other men, in addition to Edbert, had taken their positions—at least he thought them to be men based on the shape of their robes. He was right. No women were allowed here.

"Have you brought them, Brother Yellow?" a booming voice asked He recognized it; everybody in Leporidae Lop did It belonged to the kingdom's judge and jury, William Breheny, a scary man who took pleasure in punishing the wicked. Breheny was a huge man somewhere between a bear and a rhinoceros. He also did the executioner's part of justice. Edbert, like many in the kingdom, had witnessed his skill with the hangman's noose. Edbert found that to be a very distasteful way for an aristocrat to spend his time.

"Yes, Brother Gray, I brought them," another voice said hesitantly.

Edbert recognized that one, too. George Morgan from the party, the banker. Unlike the previous man, Morgan wasn't feared, but not liked, either. He held his purse strings tight, only lending money to his acquaintances. He demanded complex written explanations from other people with their loan requests—a trick he'd perfected to such an extent that it kept the rich rich and the poor poor.

Brother Yellow—George Morgan—put a small brown sack on the altar. He opened it and took out with his thumb and index finger a string of mice heads.

Edbert's stomach tightened and his breath caught in his throat. This had to be a joke.

The mice heads were tied together via their ears, ready to channel Edbert's inner wishes to the gods.

"Here we are, lucky little bastards, in the innermost sanctuary, where no goat's head will ever go," they whispered to Edbert, their voices dripping with mockery. They smirked through their broken dried lips and almost lost teeth.

"Here we are."

The panic rose inside Edbert. It wasn't only the mice's head. No, something was screaming inside him that this wasn't right. He kept shifting from one foot to another, but there was no escaping—not that he wanted to. He smothered all the useless noises inside him and focused on the ceremony about to begin.

* * *

"We want your help," still rang in the audience chamber. Harriet tried to wrap her head around it. Of all the requests in the world, help wouldn't have crossed her mind first. There were better reasons to trap her, most of them ending with her head on a spike, but to ask for help? That had to be a first. The

Gainsborians clearly needed luck and her, that was for sure. There was no one better to get people out of their messes than her. In a way, she understood why they had taken her. In a way, it was kind of nice to be appreciated rather than feared for her ability to fix everything. Still—there was always *still* in play—you really didn't go and kidnap people just because you desperately needed something. You asked, you sent letters, you did it through proper channels.

There was a nerving feeling inside her that she'd seen a request for aid somewhere in her papers years ago, but—another word that had a habit of sneaking into sentences, making everything what wasn't alright right—but things hadn't been right then at Leporidae Lop, either. There had been floods and storms raging over the land. No, it couldn't be... She had to misremember things.

Yet there was no denying the hardships the Gainsborians had endured. It was carved into their flesh. The lines were deep, and the skin was thick and coarse from all the sun and work. They didn't choose this simplicity surrounding her, them. It was clear from the way the stones were pressed and the walls darkened that there had been cushions, paintings, and other things to decorate the room they were now in. But nothing of it was left, just the stones and the people. Part of her argued it was her moral duty to help, but then again, she had to reconsider her loyalties toward her own people. They should come first, even if they hated her, and if given an opportunity, would gladly burn her at the stake. But Harriet understood people rarely knew what they wanted, or even more so, needed.

"You are asking the impossible. How do you expect me to help you when you say your land is bare and dry? What do you think I can do?" Harriet asked, straightening her glasses. Even if she said no or yes, she had to see if they'd thought this through, which seldom the case with these kinds of crude actions. Desperation bread mistakes. A proper action should be taken only after having stepped back and seen the whole view. Or so Harriet handled any given situation.

"You…" the woman stuttered. The older bearded man steadied the woman.

"Yes?" Harriet asked. She knew she was pressing it, especially after the tears and the distress she'd witnessed, but this was not the time to play soft. Soft meant she would let emotions cloud her judgment with what was the right call. There Harriet got it all wrong, but even the mighty had to fall sometimes. Emotions weren't there to be the boogieman. No, they were there as information to make people notice something made them happy or uncomfortable. It was all about what you did with them rather than having them around.

Harriet tried not let the Gainsborians, shuffling their feet as their children clung to their parents, to the hope they couldn't promise, get to her. She had to make an informed choice. She had to look away as their leader searched for words, and her people knew she wasn't delivering.

"You can help us turn our kingdom around," the woman hesitated. "To provide the same guidance and fresh start you did for Leporidae Lop. My grandmother told stories about you, and how you turned Leporidae Lop around from chaos to the kingdom it is now. And I know you do more for them than monitor monetary affairs or negotiate political issues, or else our nightmare wouldn't be true." The woman grasped for any notion where she could find reason. She wasn't that far from the truth. Harriet did more; she guided luck to the whole, battling every day for the wishes of the individual against the many. To the misery of the gods. And, as she had done that for her people, she had, in the process, robbed a good life from these people, but that couldn't be the whole truth. Surely, their own misguided actions had left them worse off.

"Your land needs more than guidance. What do you envision me doing?" Harriet asked. She lifted her hand before the agitated woman answered. "No, save your words for later. You'll need them. Let me think."

They gave her time. The woman, the bearded man, and the young boy who had welcomed her shooed off the restless people. The convoy out of the audience chamber created a rustle into the room. Harriet let it be. She sat down in the middle of the cage. "Hmm." Her mind was already solving the problem, not because the woman's reasons had been good—they hadn't been—but because she liked a good challenge more than anything, and of course, there was the whole business of dying. She wasn't that keen on letting a whole nation cease to be on her watch, for her actions, and the actions of her people. She'd never thought that her whole nation was sucking wealth and health out elsewhere with all the little asks they did.

Whatever way she was going to solve this, entrapping a god was out of the question. She was never doing that again, not for anyone. It had to be done the old-fashioned way, with hard work, and, for starters, with a ritual of luck. She had to draw in what was lost even to begin imagining altering the customs and care of the land. Curiously, a nagging voice inside her begged to differ, saying she should stop messing with this whole luck stuff, that it was a gift horse. Harriet silenced all her doubts. She didn't have the luxury of taking their counsel in this dire situation. *Crit it*, Harriet thought.

So there it was. She could help them and even turn things around, but all this was tricky when it came to her position as the prime minister of Leporidae Lop. She might argue this to be humanitarian aid, but there was no fooling herself when it came to some of her own citizens and what they thought about helping others. *Crit it*, Harriet thought, *they are wrong*. Harriet looked up to the expecting faces of the woman and her companions. They had taken seats on the stone steps, resting there, waiting for her. All of them knew her fate was already sealed when she was taken.

Crit, Harriet thought again.[12] She didn't care about old-

---

[12] A note here. The word 'crit' is dangerous to use, because it should never be said too lightly, and it might bring misfortune upon the sayer. Crit symbolizes everything bad in the world, and it is the other side of the coin no one ever wants to flip up. Crit is an abbreviation derived from a name, a name which should never be mentioned, a name which when said aloud, would instantly cause bad luck. A name belonging to the god who released

fashioned superstition or about what the Leporidae Lops thought. She cared about doing the right thing and mending what she'd broken. "I will help you," she said. "But I'm not a miracle worker; I can't conjure food out of thin air. If you want to survive, it means hard work and doing precisely what I say, nothing more and nothing less."

---

misfortune to the world for all creatures tall and short, furry and bald, wise and stupid. The god whom other gods hate. His name is Cornelius Rustika Inconnation This. Crit is a somewhat safe curse word to rely on, but not too often and not too passionately so as not to tempt fate.

CHAPTER FIFTEEN
A Smile Goes a Long Way

he rabbit god of luck could sense it. It was there, hanging in the air under the Leporidae Lop's sky, outside the pathetic shack. What it was, it wasn't entirely sure, but it felt a lot like Fate messing with it and something else, maybe another brother or sister there, lurking in the shadows. The rabbit god of luck was the personification of the real deal. The force that came from the minds of people with their believes and hopes. The rabbit god of luck was formed from the imagination and stories told beside the campfires like many of its siblings were. Then, later, came the named ones, the legends. The ones who got the temples. The gods people actually prayed for to alter their lives. The rabbit god of luck had never understood why and where people needed Bhaltar, Gertrude, Cornelius, Tamtue, and the rest. But as soon as they were birthed, they were everywhere, running around like they owned the place, and those like the rabbit were pushed aside. And now, it had an inkling they were coming, and it wasn't going to be pretty. And now it found it was going to be drawn into the whole mess just because of a random encounter. It refused to believe this to be its luck.

Harriet's name still ringed in its ears. The woman who had

ruined the last couple of years for it, making it pure torment. Of course, it could shrug it off just like that, but what was the point? Holding a grudge made life that more exciting and gave it a perfect purpose to hold on tight.

The rabbit god of luck groaned. It hated when it had to be the bigger person. It hated when people had attached to it human-like qualities like honor. What a useless concept. It'd rather swindle more carrots out of the small human female and be on its way. But the nasty thing, compassion—or pre-step of it, as the rabbit was unwilling to admit it had any of it in it— found the keen, honest, bleeding eyes of the small human female made it feel something. Sometimes it wished it was more like its brother Coyote. But luck was not a that kind of trick, even when it wasn't to be trusted.

"I see. Are you sure you're willingly give up your one wish for her? I could get you a pony. How about that?" the rabbit asked, shaking its pink nose and flopping its ears up and down. It had taken the rabbit a few centuries to master the movement, but now it came just like that. In the right kind of situation, they had the potentiality to hypnotize any onlookers.

"Yes, I'm sure," Sigourney said and shrugged. What else was there so worth having? Money? Sigourney didn't want that. Fame? Only for lunatics. Clothes, jewelry? Not for her. Freedom? Yes, but she already had that. Love? For fools. And ponies scared her.

If the rabbit knew all of what was running in Sigourney's head, then she'd rather stick with finding Harriet Stowe, her only friend. It wouldn't have even tried to press on her, but it didn't.

"Truly, you haven't thought this trough. I'm luck. I can give you anything you want. Just wish it and it will come. Anything you want, name it."

Sigourney shook her head.

"You don't understand. I can make you a queen."

What it got in response was a stunned, horrified expression. The one with slight bulge of eyes and mouth open. Not that dramatically, as Sigourney had always been bad at giving out the inner-workings of her mind, but something close to it.

"I truly can. Give me your hand. I have enough spark left in me to make you one." It left out the fact that maybe not the queen of Leporidae Lop or a kingdom as big, but there had to be some place with a potato field and a hut in need of a queen. There was, but they actually preferred a plow over any kind of bossy creature.

The small human female bit her lower lip, and the rabbit knew it was getting this all wrong. It was just that she was wasting a perfectly good opportunity to change her life around and not to be just an owner of a pathetic shack, clearly sneaking in here while no one was looking. The rabbit was right about the last part, but not about the other part. It was its perception how a life should look like. People had funny expectations of such things. So funny, that it made them cry more than often for not fulfilling their perceptions of a good life. What they never realized was that their good life was all wrong, especially if focused in the pursuit of money. You can ask any sociologist or psychologist if money brings happiness, and their answer will be, no. Of course, they can be mistaken. In a way, they are. Not about the pursuit part, but the money part to some extent. Up to a point you need money to make a good life, especially in a world where money does all the talking. Or in Leporidae Lop's case, luck, but let's leave that beside. But you don't need an excess of it. That's its false promise, especially if you dedicate your whole life in search of money rather than spending your time with a worthy task surrounded by somewhat decent enough people. Not everyone around you has to be a saint; the devils have their entertaining value as well. But none of that mattered here and now. Money wasn't the issue.

The rabbit gave in, tasting every single word it was about to say, not truly wanting to let them out, but having promised anything for the small human female, and it had to keep its vow. "If that's what you want, I'll help you."

Sigourney nodded, then she lifted her eyebrow like a question mark. To the rabbit's dislike, it understood the meaning. The small human female waited for it to perform a miracle as so many did upon meeting a god. Always wishing and wanting and never getting to know the god in question. Oh yes, humans, knew tiny little details about them like, what the god liked and what not, but how about the real stuff that mattered? How about its soul and inner wishes, eh?

"I'm not a miracle worker," it said with a tight voice. Not with this subject at least. Luck took time to work. Okay, not to it, but in this case it did. Even becoming a queen would have taken—let's say—a week or a month or a year to work. But it wasn't lying. It could have made the human female a queen if she'd wished so, which was all wrong she didn't. Didn't every girl want to be a queen? Now that it thought about it, they didn't. They wanted to be princesses according to popular concepts. But there was the trouble; at some point, they had to grow up to be a queen or a sister to one at least.

No answer, which was a good one, especially with all the thoughts running inside the rabbit.

"I might be a god, but I can't just whisk her here," it added.

No answer.

"Would it help if I showed you where she was taken?" it asked, giving in to Sigourney's magical way of dealing with others.

Sigourney's eyes lit up.

"I take that as a yes," the rabbit said. Getting the woman to answer even with her eyes soothed it.

Sigourney smiled, and the rabbit shook its nose. There was something wrong with the small human female and her smile. It didn't doubt for a second the effort was not sincere, but it looked as if no one ever explained to her what a smile was, how to do it, and what it was for. "Then you will have to follow me," it said. The rabbit turned to face the rooftop's edge and reluctantly offered its paw to the small human female.

* * *

The rabbit took Sigourney to a part of the palace's sewer

system she had never been in, which was odd because as she had a bad habit of wandering around when she had any time to herself. Sigourney had searched every inch of Leporidae Lop with meticulous passion, which was supposed to be a short stop in her journey to getting as far away from her brother and parents as humanly possible. Now, after several years, she still worked for the prime minister without a decent reason to do so, except her misguided notion about their friendship. Not a bad reason when it came to reasons in general.

Sigourney followed the rabbit through a narrow sewer corridor, listening to its quiet breathing and occasional muttering about how no one chose to use their one wish like this—all making Sigourney highly anxious. Not about the choice she'd made—she could stand with her own two feet behind that—but about no one doing the thing she'd done. It was nerving to be unlike the others. Something she had been all her life. Always looking in from the outside because of being labeled and feeling abnormal. She'd tried to be friends with others before Harriet, but she kept messing those relationships up. They always canceled their subscription to her, whatever that meant. There was something fundamentally wrong with her.

She had to get Harriet back, and from the sound of it, she had been kidnapped. But by who and why was still mystery. The rabbit had shrugged off when she'd asked. Unimportant details had been the only answer she'd received. Sigourney was starting to doubt the rabbit's eagerness to help, but she had no other choice than to trust it.

Sigourney concentrated on not stepping on the rabbit's great paws as she followed it. It kept creeping in slowly as if it waited for a monster to leap out anytime soon. Sigourney didn't believe in monsters. There were bad people. There were hurt animals. There were a lot of things that made living scary. It was just that she didn't see them as monsters. There were always reasons behind an action or a face. Even when her brother had been horrible toward her, and her sociopath mother and drunken father had left her ill equipped to everything truly, she saw why they had been like that. They had their history, just like she had. She had forgiven them a long time ago, but that didn't mean she wanted them around. She wasn't stupid.

The sewer kept twisting deeper underground. The corridors got bigger as they went and the rabbit straightened itself to a full height, which was massive. They had been walking a better part of fifteen minutes already, and in a way, Sigourney didn't want this to end. Having the rabbit around was reassuring. There was an aura around it that told Sigourney everything was going to be alright, and she didn't even think auras existed. It was that some people made the world a better place and you felt great just by being near them. The rabbit did that to her. The rabbit would have disagreed, and so would have many of its brothers and sisters. They would have argued it was moody, always complaining and sulking, and constantly in motion. Sigourney ignored all the warning signs. You could say that the god was her cup of tea.

The rabbit god of luck stopped suddenly, pulling Sigourney aside, away from the dripping goo as they stepped into another corridor just like the one before with all the stones and moisture and the odors left to be desired. The goo splatted next to her feet and melted away the top layer of the stone floor. They half-expected a predator-like creature to watch them from the ceiling, but the goo was just the waste Leporidae Lops produced.

Sigourney let out a string of noises no one could decipher, not at least the rabbit. Neither could the earlier detective, who certainly would have gone mad by now if sticking around with Sigourney. However, the rabbit rightfully expected the noise to mean "Thank you" as Sigourney had meant it. None of the earlier thoughts she had indicated that she could speak more freely around the giant bunny. The opposite was true, in fact. Being around it made her feel like one misplaced word or action would make it all go away.

"There, there," the rabbit let out and hurried to lead the way past the goo and other unrecognizable materials left there to rot.

Getting into the spot where the cage had been was surprisingly easy. It was like Harriet's absence had made the place less hidden. In fact, it had. While there was nothing magical about the prime minister, she still had her ways to make the world yield to her wishes, and not only through the rabbit and its luck. Some people were gifted like Harriet; they could make the laws of the universe obey them just by their unbending iron will. It was all down to the fact that the universe and more so, people, disliked contradictions, and if someone was unyielding, then there were two options: walk away and bring about a new multiverse or change your views. The latter was a lot easier to do than getting another multiverse working. All due to the social condition the brain came equipped with.

The cage was gone. Only a darkened circle was left of it. Sigourney pressed her hand on the circle, which was cold, indicating the cage and its occupant were long gone. Sigourney looked around, but there was nothing much to look at. They were in a huge opening with three tunnels leading out and stairs leading up to a door. She half thought there should be a draft, echoes of the outside world booming in, and a bad smell of sewage, but all of those were absent. The place was, in a way, nice when it came to controlling the environment. But this was no place to spend longer than fifteen minutes. And from what the rabbit had explained, it had spent more than a year here. More than a decade.

Sigourney bit her lip and tried to not let her upset stomach get the better of her. Yet inside her mind, she screamed loud and clear that Harriet had done this to the rabbit. She'd kept it here and used it for her personal means. And Sigourney still wanted to find her, even though, most likely, she should rot in the cage for what she had done. But Sigourney knew that such line of reasoning was just the top-most layer of her primitive mind. The mind which was willing to hurt others to save her face. A useless part of her that needed close monitoring or she would became that monster she didn't believe in.

She stood and shook all the thoughts away, concentrating on the immediate. Despite what Harriet had done, she was a lot better person to be in charge than Huxley would ever be. And it was clear as day that Edbert wouldn't be a match against the goblin man.

But this was all disappointing, and Sigourney had expected more. She'd expected some kind of revelation which explained everything. She gave the rabbit the same look she had given it earlier, with one eyebrow raised, a slight curl in her lips, and her eyes wide, ready to absorb any word it said.

The look unnerved the rabbit. "All right, all right," it said. "A small human male snuck in here a couple of days ago and promised to free me in exchange for helping to entrap that horrible woman. I told him how the cage works, how to free me and entrap her. With the help from a taller human male and his almost as tall companion, they moved her out of here. I exchanged my freedom for knowledge and all the luck I could muster. That's all I can tell you. That's all I know.[13]"

Sigourney raised her eyebrow one more time.

"What more do you want from me?" it asked.

"Who were they?" Sigourney asked.

"Nice to hear your voice, it's lovely by the way," the rabbit said. It hurried to say something else when it saw a tormented expression slowly morph on her face. "I don't know."

"Please," she said, prolonging the last syllable.

"I can't tell you what I don't know," it said and paused to think. "Would it help if I described them?"

Sigourney gave the rabbit an awkward smile.

The god took a moment to think. "Let me think. You humans look all the same. Nose, eyes, a couple of holes here and there, and lousy patch of fur, and there you are standing with two feet." It glanced at her. "Okay, okay, you look like your own person. So did they." The rabbit paused to think, scratching its ear, and then licking its paw.

---

[13] A slight misconception of the truth wouldn't hurt anyone. A gist of it was the same.

Sigourney sat down on the ground, cross-legged, and waited patiently.

The rabbit shook its nose. "Would a nose help?"

Sigourney nodded.

"Then the tall fellow had a wide nose, flat and huge," it said, swinging it paws to elaborate its words. "And, of course, there was his eyebrows. They were bushy and tight together. What else can I say? Oh yes, he was muscular, angry, and bald."

Sigourney shook her head. The description could mean anyone in Leporidae Lop.

"And his companion?" Sigourney asked in a quiet voice.

"Almost as tall. He, on the other hand, had some of his hair intact, but not all. He was jumpy, and he had shifty eyes," the rabbit replied. It was its turn to shrug.

Once more, the rabbit's description could mean anyone. Sigourney raised her eyebrow again. This time for the last time, but no promises.

The rabbit's pink nose shook rapidly. "What, more? Oh, yes, the one who snuck in. He was skinny and tanned, with a weather-beaten face."

"With crooked teeth?!" Sigourney asked.

"Show me yours?"

Sigourney bared her teeth.

"Are those straight?" the rabbit asked, licking its huge front teeth.

Sigourney nodded.

The rabbit scratched its neck. "Then yes, he had crooked teeth."

"A rat-like face?" She gasped for breath, strained by all the talking.

"Oh yes, now that you mention it, he had a face that looks like a vortex is trying to suck him in by his nose. Do you know him?"

Sigourney nodded. 'Know' was too strong a word to describe their relationship. 'Know of him' might be more accurate.

"Don't keep me in suspense," the rabbit said.

"I have to show you," Sigourney said, and this time, her voice had more strength.

CHAPTER SIXTEEN
My Luck or Your Luck?

he ritual continued within the royal palace of White Cuniculus's secret room. Edbert and the others performed the ritual like a well-rehearsed play. The hooded men circled the altar, shaking their legs and reciting ancient words none of them understood but were guaranteed to bring luck. They twirled around and walked in the other direction, shaking their hands and saying the words backward. Then the ceremony master's shouted, "Gertrude, bring us your blessing."

They all dropped to their knees to chant.

"Gertrude, Gertrude, Gertrude," Edbert repeated. He never thought to chant 'Gertrude,' as the name didn't seem an appropriate name for a god. He had seen her name in his book *The Pantheon of Gods*, but her legend of this fair maiden, the mother of kingdoms, and the leader of men had seemed nothing to do with luck. She was maker of kings, not a good life.

"Gertrude, Gertrude…" he repeated louder, thinking, *Oh, please, oh please, don't read my mind.*

They went around the room once more to chant their wishes—wishes Edbert wasn't quite clear of. Most likely wishes for power, prosperity, and Leporidae Lop to succeed. He snuck in a personal wish, for his book shop to thrive. Edbert couldn't help it. It was the one thing he'd asked always at the end of luck ceremonies. With this group, it would have to work.

They lowered to the floor, their heads pressed down to show their respect for the god. There was a slight tremor, almost unnoticeable. Edbert kept his head down, as did the others, even as the stony floor maimed his knees and the pose put pressure to his hips. Somehow, he couldn't help but feel disappointed. He'd expected more, like the gods themselves coming down to greet them, but no. The only thing he'd gotten was the end flutter, and it was over fast. This was the same old boring stuff he did with his own group, maybe in a nicer setting, but that was all. And the mice heads still smirked at him with their chipped teeth. Mice couldn't be the secret to the success of Huxley and the rest enjoyed. Also, success couldn't be because of Gertrude. Despite what the legends said, she never struck him as a god who could deliver. Something else made these men powerful. He mentally reviewed all the ceremony details, but still, the key to unraveling the secret hid somewhere out of his reach.

Someone got up next to him, and others followed. Edbert kept his head down a little longer, but when there came a cough, he got up.

"Come and meet everyone," Huxley said, giving Edbert his hand to help him up.

He took it.

'Everyone' was William Breheny, the judge, George Morgan, the banker, the king, Udolf Huxley, and Adolf Huxley, as he'd expected. The only one he'd missed was Adolf Huxley, Huxley's younger brother.

"Adolf Huxley," the younger brother said, offering his hand to Edbert.

Edbert knew of him. He ran the university. What he'd heard was Adolf to be a nice and intelligent man, and that everyone was enchanted by him.

"Edbert Pollock," he said when they shook hands. Edbert's dry, paper-thin skin hurt under Adolf's youthful handshake.

Adolf was at least ten years younger than his brother. He had striking features and dark brown hair that could dazzle anyone, along with his shining hazelnut eyes. One could mistakenly think he was content with his life, having such an esteemed position, always being surrounded by beautiful women, being highly intelligent and rich and liked by everyone, but still, that wasn't the case. Everyone in the kingdom knew how Udolf had stolen Adolf's fiancée. It had been a big scandal back in the day, and the whole dismal affair had been reported in the newspapers. Edbert hadn't understood back then, nor now, why it was thought as newsworthy. But clearly, the man carried it still with him, otherwise there hadn't searched recognition in Edbert. Edbert portrayed ignorance to the best of his abilities, which was kind of lousy.

Adolf sighed and released his grip. "Nice to have new blood amongst us."

New blood, Edbert silently snorted as he flexed his hurt hand.

Adolf turned back to face his brother, leaving Edbert alone with his thoughts. "How is Mabel?"

"Fine, as always," Huxley said.

"You?" Adolf asked.

"Perfectly healthy," Huxley said.

"Good." The man turned back to him, just when Edbert thought he'd escaped the social awkwardness. "So, Edbert, have you acquired any exciting new books in stock?" Adolf gave him an encouraging smile.

Edbert shrunk a little. The thought of not acquiring even a single book in days made him miserable. Edbert couldn't offer the most intelligent man in the kingdom anything but a meek sound.

Huxley nudged him, and Edbert blurted out, "A few you should come to see." Tomorrow he would have to contact his sellers: the University Press, the Leporidae Lop's Religious Order of All Gods Press, Press and Sons Press, and a few others. A relationship with the head of the university could mean a constant stream of revenue. Maybe the gods had actually delivered in a weird, twisted way beforehand. He vowed that tomorrow, bright and early, he would acquire at least ten new books.

Adolf and Udolf guided him through yet another secret door to a parlor, and again, Edbert was taken to drink his night away. Lately, drinking had seemed to be the way he spent his nights, but this time, he had someone to talk to. He enjoyed spending time with young Adolf. Here was a man who understood the value of a good book. He found out they had a common passion for Bradley Sheth's collections. He'd reread them cover to cover last year, as Edbert had done after the release of every new book. Then they discussed all the promising new writers whose first editions he'd secured in his collection. Edbert and Adolf had more in common than they knew—they had been competing with each other in acquiring those books. The night went by pleasantly, but Edbert was sure the constant drinking would be his doom if Harriet didn't suddenly appear and do the job for his spleen—the one that was already contemplating giving in.

Edbert didn't even notice as the other men huddled at the corner, speaking in quiet tones and occasionally glancing at him. He was too mesmerized by the young Adolf and his canter. Occasionally, he wished he hadn't followed his family's footstep to go into being a book dealer. If he hadn't, he could be sitting there in Adolf place, running a university and creating his own books about the gods only knew what.

Edbert found himself laughing at all the jokes Adolf made, making him wonder why any woman would choose his brother over him. All the socializing made him forget this had been supposed to be an important night according to Huxley. That was not all he ignored. There was a gentle buzz around him, like this little electric tingle as luck poured in, concentrating on him. But that was not all, there was a quiet vague murmur going around him as the wishes and wills of the gods circled him. You could say he was an oblivious linchpin, and if he wasn't so tuned to the material, immediate world, he might have noticed all the bustle and used it for his advantage. Now most probably he was just going to be another victim of the whims of the others. Not that it truly made a difference compared to any other habitant of the world. The question about determinism and freewill was just a theoretical debate as either way things went as they went, unknowable if it was predestined or had you chosen to act as you had. If there was ever a reckoning when the curtain to the backstage was drawn, then maybe there was some hope of truly, actually, absolutely knowing. Until then uncertainty was the forced precedent of life.

The same gentle buzz continued the day after when Edbert was back home, just waking up from the last night drinking, but Edbert was as ignorant. He was trying to survive the Wednesday morning, and the throbbing headache and nausea he was experiencing was made worse by the heavy banging on his front door. He wished the pounding would stop and turned over on his other side, drawing a blanket over his head.

The banging went on, turning louder every second he didn't answer.

"For Lop's sake," Edbert murmured and got up. He would have liked to curse and even throw out the word 'Crit,' but his headache didn't allow to make such a racket.

"I'm coming, I'm coming," he muttered as the banging continued with vigorous urgency. He dressed in his red and brown morning robe and left the comfort of his bedroom. His journey from bed to the front door was wobbly. His head felt like it was full of porridge, and his stomach had a storm brewing inside. He opened the door and peered outside. The bright light hurt his eyes.

A young boy pushed in, startling Edbert with his audacity.

"Sir, sir, you have to come with me straight away. Please hurry, sir," the boy said. His fast words came at him like tiny little hornets. Edbert batted his eyelids, trying to fend them off, but the boy was relentless.

He groaned. "What on earth are you talking about?" At

153

least his stomach had settled. Maybe his gut was getting the hang of drinking, but his tongue disagreed with his stomach. His tongue tasted like old cheese marinated in a sweaty shoe for a week and then rolled in garlic oil. He was sure he hadn't eaten any such things, yet there it was, reminding him that life was covered by thermodynamics.

"Sir, they need you. Something horrible has happened. They asked me to get you." The boy fiddled with his fingers and took a step back from Edbert's vicinity.

"All right. I'll change my clothes, then we can go."

"No time, sir."

"Don't be silly, I can't go dressed in my pajamas," Edbert said, tying his morning robe tighter around him.

"Sir, please, sir. It's an emergency."

And that was that. It was easier to go with the boy than argue with him.

They rode to the palace in a coach decorated with Leporidae Lop's crest. The boy rocked back and forth in his seat.

"What is going on?" Edbert asked.

"You better see it for yourself," the boy said. "Or you won't believe me."

The drive was short and fast. The horses and coach were pushed to their limits, which was a good thing or else Edbert would have done something drastic for the rocking boy, who was making him feel sicker by every prolonged second they spent together. At the palace, Huxley awaited them on the steps. He gave Edbert no time to breathe and ponder the climb down the two steps off the coach. He instantly asked, "What took you so long?" But Huxley didn't give him time to answer, either. The man rushed him into the palace, taking long steps. All around them, clerks ran here and there, visibly alarmed by something. Edbert tried to avoid them and keep up with Huxley.

"Slow down, boy," Edbert gushed.

Huxley grunted but kept up his fast pace. The man disappeared around the corner, forcing Edbert to take running

154

steps, only to see the man's fleeing back. Edbert's slippers moved as fast as they could, while around him, clerks and other palace staff rushed past him. He felt more than humiliated, having to parade around in his morning robe and receiving side glances from everyone. Whatever had happened had to be good or else Huxley wouldn't hear the end of it.

Huxley made a stop before he disappeared around yet another corner. He waited at Edbert there, fielding a deep frown. Edbert slowed his pace and walked to the man. He'd had enough with all the rushing. The world hadn't come to an end, so there was no point hurrying anywhere. Death waited for all, and it didn't ask if it was convenient for you.

"Sorry," Huxley said, seeing Edbert's expression.

Edbert was surprised but grunted approvingly. Somehow sorry and Huxley didn't seem to belong in a same sentence, let alone in the same universe. Huxley worked by his own laws, which had nothing to do how others functioned.

Then on, Huxley slowed his stride, enabling Edbert to keep up. He took him past the common rooms and other confusingly necessary parts of the place to a secluded hallway packed with royalty, politicians, academics, and all the rest who made themselves matter. Edbert straightened his morning robe and stepped in.

The crowd took no notice of him. They swarmed outside a doorway, leading to a round, decorated balcony where the king and his queen usually had their breakfast. Huxley pushed through the crowd, carving a path for Edbert. "Everyone out!" he snapped, driving everyone away, even the royal couple. Huxley pushed Edbert to the balcony, where Edbert saw what had caused all the stir past the golden rabbits with sparkling green eyes molded onto the balcony railings. He held his breath.

Two huge sinkholes had destroyed a great part of the kingdom. They had taken part of the palace with them, and a huge chunk out a residential area with factories Edbert couldn't quite name now. The only thing he could say was, "Holy Lop."

Huxley motioned for Adolf Huxley to come in. A smaller man trailed after him, who looked like he hadn't seen the light of day in decades. The man batted his eyelids constantly and straightened a stack of papers tucked underneath his armpit every other second.

Edbert greeted Adolf.

Adolf gave him a small nod.

The small man spoke right away. "We have done some measurements, and we have come to a conclusion that there are three possibilities which might have caused the sinkholes. They are either natural, made by an enraged god, or someone else has done this to us…"

"Done this to us, you say?" Huxley interrupted him, rubbing his jaw.

"Yes, but only a slight possibility, you see. If those things were made by humans, it would mean with a weapon with a great destructive capability, and from what we have gathered from all the witnesses, they didn't hear or see anything. Most likely the cause is natural, or even likelier, is that it's the work of a god or gods… For now, we can only guard the holes until we come up with a reasonable way to fill them. However, our first priority is to find out if there's some divine reason for them. We wouldn't want to offend our gods by…"

Udolf Huxley waved his hand, and Adolf dragged the man away.

"The sinkholes aren't the worst part," Huxley said, pointing to the nearest hole. "Look at that small opening there on the wall."

Edbert nodded.

"That's the corridor to the palace treasury. To your domain." Huxley took a deep breath before he said, "It's missing. All our wealth is gone." And for some reason, Huxley didn't sound to be too sorry about it.

* * *

As a mortal, it would be highly paranoid to think the universe and the gods were plotting against you, but sometimes they were and you weren't even aware of it. They were sneaky about it, making you believe in probabilities and bad things coming in threes and all you could say was 'So it goes.' At Gainsboro, far from Edbert and the buzz around him, Harriet Stowe had no clue of any plots going on. Her bones ached, feeling odd and hollow, and she had the sense of a threat lurking inside her. Something was wrong at Leporidae Lop. But she pushed such notions away as her being paranoid. The Leporidae Lops could manage without her for a couple of days. They were most probably throwing a big party in her absence. Nothing she couldn't fix once back.

Harriet watched as the older woman, the leader of the Gainsborians, worked to free her from the cage. She read the letter she'd stoved inside her pocket and frowned. She walked to the cage, touched it, and simply said, "Dissolve," and the cage's bars crumbled. The woman looked highly confused, but Harriet didn't. It wasn't about the word; it was about the intent and the letter. Harriet had sensed all the luck stored in the piece of paper pour into the cage. But now it was gone. What was left was the indescribable and confusing sense of relief washing over her.

Harriet carefully stepped out of the cage. Outside the air felt colder, making Harriet's skin pebble with goosebumps and her to take a step back inside, but she forced herself out. After the relief came the need to tear someone's head off, but she didn't accept such a primal part of her, and she drowned the foolish notion. Instead, she said with a tight voice, "We have to perform a ritual of luck tonight before the night draws to an end. But before we can do that, I need you to arrange a few things for, whoever you are?" Harriet looked at their leader.

"What?" she asked.

"Your name, please, and then we can move on," Harriet replied.

"Oh, I'm Bethan Ellis. This here is my brother, Harri Ellis." She pointed to the bearded man next to her. "And he's Idwal Lewis," she added when Harriet looked at the boy.

"That will do for now," Harriet said before Bethan summoned all the Gainsborians back and named everyone alive. "You already know my name, so let's not waste time with it. Now we have to get on with performing the ritual of luck. We need a head start right away. I have a feeling we need all we can get." Harriet left out the fact that she was still feeling sick to her stomach, having the sense of threat hanging around. But she tried not to put too much weight on her intuition—the one compiled from all the years of knowledge and lived experiences, that sometimes, but very rarely, led her stray. She tried to think she was just rattled by the kidnapping, by not being home, monitoring the reckless Leporidae Lops, and by being in somewhat novel situation.

"A ritual of what?" Bethan asked.

"Luck," Harriet said. "It's the thing that had robbed away your wealth and land. It's what we have used at Leporidae Lop since the beginning of our kingdom, and throughout the years it has gotten more sophisticated and into a whole industry of its own. It's the most well-kept secret that everyone knows to exist. Everyone in Leporidae Lop uses it and everyone knows to keep their mouth shut." Harriet snorted. She'd never had put it into actual words how their nation worked, which was built around silence and secrecy. "How it works is you do a ritual and pray for the gods to grand you luck and success to your wishes. It's a way to gain little advantages in life. In Leporidae Lop, you can't survive without it, or else you will be run over by others' wishes. You will be the sucker left out, begging people to buy matches from you and starving to death." Harriet winced as she looked at the malnourished woman in front of her.

Bethan Ellis stood there silent, looking at Harriet with disbelief. Then she shook her head. "We cannot. That's sacrilegious. Our gods—"

"Where have your gods been in the time of your need?" Harriet interrupted, knowing well she shouldn't have.

Bethan's mouth turned into an angry line. "You know nothing about us—"

"But I know about gods, Bethan. If I may call you that."

The woman nodded, despite the anger.

Harriet gave a smile. "I know what I'm saying sounds all wrong. But as you know, gods exist. They hold our destinies over us and the luckiest of us fly under their radar and decide our own paths. But I haven't been that lucky. When you start to shape things, be in charge, invent things, anything that might alter you and your people, they latch onto you and want to suck you dry and use you to their personal gains. Our gods squabble and fight each other for power and the hearts of men. I don't know about your gods, maybe they are more kind toward you and do it out of love, but I highly doubt it. Gods are vainglorious, petty, and spoiled, and they do everything they can to advantage their position over each other. Playing with the gods is dangerous, but it's the only game in the town, and you either strike out or luck out. I'm not saying there aren't good ones around. Clearly, there are or else our world would look a lot different. And the ones who play their games have to take prisoners' dilemma and other social conditions into count not to fully lose their position, but that still doesn't mean they are there for the little guy."

"And you are?" Bethan snapped.

"I could have declined your request, but I didn't. I have no moral obligation to help you, Bethan Ellis of Gainsboro. "What I have done, I have done for my nation and my people. My conscience is clear. So, I let you talk it over with your people what you decide. But before you go, tell me your god's name and we'll pray for them to see you, if that makes it easier for you."

Bethan Ellis paused to think. "Tamtue," she whispered.

The others around her made cross signs on their shoulders as the name was spoken, but Bethan didn't. She kept her stern eyes on Harriet.

"Talk it over, and if you accept, I'll go through what we have to do. Otherwise, you better start planning how you'll take me home or kill me."

Harriet sat on the stone bench next to the cage. She

watched the woman walk away with the bearded man and the young boy, speaking in hushed voices. Harriet knew she had been harsh—that her truth wasn't fully the truth. Gods could be bastards, but they had their merits too, even when she couldn't think of one right now. But one thing was sure, the ritual had to be done to balance out all the wants Leporidae Lops had sent to float around the cosmos.

This would be the first ritual Harriet would attend since becoming the Prime Minster, but she'd kept with the times and listened to the quiet murmurs how the rituals should be done. To be effective, they needed blood, a sacrifice, and words, but fire would have to do for now.

The Gainsborians needed a miracle to survive the upcoming winter, and when it came to rituals of luck, they were best done as soon as possible. She hoped Bethan would make up her mind and soon. There was truly no downside doing the ritual. If the gods didn't want to listen, they simply tuned out.

Bethan finally came back alone and said nothing but nodded and motioned for Harriet to follow. Outside the audience chamber, the Gainsborians waited for her instructions.

"We need to do it under the full moon, out in the open. I need all the candles you have to spare."

Harriet Stowe was showed to their backyard, where statues, the garden, everything from their past days had deteriorated into unrecognizable forms. It would be nice if there was one place in the world where you could escape entropy, but there wasn't, not even under a scalpel. So here the broken statues laid scattered on the dried desert sand. Only here and there grass fought for its existence, sucking all the moisture it could from the night air.

The settings didn't make Harriet entirely happy. The lack of an altar made the situation iffy, but she had to do without one. The Gainsborians brought all they could. They needed even more candles. Decent rituals needed flames to aid the performance, but Bethan said there were none to spare. Harriet entertained the thought of starting a bonfire, but that went a step too far to the demonic side of rituals and the situaticn wasn't that dire yet. Luckily, the moon still shone bright and the wind had calmed down a little. The backyarc was sufficiently illuminated to drive away any unwanted bogeymen and their doubts. So, Harriet and the Gainsborians continued with what they got.

Too many of the shiny, flashy, bloody, bony things the gods liked were missing, forcing Harriet and the people to rely solely on words and their strength in numbers, which had to mean something to someone.

Harriet smoothed out a flat surface in the middle of the withered garden. She drew a huge circle around it to make room for all the Gainsborians who'd agreed to attend—only a few had declined on religious grounds, and she let them be. They had no luxury to afford any fear or hesitation during tonight's ritual.

"Are you sure this will work?" Bethan asked when she took her spot.

"It will, trust me, Bethan. It will make all the difference," Harriet said in spite of her distrust of the whole process of begging for the gods to be merciful. What did they know about being a mortal. But Harriet couldn't deny rituals and luck didn't work.

"Take your places and do everything exactly as I do," she said and showed them the circle. Everyone obeyed and stepped into the line. The day when nobody complied with her orders was the day when she had become obsolete. Hopefully, that would be never.

"Join your hands together," she said. It wasn't usually dene in Leporidae Lop's rituals, but she thought the act would help relax the Gainsborians.

"Tamtue, hear our call," Harriet began. She would have liked not to use a precise name, not knowing anything about their god. A generic god would have been better to increase their odds, but she needed the Gainsborians to believe, and that was the secret to any ritual, not to mention the general loudness might draw attention of any god who wished to steal a little bit belief to them.

"Tamtue, hear our call," Harriet repeated because the Gainsborians hadn't followed her example. They shivered and looked around, waiting for someone to punish them. Harriet squinted and swirled her hand. She could show them real fear and punishment if they didn't obey, and soon. She and the night weren't getting any younger.

"Tamtue, hear our call," every man, woman, and child repeated in a low, unsteady voice.

"Tamtue, hear our call," she said with more strength, and this time, they got the tone right, and from there on, they did exactly as she did, fearing her more than the sins they committed. Harriet made them shake their bodies, repeat ancient mantras of luck, and drop onto the ground to worship. They repeated all the gestures with OCD precision. The ritual seemed to come out of them like an endogenous action.

The ritual kicked a dust cloud into the air, tainting the performance, but to their luck, the god didn't mind. Why would he?

The chant was both intoxicating and obnoxious.

"Tamtue, give us enough luck to prosper to gain food for our table and fertile land for our future," Harriet said, and everyone repeated the words. Harriet had found out it was good to use clear demands since gods had a habit of misunderstanding everything. After the silly ritual, the real work would begin, with or without the help from the gods.

The gods chose to help. The land shook with the intensity and determination only reserved for landmasses. Gainsborians screamed and ran to take cover inside the palace. Harriet ignored the shaking and pushed her hand to the ground to feel its silent tremble. She should have run, but it was too late.

The ground underneath her opened and swallowed her whole. The ground continued shaking, but then it stopped as suddenly as it had begun.

Harriet Stowe lay unharmed but bruised in a deep hole, sprawled on top of a pile of treasures. She took a few of them in her hand and flipped them between her fingers. She snarled.

Bethan Ellis peered into the hole. She had come to her rescue, but instead of helping Harriet up, Bethan stared glassy-eyed at the loot. There was a shine in her eyes which Harriet disapproved. No one should have that gleam when it came to gold and the rest of the glitter. To Bethan, the treasures filled the empty hole in her soul. To Harriet, they were the necessary misery in the world which one should stay clear of after a certain point. Too much gold and the happiness it brought was gone, and too little made life too unbearable. There was a fine balance. Harriet was sure she would find out someday what it was and finally find a religion to preach about.

"Crit," Harriet said, looking at the treasures. This wasn't even close to what she'd ordered. A sandwich delivery would have made her happier.

Her cursing was muffled under the joyful cheers of the Gainsborians, who rushed to their leader's side. They cheered even when the gold didn't instantly ease their hunger. They cheered for the opportunity to change their lives for the better, and they cheered as the glint of the treasures ignited their inner Magpie, the thing that lives in all of us—except inside Harriet, who doesn't let any animals inside her, only proper things, and maybe a few wildflowers with spikes.

Harriet climbed up with the help of Harri Ellis. The man had come to her aid without needing to be asked. Thank the gods. It would have been awkward to lay on the treasures for the rest of her life like some kind of dragon. Now, instead of biting off the fingers from whoever approached them, she could reason with them on their own level.

The ground shook again, but this time, no one fled. Everyone wanted to see. They hoped for a nice simple snack because they felt hungry, but they got an entire baking district dropped from the sky. The buildings made a loud thud and lifted a small cloud of sand.

Harriet's "Crit" echoed through the backyard, but it was buried under a loud cheer when the smell of freshly baked bread wafted through the air. She should have known that the gods were ready to start their games—she knew her history—[14]that there was more than the normal luck in play. She'd feared this to happen so long, for generations, that it had become a part of her existence, but now it had finally come and Harriet wasn't sure what to do to save her people and the Gainsborians.

---

[14] A reason she'd trapped the rabbit god of luck. She'd needed it to balance out all the other forces in play at Leporidae Lop, and now she'd lost it and everything was doomed.

CHAPTER SEVENTEEN
Animals of Misfortune

ate autumn turned the leaves from colorful to a dead brown. Those who were wise had already collected all the berries nature had to offer, not to mention the mushrooms and other wild plants and herbs, but the fat man wasn't amongst the wise ones. He had other things to worry about in the wee hours of Tuesday night. Soon the day would turn into Wednesday and all the troubles would begin. Harriet wasn't the only one who knew what the gods were playing. The fat man, one god, who wanted to avoid the upcoming blood path, knew what would happen next. So it always went when the party had run its course and it was time to pay the debt.

Cornelius breathed in the cold air and slowly let it out. He took a few more deep breaths to ready himself for the spectacle that would start the events. As his lungs inhaled the last sip of air, the earth swallowed a garden and left a perfect deep circle in its place. Cornelius peered into the newly formed sinkhole, pushed gravel into the hole, and grunted. Then he looked away and made a red apple appear. The horse snatched it straight away. Cornelius patted the horse on its side. It was a good horse, never flinching and always obeying. They had been together for twenty years now.

165

The autumn wind, which would have rustled flowers and trees, now made an eerie hollow sound as it circled the hole. The sound aroused the neighborhood's cats and dogs as a chorus of whimpers echoed through the inner kingdom. Cornelius listened to the sad sounds, making a note of all their complaints for a later date.

Cornelius took a bite from another red apple, which he held close to his chest. The horse next to him neighed in protest, and Cornelius shook his finger, causing the horse to lower its head. For a while, he listened to the eerie sound coming from the sinkhole and the neighborhood's upset animals.

Eventually, Cornelius had to move on. He said to his companion, "Come along, we still have work to do."

They walked to the other side of the kingdom where the air smelled of cinnamon. Soon the smell of cinnamon rolls and freshly baked bread would be gone. Actually, right about now. The ground shook in the baking district, and it gave way beneath a few residential buildings and a factory. Again, the animals woke and whimpered. The whimper grew louder as the wind encircled the new sinkhole and made the same eerie sound.

Cornelius sat next to the hole and began to breathe from his belly, puffing and flattening it, giving him enough oxygen to think. He shut his eyes and continued his breathing cycle.

The sinkholes would bring out the bad in human beings as was meant to. They would tear each other apart, giving the gods what they needed. He felt vexed over how this had to happen over and over again after every third generation, all due to the irresponsible use of luck. Humans were always ready to take what the gods gave them, always ready to fight each other over the worthless tokens, and always ready to destroy everything they could get their hands on. How could he stop the same failed pattern of abuse and destruction when the humans and gods did everything in their power to repeat it and refused to listen to him?

Cornelius would rather be on a beach, basking in warm sunlight, listening to the waves hit against the shoreline. He wasn't that picky as to where, as long as the beach was far away from here, but… no. It might be time to release his own name upon the world. They said he was a bad omen, that he caused all the misery. They blamed him for all the bad they did to others and themselves, both humans and their gods. He saw himself more like the balance between sweet and sour, and the only sensible person in the world who saw through the bullshit and lies.

"Cornelius Rustika Inconnation This," he said, speaking his full name aloud. His words echoed from the sinkhole and resonated through the kingdom. It was the first time in a long time his name had been spoken aloud. Years and years had gone by without anyone uttering it, not even whispering it. It was about time someone said it and put some sense in the world.

The dogs howled and the cats hissed.

Cornelius Rustika Inconnation This breathed deeply in and out. His mind was at peace. He promised he would make a difference this time around.

CHAPTER EIGHTEEN
They Sank Into a Hole

Edbert swayed as he looked at the sinkhole in front of him. Edbert and Huxley, along with a few others, had moved into the collapsed corridor which led to the treasury, which in the jolly old good days, ensured a happy, carefree life.[15] Now the corridor was full of debris and the light seeping in from the sinkhole. Edbert peered into the hole again, but it made his head sway and his heart beat faster. He stepped back and took hold of the wall. He'd seen enough of the black emptiness to know his head was completely wrong when it gravitated toward it.

"This might look dire, but don't worry, we'll bluff. At least for now," Huxley said. "Everyone thinks us to be the richest nation on the continent, and so we are." Huxley tugged the vest underneath his frock coat and looked down at the hole. There was an unsure expression on his face, as if he couldn't decide if the sinkholes were a good or bad thing. The hole itself didn't seem to affect the man the way it affected Edbert.

"What do you think is down there?" Huxley asked.

---

[15] To some.

"What does it matter? It's more important we do something about it than wonder why it exists at all," Edbert replied. The two sinkholes were devastating and shouldn't be taken too lightly. The missing treasures would make the kingdom and their neighbors restless. Edbert saw how the whole deal unraveled—the kingdom on fire, all his precious books stolen and destroyed. How could Huxley so easily ignore the impending doom? This needed more than 'We will bluff it.'

"Of course, we do, but don't you stress yourself about it... You better go to your office and deal with the day-to-day matters. Your office must be packed with people. We'll deal with the rest and come get you when there's some sense to it." Huxley hurried him off, but before he left, Huxley said, "And that negative attitude of yours isn't helping anybody. This is an opportunity for us to seize."

Edbert walked back to his office, his slippers making a soft *scuffling* sound. He scratched the back of his neck and snorted. "Deal with the day-to-day matters. Don't worry. Your negative attitude." He wasn't some old, senile thing to be set aside; he was the Prime Minster for the love of gods.

As Edbert debated what to do to be taken more seriously, a man bumped into him, hurling Edbert down to his bottom. All this made him think the universe was out to get him and utterly humiliate him. He knew he looked like a fool in his slippers and pajamas, but still, there was no excuse to treat him this way. "Watch where you are going," he snapped, trying to regain some dignity by using an angry voice, which truly never amounted to anything good. It might work in the situation, but usually it would snowball and who knows, even take a whole town with it. You got further with empathy and understanding, but those two bastards weren't easy to use. They were actually quite painful and downright dangerous. With aggression you knew what you got, either submission or a slap. Both quite alright, but with empathy, someone might make a fool of you or became your best friend, and there lied the danger.

"Sorry, sir, I didn't see you there," a familiar voice said and offered him a hand.

169

Edbert tied his fingers around Upwood's hand and soon he was upright.

"It's all right," Edbert said, massaging his right hip, which by the end of today, would be black and blue. He liked Upwood enough not to make him feel too bad about his one mistake when it came to him.

"I'm sorry, Edbert. I assure you, I completely missed you there. And I would like to stay and chat and apologize properly, but I have to see Huxley straight away," he said. "I promise to make this up to you later when I'm not in such a hurry."

"Then you better go," Edbert said. Upwood's comment, "I completely missed you," rang in his ears. It sounded like an offense.

"Will you manage?" Upwood sounded sincere.

"Of course I will—"

He didn't get to finish his sentence before Upwood hurried away.

"Go, go, I'll manage," Edbert mumbled to himself. "I'm just your prime minister, but you better go see *Huxley*."

Edbert continued to the office at a slower pace. His slippers scuffled against the marble floor, and his hip burned with agony. His steps sounded old and tired. All he craved was some peace and quiet after the morning he'd had.

The universe had better use for Edbert than to let him hide in his office. The office corridor exploded with noises as soon as he made an appearance. It was full of angry people, yelling and screaming in unison, sounding like a chorus of hungry cats. Edbert looked for his assistant to safeguard him, but the boy was missing. He ignored the public and limped to his office, closing the door behind him, and causing a riot to break out. Edbert didn't care, not any longer. If they wanted to see him, they would first have to learn how to behave.

He walked to his desk—or as he still saw it, Harriet's desk—and slumped down in the chair.

Deal with the day-to-day matters, ha, he thought.

He opened a random desk drawer and took out the

topmost folder to read. A menial task to take his mind off things. Where on earth was his assistant? He would know what Edbert should do. He opened the folder and read the first document in it.

Edbert's face reddened. The first document was the permission to tear down his bookshop. Edbert shut the folder and threw it on top of the desk. It was like someone had purposely put there to mock him.

He stood with force and walked to the door. "First," he shouted.

The riot outside simmered down to a shared sound of confusion. A bold woman, who grasped the situation first, rushed in. The riot began as soon as Edbert shut the door behind them.

"How can I help you?" Edbert asked.

"My home is gone…"

Every story after the woman's was the same. The two sinkholes had taken either the people's home or their livelihood. Some stories were even more tragic because children, wives, or husbands had also been lost. Edbert felt helpless against their tears. The only thing for him to do was write down their stories, names, and addresses—if they had one. After the audiences, he decided to find someone who could help him help them. He found no one willing to do that. They all were too busy with their own tasks. It was up to him to do something.

Deep in thought, Edbert returned to his office. He was sure Harriet Stowe, the miserable witch who happily tore down anything in her way, like his precious bookshop, was the cause of all the misery. She had to be.

In the office, the folder still lay on the desk. Edbert took another look at the folder as he passed it on his way to the chair. His face turned pale and his knees trembled. He hadn't seen the rest of the papers in the folder before. They were completely different from those he'd received. If he had, he would have happily given up his property. Gods, he would have been there to see the building be demolished and given a fanfare to Harriet Stowe as it was done.

She'd planned to build an orphanage in his shop's place. But that wasn't what would have made him let her do unspeakable things to it; it would have been the relocation and a huge pile of gold for the inconvenience—more than a fair proposal. The relocation to the busiest street in the kingdom would have saved his shop, but instead, he had been tricked and made to look like a fool. Edbert turned red. He was no fool.

Someone had to pay for this.

* * *

Norville Upwood forced his way to see Huxley, who'd returned to the balcony room. Two noblemen tried to block his entry. "This is important and can't wait," he said, pushing them aside, not letting them make him seem foolish in front of all the important people in the kingdom and in front of Huxley. He wasn't as compliant as Edbert. Forcing his way in came easily to Norville, who had the farmer's upper body strength even in his old age. Norville was a man who didn't shy away from hard work. It gave him pleasure. In this kind of situation, his well-equipped arms and tongue could do real damage.

"Huxley," he said, his words cutting the air and startling everyone in the room.

"What is it?" Huxley asked, giving him a look which said Upwood would pay a heavy price for his impudence. Upwood shrugged the look off. He wasn't in a mood for Huxley's silly power games. The man had a hold on him, that was sure, and they both knew he was at the mercy of Huxley's silence, but that had a time and place, and this wasn't it.

"I need to talk to you, alone," he said.

"Be done with it and say it aloud," Huxley said, spitting out his words.

"I rather not." He glanced around and saw the whole room watching them. The men in the room made Upwood sick to his stomach. They used him as their lackey. He'd even grown to detest Huxley and their friendship. There had been good times between the two of them, but lately, Huxley had been spinning out of control, even putting a threat between them. Upwood understood why. This was the only opportunity the man was ever to get, and he wouldn't let it slip away from him despite the cost—not wanting to hear Upwood's cautions. And then there was the rest of them, the so-called noblemen. They knew nothing of real work and real responsibilities. Delivering lambs and working at his farms had given him a proper perspective on life. But these men thought the real world happened inside documents, courtrooms, and banks. They knew little of building something from scratch as he'd done with the farms he'd bought. Not all in the room were those Huxley had bribed, bought, and extorted to do his bidding and take part of the coup against Harriet Stowe; some where there as it was their birth right, and still a threat to Huxley and his plans. Plans that one day would remove the king and queen, that much Upwood was sure of.

Huxley dragged Upwood to a corner and whispered, "What is it? Can't you see we are in the middle of something a bit more important?"

"Your contacts at Ferrum demand payment for the shipment. Right away. I thought that as we have no need for them any longer, we could apologize for the inconvenience and send them back," he replied in a hushed voice, knowing the last sentence wouldn't fly with Huxley. But he had to try. Guns in the man's hands would be bad, especially now with the two sinkholes. There were already rumors circling around the kingdom about an invasion and attack. Upwood was pretty sure who'd started them or who at least fed them.

"Don't be daft. We apologize nothing for no one, least of all to arms dealers." Soon a scary grin spread across Huxley's face. "Pay them and get the weapons at once."

"But—" Upwood opposed for nothing. Huxley had responded just the way he'd thought, yet he'd come to ask.

Huxley shooed him off.

"No," he boomed, making the whole room stare at them. Huxley narrowed his eyes. "Don't make me break my word to you. I value our friendship too much for it."

"If you did, then you—"

"I mean it. Now please go and handle the weapon shipment and bring it to me."

And Upwood let him push him again. There it was in Huxley's eyes, the hunger like no other. Hunger that had made him lose all his senses. Upwood couldn't deny his fear for his dirty secret to come out. His reputation would be ruined, and what was worse, his family would be shunned out of Leporidae Lop. He had once thought them to be friends, but growing up together meant nothing to Huxley, or so it seemed.

Upwood's stomach churned. His breakfast—two eggs, two slices of bread, and a bowl full of good old porridge—wanted to come out, but he forced down the acid taste in his mouth. The bile burned as it slid back into his stomach. Illegal arms deals were too much for him. He'd protested against them from the beginning, but with every day, Huxley went further and further to the side where no honorable gentlemen should ever go. Yet he went along with him. Not only because Huxley had a hold on him. No, he had done all this in full awareness. He'd needed as much as the others in this room to overthrow Harriet Stowe and her army of clerks to give room for others' opinions. Harriet's iron rule had to be stopped.

Edbert Pollock's little fight against Harriet had made it all possible, obviating any need for weapons and violence. Then Harriet had gone missing, which had been a godsend. Their coup had been nice and simple, without blood and grief, just luck working perfectly. For a second there, he had been able to enjoy his newfound freedom by acquiring a new farm, but now the sinkholes and Huxley's madness robbed him of his good feelings. Upwood squeezed his right hand into a fist. He had only wanted to raise more sheep, but no, Harriet had to refuse him. Just because he didn't tick a right box, include a right kind of document, and do a demeaning monkey dance in front of her, and all this had happened. Harriet always had to know better. Two new farms would have been a great addition to the kingdom's economy.

And now, whatever came from this, he was to be blamed. He could have stopped Huxley several times, but he was a coward and a fool... and he was being a fool even now.

Upwood fled the palace, his heels rapidly clicking against the marble floor. Damn the reputation! He wouldn't let Huxley get his hands on the weapons. He would hide them and face the music if it came to that. So what if he was exposed for what he truly was? It was better than the constant acid taste in his mouth.

CHAPTER NINETEEN
All the False Promises

an't we leave it at that?" the rabbit asked again, its voice echoing in the sewers. "Isn't it enough that you know who took her? We can do something else. There's a brave and vast world out there, which really doesn't need a busybody like Harriet running around. You could still be a queen. I can make that happen."

Sigourney gave the rabbit an awkward glance after she shook her head.

The rabbit twitched its nose, and said, "Guess not... Oh, crit. Let's go and find your kidnappers, then."

Sigourney offered her hand to the rabbit.

"Hmm, what do you suppose I should do with that?" the rabbit asked, gazing at her hand like it contained a dead fish which had been left in a trashcan for a week and then rolled in dirt and the small woman was trying to pass the fish off as a bouquet of flowers.

"Just take it." She extended her hand and shut her eyes. It's amazing how much social anxiety and fear can fit into a person of Sigourney's size—who, for that matter, was on the short side of the spectrum and made many think she could fit inside their pocket. The answer was a lot. Anxiety was altogether a silly bugger. You never actually went out to get it, out somehow it found you, latched on to you, and made your life a living hell. It was like this broken alarm system that made you fear even a friendly smile. And not always because there could be something sinister about it, no. More like the alarm system was telling you that you were going to mess things up. Someone might say anxiety was like a demon, there to guide you wrongly to a seclusion and world of torment. Somehow that demon had snuck inside Sigourney and she needed all the help in the world to get rid of it. But she couldn't ask for help; she had no voice for it.

The rabbit's soft paw clutched her hand. It also held its eyes shut and hoped nothing too bizarre would happen. They disappeared. All right... quite acceptable. What next?

Sigourney stood still, savoring the moment. Somehow the paw's velvety touch reassured her and made her feel more whole than ever before. She wanted to stay in that precise moment forever and ever, with the rabbit's paw pressed against her hand.

"Ahem," the rabbit said, clearing its throat and taking away the short harmony Sigourney had achieved.

Her social anxiety came back, and holding hands with the rabbit became a horrific experience. All the 'what-ifs' and 'does it hate me?' stormed inside Sigourney's mind. She tightened her grip around its huge paw, searching for that perfect moment, but it wasn't there anymore.

"So, you are one of those monks?" the rabbit asked. In fact, it meant Mount Jalaya's nuns, but 'nun' as a word gives the wrong impression. Nun inclines women who sing songs, pray for a dead man, and dress into dark clothes, and they were nothing like that. Yes, they wore dark clothes and sang obscene songs, but they prayed for no man. They knew it was Mother Nature who'd made everything, and the dead man and his father had stolen her glory. Men were like that, at least in their opinion.

Sigourney shook her head. She wasn't a nun, not at least in the sense the rabbit had meant.

"No? Then how?"

She shrugged.

"You are an odd creature if I have ever seen one."

All the emotions one can have—the horrible kinds—moved across Sigourney's face and settled into a stoic stare. "All right, take me to the fellow," the rabbit said. It was better to get things over with. Holding hands with her might turn out to be fatal. She could have other bizarre tricks up her sleeve.

One could think there was no one to watch them at this precise moment, but that was not true. The dead were always watching, along with all the other critters in the world. For example, five spiders watched them and dropped off their webs when the rabbit and Sigourney disappeared. Human disregard for the basic laws of nature had left them highly confused. So much so that they were sure a philosophical pondering was their only salvation. But they never got that far; they were too busy multiplying and filling the earth.

As the rabbit and Sigourney walked out of the sewer system into the palace, the rabbit let out a tune, a whistle. The song sounded too familiar, as if someone had already let it loose in the kingdom. A passerby got frightened by the sudden noise. The poor clerk twitched and ran away, hitting his head on a swinging door, but his scare kept him running.

The god smiled as Sigourney as it watched the clerk flee and said, "Fun, huh?"

Sigourney laughed. The rabbit was right, this was fun. Then she stopped herself, seeing her brother's face clearly in her mind as a tight feeling seized her chest. The memories she hated came flooding back. Sigourney wanted to let go of the rabbit's paw for the second time and flee, but she couldn't. She had to do this for Harriet. She had to try to be social.

Sigourney took heavy breaths and walked onward in silence while the rabbit continued spooking the palace staff.

Soon they arrived outside Edbert's office. The culprit sat there as she expected, all innocent. "Is that him?" Sigourney asked, pointing at the assistant.

The rabbit nodded.

Like the rabbit had said, the boy looked as if the universe was trying to swallow him whole, using his nose as the starting point. But that was just a perfect imperfection; the one thing that made him unique and somewhat charming.

The lines between Sigourney's eyebrows turned deeper as she frowned. The assistant clearly was a great deceiver. He looked so harmless even now, but if he had been able to kidnap Harriet Stowe herself, then he was a dangerous man, indeed. She hated him. He was another man like her brother—nice to some and evil to others. She wanted to sink her teeth into his ankle. But—there was always a 'but,' and she hated it. All the 'buts' in the world made her head spin and her heart burn.

Maybe one scare, a tiny little one, would show him what was right and what was wrong in the world. And she wasn't being bad, as there was a good cause, but first, she had to get him alone.

Sigourney took them closer to wait. The boy stubbornly stayed behind his desk, occasionally stretching his legs. At some point, Sigourney expected the rabbit to get bored with their constant hand-holding, but its touch stayed soft and relaxed. Again, she felt comfort, solace, and the promise of a better future, making Sigourney happy—happier than she had ever been, almost forgetting the dark thoughts that had nestled inside her. All the heaviness and the rest of the critting things life came with had melted away.

Sigourney purred.

The air turned colder outside as they waited, making the windows moan and creak. The hallway grew darker, but the boy remained as Edbert remained. So did Sigourney and the rabbit. There was no other place Sigourney would rather be. She had decided to see one thing through in her life, and this was the best moment to start. Harriet Stowe needed her help.

* * *

Harriet indeed needed help, but not in a way Sigourney thought. The fallen buildings stood solemn on Gainsboro's landscape. They'd brought with them a scent of baked buns and bread. It smelled nothing like the Gainsborians had experienced for decades. To Harriet Stowe, it smelled like a false promise, but to the others, it was sprinkled with hope, making the famished women, men, and children rush to the huge building without a second thought. The ground had stopped shaking, and Harriet hurried after the people, wishing for no bodies or conflict, knowing there would always be those two. Unavoidable calamity of human existence.

As she got in, she saw the Gainsborians stuffing their mouths full of bread, cinnamon buns, and delicate pastries. Also, she saw everything that was wrong and could go wrong. The bakery was full of other people, the bakers. They watched with horror in their eyes as the dirty, malnourished people indulged in their ravenous behavior. Most of the bakers reached for their knives and spatulas, but one sought comfort in cookie dough instead. He was a black sheep, the one fellow who was always in the lot. He gulped down the dough. Harriet lifted her finger and all of them released their chosen weapons, except for the black sheep, who only increased his rate of eating.

In the meantime, the Gainsborians munched away on the delicate pastries with a hint of vanilla and raspberry with such vigor, it left no room to taste the beautiful balance between sweet and sour. Harriet Stowe wanted to turn her gaze away, but she forced herself to witness their deprivation.

The Gainsborians ignored everything else except for the food.

All around them the magic of Harriet's raised finger died down.

Harriet beckoned the head baker to her before anything irreversible happened. Harriet knew him to be a reasonable man, and together, they had a chance to somehow salvage this until everything got too dark to be fixed. Already she saw the hate and anger building up inside the Leporidae Lops. She understood them. They got ready to defend what was theirs, which was a good thing in a way. But Harriet couldn't let a river of blood to be the first moist substance the desert land had seen for decades. She couldn't let humans get it wrong again, especially not when the gods were using them. She still remembered the stories from the last time. They were a faded memory now, but her father had killed himself for the horrors he'd witnessed, for the wars and hate he'd endured in the name of his kings and lord and saviors. She still remembered him holding her in his lap, rocking her in his chair as he sang the old war songs. But she had been four when he'd left, and she couldn't trust her memory. Her mother had cursed the gods and their taste for blood. And for what? Glory, resources, and their own pettiness. Yet, it wasn't that simple, and Harriet knew that. She also knew the new generation had forgotten what would always follow after running out of future bonds, running out of luck.

The head baker obeyed her, even when his body shook with anger. He walked to her with his fists clenched and said, 'Good morning, prime minister. To what do we owe the pleasure?' The head baker, Otto Hobbs, forced a smile to his round face. Otto smelled of sweat and flour, and his white jacket barely closed around his belly.

Harriet gave him a smile, making Otto flinch.

"It's good of you to pretend everything is as it should be, but I prefer reality over pleasantries. I presume you are angry and devastated by the sudden invasion. I ask you to restrain yourself and your people from lashing out. Explain to them that you and I'll resolve this together, outside, and stress the fact that if they lay even a finger on these people, they'll have to answer to me. Do you understand?"

Otto turned pale, nodded, and did as he was told.

Harriet silently observed the room. She straightened her thin silver glasses and thought of ways to deal with the mess.

When Otto came back, Harriet took him straight outside. He had to know and see the situation for himself in order to understand it. If the facts came out of her mouth, it would sound too silly, and Otto might do something he wasn't supposed to do.

And as Harriet thought reality had a habit of bringing even a grown man to his knees. Otto collapsed outside as soon as he noticed he was no more in Leporidae Lop. Harriet steadied the man four times bigger than her and half her age. "Breathe," she commanded.

Otto gulped in air, taking his time on the ground. Harriet had always wondered about the command to live in reality. There was nothing kind or welcoming about such a life, but she'd chosen to live in reality despite its flaws; despite the fact that sometimes those who had their heads in the clouds lived a fulfilling life, ignorant of the horrors existence brought. She was envious of such minds.

Otto detached himself from Harriet, pushing her hands away. His fingers felt coarse against her thin skin. She let him go, though he still staggered. She knew she couldn't afford to offend the man.

He dropped to his knees.

"Where are we?" he asked, his words coming out in a stutter.

"You are in Gainsboro."

"Gainsboro?" he asked with a much clearer voice. The initial shock was wearing off and he pushed himself up.

"A few days ride from Leporidae Lop to the south."

"What happened?" Otto let his eyes glide across the landscape to the three-story-high buildings which had arrived along with the bakery.

"Luck."

Otto nodded. "Not ours, though?"

"No, I guess not, Mister Hobbs." Harriet watched the buildings as well. The situation was turning more dangerous by the second. "I want to clarify for you that nothing here has been done on purpose. This is all a huge mistake."

She had to cut her words short as people came out of the apartment buildings. They aimlessly drifted around their homes, looking for anything to make sense.

"I have no time to explain everything. I need you to lead your people before anything bad happens. I'll get the Gainsborians out of your bakery. Then we will all resolve this."

Otto opened his mouth, but he quickly closed it when he saw familiar faces out in the cold desert. He hurried to give them solace and ease their fears. Harriet hurried into the bakery to stop the immediate violence. She ushered the Gainsborians out. who fought against her, but the sickening feeling of eating too much, too richly, left them too weak to argue against her. She instructed the bakers, the Leporidae Lops, to go to Otto Hobbs, telling them that all would make sense soon—even when she doubted that sense had anything to do what was going to happen. She had to work fast and be more than diplomatic to defuse the situation.

Her fears were right. Soon the sick Gainsborians and the confused Leporidae Lops stood facing each other. She stood in the middle of them, trying to navigate between the hate and the shame. Harriet assumed a posture of authority and silently assessed both sides. She could face the armies. She would face the music. She would never let the innocent die.

A tall man with an angular face—the kind you could imagine belonging to a man on horseback wearing a badge, and dark set of brown hair—Peter Thacker as Harriet remembered his name to be—clenched his teeth, making his jaw tense. He squeezed his hands into fists and spread his legs apart, mirroring Otto Hobbs's posture, and so did many others behind them. Their tragedy needed a scapegoat, and that goat had to be killed, sacrificed, and stuffed for their peace of mind. It was the easier thing to do than accept the situation as it was and do nothing. Doing nothing was the hardest part, as it was with everything in life.

On the other side, people averted their gazes. Idwal lowered his head, and the rest of the Gainsborians followed his example. Their limp physiques were ready to take the beating they deserved. They wouldn't even fight back for their own rights. To them, their natural reaction from their long deprivation were punishable. And in a way it was, especially in the point of time where so-called civility had forgotten what it was to be human; what it was to meet misery rather than having all the wishes filled just by asking.

"I know you are angry, and rightfully so," Harriet said. "I can't blame you, but—" Harriet didn't get to finish her sentence. Not in a situation where words often failed.

"You'll pay for this!" the angry shouts filled the air. It was such a cliche that if there had been any supreme being hovering above, watching the situation unattached, even they would have face palmed. As it happened, there were several gods watching, but they were far from supreme beings and far from unattached. They were made of the minds of men, and men got what they asked for.

The knife pierced the air, flying towards Harriet. It wasn't the lousiest choice when it came to solving things; it was just a choice you would have to own up to whatever the consequences were. Not by the knife though, which flew without having a single malice thought.

At the same moment, a loud growl rang out and a sudden flash. A girl, not more than six years old, dashed past Harriet to attack the man who'd yelled. Harriet watched the girl go and lifted her gaze to meet the knife. She crossed her arms and stared the blade down. It dropped in front of her feet with a sad *thump*. Maybe she possessed some magic, after all; maybe it was the gods or plain luck working for her, but then again, her sheer willpower could do that. The kitchen knife glimmered in the morning sun, which had gradually snuck up and soon made the desert scorching hot.

The girl hit the man with fury none had ever seen before. She bit him every chance she got. The huge man had difficulty defending himself against the small girl. He wailed and fought her off the best he could.

Harriet picked up the knife, walked up to the man, and said, "Care to trade?"

Harriet snatched the girl into her arms.

The girl sunk her teeth into Harriet's shoulder. Harriet wanted to scream, but she clenched her leg, gave the knife back to the man, and said to the girl, "Thank you, but it's time to let go." She lowered her, and the girl ran back to her parents.

"You can't let her leave; I want her to pay for this," the man wailed. He was bleeding from several places.

Harriet thought his wail was a joke at first, but when she understood he was dead serious, she said, "Put that knife down." Her stern voice slashed the man.

He dropped the knife.

"Do you seriously ask for blood to be drawn? From that little child? Or from your own children? Do they have to witness their fathers and mothers butchering innocent people who were just hungry... hungry beyond our comprehension? If you agree, then go ahead, they are waiting for you to do it, feeling ashamed of their moment of weakness. They are ready for you knowing they have no future without your mercy." She paused. "Pick your weapons and do your worst or choose the decency that I know lives in all of you. But you have to choose now, or I'll lose my patience."

CHAPTER TWENTY
Is It Too Much to Ask from the Universe to Intervene?

igourney and the rabbit had to wait until midnight for Edbert's assistant to leave. When he did, Sigourney readily chased after him, searching for any opportunity to corner him for answers, but there were none. He stuck with the crowds. She and the god followed him across the inner kingdom to the bad part at the outskirts where the low-income people had escaped the cruelty of Leporidae Lop. It was foolish to think there wasn't such a part in the luckiest kingdom in the world, because there always was. Not out of necessity, but out of disregard, cruelty, and the failure of human nature. As soon as they entered, a fruity, rotten smell took over. Sigourney was sure all the dirty, dark figures gathered in the shades followed them with their sad, angry eyes. But they looked past them to the looming future. Not even the most imaginative person could manage to escape the hell created here. Sigourney avoided this place as best she could. She just couldn't handle all the misery, and deep in her heart, she suspected she'd failed some test. Yet, the assistant navigated the street easily. He didn't seem to mind the sadness or the dark figures, and they didn't seem to mind him. He even got a nod from a few.

"What's wrong with them?" the rabbit asked, looking around with bewilderment at the people who had their faces cut from deep lines.

"Bad luck," Sigourney replied, not wanting to go farther. She couldn't, or else she would have to reconsider all that she'd done in the name of the kingdom, who let the large part of its citizens suffer at the hands of those luckier, forgotten in the motto winner takes all' and everyone according to their skills. It didn't work that way. But she kept all that locked away, out of reach of her thoughts to protect herself from the fact that she was favored by chance to be able to live her life as she wished and concentrated on her own existential suffering.

"This can't be bad luck; it has to be something else, or else…" The rabbit cut its words short. Or else it had to admit it was to be blamed, and that there was something sinister when it came to luck.

The rabbit didn't have to think on the matter long. You could even argue that it was out of good fortune, but then again, sometimes things just happened without need for labels like good, bad, lucky, and unfortunate. The assistant disappeared from view, making Sigourney twirl around, not paying any attention to the rabbit's last words. It gave the rabbit an excuse to push the matter to the buried memories file, which was not to be opened in any circumstances or the hardware would corrupt.

The rabbit tugged her, and said, "Follow me, I can smell him." It took Sigourney through the narrow alleyways, taking long strides that made her half-fly. The assistant must have sensed them because he made erratic movements as he half-ran to wherever he was heading.

When the assistant came into full view, a homeless man blocked their entry. The rabbit and Sigourney squeezed past him, losing sight of the assistant once again.

Sigourney's moss-green jacket sleeve got caught in the homeless man's hand. She almost lost her grip on the rabbit's paw, revealing them to the world, but the homeless man let go of her just in time. Sigourney wobbled forward, managing to hold on to the rabbit's paw.

In turn, the homeless man thought he had been touched by the gods—and he wasn't that far from the truth. He dropped to his knees and shouted, "Dear gods, finally kill me. I can't take this any longer."

If the universe, luck, gods, or Sigourney and the rabbit had been merciful, they would have struck him down, right there and then. Instead, he got up, and at the next corner, luck intervened in his life. A fat, wealthy philanthropist woman with the widest smile in the world fell in love with him. From there on, he had a plate of food in front of him four times a day, a house so hot he walked half-naked—even during the wintertime—and he had never a dull moment in his life. His wife's constant chatter gradually made him insane, but he continued loving her, nonetheless.

That said, the rabbit soon found the assistant's smell over the stench of cabbages in addition to the questionable smell of foods which surely didn't contain any carrots. The assistant wasn't far, and when they found him, he slipped into a shack that was more pathetic than Sigourney's. The shack stood behind a bigger, but equally pitiful, four-story building, which looked like it might collapse at any time. Loud noises boomed out of the building, piercing both Sigourney's and the rabbit's ears—arguing, children crying, and fists pounding against tables. The racket almost made them turn away. For someone like Sigourney and the rabbit, the noises coming from people's domestic life was too much to handle. For them, the noises triggered their flight or fight response.

Despite everything, Sigourney pulled the reluctant rabbit to the pathetic shack, ignoring her inner guidance system to flee. They entry made the assistant jump with fright. He was packing his possessions into a black sailor sack. All his clothes flung from his hands, along with book, *The Rule and Laws of Leporidae Lop by Harriet Stowe*. It thudded to the floor as the boy swung around to face the door as it slammed shut behind him. "Who's there? Show yourself," he let out, making his stance wide and firm. He looked more harmless than intimidating, but

Sigourney didn't have the heart to tell him that. He was trying so hard.

Sigourney untied her fingers from the rabbit's paw, revealing herself and spooking the assistant even more. The boy instantly got agitated, backing away from her while letting out, "Please, please, don't let her near me." His legs hit the low wooden bed and he stumbled down onto it.

The rabbit tilted its head, looked at the boy, and then at Sigourney.

Sigourney said, "Huh?" Her heart pounded heavily, and she glanced at the door and then back at the assistant, and then at the door. She bit her lip and stood her ground.

"Get that wicked thing away from me," the boy pleaded. He tried to get up from the bed and flee from Sigourney at the same time by scooting farther back into the bed. Clearly, his body and mind weren't great co-operators.

Sigourney's stance turned into frozen, mortified existence. She knew there was something wrong with her, but this seemed a bit extreme. She bit her lip harder, tasting blood. She fought to get words out, to shout out, 'Where is Harriet?' But all she managed was a low grumble and some sort of swallowed whimper. Sigourney reminded herself that she was here on a noble quest, but none of that helped. It actually made things a lot worse.

"That's not very nice thing to say," the rabbit said, his head still tilted. You could say that it was growing unusually attached to the small human female and finding it difficult to let things, such as calling someone wicked, pass.

The assistant stuttered in the face of the god, blurting out, "But there are rumors that she's vile. That Harriet employs an innocent-looking, but actually demonic, child as her secret inquisition to fish out your innermost secrets. And she can do that just by looking... That... that her eyes are cursed... They hate her as much as they hate Harriet. They say not to look into her eyes." He shut his eyes and opened them again.[16]

---

[16] A fighter should always face the horrors and not hide under the blankets.

The rabbit looked at Sigourney with a confused expression. Sigourney took a step back and fell to the floor as if she had been hit. She'd always thought no one knew about her, which, in a way, was as almost as painful as this, but she preferred that over hate. Sigourney's lower lip quivered. To be thought of as vile and wicked was too grim, and to have him confirm her thoughts about the matter was even worse. Sigourney felt oddly numb as her whole life crumbled down.

"Hogwash. Her to be vile, there's a novel thought. She's as innocent as they come, and I know these things. In my line of work, you get a sense of who's wicked and who's nice. Oh yes, she might be working for *her*, and yes, in association she could be seen as evil, but still, look at her…" They both did.

Sigourney wanted the ground swallow her whole.

"Is that a face of someone evil?"

The assistant hesitated, yet kept his eyes upon her.

Good gods, Sigourney needed the earth to take her as its own, right now, thank you ever so much. The universe refused to cooperate—it had other things in mind for her. It saw this as a friendly reminder that you were what you did, and not what you thought. And it was high time Sigourney started to pay attention and understand that her actions mattered. Maybe not in the grand scheme of things, but there was a potential of little ripples to drip to other places and cause avalanches and other such things. Like a hurtful word, passing on and on its curse until someone broke.

"No?" the assistant tried. It was highly debatable if he said so because a giant bunny asked him, but nevertheless, there was high concentration of altering one's mental state going on here. The question was if for the good or the bad, but again, you could only get things wrong with such black and white thinking. Good and bad were highly subjective and a very inflexible way to see the world.

Tears began to well up and Sigourney sunk her teeth into

Nothing good came from that.

her cheeks so as not to let them escape. "Later," she whispered to herself.

"There we go; that wasn't so hard. Now shake hands and be done with it," the rabbit said.

"No," the assistant let out, this time with more strength.

The rabbit pushed itself to its full height, causing its head to thump against the ceiling. It squinted at the assistant.

The assistant screeched, got up from the bed, and offered his hand to Sigourney. There's nothing like a several feet tall rabbit to motivate your actions.

Sigourney's hand trembled as she touched the assistant, and they disappeared for a second. But the boy was too mesmerized by the touch to notice. As their hands met, something instantly kindled in both of them. The universe seemed to line up and bring two people, who were on the same wavelength, together. They just had been ignorant of the fact.

The assistant blinked.

Sigourney blinked. Her tears were gone, and she felt his warm breath against her face when he pulled her up from the floor.

His brown intelligent eyes and his gentle heartbeat enraptured Sigourney when their eyes met again.

The sensation scared her, and she snatched her hand back.

"Where's Harriet?" Sigourney blurted out, wanting to do anything to erase the earlier moment. She would rather go back to the time when he hated her and none of this had happened. It was so much simpler.

"She's in Gainsboro," the assistant replied. He felt panicked, but not from fright as Sigourney had, but from the pure shock of finding his soulmate—which he didn't believe in, in the first place. Soulmates were reserved for the romantics, and he was a pragmatic man. He'd made sure his heart had stayed shielded because fighters had souls as hard as stone. That was what his father had taught him. He and rest of the Gainsborians had sacrificed everything to get him here, and he wasn't going to let them down, not now, not ever—and least of all because of a girl… no matter how lovely she was.

"Why?"

"I took her."

"Who are you?"

"Siarl Ellis. I'm a freedom fighter, and she's ours. You can't have her back. I'll fight you if you try," he said, not really meaning the last part.

"Huh?"

"What's going on? And, and... who are you?"

"Sigourney," she said. She took a deep breath and added, "Perri... I don't know."

The rabbit watched as the two humans played a weird game of verbal sparring, which looked and sounded a lot like Ping Pong. It laughed aloud, knowing full well what was going on. "This is wonderful. All the creatures united under my name, under Lepus Cornutus Bonnee." The rabbit's voice boomed, filling the little shack with vibrations. For a while, the air outside turned dead silent as the god's name filled the entire kingdom.

Both humans lifted their hands to cover their ears as the name twisted into them. For the rest of eternity, it would stay inside them, bonding them and never leaving, not even in death. Hearing the name had to be sacrilegious, yet they felt pure bliss.

Sigourney shifted her gaze from the rabbit to Siarl, and their eyes met again. This time, instead of wonder and excitement, there was softness and hope. Sigourney turned her head away. Still, she wished to glance back at him, but she refused to obey such foolish impulses.

Siarl let out a low sigh. He cleared his throat and hurried to say, "I can take you there, to Gainsboro, but only if you hear me out first about why it was done. Only then." He looked at Sigourney, trying to meet her gaze. Just one small glance and his day was saved.

"Agreed," Sigourney said. She found her hands very interesting.

The rabbit god of luck, Lepus Cornutus Bonnee, laughed. This made things a whole lot more interesting. Which was good, as it was getting bored with chasing suspects and looking for that horrible woman. Still, at the back of its mind, it had a highly insistent thought saying that this couldn't be a random chance, yet this was not the doings of its luck. This was something else it should be aware of; something that should make it run to the hills and take cover. The rabbit shrugged off such a thought. Mostly because this was not about it; this was about the small human female, who was fidgeting nervously next to it.

* * *

The rabbit god of luck had been right. Something wicked was about to come. Outside, a great thick wind blew across the continent with a heavy oppressive pressure. It tasted like dust and cinnamon. It swirled around Leporidae Lop and Ferrum, looped around the mountains between the kingdoms, and made a sharp, zigzag leap over to Gainsboro's side, picking up more speed. It moved through the lands with ease and, in the end, dived into the cold sea. The sea swayed against the continent of Jadero, trying to soothe the ground back to sleep, but the ground grumbled.

The continent had gained its name after a huge mountain standing in the center of it. Mount Jadero stood solemn and mighty, gazing over the lands. Only a few of its inhabitants dared to venture there.

Its iced top was impossible to see because clouds shielded it from any onlookers. It was a place of magic. Its uniqueness came from the most meaningful force in the world, but not from the gods. They didn't dare live there. The magic came from the water, the source of life. Occasionally, freshwater surged down the mountain's rugged wall to the valley, creating life and anchoring everything in the soil.

Another gust of wind circled around the mountains, rustling the aspen trees standing in the valleys. The susurrus from the trees tried to sooth the land once again, but failed. The land groaned.

The land knew something bad was coming and it couldn't
slumber any longer, and neither could the mountain.

Lepus's smile died away.[17]

The rabbit pushed its ears up and listened. The air outside
sounded different and the ground underneath its paws
trembled. The noise and the motion felt familiar. The rabbit
had witnessed something similar happen before. It shrieked,
snatched the two humans into its arms—who tried to fight it
off—and it charged out of the little shack. Now the ground
trembled so violently that even the two humans noticed the
tremors and stopped struggling. The shack collapsed as soon as
they were out the door. The rabbit continued running, picking
up speed with its huge hind legs. Together, they became a
blurry motion.

With its final effort, the rabbit leaped up to a stone
building's rooftop, panting heavily, its whiskers fluttering. It let
the two humans down from its grasp. All of them huddled
together in the middle of the roof.

The ground shook again, and this time, the four-story
building next to the shack collapsed, lifting a dust cloud into
the air.

Siarl, the skinny human male, kept opening and closing his
mouth. Sigourney followed the rabbit's gaze. They looked
toward the palace, where the ground had disappeared. The
rabbit swirled around, and so did Sigourney.

A whole district in another location disappeared.

Siarl made a wheezing sound. "The, the residents…" he
said, not even seeing the sinkholes.

The rabbit turned its attention to the collapsed shack and
the building next to it. Inside the never-meant-to-last-building,
people died under the termite-covered wood. One woman got
knocked down by a falling vase—her prized possession,

---

[17] A side note. This is the last time Lepus's name is used. It is unsafe to use a
god's name haphazardly. Something disastrous might happen, like the true
nature of the world might be revealed. No one would or should ever want
that.

inherited from her grandmother—the thick porcelain base cracking open her skull. Maroon colored-blood oozed out, dripping onto a stitched tablecloth she'd made at the Women's Institution of Knitting.

"The… We… We have to do something," Siarl said.

"All of them are dead," the rabbit said eventually when the world stopped shaking.

Siarl flinched. "You can't say that."

"It's the truth," the rabbit said, trying to sound reassuring.

"No! They… Some of them might be alive," Siarl said, his voice lifting higher. "They have to be." He hit a high note.[18]

"I hear no heartbeats under the debris," the rabbit said, not understanding what Siarl needed from it. The gods and their like were better equipped for life. Truth and death, in general, didn't scare them a bit.

Siarl screamed and hit the rabbit with his fist, though the rabbit barely felt him. Sigourney made several attempts to touch the human male to calm him down, but for some reason, she failed every time. Her hand moved back and forth, never reaching his shoulders.

"Their lives matter to you?" the rabbit finally asked.

Siarl looked at it with a mixture of hate, contempt, and sadness.

Why? the rabbit wondered, unable to understand. He himself was alive and death wasn't that bad. There was an upside to it. For example, there was no more need to pretend to be nice. The dead could go around screaming at other people all the things they weren't able to say when they were alive. And, of course, there was no taxation, not if they didn't move to Necropolis.

It looked back at the holes, and back at the collapsed building, and then at its paws. It could sense its powers had

---

[18] Truth is a funny thing. Its popularity is overstated. Siarl was happy to choose any garden-variety lie over anything else the rabbit might offer. He frantically searched its eyes for something to make the world a better place again.

come back—some of them at least, enough to tamper with the universe. Then it said, "It means a lot to you that they are alive?"

Siarl squinted.

"Does that mean yes?" the rabbit asked Sigourney.

She nodded.

"So be it." It shook its perfect pink nose.

The rabbit nodded toward the collapsed house. Instantly, it rewound back together as if nothing had happened. No one except them would ever know it had collapsed. The occupants went on living without a clue of their own death—apart from maybe noticing petty side effects, which they happily ignored. They ignored their foul-smelling death breath; oral hygiene wasn't that important, anyway. The horrible nightmares about the upcoming doom were a mundane problem in the neighborhood. The only thing which caused them concern was the reoccurring visions of a giant, fluffy bunny embracing them and never letting go. That scared them stiff. And all the rabbit did was borrow another ending from another dimension, and the thanks it got was distrust of its godly image.[19]

"Now, we have to go. It has started," the rabbit said.

"Wh— How?" Siarl asked, switching his gaze from it to the building and then back again.

"I'll explain later. Let's go; we don't have time to waste," the rabbit said.

"But—" Siarl said, needing an explanation for his brain to function again or it would continue going around in an infinite loop.

"Sigourney, do your trick and I'll carry you two," the rabbit said, ignoring the human male. It already had done enough for him. Now they should concentrate on the sinkholes before something bad happened. Like, for example, losing its feet.

"Take it," Sigourney said, offering her hand to Siarl.

Siarl did as he was told with a distant look in his eyes. But

---

[19] Humans, go figure.

as soon as he joined hands with her, all his thoughts turned insignificant, and all he had eyes for were her soft, tiny hands.

The rabbit scooped them into his lap and jumped with a giant leap onto the ground, making a loud *thud* and cracking a few cobblestones underneath it. Then it ran away from the sinkholes, but it legs didn't obey. It kept bringing it and the humans toward the sinkholes, forcing it to think of ways to fill them, or at least how to block them fast as it knew well enough what was drawing it toward the sinkholes, not letting it go. A cork the size of several buildings would suffice, but the tricky thing was how to obtain such a thing. It was a god of luck, not someone who could conjure anything out of thin air. It might be able to persuade a mountain to move over top the holes with a blanket of an ocean, just to be on the safe side, but only might—and through luck.

The rabbit's leg muscles pulsed as it gained more speed. Siarl and Sigourney's weight added no strain to the god's running.

The only amusement the rabbit was going to get from these situations was the way Siarl looked at Sigourney. The human male repeatedly gave the human female and her hand repeated glances. Even though the rabbit came from another species, it knew what that look meant. A look so universally recognizable, even a goldfish would know infatuation was happening.

Sigourney turned her head away, turning red and feeling warmer against its arms. *Good*, the rabbit thought. She'd gotten overly attached to it every second they'd spent together.

The rabbit laughed, its booming voice filling the streets, causing sheer panic in those who roamed the streets in the wee hours of a Tuesday night. Its laughter caused Sigourney to blush more. Human courting rituals were bizarre in that way. They are better done in secrecy, preferably on a remote island, far away from prying eyes and possible threats. The whole process was so delicate it could easily be ruined by things like eating too little or too much.

They soon got to the first sinkhole, and the rabbit stopped next to the swallowed garden. "Unless we do something, these sinkholes will destroy everything, along with all the carrot fields and the rest. They are the beginning of the end. We have to fill them up before they come."

"We?" Sigourney asked, not hearing another word than that.

"We?" Siarl echoed, sounding hopeful.

"Yes, we. *How* would be a better question, though. And soon it won't matter if you two keep concentrating on the trivial. I can't smell them yet, so we have time. What do you suggest? Can either of you magic a cork or something called a cement truck here?"

CHAPTER TWENTY-ONE
Furry Little Fools

n Thursday morning, after finding out he and his shop had been used as a weapon against Harriet and he had been made a fool, Edbert stood on Huxley's front steps bright and early, searching for an explanation. The brisk shamble there had almost made him change his mind and be a coward as he had been all his life. But he refused to be one anymore. So here he was, swinging the rooster knocker attached to the front door. He did it a few more times with force.

A befuddled servant with sleepy eyes opened the door. It was the same man whose clothes Edbert had borrowed, which were back in his shop, uncleaned and wrinkled. When the man noticed Edbert, he looked at his new prime minister from head to toe, and over again. Back in another time, in a different mood, Edbert would have smoothed his jade tweed jacket, but now Edbert stared the manservant down. "I want to see Mister Huxley," he demanded.

"Sure, sir. I'll get him," the man said without welcoming him into the foyer, as was the custom. The servant closed the door behind him, leaving Edbert to wait on the porch, clutching last night's papers, and shifting his weight from one foot to another, releasing tension from his hips and knees. He watched as the morning sun rose, warming the roads and windows, wiping away last night's frost. As it melted, it shimmered in the sunlight. Soon the sun's heat wouldn't be enough to fight the cold off and everything would stay frozen, even the windows of Huxley's magnificent mansion.

Edbert wondered what kind of income one had to have to be able to afford a house like this, which put other houses on the street to shame. If he tried, he could roughly estimate the sum—basing it on to his shop's expenses and taking into account the location, size, and age difference, and all the rest. The sum was a lot.

After a long while, when he finally had come to the right conclusion as to what Huxley's yearly income had to be, the servant came back. "Master Huxley said he'll see you at the palace," he said, averting Edbert's gaze.

Edbert not only lost his final calculations, but also felt as if the servant had slapped him across his face. "But—"

"Master said it's better if you two talk there; more private, sir." The man slammed the door shut before Edbert had time to say anything else.

Edbert stood on the porch, feeling flabbergasted for the servant's and Huxley's impudence. He considered knocking the rooster again, but what was the use? Huxley was clearly trying to avoid him now that the man had only a symbolic use for him. 'Obsolete patchy' kept playing over in Edbert's head. 'Useless old man' came after, and Edbert knew he would have a long, miserable day ahead.

He shuffled to the palace, trying to clarify his thoughts, but lacked the rudimentary understating how. They only got more clouded and twisted. Even more so as he got nearer to the palace. This was why he favored books over people. They were simpler, they had rules, and they weren't messy like humans were. And you could always put one away if it made you feel uncomfortable. Edbert sighed and climbed the stairs to the palace. The guards nodded in agreement, but the initial glamor had died down. He was still the hero in their eyes, but a hero that came with the house.

Edbert expected to find a huge line of people requesting his attention in the office hallway, but the place screamed emptiness. And the assistant remained absent. Edbert sighed. His office should be full. The devastation the sinkholes had created still affected the citizens. And all those notes from yesterday about the troubles couldn't already be solved, not when he hadn't been able to find anyone to help him with them. Also, the last time he checked, the sinkholes were still there and hadn't been fixed overnight.

Edbert stopped the first clerk he could find, demanding to know where everyone was, but the only reply he got was that, at the king's request, Edbert was to be given peace to work. When he'd asked about the folder—Harriet's original plans for his shop—the clerk had shaken his head and made an excuse to leave as soon as possible.

Edbert was forced to go empty-handed, and with a heavy heart, to his office. Edbert couldn't help but think that life insisted on being composed of a row of disappointments. That if you were given only one chance at living, why couldn't it be lovely and peaceful? Edbert was sure that somewhere a mistake had been made, somewhere in the design of life, as if someone had wrongly thought stress and troubles kept humanity alive. But what was there to do to keep oneself busy. Edbert drew the huge paper mountain closer to him, left there to wait him. For a moment, the beautifully written documents, with curved lettering and round smooth loops, made him ecstatic, feel less like a throw away dish at the end of a failed dinner party. No one put in so much effort for nothing, and it was left for him to be handled. Seeing the queen's signature at the bottom of every page made his heart skip a beat. Finally, a real task. Finally, something in which he had an opportunity to excel. Edbert smiled, but then he read the title: *The Palace Redecorating Proposal.*

He shook his head, and his constant frown came back, as it had known it would. No smile stayed too long on Edbert's face—it hadn't been built that way.

The proposal turned out to be a daunting task. Time ticked away while reading it and waiting for Huxley to come. An hour passed, and still no Huxley. Another passed, and another. Edbert's stomach growled. He pushed the papers away. Why should he care about obligations when others clearly didn't? Obligations which were impossible to fulfil, or had he missed the kingdom's treasures coming back? Who cared about new chairs, curtains, wallpapers, and the rest of the lot? No one should.

He pushed himself up and left the room, taking the proof of the shenanigans which had ruined his and Harriet's lives with him. He would have been happy with a relocation and payment in gold. Edbert grimaced when he envisioned everything he'd lost. A new cozy little bookshop and a constant flow of customers, not to mention lots of new and old books lying around, flying off and onto the shelves, and turning paper into gold.

Someone would pay for this. Pay for the torture they had willingly caused an old man like himself.

As he searched for someone to talk to, no one wanted to meet his gaze and speak to him. He was pushed out everywhere he went. When he finally found Huxley, he was eating and drinking with his secret society buddies and planning things to make other people's lives miserable. Edbert was sure of it.

"Not now, Mister Pollock, we are busy with the sinkholes. I thought you had your own matters to deal with?" Huxley said from the door's sill. Laughter and banter resounded behind him as his friends consumed fine champagne and plates of delicacies. Edbert's stomach growled when he thought he saw a roasted chicken.

"The proposal in my office is nothing more than a joke," he said. "Why do I need to waste my time with redecoration proposal when there's no money left?!" Edbert raised his voice.

"Keep it down." The lines between Huxley's eyebrows drew tighter.

"Everyone knows it. It's not some secret that we lost it all.

People kept talking about it on every street corner I passed from your place to here. Leporidae Lops are not fools, and neither am I. I know what you did with Harriet's proposal!" Edbert waved the folder that had become a permanent feature in his hand.

"Not now," Huxley growled.

Edbert took a step back, as the man had actually bared his teeth and let out the low grumble.

"Mr. Pollock, with all due respect..." Huxley said, sounding more composed, "the kingdom has a more dire task at hand than you and your bloody bookshop or Harriet's proposal or what people speak off, so just take a moment and rest. Go and read a good book if that makes you feel better, but leave the state business to those who know what they are doing." Huxley looked Edbert down, and as he fought for words, the man slammed the door shut, giving him no room to argue back.

He heard more laughter come from behind the closed door. He wanted to cry. But no man, let alone an old man, should do that in public. He walked back to his office to collect his things and left. He knew when he wasn't needed.

On his way out, he dropped the redecorating plans into a wastebasket. They chose the wrong fool to do their bidding. Better if he went back to the bookshop to commiserate how whatever luck he'd gained was gone and to figure out a way to get back at Huxley for destroying his happiness.

To him, happiness meant books. Huxley had been right about that. Edbert lived for the smell of ink, paper, and glue combined together into a heady bouquet. For the feeling of thick paper covered with letters between his fingers. The feeling like none other. To him, there was solace in the written word because it made bad days vanish. A thick book was an ointment for a tormented soul. A page or two would get him back on a right track and clear his thoughts. Yes, it would. He couldn't wait.

As he made his way back to the shop, there was a warm flutter in his chest and he greeted people he walked by, which he would have never done in a million years. Now, even when things were horrendous, he was somewhat content. A thought of a good book could do that. But luck wasn't ready to make him pleased, or more like gods weren't. They still had their uses for him, and as the shop came into view, someone yelled his name, scaring him half to death, making Edbert unsure if life wanted to teach him a lesson or kill him with its constant surprising and shaming. Edbert squinted at the blurry figure standing on the shop's front steps. "You?!" Edbert let out.

"Good afternoon, sir," the mouse head man—more like a boy—said with a bow.

* * *

Cornelius Rustika Inconnation This, AKA Crit, awakened from his deep and complex thoughts next to the sinkhole in the baking district. Well, as deep and complex thoughts as gods can have, which weren't that deep or so complex. But he had been watching Harriet Stowe, altering her fate the best he could. Which wasn't easy, not when the other gods used their players. But she was his, and his alone.

Cornelius had awakened to a sudden rush of people, who came with measurement tools and gadgets to calculate theories so as to be able to poke holes in the universe. He was sure they dropped something into the hole to measure its depth. They would only end up with a wasted apparatus. Cornelius smiled. What a futile task. The hole had no bottom or top. It was what it was. The results they would get would always be wrong and in flux, as no natural law governed them.

"There's no loitering here," a man in a blue uniform said, suddenly appearing next to the god. Cornelius had been ignorant of the man with half the mass he had, with only a small fraction of his mental potential, and with a hairy maggot squirming on his upper lip. The man tried to intimidate Cornelius into obedience as the officer puffed his chest out and carefully mouthed every single word. "There is no loitering here. Leave."

"I hear you; I hear you," Cornelius replied, getting up and wondering who the man worked for. The universe had a lot of people such as the man. Always guarding, commanding, and insisting upon rules and regulations for actions to be taken. They made sure peace won over anarchy, or so they insisted as they embargoed upon others' fun. Cornelius respected their existence, despite occasions like this; he would be happy to change the human into a furry little creature to stop them from taking themselves too seriously and to stop thinking themselves better than everybody else. But changing humans, in general, into furry chipmunks would be wrong, or maybe a layer of fur and a tail would do good for humanity?

Cornelius smiled. He imagined the man being several inches shorter, with pointed ears and a brown fur coat. *Yes, much better.*

"And take that nag and mutt with you," the officer said, confused by Cornelius's smile.

"Mutt?" he asked.

The officer nodded toward his feet.

A mutt, or more nicely put, a dog, sat next to his right foot. The dog had white and gray shaggy fur and sad puppy dog eyes. They blinked several times and watched him in a supplicant way. Those eyes forced Cornelius's upcoming actions. "Oh, yes, my mutt," he said, and patted the seat on his cart.

The dog jumped aboard, wagging its tail.

Cornelius climbed in behind the dog, and said to the horse, "Let's go. We are not welcomed here."

The horse obeyed, but made a short protest to the officer, who understood nothing of what the horse said, which was, "What a jerk."

When they were farther away from the sinkhole and the officer, somewhere out of thin air, Cornelius manifested a sausage and the dog snatched it right away. Another sausage appeared and disappeared almost instantly. The horse let out a short, jealous neigh. *This was getting ridiculous,* it thought.

"Who are you, and where did you come from?" Cornelius asked, scratching the dog's chest.

The dog barked.

"Must be," Cornelius Rustika Inconnation This said and smiled. The day couldn't start any better. He'd made a new friend already. He was in dire need of one and had been for a long time, ever since he lost his true love. No one wanted or should ever have to change the world alone. "We have a humongous puzzle to solve and humans to butter up. I fear I'm taking on a task which has no good solution," he said to his companions, as there was magic in the spoken word, especially against the cold crisp morning. Such mornings needed a mug of warm cocoa and a friendly smile without the hurry to go anywhere.

The dog looked at him sympathetically. It licked Cornelius's hand, leaving a thick, wet layer of saliva glistening in the sunlight. He scratched behind the dog's ear and wished he had a bit of clairvoyance in him. The future would be simpler if there was only one true god, but there wasn't, and he had to deal with it.

Cornelius turned his loose comfortable tunic into a royal ensemble, which he thought would secure him enough credibility to make humans to do his bidding, and more importantly, to see things his way. The royal ensemble had tight blue trousers, a matching jacket—with so many buttons he didn't know what to do with them—and there were these curtain-like decorations on his shoulders which purpose he couldn't even begin to figure out. But somehow, the clothes he now wore impressed the humans. Now he only had to find the right person here at Leporidae Lop who could help him stop the cataclysm at hand.

When embarking upon this journey, he'd relied on Harriet being around. But clearly, the other gods had seen her as a threat and sent her away to stand beside the collapsing empire of Gainsboro, hands crossed in anger. Maybe it was better this way. She would do a lot more good there than here. But even when he had her on his radar, she was impossible to control. If only, but that would have required omnipotence from Cornelius part, meaning sufferings and wars got to run free and dance around humans, easily sweeping them into their madness. Not because one god was better than a bunch of them, but because Cornelius hated unnecessary violence, selfishness, and the rest of the lot.

Cornelius manifested another sausage for the dog and an apple for the horse. The apple uplifted the horse's mood, and it forgot the jealousy it had festered inside, and they continued onward without a hitch.

CHAPTER TWENTY-TWO
Surrounded by Morons

For a second or two, the Leporidae Lops thought to skin Harriet Stowe alive. She stood with her arms folded, her hands tightly clenched. Her words still sounded in the air, waiting for someone to seize them and make a massager out of the situation. They didn't. Her dry, thin smile made sure that even the most ruthless person considered their options. There was something sinister about her smile—something which told others they couldn't win, and if they did, they would pay a hefty price determined by her.

"No violence," Otto Hobbs said gravely.

There came a general sigh from the Gainsborians, but not only from them, but even some of the Leporidae Lops had wished no blood would be drawn. The gods agreed. Not that the humans noticed that. They waited for the bigger payday to come.

Harriet nodded, having expected Otto to yield, but still fearing the worst. There had been a slight chance for absurdity. It was a good thing Otto Hobbs and his people didn't forgo their humanity with one careless answer, as was the case of so many occurrences in history. As backing down, and saying, 'I change my mind,' was rarely an option. All again down to losing one's face, showing only how socially wired human brains were.

Harriet motioned Bethan Ellis to her and together, they led the Leporidae Lops inside the palace. "Choose your representatives so we can solve this predicament," Harriet said to both parties as soon as they were inside. She would have to navigate between their needs. It would be nice if everyone got what they wanted, but that was impossible, for someone always was disappointed. That was a fact of life. What came after the disappointment showed the person's strength of character and ability to take responsibility over one's own life. Harriet hoped Otto and the rest of them had good hard backbones, or else this wasn't going to work.

The Leporidae Lops agreed to have Otto Hobbs represent them, along with Peter Thacker—the one with the horseback face and dark features—who was second-in-command at the bakery.

On the other side, as expected, the Gainsborians chose Bethan, Harri Ellis, and Idwal Lewis. Harri Ellis was Bethan's older brother. That much Harriet had deciphered. He was in his sixties, with a weather-beaten face, a rough dark voice, and charismatic lines, which would have made Harriet's heart flutter as a young girl. Now she barely had even a second thought about Harri's alluring lines. Idwal Lewis was attached to Bethan and Harri, and they acted protectively toward him. Harri was always a few steps away from the thin young boy, who was fifteen or sixteen. He had silver eyes and an appealing face. Harriet was uncertain of his title, or why he followed Bethan and Harri all the time. A truth she would have to fish out later, once things weren't as immediate.

Six of them headed to the audience chamber, leaving the rest in a huge kitchen and the rooms next to it. To Harriet's dislike, they found the cage still standing in the chamber, making them all nervous. Otto and Peter eyed the cage suspiciously. Not that the sight was pleasant for Harriet, either, as it brought back bad memories. If she'd spent a few more days in the cage, she would have come out as an animal.

"All of us have talked, and we want to go home," Otto said, making side glances at the cage.

Harriet stepped between him to shield the cage from view and turn her back on her former prison. She faced Otto and said, "None of us wants anything else but for you to be able to do that, but the question is, how and when. There's a vast desert out there."

"You can't keep us here. We have a right to go home," Otto said in a tired, irritated voice.

"You do. There's no question about it. All of us want you to go back home. But let's be realistic here. You can't carry the houses shipped here on your backs. And these people have nothing to offer you. No money, no transportation, no food." Harriet wanted to scratch her nose. The golden coins, pieces of jewelry, gems, and art of Leporidae Lop, which she could catalog in her sleep, lay at the bottom of the hole. They had the means to get rid of Otto money-wise, but Harriet doubted they should. "What do you think their best transportation looks like?" she asked so Otto could see the situation they were in and stall time for her to think.

The best transportation they had was a single donkey. It grinned at them with its wide mouth. It was confused by the sudden attention and shook its head when all they walked around, judging it.

The donkey looked healthy; its brown coat had not so much as a single gray hair, but its teeth wouldn't have made a gift horse jealous.

"You are right; it can't carry us all," Otto snarled.

The donkey made a turn, showing its best sides to its audience.

"Isn't he magnificent?" Idwal asked as he petted the donkey. The donkey stuffed its muzzle into Idwal's armpit and the boy let out a laugh, ending the uncomfortable moment. He petted the animal and turned red when he saw the others looking at him.

Harriet watched as the young boy lowered his gaze to his feet, trying to hide his shame, but not able to. There was nothing wrong with showing emotions, passion. Nothing at all, even though Harriet herself preferred not to. It was like giving someone else power over you, as if you revealed your inner mind. Such things could be only done with carefully chosen company, if even then. But such was a lonely rode to be taken, and Harriet should know. She couldn't remember how she cried over her husband's death.

Harriet forced all the thoughts away. This was no time or place for them. There were worse things happening than if she had cried or not. For the matter, the kingdom's treasures laid openly not far from here, where anyone could stumble upon them. "Still and all, the donkey won't help anyone. We should head back inside and arrive at a better solution," Harriet said.

No one objected. They all kept silent, not knowing what could be done. No one dared to ask the obvious question, 'Why the gods or luck had done this to them?' They just had to survive, but that wasn't any different from any other day. You could never escape the whims of natural forces, gravity being amongst them.

As they walked toward the palace, Harriet whispered to Harri, "We need to get the treasures in right away, without anyone noticing."

Harri grunted and said, "I deal with them." He then left, making excuses for his absence.

Nothing good came out of the rest of the negotiations. Harriet did all she could to convince Otto's people to take all they could carry and go back to Leporidae Lop to alert the proper authorities for emergency aid. But Otto didn't like her proposal at all—not without transportation, not without his bakery, and certainly not without compensation.

"I can write you a letter and seal it with my coat-of-arms, if that helps," Harriet said, still trying to persuade him, showing a pendant with her crest on it. On the pendant, a dragon encircled a hare, which looked remarkably like the rabbit god of luck.

"I can't accept this without talking to my people," Otto said without looking at the pendant. Everyone in the kingdom had seen Harriet's coat-of-arms and hated the sight of it. Whenever they received anything adorned with her crest, it was always bad news.

"You do that, and we'll see if we can ease your travel back home."

After Otto and Peter left, Bethan said, "We should have paid them off with the treasures. It would have made things easier."

"If we let them leave with the money from Leporidae Lop's treasury—that is, what's out in the pit, by the way—do you think we would get away with it? Someone would notice and they would come after you. Best if we don't touch the treacherous stuff. We will have to figure out a way to get the treasures back to Leporidae Lop, and if that fails, we'll try to exchange them for aid."

"I know people. Otto Hobbs and the rest of them won't be happy at all. They might even hurt us if we give them no compensation," Bethan protested.

"It's a risk we have to take," Harriet said, ignoring the woman.

Bethan fought to keep her words back, but she caved in as Harriet refused to engage, but before Bethan could get her first word out, Harriet had raised her hand to silence her.

"I know people, too. I know Otto Hobbs better than you think I do. What they hunger for is an easy fix, and we have none available. The situation is what it is, and we do our best to mitigate whatever is going on." She left out the fact that what was going on were the gods using Bethan and her people. That she should have never guided them to do the ritual. Now all Harriet needed was time to think about how to outsmart the gods. Otto traveling back home by foot with a note from her stating what had happened to the treasures and them would hopefully mitigate the blowout Leporidae Lops would have. But then again, if she kept Otto here under her gaze, she could be able to control the situation. *Crit*, she thought.

* * *

Unlike Harriet Stowe, Edbert Pollock lacked certainty when it came to how things worked in the world. The boy outside Edbert's shop was proof of that. Also, it was proof of a lot more Edbert was unwilling to admit to himself and anyone who might ask.

"What are you doing here?" Edbert asked.

"I'm here about the book," the meek-looking boy said. In truth, he was a man, but to Edbert, most men looked like boys. Only some past their mid-sixties resembled a grown man to him. It was the wrinkles and the dimmed light in their eyes that told him they'd finally realized what it was all about. There was nothing like a reminder of decay telling one that you should have never postponed those dreams and experiences of yours for the later date. The date when the body saw even a slight change in temperature as a threat, steps as a surest way into a heart attack, and any alteration to the day a sign that chaos was there out to get you.

"Ah, yes, the book. Come in," Edbert said.

He walked past him to open the front door and let Josh, the-mouse-head-boy, in.

Edbert had forgotten all about the matter. Too much had happened ever since. But part of him disliked that he'd forgotten. He'd never missed an order before, especially not an important one. Josh worked for the Hunt's Library, and occasionally came to the shop to get a thing or two for their collection. A month ago, he'd ordered some sort of romance novel.

"Romance," Edbert snorted angrily as he walked into the back to get the book. He wasn't in the mood for all this. He had, at no time, been one for romances, or ever had a Mrs. Pollock for one. It had always been he and him alone, never caring to look too deeply as to why. Such things were better kept hidden deep under the skin and only taken out really late at night or when there was professional help around. Edbert focused on searching for the book in his storage closet. Most of the books he had at the shop were in plain view, but he kept special orders and other books he couldn't sell in his storage closet. For example, he stored there his most prized possessions, a rare books collection. It had taken him a lifetime to acquire them, especially prized five of those books. They were the only surviving copies.

Edbert let his eyes glide over the collection. Everything was accounted for, especially Bradley Sheth's books. He took the romance book off the shelf and went back out to the shop.

"This will be huge," Josh said when Edbert gave him the thick, leather-bound novel. "We already have a waiting list for it. First time since forever we've had one for a book."

"I thought libraries were for education?" Edbert sighed. His day was getting worse, and not for the first time, he had doubts about the future of the book industry as a whole. What good did a romance novel do for the world? Nothing. That was the right answer. It was a waste of money and paper.

"That too, but this will get us more visitors, and I heard it's quite entertaining. You should buy a few copies for your shop. Oh, crit, buy a stack of them. Every woman in the kingdom will want to buy this."

"Ha, I doubt that. They don't have time to spend on frivolous matters. The women in Leporidae Lop are more sensible."

Josh smiled politely. "Is it okay if I look around?"

"Be my guest," Edbert grunted from behind his desk, ignoring the boy.

Romance, nah. The boy was wrong; he had to be. It couldn't save his bookshop.

Josh stopped next to the bookshelf where Edbert kept all the cooking books and glanced over his shoulder at Edbert, who muttered to himself. "Is everything all right, sir? You seem…" He paused. "Is there anything I can do to help? I'm more than happy to."

Edbert wanted to snarl at him and say something horrible, but he unburdened his soul instead. If the mouse-head-boy was willing to listen to him, who was he to say no? Edbert told him everything: how Huxley had robbed him of his future and how he had let them sweep him into their lies. He stammered when he reached the last part.

"There's nothing you can do, but thank you, I needed to clear my thoughts to someone, and I'm happy it was you," Edbert finished, and flinched at his words. Happy? At Josh being there? The world had certainly gone mad. Maybe he was senile like the others seemed to think he was. Maybe he had to face the truth without hesitation and with a clear understanding. It was what it was, and he and the world weren't getting any better as the days went by.

Josh squirmed under Edbert's case.

Edbert thought it was for the fact that he'd made the boy uncomfortable or that the whole squirming thing was the boy's defect. But he was mistaken. Josh was actually collecting the courage to speak his mind.

Josh gave a shy smile as the lines between Edbert's eyebrows grew tighter and stricter every second he said nothing passed. "I can help. Or more precisely, I can take you to someone who can help, who you have misjudged."

His words slashed Edbert. The meek mouse-head-boy helping him, pointing out he'd misjudged not only him but someone else, and being so nice about it… Edbert sucked his teeth.

"Anyway, only if you want my help," Josh said after an awkward silence.

Edbert clamped his mouth shut. "Who do you want me to meet?" he asked after arranging his thoughts.

"Norville Upwood."

Edbert snorted. The balance of the universe was restored. The boy was a moron.

"Give him the benefit of the doubt. What do you have to lose?" Josh urged Edbert.

Josh was right; Edbert had nothing to lose. "Let's go then." It was as well. No one was coming to the shop, anyway.

Edbert let himself be guided to the Upwood residence, hating himself and doubting the outcome at every step. He thought about heading back home. He was sure he'd left one book to a wrong spot. No book starting with the letter 'F' should go before 'B.' The thought would haunt him for the rest of the day. Edbert turned around, but Josh took him by the arm and guided him back to Norville's.

"How do you know him?" Edbert asked before they used the sheep-shaped door knocker. They stood on the Upwood residence's porch. The snow-white home was simpler than the place Huxley had but bigger. It had huge windows and a more homey feeling. The house stood at the edge of the inner kingdom, near Norville's farms.

"He's my soon-to-be father-in-law," Josh said, giving Edbert a reserved smile.

Edbert would have never guessed Josh would marry one of the Upwood daughters. Didn't one of them go abroad, something to do with demons or something? There had been a celebration for her, he was sure of it. The dark brown door opened before Edbert said anything, and a girl flung herself at Josh, leaping into his embrace. The boy more than willingly wrapped his arms around her.

Edbert glared at them.

"Oh, sorry," Josh said. "Let me introduce you to my fiancée, Larissa Upwood."

Larissa gave Edbert a huge smile. It was easy to understand what Josh saw in the woman; her genuine, heart-warming smile melted anyone's soul—though not Edbert's. He expected more from humans.

She was a robust woman with honey-colored hair, huge watery eyes, and full lips.

The woman disturbed Edbert.

"I know you," Larissa said with a bright voice, making Edbert's knees wobble.

Edbert gave her his best smile, which lacked, shall we say... warmth. But he tried. Women, in general, made him feel self-conscious. They made him trip over his words and act unlike himself, like what had happened at the dinner party. He was sure all the ladies at the party had been laughing at him, but he could not be sure. He disliked laughter in general, not knowing where it came from.

"I love your chemistry books. Bought more than a few of them," Larissa said, her voice as bright as the sun.

"Yes, I remember you, too." And he did. How could he have missed her? It had to be the odd circumstances, but now he could remember every single book she'd bought. Anyone who bought more than one book got permanently marked in his memory as a good person. He warmed up to her. Well, warmed up to her a little. He couldn't see what Larissa saw in Josh, who was much smaller and bleaker—and, most importantly, stupid. *A mouse head...* Edbert shook his head.

"Come in, come in." Larissa stepped out of their way, letting them in. She guided them to her father's study without being asked.

"Dad," she said, "you have guests." The room they entered looked like any other study, with dark wooden shelves, desk and floor, and white walls. The thing that separated it from any other study were the books about sheep, pictures depicting sheep, statues of sheep, the curtains decorated with sheep. There was even a huge toy sheep head on the bookshelf.

Edbert frowned. No one could or should be so interested in sheep.

Norvile Upwood lifted his gaze from a piece of paper he was reading. "Welcome," he said, sounding befuddled.

His face lit up when he saw who it was. "Do sit down," he said, pointing to a brown leather chair in front of him.

Edbert sat down. The comfortable chair supported Edbert in the right places. He melted into the chair like a cat melting on top of a masonry oven. Soon, a gentle snore filled the room. Edbert woke to his own noise and pretended it never happened.

So did the others.

"So, to what do we owe the pleasure?" Upwood asked.

Edbert grunted, looked back at Josh and Larissa, and then looked at Upwood. "I was just in the neighborhood..."

"For the love of gods' sake, you can't be so stubborn, Mister Pollock," Josh said. "You can trust my father-in-law.

You want the same thing, which is to stop Huxley from ruining your lives. So just talk."

Upwood and Edbert gazed each other.

A twinkle entered each man's eyes.

"My daughter has lent him some spunk. But don't mind him, he can be daft sometimes," Upwood said, giving Edbert a wink. "Care for tea?"

Edbert nodded.

They stood and walked out of the study, leaving Josh confused and alone with his bride-to-be.

"Don't look so solemn," Larissa said. "You did good."

"You mean it?" he asked, giving her a shy, nervous glance.

She offered him her hand, and he took it more than willingly.

"I mean it," she said.

He smiled.

CHAPTER TWENTY-THREE
Wealth With a Capital F

Sense and obedience are the cornerstones to a working society if you asked Harriet. To Bethan, common cooperation came from carrots. Not the kind of carrots the rabbit god of luck consumed, of course, but from proverbial carrots—rewards for people who showed proper behavior. As their philosophies differed, Bethan went against Harriet's wishes, knowing it was wiser to use the Leporidae Lops' nature against them rather than intimidate them into leaving. She wasn't willing to jeopardize her people's lives because of arrogance and stubbornness. All right, Siarl sending Harriet here had been a blessing, along with how she'd arranged the food and wealth, but the old woman lacked the rudimentary understanding of people.

The next day, Bethan pulled Otto aside and took him on a tour of the lands of Gainsboro, showing him their misery and why he and his people had to go home with haste.

"The underground water sources are drying up. There's no good soil, and the water doesn't renew," Bethan said in passing as they walked through a withered vegetable garden. Her people had already preserved all the food they could for the upcoming winter. Their resources weren't much, but with them and the food from the bakery, they might survive. Last winter had been bad. Fifteen people had died, including some strong, capable men. Her own husband and children were gone, and she luckily had escaped death. She didn't count herself as fortunate as one might think, however, but she continued on for the sake of her people. Otherwise, the sacrifices would be empty.

Otto looked disinterested. He barely glanced toward the yellow-green spots on the ground.

Bethan continued showing Otto the barren land with enthusiasm, much to Otto's uneasiness. He clearly found nothing to celebrate in their dying land. He wanted her show-and-tell to end, impatient for her to get to the point. To top it all, his stomach grumbled loudly from eating nothing but bread.

They walked through the palace's backyard toward the deteriorated houses. Once people had lived in them, but most of them now occupied the palace. It was simpler if all of them stayed close to each other.

"These are what connects us to our past," she said, showing him murals on the houses' walls. "It's the only way to remember."

Once the murals had shined in vivid colors of bright yellow, orange, cobalt, purple, and all the rest of the rainbow. Now the rough weather with an ax to grind had worn them out, except for one, which had weathered the storms well by being sheltered under a huge rooftop.

She took Otto closer to the mural. In it, men hunted a snake-like creature, which was hidden amongst the beautiful flowers, majestic trees, luscious wildlife, and little delicate birds. The mural was more alive than anything around them, even livelier than Bethan and Otto, who had been mortified into numbness. For a short moment, Bethan escaped into the dream-like art. She wished the lush, glorious days the picture depicted would come back.

"It's a hunt," she said, shaking off her trance.

"A hunt?"

"Yes. See those riders? They are hunting the beast in the upper left corner."

"What is it?" Otto asked, squinting, trying to separate the snake from all the flowers and trees.

Bethan looked around uncomfortably, and then she whispered, "Tamtue."

"Tamtue," Otto repeated.

"Shh… Please don't use that name."

Otto swallowed his words. When he assumed Bethan wasn't looking, he spat over his shoulder three times and made a little chant to fend off any evil spirits lurking in the area who were harboring gloomy thoughts. There were none; they all were back in the attic.

"May I touch it?" he asked.

"Sure." Bethan watched as Otto moved his hand around the mural.

"They don't make them like this anymore," he said.

"No. I guess not." Bethan had no clue what they made these days.

"Your artist knew how to use composition to advance the picture's motion and colors to make it come alive. I like it."

"That's good to hear."

They admired the mural for a few more minutes.

All around them, old pieces of history lay scattered, broken, and forgotten. Just plain old pottery and idols no one used any longer, none of which would entice him to leave.

Bethan took Otto indoors, to the room where she'd asked Harri to lay up a few of Leporidae Lop's treasures—items she could pass off as being left behind by their beloved emperor. Otto's eyes widened when they entered the room decorated with mahogany and silks. The room was well-preserved, as if time had stopped, showing no residue of the hardship Gainsborians lived in.

"Our last emperor lived here fifty years ago. Since then, the room has been kept like this," Bethan said, "or else it's pointless." She said the last remark more to herself than to Otto.

As Bethan chattered away about their history, she watched Otto tune her out to calculate the value of everything he saw. His lips moved as he added value on value. He took the most interest in the old paintings on the walls.

"Our emperor used these as toys," Bethan said, opening a closet full of Leporidae Lop's gems and trinkets.

Otto gasped. His eyes moved from the worthless silk, paintings, and sculptures, which had value a moment ago, and moved on to calculate the value of the mother-load inside the closet, which could be snuck out without Harriet noticing.

"You might consider selling those things to make life easier for your people," he said, jumping at the opportunity too quickly.

But Bethan was relieved. She forced a confused expression on her face, but she had a huge smile deep inside. It was always nice when an easy opportunity had the power to turn an honest man into a cheat and a liar. Life was good that way. She turned to face the man holding the closet doors open.

"I couldn't..." Bethan said, giving Otto an awkward glance. "They are valuable to us; they are our history."

"I would sell them if I were you. It will give you an opportunity to buy food and farming equipment and all the rest," he said.

"I don't know... We would lose our past along with them. Do you truly think this stuff is valuable?"

"For a collector, yes. For example, it might be enough to buy a few horses with wagons to ease our travel back and to get you the emergency aid Harriet asked for."

"Are you sure they aren't just trinkets? Would they really get you back home?" she asked with wide eyes.

"Yes," Otto said more than eagerly.

Bethan bit her lip to hide her smile.

Otto tried to suppress his excitement, but failed horribly when he let out a repressed giggle.

Finally, Bethan had done something for her people. They would now survive.

* * *

Elsewhere, out of Bethan's reach and to her misfortune, Huxley walked back to the table after hurrying the confused Edbert off. He eagerly resumed eating the carrots laid out on the table, and he savored the roasted chicken garnished with garlic and thyme, washing it all down with honey-flavored champagne.

He continued enjoying the company of his secret society mates.

He was ecstatic beyond his dreams. The last couple of days had been just perfect. The weapons Upwood would bring were a godsend. They would come in handy. They were real proof his luck worked impeccably. Only a good skirmish would make him more ecstatic. A war, skirmish, anything to kill the tumultuous mood amongst the people. A common enemy would make the Leporidae Lops forget the sinkholes, missing people, and upcoming problems with paying wages. Most of all, the need to raise taxes could be avoided. Taxation was always unpopular amongst the people, anyway.

This was going to be fun.

Huxley grinned. "So, how about we punish those who have done this to us, who threaten our existence with their untoward intentions?" Huxley asked, looking around the table. He had pictured this moment a thousand times in his head, and now it was finally coming true—and it was as good as he'd thought. All it had taken was one shabby bookshop owner going against Harriet's tyranny. If only he had known sooner.

Tableware clinked as the king, Adolf Huxley, William Breheny, and George Morgan put their forks down and looked at Huxley. They were unsure if his question had been serious. They searched his face to see any sign he told a joke.

When they found none, the king said, "I'm not so convinced about the revenge and punishment business. It's an inconvenience, and we still don't know who did this to us. It might be the gods, and you can't go around punishing them. And people might not like it."

It was typical of the king not to see the upside of new things. He would rather continue living his cushy life, acquiring more clothes, jewelry, and those apparatuses the kingdom's inventors came up with, flaunting them all at his stupid, boring parties. The king was a simple man, too easily entertained.

"I agree; caution is a virtue here," William Breheny said, but in truth, he was already imagining a war. Breheny had a taste for blood and mayhem, but he fought those urges and prayed for forgiveness for his vile thoughts every night. He was an evil boy and should be punished, just like his mother had said.

Breheny shuddered. "There has to be another way."

Not him, too, Huxley snarled, letting out a low grumble. These men lacked basic imagination as to what the future could be.

The other two men stayed quiet.

"We have a moral duty to protect our citizens. The wicked have to be punished." When that didn't get the rise he wanted, Huxley added, "We have to fight for our way of life and protect it at any cost."

Adolf Huxley laughed. "What has gotten into you, brother?"

"Stop laughing! Nothing has gotten into me," Huxley replied. His face reddened. He wasn't a joke and never would be. "I see only glory and well-being from this. We all benefit from a war, let alone the citizens. They get to be brave, earn medals and respect amongst themselves, and most of all, protect our kingdom."

"I still don't see the point," the king said, leaning farther away from Huxley.

"The other option with the missing treasures is a revolt, and you don't want that."

Huxley was right; the king didn't want that. He had reoccurring nightmares about revolutions. Sometimes they were made by the rats living under the palace, but more often, it was his people rising against him. He always woke up soaking wet.

The king swallowed.

"And as you know, the most beloved kings in the history have started wars. Wars are good for business; it makes the money move around. Banks will gain from it, I'll gain from it, you'll get richer, and our judge here gets to try possible deserters, and so on. There's no downside."

"What about the casualties?" the king weakly protested.

"Oh, it only balances the population and gives us an excuse to build new things to stimulate the economy. It's not like we or our families will be in danger. So, what do you think?"

There was a moment of heavy, oppressive silence. Huxley's heart was racing. This is it, now or never. They had to take him seriously.

"I guess—" the king started.

"Splendid!" Huxley said, smiling a boyish smile.

It was a good thing that even when the other men weren't as imaginative, they knew when to follow reason. Except for his brother, who was as bright as a button, whatever that meant. All buttons he'd met were closed-minded and inactive. Huxley gave his brother a glance, who was still smiling but kept his mouth shut. He hated that. Maybe he'd colored the picture a little too much to his and their advantage, but all he said was true. War had an upside for everyone, including the casualties. They died as heroes, which was more than they ever would amount to if they lived out their lives with their boring families and jobs.

Some remote country with a moderately weak army would be perfect. He hoped his luck would arrange that as a war here on their own soil was too iffy. But he would even take that if necessary. Anything to get Leporidae Lops' blood boiling.

Huxley hummed the tune Cornelius had let loose on the kingdom, and for a second, he rethought his plans.

He stopped humming and began to eat his chicken.

225

CHAPTER TWENTY-FOUR
Horrors One Can Do with Words

n a cold Friday morning, Harriet watched Otto's people leave in an orderly fashion. Bethan joined Harriet on the palace's highest point. They stood in a small tower on the left side of the building. The tower hadn't seen much use lately. Sand covered floor and the stairs leading up to there were rickety. However, it was the greatest point to observe their future disappearing into the horizon beneath the clear sky. From there, Harriet could see far beyond the desert to the mountains rising at the border of Ferrum, Leporidae Lop, and Gainsboro. Harriet squinted and tried to spot the safest trail back home. Bethan stood restlessly next to her, sighing and shifting her weight. Harriet wanted to push her off the roof if she didn't stop soon.

A wind howled in the valley. The same wind which had lost the earlier wager. It had come back to witness Harriet's defeat. The noises it made twisted into the sound of Harriet cracking her fingers. When they felt flexible again, she wrapped her hands around her arms. To her, Bethan giving Otto the treasures was dangerous and naïve. Undoubtedly, there would be ramifications. Someone would notice the gems and whatnots appearing on the streets of Leporidae Lop if Otto and the rest of them got that far. And by now, someone must have noticed those same gems and trinkets had gone missing, along with the whole critting district. This would turn ugly. All the horrors money and its gods could produce would come here.

Let them, Harriet thought. She would deal with them as she did with everything else.

If Bethan had let Harriet do what she did best—persuade people to do exactly as she wanted—then they would have had a chance. Harriet squeezed her arms tighter. Now Otto returned home in a way that was out of Harriet's control. He was free to act as foolishly as he wanted to.

What a waste.

"It's a good thing they are leaving, now they can't harm us," Bethan said, but Harriet said nothing. "If you are worried about the gems, they'll spend them on horses and carriages. They have to. Otherwise, they won't manage to get back home."

Harriet cleared her throat and tried to squeeze her arms harder, but she had to release her grip before she did real damage. Bethan couldn't be that stupid. In her haste, she had missed the tiny, yet important, details no leader should miss.

"We have new housing and there's food. This is a good thing. They left so much behind," Bethan said, getting more anxious every second Harriet refused to say anything.

Harriet listened to Otto's voice echo in the valley as he gave orders to his people. It was a very sad voice. Otto got all the Leporidae Lops to leave. Peter Thacker, at first, had tried to persuade Otto to let him stay to keep an eye on their things. Otto refused. He wasn't coming back, and he wouldn't say a word about their peril, Harriet was sure of it. She snorted. She wouldn't let them wipe these people out, not even when she loved and cherished her own people. It was no reason to sanction a genocide.

"Now we have to find a trading partner and put what we gained to good use," Bethan said, sounding nervous when Harriet still refused to speak. Her voice was fast and higher than it usually was. Bit by bit, Bethan understood she'd offended and disappointed the great Harriet Stowe. *Why had the gods done this? What would be their next play?* Harriet wondered instead of listening to Bethan. The treasures and the lousy food weren't the salvation they needed, not even close. Something had gone wrong. And Harriet didn't have even the first idea how to fix it. She needed guidance from the gods or luck, but the only god of luck she knew was long gone and probably snorting carrots. Harriet wasn't that far off with her thoughts. Not that she was right what the rabbit god of luck was doing, but she had its thoughts peg-down. This would be so much easier if she could summon the god again, but it would fall again for the same trap. The rabbit wasn't stupid. Harriet searched the reaches of her mind for another way as she watched two smaller dots part from Otto's convoy and head back. It had to be Harri and Idwal returning. They had gone to the help Leporidae Lops get a start on their journey to home.

Harriet's silence was gradually getting to Bethan more and more. It made the younger woman feel nauseated. She tied her loose jacket around her, but sneaky thoughts of doom still found a way in. Little by little, her doubts began to chip away at her self-confidence, slowly reducing her to an insecure wreck. Disappointing Harriet was like disappointing one's own mother. Surviving it took a lifetime, or more likely, several lifetimes, to recover, and most likely, with a help of a great professional. The one who finds themselves overworked.

"I did well?" she asked.

Harriet's lips curled into a snarl.

Bethan did all in her power not to crumble right there and then. Harriet was being cruel, even though she didn't have to be, but Bethan had ruined everything and put even her in jeopardy. She had to learn if she wanted to rule her own people and succeed.

* * *

Back at the source of all the misery let loose in the world, far away from Harriet Stowe, the rabbit god of luck shivered. It, Sigourney, and a love-struck Siarl stood near the sinkhole next to the royal palace of White Cuniculus. The rabbit looked at its paws, then at the hole, then at Sigourney and Siarl. It rapidly squeezed its paws, opening and closing them in milliseconds. Then it shifted its gaze back to the hole and shook its pink nose. It had used all its powers to bring back those dead humans for Siarl. There was no way it could persuade a mountain to move here. And to top it all, whoever had pulled it toward the sinkhole wasn't letting go. It should have argued better against Siarl that there was nothing wrong with death and dying, all creatures did that, but it had tried to satisfy the mortified human without a good reason to do so. The first theories about social pressure snuck into its head. The god didn't like them, not at all.

Sigourney's 'we' spun back out of the hole with a gush of air. Siarl's 'we,' which had been too soft and hopeful to gain speed, still it rang in Sigourney's ears, to whom it had a surprisingly strong tone. Along with the personal pronouns came a sweet, beautiful melodic song which instantly began to lull those around it. Except for the rabbit, who said, "Oh, crit, not yet, not so soon... Crit, crit, crit... I should have smelled it was her. We have to leave, now. Come along, right now!" Its nose twitched as it tried to think, tried to free itself from the song and the pull. The two humans were extra dead weight. Dumping them would help it flee, but... Like so many others, the god hated all the buts in the world. Once again, it was faced with the fact that it had gotten itself somehow attached to the small human female and her newly found friend, and it was pretty sure a decent person would save them.

The rabbit debated with itself if it was a decent person or not. It could be, or so its sister Justice insisted, but then again, its other sister Calamity saw the rabbit as trustworthy as a banker on a sinking boat and thusly never to be relied on. Itself knew it could be both. All depending on the circumstances and the mood.

It decided to take both Sigourney and Siarl with it as unlike Sigourney or Huxley or anyone else, the rabbit knew who'd made the untoward holes and who was coming up and what for. The gods were here to collect all the favors given. This was never about humans, the wars, or the hatred amongst the men—they just thought it was. It was always about the power of the wealthy and the few playing games with the mortals to advance their own status. The rabbit's feet itched. They could continue itching as long as they were fleeing and attached to its body.

"It's too late," the rabbit said, sounding distraught. Like a repeating nightmare, it would end up a mascot, a pawn for the named gods, being a mere deity. It again thought to leave the humans and flee. The universe[20] decided otherwise, for at that same precise instant, a head poked out of the hole, not a horrible head, nor a scary head, and most certainly not an ugly head. Actually, it was quite a nice head if a small, female, elvish-looking face did it for you. It was unlike Sigourney's face, which looked like a face hit by a pan several times when compared to the elvish woman's face. The woman's face wasn't even close to being as hairy as the rabbit's face or as disproportionate as Siarl's face. Altogether, the face was perfect.

Oh, crit it, the rabbit thought, swinging both humans into its lap.

Siarl's head swayed from side to side with the melody. The hopeful 'we' from earlier began to fade from his memory. He fought against the rabbit, not wanting to be taken, not now, not when the most beautiful woman he had ever seen was here and… and… he wasn't sure what next, but he knew it would be something amazing.

The rabbit didn't care. It hauled them away—well, like a rabbit, using all its residual luck to free from the pull, leaving behind a trail of half-ignited sparks. The rabbit had a very good

---

[20] The bugger which had refused to cooperate with it ever since it met Harriet Stowe. The woman had given the rabbit god of luck terrible mojo.

reason not to let the two humans stay. When the elvish-looking woman fully emerged, she would kill them all, cut off the rabbit's feet, and use them as a conversation starter.

The woman coming up was even more horrible than Harriet Stowe, if that was even possible.

"Huh…" Sigourney asked. Her question mark got lost as her mind wandered into the land of what-the-heck-is-happening-and-who-is-she? A land where it's easy to get lost.

The rabbit god of luck continued running non-stop, not caring if people saw them as it zigzagged through the kingdom. The faster it moved, the better it felt. When it had run out of the inner kingdom into a huge empty field and had stopped under a tree, the rabbit said, "That's gods for you." It was unsure if it had gotten far enough and looked around. It preferred to have at least one ocean between it and her, but for now, the meadow would do.

It panted a little, actually a lot. However, even its panting was cute and soft if you asked Sigourney, who hadn't become enraptured by the melodic song. The elvish-looking woman should have come with a chocolate box if she'd wanted to get Sigourney on her side, or preferably, chocolate-covered biscuits.

The small human female staggered off the rabbit's lap and asked, "Gods?" Sigourney swayed from side to side. Her body was recovering from the sudden spurt, trying to adjust back to the planet's normal rotation, which her body thought moved too slowly. It had gotten a taste for going fast and far.

"Yes, and never ever look them in their eyes. That's how they entrap you, at least that's how she does it," the rabbit said, looking at its feet.

It took its ear into its paws and began to bite it.

"The god of all things graceful," Siarl said with a deep, lovestruck sigh. Siarl stood still as his mind orbited around the elvish-looking woman.

A tormented expression leaped onto Sigourney's face, made a pirouette, took a bow, and hid behind the curtains. Despite the rabbit's mood, it noticed the subtle shift and felt bad for her, but then it remembered its own destiny and continued biting its ear. It could remember a time it had been in Siarl's shoes.

Siarl made more pining sounds, and the rabbit was sure the small human female would begin to cry, and soon. It patted her. "Not a graceful being, far from it. That thing you think is lovely has come to collect you and pulverize you into pieces," the rabbit said, continuing to stroke her.

"Collect me?" Sigourney asked, wiping away her tears, which had snuck out without her permission.

Siarl let out a huge sigh. "She can collect me any time." He sat and began to pull out withered grass and flowers from the ground with a gleam in his eyes.

"Collect what?" Sigourney asked and turned her back on Siarl. That seemed to stop her tears, but it didn't do her mood much good.

"Souls," the rabbit said.

"Souls?"

"Their life-force, your life-force. Gods are as powerful as the number of their worshipers... most preferably, dead worshipers. Dead worshipers are like wealth."

"Wealth?"

"You know, capital."

"Gold?"

"Yeah, gold, in a sense. Gods need souls to stay in power and to use their powers. The more dead souls, the merrier. Or more simply put, the gods need you to die, fattened, with their name on your lips. Not by a natural death, as it's the worst kind of death for them, for it means lost souls. You see, the key is blood. All this means is we have to leave before the kingdom burns."

"But you are a god?" Sigourney asked.

"No, not actually a god, per se. I'm a deity, a manifestation of pure luck, unlike the named gods. Gertrude, Bhaltair, Tamtue, Sisirus, Cornelius, and the rest have risen out of your minds, of the whisper and stories you tell. Don't get me wrong, they are real; realer than most things in the world. They believe in themselves. They can make heaven and earth move for them, not to mention you and your destinies. They can tap into anything you have touched, you have thought, your desires, but they need you to believe in them, power them, love them, die for them. You get what I mean? Not me, though; I'm just pure luck formed from your unconscious thoughts." The rabbit looked toward the ground and pushed its ears against its head. "And I wouldn't do such things to anyone. But we don't have time for semantics now; we have to get out of here."

"To her? Can you smell it? That scent of jasmine. So sweet, don't you think?" Siarl lifted a flower to his nose and took a deep breath in. It was a flower which had seen its "Best By" date long ago, but Siarl saw it as it once had been. "Would she like this?" he asked.

Sigourney gave him a menacing glance. She muttered to herself, "She can go ahead and pulverize you all she wants. See if I care. I might even lend her a hammer or whatever she needs for the job." She looked dazed by the fact she'd said all those words aloud.

The rabbit patted her again. "There, there… Of course, if you want to stop her, then we have to find someone who hates the gods as much as I do. We have to find Cornelius Rustika Inconnaton This. He might help us," it said. "But only if you want." He hoped the small human female would be more sensible than to go against the gods. No mortal had ever won, at least, not by playing fair.

CHAPTER TWENTY-FIVE
The Cruel Gems

here's luck and then there's misfortune. At first, one might seem like the other, like for Otto Hobbs. The aberration that took him to Gainsboro had first been bad luck, but then the gems had entered into his life and life had had the potential to be good. But now, as he trekked onward across the dry, scorching desert, the gems seemed both unimportant and a curse.

Otto wiped sweat off his forehead and spat over his shoulder.

He and the rest of the Leporidae Lops had made it to the mountains which stood somewhere near their kingdom their goal. He could see the high peak of Mount Jadero rising into the sky.

People trailed after him as if he knew where to go. The map Harri Ellis had given to him was no use. All the directions drawn on it were wrong, and they seemed to take him away from the mountains, not toward them.

Otto stopped to look around and sneered at the map. He clasped his shirt's neckline and violently tugged it down. His shirt was wet, and it felt uncomfortable against his hot skin.

Peter Thacker came up next to him, peering over his

shoulder at the map's outline of the lands.

"We should go that way," he said, pointing away from the mountains and deeper into the desert, which didn't seem to end.

Otto was sure dangerous monsters with huge pointy fangs, who responded to even a slight tremor beneath their feet, lurked there. "No, we'll die if we go there," he said, turning his head back to the mountains.

His stomach growled. The food they had with them was useless and wouldn't get them far, and neither would their equipment. Otto was sure he would die. "The map is a ruse against our people. We were given it only to stop us going back home," he said.

He crumpled up the map and threw it away. "Not a single landmark on it is right. We go toward the mountains!"

When Otto continued onward, Peter picked the map. He smoothed the wrinkles and peered at it, then put the map inside his dry pocket. Otto saw him do that but chose not to say anything.

They kept wandering the long route to the mountains for hours, steadily becoming fatigued, thirsty, and hungry.

After a few hours, their possibly gloomy future began to dawn on them all. First, they blamed bad luck and crit for their misfortune, but then a mutiny began to spread behind Otto's back. Peter tried to stop the upcoming attack on Otto. He tried to reason with Otto to look at the map again, but Otto refused and shredded it. The Leporidae Lops began to think Otto was being reckless by how he rationed their food, where he was taking them, and how the constant rests he took slowed everyone down. One of them even thought to kill him. It would resolve their protein problem at once, but he only entertained the idea and hadn't time to say it aloud before someone said, "I say we do a ritual of luck."

"We can't, it isn't night and we don't have the right materials for it," Otto said.

There were more murmurs, which grew louder with every step they took.

Otto's feet were killing him. Walking beneath a scorching sun was making him feel lousy and irritated. "All right, what's the harm?" he said.

They set up the ritual in the middle of nowhere, surrounded by nothing but sand. They gathered around Otto, who led the ritual as he best saw fit. It was a very simple and plain ritual where they resorted to shouting their words in agony.

They had barely even started before a dust cloud began to lift on the horizon. They sped up their ritual. Those who had extra stamina constantly waved their hands in the air.

The dust cloud drew closer.

More words were shouted.

It was almost visible, and when Otto squinted, he saw caravan after caravan. He chanted his words and dropped to his knees.

Soon, the convoy was upon them. There were fifteen carriages, each driven by one driver. A man in the lead shouted, "Hey there, need some help?"

Otto tried to push himself up, but he dropped back to his knees. His mouth felt dry, and he wasn't sure if his imagination was playing tricks on him.

Peter stepped forward and said, "Yes, we are lost."

"Where are you heading?" the man asked.

"To Leporidae Lop."

"That's where I'm heading. Hop on."

The Leporidae Lops greeted his mercy with a loud cheer, their voices sounding somewhat hoarse. "Thank the gods," Otto said. He turned to the convoy's leader. "Thank you."

The man offered his hand to Otto, who more than eagerly wrapped his fingers around the leader's wrist and got onto the caravan.

"Don't mention it. We humans have to stick together here with her," the man said.

"Her?"

"The desert. She can be a real bitch."

"Sure," Otto said, feeling sweat find new channels inside his clothes, "a real... bitch." As of now, when he got back to

Leporidae Lop, he would be a rich man. No more working, no more slaving to perfect a meringue cake. He could retire and paint pictures. Otto smiled, already imagining his first painting.

"Yeah," the man said, and hurried the caravan into movement.

"I'm Otto Hobbs," he said, offering his hand.

The man shook it and said, "Hmm, I have heard that name somewhere." A smile spread across his face from ear to ear, revealing a row of teeth in between.

Otto's hands began to sweat, and he kept his eyes locked on the man, seeing only the smile. He withdrew his hand back. "I'm the head baker of the finest bakery in Leporidae Lop. You must have eaten something I made," Otto said.

"That must be it. Mister Baker, you are a long way from home, how come?"

"I—"

"I have to say, it's very foolish of you to be ill-equipped to traverse the desert. You didn't take her temperament into account, did you?"

"We—"

"But sometimes you can't help it, eh? Sometimes you find yourself in a miserable situation without choosing it. That has happened to me more than often. The key is to avoid them beforehand."

"Yes, I think—"

"You know, I think it, too. Yes, the key is to avoid everything. You can't see what lurks behind a corner," the man said.

Otto was getting red. He took his gaze off the man and locked forward. He could see a city rising in the distance. He hadn't known there was something between here and Leporidae Lop. He measured their distance and looked forward to a rest. Maybe he could disappear into the city and be done with it. Otto half-listened to what the man said and grunted. Otto was calculating the value of the cold gems pressed against his chest.

"…but life can be fine when you really think it. Like a gem

in the darkness," the man said, waking Otto up. "I had this jewel once—"

"You did?" Otto interrupted.

"Yes, the finest woman there can be. She made me dream big. That's why I'm riding in the desert now. Anything for her, anything to make her dreams come true. There's nothing you wouldn't do for a fine woman, eh?"

Otto sighed. "I guess not."

The city was getting bigger; green spread around it and soon embraced the convoy. Still, the city was farther than Otto thought was possible. "Where are we going?" he asked.

"To home, where my heart lies."

"Hah, you have it bad. I'm sorry, man," Otto said, slapping his huge hand on the man's shoulder.

"Yes," the man said, shaking his head. "I appreciate your sympathy; it means a lot to me. Sometimes I think my destiny isn't mine."

"Whose is? All we can do is hope for the best," Otto said.

The city was getting closer, its huge buildings rising higher behind the stonewall. Only a moment ago, the city had been unreachable, and now Otto could almost touch it.

"You are a wise man, it almost makes me feel sorry," the man said with a frown.

"Sorry about what?"

"About this," the man said.

The caravan stopped.

Someone took Otto by his arm and pulled him down.

"What are you doing?!" Otto wailed.

"Officers, I found this man trying to buy my services with these," the man said, tossing Otto's gem pouch.

Otto's hand reached for his chest but found nothing. His mind disconnected from the world around him. Everything that happened next appeared to happen to someone else. Someone else was taken into custody by Leporidae Lop's guards.

Otto looked at the driver, who was smiling again. He could see his mouth moving and heard the words coming out, but he couldn't quite make out what he said. Otto went limp in the guards' arms. They dragged him and the rest of the Loos straight into the palace dungeon. Otto was still dazed. He was sure he was still between his sheets and none of this was really happening at all. It was just a nightmare from which he would wake up any time now.

Hours passed, and he still didn't wake up. He refused to believe he truly sat inside a damp cellar and that a rat had just scurried past him.

"Mister Hobbs," a voice said from the doorway.

"Who are you?" he asked.

"I'm the magistrate, and I have come to talk about the circumstances of your arrest."

"I'm innocent. I have done nothing wrong, so you can wake me up now."

"Wake you up? This is serious. You are accused of treason. You will be hanged if you don't talk with me."

Otto tied his arms around his chest. They felt so real.

"But I have done nothing wrong. I should go now. The bakery is waiting."

"There's no bakery. You were found with the gems stolen from the kingdom's treasury."

"I have no gems."

"Of course, not anymore, but you did have them. I need you to tell me everything that has happened to you, and maybe we can spare your life."

"Is this real?"

"Quite real, I'm afraid."

"I'm really sitting in a cell?"

"Yes."

"And everything that has happened in the past few days is real? Edbert Pollock is running the kingdom and not her?"

The magistrate hesitated. "Yes," he eventually said.

"Then I speak only to Edbert Pollock. He will understand me."

The magistrate tried a few more lines of inquiry, but he got nowhere. Otto didn't say a word, just like he'd promised. The magistrate left Otto alone and rushed to Huxley, who cursed his bad luck. Huxley had somehow misplaced the miserable old fool.

Down in his cell, Otto dropped to his knees to pray for a miracle. He needed luck more than ever before. Life couldn't be this cruel. He hadn't done anything wrong. One small blessing and everything would be fine again.

The gods ignored his pleas. He'd served his purpose and nudged everything into motion. For all they cared, he could go and die, preferably with their name on his lips. Not a must, but it would be nice.

The gods had their target set on a bigger payday.

CHAPTER TWENTY-SIX
One Last Ritual for Our Youth's Sake

Edbert sat outside a mansion, drinking a nice hot cup of tea with a twist of lemon but without a single drop of honey. Edbert hated those who poisoned good tea with sweetness. They got no sympathy from him.

Josh sat next to Edbert. Both of them basked in the sun, which felt good against the skin after so many cold days. Edbert hoped to skip winter altogether and continue straight to summer. It was better for his hip.

They were at the Upwood's family estate. Edbert had thought the Upwoods had always lived inside the inner kingdom where everything happened, but he had been wrong. He couldn't understand why they had ever moved away from the mansion. From the porch, he could see green fields spreading toward the sea. In the distance, he could hear the remaining seabirds screeching. Here, a mind could rest. Before they had come here, Norville Upwood had warned him about his dead relatives and their bad habits, but he found them mild and amusing compared to his own family.

They'd come here to bury Huxley's weapons. Together, Edbert, Upwood, and Josh had hidden them in the family plot. His back burned from the effort, and the first blisters of his adult life felt raw against the warm tea mug. He took another sip, nourishing his body before he had to go inside to do a ritual of luck. It had been decided that they needed all the luck to battle against Huxley. But it wasn't like they went to war without a plan. Luck was there to boost their success. What they planned was to secure support from those aristocrats who hated Huxley and his hold over them. Edbert had found out that Huxley spied on everyone he could, assuring him ways to extort people into obedience—Upwood included. Thought Edbert had detected sadness in the man's voice. From what he'd gathered, Upwood and Huxley had been friends, but Huxley couldn't help himself. He'd needed control even over his closest friend. Anyway, all the spying was how Huxley had found out about the little debacle Edbert had with Harriet Stowe and altered the course of events more in the hope of distracting the prime minister from the upcoming coop. But the gods had intervened.

The whole idea made Edbert shiver as he took another sip from the mug. Gods should not see men like him. But he'd begged them to notice, and here he was, stalling the unstoppable future by stayed with the Upwoods. He had been with them for a couple of days now. Oddly enough, having his shop closed during that time hadn't bothered him. All the planning with Upwood had given him newly found strength. The whole effort had given more meaning to his life than being prime minister, or the struggle he had with his income. He even felt proud of the blister he'd gained.

Edbert and Josh were the only ones sitting outside as Upwood and his family were busy preparing the ritual inside the mansion. Edbert drank the bottom of his tea and grimaced at its bitterness. All the acid from the lemon and darkness of the tea had coagulated on the bottom. The restless young man next to him moved on the bench, scratched the back of his neck, and fiddled with this or that. Had he been like that once?

"You like it with the Upwoods?" Edbert asked.

His question made the boy stop.

"Er, I do."

"So, the mouse head worked for you?" Edbert asked.

"Er, I... I guess so... That's not why I met Larissa, though," Joshua Felis said and turned to face Edbert.

"It's not like you moved in the same circles as her," Edbert replied.

"No, I guess not. However, she still loves me." His words sounded more like a question to Edbert than a statement

"She must, or why else she would be with someone like you?" Edbert asked.

"Eh?" Josh managed to say, but thankfully, Norville came to get them before Josh had time to recover.

"The ritual is set," the man said. "You may come in." He held two black robes, offering them to the two men. Both Josh and Edbert tied the black robes with silver sheep brooches over their shoulders. The robe wasn't as well made as the one Edbert had worn at the palace, but it was better than his own. It felt so natural to wear the smooth thick garment, as if he had been born to do this. Sometimes it felt like the rituals were more important than the results they brought, and more so now. All Edbert's cautions about the gods and what a ritual might bring was gone. Such things were irrelevant against how things were done.

"Just as you know, we met at the library," Josh said. "She loves who I am, what I do, and everything about me." But Josh said his words so quietly, they went unheard as they stepped into the mansion.

Lady and Larissa Upwood awaited them near the ritual circle. Outside of the circle, the dead relatives whispered their advice. Truth be told, listening to them would have been a better choice, but they ruined it by spitting out useless facts instead of sticking with the matter at hand. No one ever said the dead couldn't be faulty. They thought little snippets like insisting getting up from the bed backward on Sundays and sing the Temporary Disturbance song while doing so was golden advice. But as Edbert and the rest of them knew it, they turned the dead relatives out and readied themselves for the ritual to come. In the background, the dead Upwoods started a perpetual argument over an old, missing silver soup spoon. They had to do something to spend an eternity. On and on went their grievances, keeping them happy. The ritual began. The chanters instantly dropped to their knees and crawled onward in a circle, repeating their appeals. After doing that for three minutes, Upwood got up and the others followed. He removed his brooch, flicked open its sharp needle, and poked a hole in his finger. The others followed suit. One at a time, they sacrificed their blood on the altar while they kept chanting. The Upwoods had used blood for generation after generation, knowing it was a sure way to gain favors. They knew what the gods liked, just not what degree.

When it was Edbert's turn, he hesitated, but still, his needle moved into his thumb. A pitiful amount of blood came out. Somewhere along the line, all the red fluid flowing inside him had clotted. He walked to the altar and wobbled as he tried to produce at least one drop. Edbert groaned and tried again with the same result. Upwood came to get him back in line. They moved on, swinging their hands in the air, and then they turned around in the other direction, doing the moves backward. Then they swirled back to face the altar like clockwork, making cadenced noises. Edbert's thumb ached every time he swung his hand.

The ritual was going great. Their chant resonated with the free luck floating around Leporidae Lop—a luck let out by so many gods carelessly running around the kingdom, trying to obtain favors for themselves. Still, it was too late. In the middle of the group's next swirl, men with drawn weapons, straight backs, and hard muscles stormed into the room. The Upwoods and Edbert froze in their positions, hands in a Y-shape and one knee lifted. They stood there in their crane stance, waiting for something to happen.

"Edbert Pollock?" an authoritative feminine voice asked. She searched for Edbert amidst all the people wearing black.

Edbert slowly lowered his leg and both of his hands. Then he took off his hood. "That would be me," he said, knowing there was no other choice. Something like this had to happen, eventually. He just wished their ritual had had time to work in their favor.

"You're coming with us," she said.

"No, he isn't," Norville Upwood interrupted.

The woman gave him a stern look, which would have silenced almost anyone, but not Norville. "By whose authority are you taking him?" he continued.

"By the king's," she responded.

"It's all right, I can go with her," Edbert said. Her voice could make him do anything, even dance naked and howl at the moon, making Edbert forget his fear of being humiliated. Not obeying her proposed a far worse fate.

"I'm coming with you," Norville said.

"And me," Josh said. The woman glanced in Josh's direction, and he shrunk a couple of inches under her gaze. Yet he didn't take his words back.

Edbert heard Norville whisper to his wife, "If we aren't back soon, get help." What he forgot was his wife wasn't the getting help kind of woman, and neither was her daughter. They both were the help.

The three men were accompanied out by an armed contingent and were crammed inside an open carriage. The chilly outside air felt cold against Edbert's chest. The sun was already lowering down. Edbert was sure he would catch a cold and die. He sniffled.

They rode across the fields where the farmers were preparing their fields for the winter. The men and women looked at the passing carriage full of soldiers with disinterest. The life inside the kingdom's walls wasn't their concern. They cared about the crops, their rental houses, and the animals that kept them alive.

Edbert, Upwood, and Josh were taken to the royal palace of White Cuniculus and straight to see the king, Huxley, and rest of their buddies. The remnants of their lavish dinners still lay around them. Underneath the plates, maps were laid open, and on top of them, tiny tin soldiers fought with each other around the glasses and forks.

"Where have you been? Where did you find him?" Huxley asked as soon as they stepped in. Before anyone answered, he looked at Upwood. "Never mind."

"Get the baker," Huxley snapped at a palace guard.

The guard hurried out.

"Sit down, sit down," the king said. "Make room for our prime minister." The king gave him a smile.

Ha, Edbert thought.

Norville followed Edbert and stayed near him; Josh followed Norville and stayed in his vicinity. Huxley eyed them all with hate and contempt.

It was an awkward wait. No one wanted to be the first one to say anything that others might use against them.

Everyone felt relief when Otto Hobbs got pushed into the room. He had a bewildered expression on his face, but he relaxed when he saw Edbert Pollock.

The whole time the man told his story, he looked only at Edbert. "We rushed here to tell you about Gainsboro as soon as we could. All of us knew it had to be important, Harriet being involved and all. And what they say about the gems isn't true; I took them as proof of her treachery," Otto said, ending his story, then was instantly taken away.

Edbert watched as the guards marched to seize the baker and accompany him out of the room. The man wailed, "You must help me. I'm innocent. Don't let them hang me."

"What are you going to do to him?" he asked.

"What he deserves," Huxley said. "We have more important things to worry about. Did he say Gainsboro?" He put his hand under his chin and massaged it. "Where's that?"

Huxley turned to the table, making all the silverware and crystal glasses fly off it, along with the tiny soldiers, which broke into pieces as he searched for his target. "There you are," he said, slamming his finger against a map.

Edbert felt an enormous sense of relief. Not because things were looking good... quite the opposite, in fact. The calm, warm feeling was more about the worst coming into being and no longer having to wait for it.

* * *

Three days had passed since Otto and his people had left. During that time, Harriet and the Gainsborians had gone over all the new materials they had. Like Edbert, Harriet's mind was serene, and like Edbert, her mood wouldn't last long. Both of them had sensed what was to come.

Harriet made the Gainsborians catalog and ration every single item and give them a use-by date. Her pedantic working style caused nightmares for many. They hoped for a day without lists and orders, a day with just a hint of chaos and chance. By following her guidelines, life was full of hard work, proper things, and a lot of bitterness, but in the end, they would survive, which was the whole point. Dreams and hopes were good for now, but you couldn't build a future upon them. All her life, Harriet had brought order where there was none. She could still feel her husband's kiss on top of her head as she'd organized all their wedding gifts in their first home. She pushed the memory away. What was the use of thinking about him? He was gone and had been most of her life. She'd learned to live on her own.

As of now, if nothing sudden happened, the Gainsborians had the means to survive the whole dry winter. Next year would be devoted to cultivating the land. It would only be a slight chance to make the place liveable, but a chance they needed to take.

All very well, but it still didn't remove what Harriet suspected about the gods and their play. Luck didn't just deliver bakeries and treasuries out of the sky. The gods were aggravating the use of luck, and she didn't like it for a bit. So, while the Gainsborians did as she'd asked, she worked on a way to trap a god. Any god would do, but she had one in mind. The best solution she'd come up with thus far was to use the cage and a ritual of luck. Those in such a way that it provoked the god's vanity. Harriet had been all over the palace, trying to find more about the Gainborian's god, Tamtue. But none of the Gainsborians were willing to talk freely. They feared something, but what, she was unsure. Yet, what Harriet had been able to piece together from all the fragments was that last time there had been a reckoning and the Gainsborians had drawn the short straw. Their lands had been sucked dry. In a way, Harriet should feel relieved to know that it hadn't been only her and her people who had done this to them, but she couldn't. She would never be happy when the innocent got robbed. And what the gods had done to these lands and to these people was barbaric.

Despite all that, Tamtue's name hold awe in the Gainsborians. Some whispered his name with hope, while others, the ones who still remembered the tales of their grandparents, treated it as a curse. Tamtue had showed them that even the god of gardens and prosperity would collect when the time was right. That was all she got out of the Gainsborians. The books had been destroyed. Burned, Bethan had said. Someone had not wanted them to remember. Not out of pity, Harriet had suspected, but out of control. If you had the hearts and minds of the men, you could do anything.

Harriet understood the sentiment, but she despised it to her core. No knowledge should be lost or treated with such a shame that people feared to touch it. Such deeds would only lead to ignorance and repetition. The end of listening. It was no wonder history was cyclical.

At the end of the day, Harriet gathered everyone into the audience chamber. The Gainsborians slouched on the stairs and had empty expressions on their faces.

"We need a long-term plan," Harriet said, her tone firm and relentless. "And a plan about what you'll do if the Leporidae Lops come here with either aid or demanding the treasures. Or if they don't come at all. You need to tell me what you want." She would rather tell them what to do, but helping meant making room for other people's opinions—opinions she could later say no to, especially as she didn't wish to tell them about her plans toward Tamtue. She would have to go with the same route as with the rabbit god of luck. Though, then she'd had a personal knowledge about the god and its obsession with carrots, females, and being pampered, never having to make ends' meet. The only thing she could think Tamtue wanted was more followers. The Gainsborians wouldn't be enough for it to win one over his fellow gods. But she couldn't just snap her finger and manifest more people. Or actually, she could. She could use the miracles brought by the ritual of luck to gain a following. But that took too long. Harriet let her gaze wander around the room, meeting the eyes of those who mattered. Harriet straightened her glasses. The Gainsborians stayed silent, tired from all Harriet had made them do, confused from having their worldview robbed. They looked at their feet and scuffled them.

"I appreciate that your decision-making is a communal effort, but it doesn't mean you all get to be silent." The silence worked for her. Still, she had to give them a chance to say their peace before she opened her mouth.

Bethan took the opportunity. "We have a future now, thanks to you. We are grateful for that, but we need more. We can't live from others' scraps. We need to trade the gold obtained to make this land liveable again. It's the only way. I know you oppose it, but still, I say we do it and let the Leporidae Lops come if they want. We have done nothing wrong. It was the will of the gods."

Harriet was ready to argue against the woman, but Idwal, the young boy, was faster than she. "I say, as I have said before, that we leave. This land has nothing to offer us. It's bone-dry and nothing will change that. And with no offense, getting Harriet here hasn't been the blessing we thought it to be. All this thing with Leporidae Lop's treasury has just put us in more danger."

He blushed when he saw Harriet look at him with her eyebrow raised.

"You should respect Bethan and what she did, and all the others who sacrificed their lives to get Mistress Stowe here, my son included, and most of all, Mistress Stowe herself for helping us," Harri said. "We have gained a lot."

"It's all right. Idwal has a right to state his opinions, even when we have a way to survive the winter and make this land ours again. I say we don't leave. This is our home and our legacy; we belong here," Bethan said. "We'll negotiate with the Leporidae Lops if it comes to that. If they are as reasonable as their prime minister is, then we have nothing to worry about."

"Aye, aye," the older Gainsborians responded.

"You can't dismiss him like that; he's our true emperor," a girl in her twenties interrupted. She wore a nice dress, courtesy of the latest Leporidae Lop fashion. She somehow looked out of place. Not because she didn't deserve nice things. No, it was just that, here in this bare room, she reminded Harriet of home.

Harriet shifted her gaze from her at the shy boy who'd found the courage to speak his mind with newly found interest.

"I'm not dismissing it. What I'm saying is, if he wants to be the emporer, then stay here. As a refugee to Ferrum or Leporidae Lop or somewhere else, he would be nothing," Bethan said.

An argument broke out.

"That's enough!" Bethan said, taking Harriet's words right out of her mouth. "There's no point in arguing. We need to do another ritual. It will solve this all."

Harriet couldn't help but grimace, despite getting what she'd wanted. She wished she could argue against the proposition and show the failed logic, but she kept her mouth shut as everyone in the room instantly agreed with Bethan. They all turned to look at Harriet with their demanding, pleading eyes. Eyes she might grow to dislike.

Harriet shook her head. "It's a shortcut to happiness," she had to say; she couldn't help herself. "And there's no guarantee it'll work. You have to remember there are always ramifications. It's not like the last time came for free."

"But we have nothing to lose. We got so much out of it already. The good overwrites the bad," Bethan said.

"With a detailed plan we would be on a firmer ground," Harriet protested.

Everyone groaned.

"We can do both," Idwal said, his voice hitting the high note of the young.

The sound made his people laugh, releasing all the tension felt earlier.

Idwal blushed.

It had been settled.

"Hmm," she said aloud.

"What do you want us to do?" Harri asked, startling Harriet by having moved next to her.

Harriet composed herself and answered, "We need more than words this time; we need a sacrifice. We need blood, bread, some of the treasures, and the cage. They all have to be taken to the backyard and to the pit. And we need lots of candles."

When the Gainsborians stared at her in disbelief, she added, "Now."

She watched them obey her. She followed some of them out to the diminishing light to strengthen the drawn circle. The stick she used ran smoothly on the sandy ground as she added symbols to trap the god—the ones she'd used with the rabbit god of luck. This time she just added Tamtue's name there. It had to work, she was using everything she could: flame, blood, food, and greed, the essence of human existence. And if it didn't work, then Idwal had the best solution. They should leave this cursed land behind them and head to Ferrum.

Harri came to help her arrange the candles in their places and light them. Harriet finished her scribing and drew the lines from the symbols to connect them to each watching the bearded man work as she did. He was a good man.

"Can I ask? Does Siarl Ellis hold any relation to you or your people?" Harriet asked as she stood up once more and descended to the bottom of the pit Leporidae Lop's treasure had made. She lowered a sack of white bread on the sandy ground next to the cage. Harri had mentioned his son, and the assistant carried not only the same surname but he had looked a lot like Harri and Bethan and the rest of them.

Harri concentrated on the candles, keeping his eyes on them. "He's my son, and don't you go holding that against him. Siarl did what he had to do to save us. You seemed like the best help he could send here, writing that if anyone could turn this land and our misery around, it was the prime minister of Leporidae Lop. He begged for your forgiveness in his letter."

"He's a good boy," Harriet said as she began to draw symbols around the food. "Where's his mother?"

"Dead... Dead like many of us," Harri replied after a long pause.

"I'm sorry."

"It's useless to be sorry. Death and dying are a fact of life. Will this help us?" Harri asked.

"It can't hurt. Get me a few dozen needles."

When Harri left, Harriet cursed under her breath. She shouldn't have let him go. Now she was stuck at the bottom of the pit. She tried to climb up, but tumbled back down. Her life had come full circle. Going from helpless to helpless, unable to use her feet as they were meant.

Harriet nibbled on the bread while she waited. They tasted like heaven, light but rich with a hint of sweetness amongst the saltiness. Otto could sure bake loaves.

When Harri got back, Harriet stashed the eaten bread on the bottom of the food pyramid and accepted Harri's offer of help. He gave her his hand without saying a word, understanding Harriet better than she liked.

As soon as she was standing upright, the ritual began. Everyone took their place, and, taking Harriet's lead, the Gainsborians chanted their pleas aloud. Their chant was rhythmical and intense. The ground trembled slightly, but it was repressed by their shaking bodies. They shouted their words louder and louder, putting themselves into a trance. With beating legs, words, and swinging thumbs smeared with blood, they made the world yield under their will. This time, all the people attended and none of them had trouble saying their words.

Harriet constantly watched over her shoulder, waiting as she fed them words to draw Tamtue here, promising their hearts and minds, promising Tamtue the kingdom to come, promising Tamtue more blood.

The Gainsborians hit their hands together and roared, giving no thought that they were giving their souls and bodies to their god without asking what he wanted of them.

Harriet waited.

Again, the Gainsborians roared.

The ground shook, knocking the candles over and killing their light. This time everyone kept to their places, shouting louder and clapping. Every clap made Harriet wince.

The Gainsborians continued chanting, but Harriet herself had stopped. She looked around, searching for the source of the tremor.

She found it.

CHAPTER TWENTY-SEVEN
Could You Pass Me the Rat?

he world would be a lot simpler place if we received a script to follow upon birth. No decisions to make, just one action after another. No surprises lurking behind corners, just calm marches to a dull destiny. Unfortunately, the world didn't work that way. Not for Sigourney, not for the rabbit, nor for Siarl.

"So, what have you decided?" the rabbit asked. "Shall we flee?" The morning sky behind the rabbit was painted light blue with a touch of purple, yellow, and everything in between. The rabbit's nose went up and down as it patted its fur and looked deep into Sigourney's eyes, making her sway back and forth.

Sigourney's head swirled while she tried to piece together what was happening. She understood nothing of it, least of all the new rules of divinity. Then there was the rabbit's fear, the threat of souls being collected, and Siarl. She glanced toward the spaced-out boy. What if she made the wrong choice? "I..." Sigourney said, but she found no words to continue her sentence. She wanted to help Harriet, and of course, she didn't care for anything bad happening to anyone else, but... This was not fair. She wasn't supposed to make these kind of decisions. She was just Sigourney, and Sigourneys went on with their small lives, struggling to keep up with everyone, and trying to find one dream to believe in.

"If you ask me, we better leave. There's no sense putting ourselves in danger. We can let them sort out their own mess. Humans and their gods deserve each other, always pursuing worthless things and fighting with each other. Let's go and do something fun instead," the rabbit said, its black eyes shining in the dawn's light.

Sigourney said nothing.

Siarl only partly registered what happened around him. A slight breeze had brought the scent of jasmine the elvish-looking woman wore, lulling him into a trance. He looked happy and serene, as if he'd found the meaning of life. He moaned.

Sigourney flinched. A surge of pain left her chest and flowed all over her body. "I—" she shrieked.

The rabbit looked toward the boy and let out a deep exhale. "You are right; I'm being unfair toward you and him. You didn't choose this," the rabbit said and shook its nose. "And it's cruel of me to force you to decide when you have been nothing but nice to me. It's far easier to let luck do all the work. You know, give me your hand," the rabbit said, smoothing its paw against its fur before offering it to Sigourney.

Sigourney gave the rabbit her hand and clutched her fingers around its soft paw. As soon as they touched, an ecstasy swallowed Sigourney. A tingle moved all over her body from her first finger through her arms to her cheekbones, and from there, to every appendage she had, even to her failed tailbone, which never grew the tail it promised. The touch felt like a thousand little fingers embracing her.

Sigourney shut her eyes and let the sensation sweep over her.

After the surge of luck, the rabbit fell, cold as—well, a stiff, dead rabbit. Maybe not as cold as everyone liked to think, but enough to be left alone and get far away from the horrible mess created here to a nice short rest in some sort of limbo, where it could decipher the ultimate answer and enjoy endless field of carrots. Where else did they go after it had eaten them?

Sigourney tumbled down along with the god. She pushed herself up and shook the rabbit, but the god remained lifeless. She put her ear against its nose and felt no warm gush of air. Tears began to pour out of her eyes, and she sniffled.

Sigourney shook the god again.

Siarl moaned in the background, at only the gods knew what.

"Oh, shut up," Sigourney said and touched the rabbit's neck. To her luck, she found a heartbeat. To the rabbit's disappointment, its small purple heart began beating again, and a whole lot of luck it had given to Sigourney floated back in. It had been happy being dead and contributing to the survival of the human race by releasing all its life-force into Sigourney, especially as it had already made up its mind about what kind of afterlife it wanted to experience before its ultimate rebirth. It had something simple and nice planned, with lots of carrots and no humans around to bother it, specifically nasty beings like the elvish-looking woman or Harriet Stowe. It might have let Sigourney come to visit, but only if she behaved. But just like that, the small human female took its plans away. The rabbit sulked, refusing to open its eyes. Humans never did what they were supposed to do. That's why the gods could never win. They might kill a whole bunch of them, but humans had a habit of recuperating. Maybe there would come a day when they fought back and changed the whole system. But it demanded knowledge, education, cooperation, and persistence, and a whole lot of intent. And even then, there was a great possibility that they would get it all wrong and create yet another system that oppressed some and favored the few.

Sigourney kept shaking the god, but the rabbit remained motionless.

"We have to do something," Sigourney said to Siarl, abandoning her somewhat nonsensical way of doing medical aid. She wiped snot off her face and looked at him expectantly.

Siarl said nothing. He only managed to pull a flower off the ground and separate it from its dried petals.

"Help me get it up," she wailed, but her words fell on deaf ears. Siarl just stared back at the city, blowing petals off his hand and making a wish at the same time. He clearly didn't know how flowers worked.

"Oh, for the sake of yourself, stop pining over that horrible woman and be useful," Sigourney said to her own and Siarl's surprise. She tried to swallow her words, but it was too late. They were already out and about.

Siarl finally understood it was better for his health to stand up to help, but even with the two of them working together, the rabbit stayed where it had landed. It was too heavy for Sigourney and Siarl to handle.

"This is useless. Look after the rabbit," Sigourney said. She had to go back to the kingdom and look for help. Get something to aid them to carry the god to safety and allow it to be able to recover in peace from whatever it had done. She had a sneaking feeling that it had done all this on purpose to teach her a lesson. It hadn't, but such were human thoughts for you, often getting it wrong. Often thinking everything about a very narrow self-centered respective. And often ignoring the fact that the other person had wants, needs, history, and their own baggage when it came to all social. For example, the rabbit not wanting to be there when the shit hit the fan. It was far easier if Sigourney sorted everything out. It had given her the opportunity to be the hero.

Siarl nodded, though his eyes looked like they were millions of miles away.

"You could just sit here until the end of the world, couldn't you?" Sigourney snarked. She slapped a hand against her mouth to silence anything that might slip out next. She hurried to the kingdom, leaving Siarl behind.

* * *

If the rabbit god of luck or Sigourney thought their lives had gotten complicated and were not going according to plan, Edbert could top them all.[21] After listening to Otto, his life had taken a darker turn. "You can't do this!" Edbert protested.

"Of course, I can," Huxley said, guiding him, Norville Upwood, and Joshua Felis toward the palace's prison. They might have been able to escape if only Huxley was there, but he'd thought 'the more than merrier' and brought a bunch of guards with him. "It's for your own safety." What the charges were was a mystery to all, even to Huxley. But such things were small details and shouldn't be held important. They could always be invented and had been throughout history. It was all about marketing, and they knew how to do that, even in the ancient times. The threat of a whip and beheading made you see the light.

"You can't seriously expect us to believe that," Norville said, who now owned a black eye, but so did a few of the guards. Guards who wanted nothing more than to show the giant nob what real working muscles could do to a neck.

"This has got nothing to do with what I believe. You are doing what I want and staying where I want, for as long as I want," Huxley said, seeing no fallacy in his logic.

"You won't get away with this," Norville said when they arrived outside a prison cell.

"You might go free if you tell me where they are," Huxley said.

"What are?"

"Stop playing games; you know quite well what I'm talking about," Huxley said and squinted. He was ready to tear Norville's head off, or at least a few of his limbs off for swiping the weapons.

"I don't have a clue what you are talking about," Norville said, trying to put a blank expression on his face, but it was impossible. His left eye had swollen shut and was wet from tears. He looked more deranged than deadpan.

---

[21] At least in his own opinion, though many people might differ with him. That was humans for you.

"Maybe a night in the cell will refresh your memory."

A guard opened the cell door, and they were escorted in Josh clutched the door frame and fought with the guards, but it was a feeble attempt. Two guards easily separated him from the frame and carried him in by his legs and torso. "I'm getting married Let me go," he screamed.

"Yeah, sure you are," one of the guards said.

They dropped him to the floor, and Josh let out a horrible sound.

Edbert went to the boy and helped him up. "Are you alright?"

The boy nodded, but his face was white as a sheet.

"Huxley," Edbert said, turning around to face the man.

"Yes?"

"You are a waste of a human being."

Huxley winced, but then snorted. "Frankly, I don't give a crit what you think. Shut the door," he said to the guards, turning his back on Edbert and the rest of them.

The heavy wooden door, which was reinforced with iron, slammed shut, and a latch shrieked into place.

"Are you sure you are fine?" Edbert asked, lowering down to help the boy up. The boy took his helping hand but put no pressure on it. When he stood next to Edbert, he took laborious breaths.

"I'll be fine," Josh said, but his face twisted with pain.

"You were brave," Norville said, coming to them and helping the boy sit down.

Some color returned to Josh's face.

They stood there in silence, watching Josh for a while. Edbert let his gaze wander around the room. Unlike the normal prison cells with rats and all the other perks, Edbert, Norville, and Josh got the royal treatment. Their cell couldn't be called a prison, as velvet and soft-cushioned divans, a huge table with golden tableware, and a relaxed atmosphere welcomed them into their dungeon. Meanwhile, Otto and the rest of them were locked inside the proper cells, which had dampness, rats, and the opportunity to meditate on ones' life choices. They ate stale bread and prayed for a miracle that their new companions didn't bite them. Edbert would soon be praying for a miracle too, but stale bread wasn't his problem— more like a tray full of delicacies with quail eggs, garlic roasted snails, and frog legs. Thank the gods there would at least be chocolate cake on it.

After a while, as long as it takes to make a cake, a guard carrying their tray entered the room. This was the first time the guard had prisoners and there were clear instructions about how to treat them and what to offer. For the vegetarian guard, the frog legs had been especially difficult to make. They still upset his stomach, but he had really enjoyed mastering baking a chocolate cake, which was a bit uneven and dry. Before entering the prison cell, he'd wiped the cake with his forefinger and scooped a thick layer of frosting inside his mouth. The rich buttery chocolate melted on his tongue, and he seriously contemplated not taking the cake with him, but that could be counted as treason, so he kept the cake on the tray.

"You let us out of here. I'm your prime minister," Edbert said when the guard entered the room. He'd found a spot on the divan and was nursing an upcoming headache. He had already envisioned all the possible ways he would die in the cell—one of them involved being eaten alive by rats, which were nowhere to be seen, as the rats avoided these parts because the pests in it could be a bit too fussy for their liking and prone to screaming. They scuttled off to where the prisoners knew how to share their misfortune and be kind.

"But not my king," the guard replied, looking at the cake without so much as a glance toward Edbert. He left the tray and departed before he did something he regretted. He knew men had killed for less.

Edbert gritted his teeth and yelled after the guard, insisting that prime ministers triumphed over all the kings and queens, leaving out the fact that maybe not over despots or dictators or kings and queens with more backbone than the ones they had. That the guard was marching to the beat of a small goblish-looking man rather than anyone wearing a stoat cloak and carrying on their enormous head a crown that didn't weigh their head. He left all that out, giving only a pitiful plea for his status. The guard took no notice. He was still thinking about his life without the cake.

"Relax," Upwood said. "We are not going anywhere."

"How can you say that?" Joshua asked. The boy rocked back and forth on his seat. Occasionally he touched his side and winced, but he said nothing about it. "I have to get out."

"We all do, but not by force and not by panicking. We need to think. So breathe and let's collect ourselves. And we might as well enjoy the dinner," Huxley said.

Edbert looked at the younger man and felt silly for all the hassle he'd created. He might as well enjoy himself. He got up and joined the others at the table. "You know, pass me the—" He paused. Their food's edibility could be questioned. The odd assortments of delicacies made his stomach turn, and he hated chocolate.

He got up and banged on the door. "Bring me proper food. Porridge and a hard-boiled egg!"

A voice behind the door said, "That I can do, but in exchange for a slice of cake."

"You have a deal," Edbert said and went back to the others. Norville was already eating, and Josh had sunk his head on his hands, muttering things under his breath. The only words Edbert picked up were *Larissa* and *wedding* and *doom*.

"She won't forget you," Ebdert said. "Not with the way she looked at you." He settled back to moping and ignored Josh's pleading looks toward him. That was enough said and done.

CHAPTER TWENTY-EIGHT
I Think I Need a Hug

ornelius Rustika Inconnation This was forced to live through the same chaotic and miserable existence as Sigourney, the rabbit, Edbert, and, for the matter, Harriet Stowe. Even his godly powers couldn't shield him from the way life could cheat you. The whole dolorous affair with the gods and humans should have been left alone, but being a decent person, Cornelius ran straight to fix it instead of going to a sunny place where fruity drinks are always on hand.[22] And he tried to do it the right way for the same personality defects that made him come here in the first place. Those effects that didn't help one function well in the world of everything-is-up-for-sale.

The dog—or 'mutt,' as the officer had called it— sat next to him, tilting its head and looking at Cornelius with sad eyes. "Wait here with the horse," he said. "I'll mend this and then we can be on our way." The dog scratched its back and laid on the cart's bench. If one cared to glimpse inside the dog's head, they would have sigh of futile efforts and humans always

---

[22] Though not the same place the rabbit had planned to go.

thinking they had to alter reality for the good or worst. It might have even added that humans over complicated this whole existing thing by always pursuing tomorrow. But no one cared to look into the mutt's head.

Cornelius left the dog and the horse near the palace, hiding them from view. He climbed up the palace's stairs. People rushed around, paying no attention to him. He had a clue why. He watched as an elderly man in his pajamas was pushed past him. The man looked miserable, which Cornelius could fix, but he was off before he got to him. Instead, he stopped a clerk who was holding heavy boxes in his arms.

"Hello there, do you mind telling me where I can find the king?" he asked.

"Hmm?" the clerk said.

"The king," Cornelius said.

"I don't know," the clerk said, looking at Cornelius funnily.

"I'm here to have an audience with him," Cornelius said.

"Oh, why didn't you say that? Follow me, I'll show you," the clerk said.

Cornelius went with the clerk, who took him down the corridor, then turned left and went through a set of huge doors.

"You'll have to talk to him to get an audience," the clerk said, pointing at a man sitting behind a desk who only had a book for company.

"Thank you," Cornelius said.

"Don't mention it," the clerk said as he left.

Cornelius made his way to the clerk, who put his book down as Cornelius approached. It would have been better if Cornelius had turned around and did something else with his life because he was about to meet the biggest obstacle ever known—a common government clerk with too much power and a habit of matching the stereotype. Even Cornelius's fancy new clothes made no impression on the creature. Something funny was going on when humans had stopped caring about the esteem appearance brought. The clerk just looked down his nose at Cornelius, keeping a hand on his book as if he would resume reading at any moment.

"What can I do for you?" the clerk asked. The words came out like a hiss between his teeth.

"I'm here to see King Enniaunus of Leporidae Lop," Cornelius replied.

The clerk snickered, but soon his face turned serious. "Then you better take a seat."

Cornelius took the seat and waited and waited, but nothing happened. At the end of the first day, he was forced to leave without seeing anyone. The same happened on the second day, the third, and the fourth—and then Cornelius lost count. His head swirled, and he looked with sad eyes at the same clerk who'd tormented him for eternity.[23] Still, he insisted on doing things by the book. Just because his opponents were willing to go with the less virtuous path, didn't mean he had to. He held on to his morals like they were the last sail on his sinking boat.

"Tut-tut-tut-tut." The clerk wagged his finger for the tenth time.[24] The clerk pointed with the same finger at the line no one could cross.

"Tut-tut-tut-tut," he said again.

Just to spite the man, Cornelius moved his left leg over the line and twisted it, enjoying his private victory of disobedience. Afterward, Cornelius Rustika Inconnation This obeyed and sat back down to wait his turn. "There's no one else but me, and hasn't been for days!" he said, getting frustrated as soon as his ample behind hit the bench.

"When the king is available, you are the first one to see him," the clerk said with a perfect mixture of authority, annoyance, and sympathy, enough of each to confuse the listener. The clerk gave Cornelius an encouraging smile.

Cornelius's frustration went through the roof. He wanted to show the man who was the god here. He gave the clerk a

---

[23] Or so it felt. The funny old feeling of everlasting now. That torment which isn't to go away.

[24] Though it felt more like the thousandth time.

similar smile. "What if I can make your every dream come true?" he asked, stooping to the easiest and cheapest way to get someone to go against their morals, wishes, and, in this case, their duties as guards of civility. He hated every word he said.

The clerk's face stayed the same. "Sure, make my dreams come true, but I have to warn you, it won't help your cause at all. The king is busy, and I can't change that."

"Can't you just take me to see him—" Cornelius paused, reading the clerk's mind. "I'll make Jane fall in love with you and move to the countryside to raise chickens," he said.

"Who told you?!" the clerk demanded, pushing himself up from his chair.

It was the first rise Cornelius had got out of the man. His fingers tingled.

"I—" Cornelius never got to finish his sentence.

"Never mind. I won't take kindly to threats against my life. You need a miracle to get to meet anyone. Otherwise, you'd better leave, or I'll call the guards." The clerk gave Cornelius a smug smile and sat back down. Next, he thought to usher Cornelius off for today, knowing full well he would be back tomorrow.

He sneered, but Cornelius looked at him funnily, and the sneer melted away.

"As you wish," Cornelius said and nodded.

In the blink of an eye, an overly cute chipmunk with black and white stripes on its back sat where the man had been. It made a cheeping sound as it jumped up and down in its seat.

"So, is that enough of a miracle for you?" Cornelius asked, giving the chipmunk a huge smile. If you think about it, life is truly composed of a string of all the small victories we can get. To Cornelius, besting the clerk felt like beating the world champion in a boxing match or cycling around the entire world on a unicycle.[25]

The chipmunk-clerk's cheeping turned to a rapid tweeting,

---

[25] Which, incidentally, he didn't happen to own.

and he continued pacing on the chair.

"I don't speak chipmunk, but I take that as a yes."

Cornelius turned the clerk back into himself—well, not fully himself, because for the rest of his life he got to keep the back-hair with white and black stripes and the furry chipmunk tail. That's what you get when messing with a god who tries to do the right thing. To Cornelius's disappointment, or honestly to his solace, the back-hair and the tail worked well for the clerk. You could say luck intervened in his life, which would have been damn boring otherwise. He got his beloved Jane to marry him because of the tail. It drove the woman insane, keeping him always on his toes as his wife chased him around the house to pet him for the thousandth time that day. And they moved to the countryside. So what if he had an additional appendage?

But now the clerk dropped to his knees on the marble floor with a look of terror and admiration in his eyes and an uncomfortable feeling in his pants. "I'll do whatever you want, my god."

"There's no need to go that far. I just need to see the person in charge."

There was a flash of terror in the clerk's eyes, and his tail began to flip.

"What is it now?"

"I... I don't know who's in charge."

"That can't be. I want to see the king."

Again, the clerk's face contorted in torment. "I wouldn't say that the king is in charge. It used to be the prime minister, but..."

"But what?"

"But I think it isn't any longer."

"Then who?"

"That would be Udolf Huxley."

"Who?"

"Udolf Huxley, the most ruthless man in the kingdom." The clerk swallowed as he saw Cornelius' expression. "I can take you to him."

"So, what do you want in exchange?"

"Nothing, nothing at all. Just let me be a human and leave me out of all of this."

"As you wish. Take me to see this Huxley fellow," Cornelius said, and sighed for the repeating patterns the universe seemed to favor. Sometimes he thought the whole thing was run by renegade stories, which had escaped a realm or two and come here to bring forth havoc. Or the other more logical conclusion was that human brains were funnily constructed. So funnily that they built empires that would always end up collapsing because of the greed of the few. The way they went down ranged from inward or outward explosion with one exception always holding true—the streets ran with blood. He just wished that he could prevent some of it, and maybe one day find a new story, which patterned the world a tad better for all. Cornelius knew that was wishful thinking, but one had to hope. What else was there to do? He followed the clerk out of the corridor that had tormented him for the last couple of days, and was relieved to have some action to call his own. It was all needed to be an agent of motion.

* * *

Sigourney rushed to the kingdom to get help for the rabbit. The luck it had given her had an idea how to serve her inner wishes. It knew Cornelius was somewhere in the kingdom, and it only had to make Sigourney and him to meet. It was just that elvish-looking god was there too, and Sigourney and she shouldn't cross paths by no means. Also, there was one thing making the job for the luck a tad harder—all the contradicting thoughts the small human female had. Underneath the pressing urgency to help the rabbit, she had funny thoughts about finding the missing Harriet and even saving the world from the gods to come. That was not all. She reserved a few thoughts for Siarl and biscuits, but only by accident. Okay, not so accidentally. Her thoughts kept going back over and over again to Siarl and the pining expression the boy had. Such were

267

human thoughts for you. They never knew how to behave. The only way to get them under control was through excessive meditation and even that wasn't a failsafe way to know what the crit was going on in one's head. It had to be all the quantum stuff that caused interference in synopsis and brought out chaos.

Not that Sigourney noticed any of that. She had her full focus on her feet beating against the grassy field and her heart feeling like it was ready to leap out of her chest as she ran. Sigourney ignored both of them. She needed to get the rabbit back up, and fast. She made herself invisible, affecting the minds she came across to disregard her and her existence. She had no idea what she was looking for, but she was sure she would know when she found it. That was how luck was supposed to work. She wasn't completely stupid. She knew what the rabbit had done. It had given her part of its powers; she could feel it in her bones. She just didn't have time to consider all it meant, nor did she care for having all its godly powers in her. It didn't feel right.

All around her Leporidae Lops had awakened to the morning the two new sinkholes had appeared. They were doing what they knew best—going about their day, trying to steer a little luck toward them like nothing had happened. Humans were weirdly good at ignoring the impossible.

It was a surprisingly beautiful morning. The crisp air felt good against Sigourney's skin, making her cheek turn pink. She was a bit busy to notice such small things. Mostly because a cart full of carrots crashed into her, burying Sigourney under a mountain of carrots. She fought against them, but there were too many. Sigourney stopped caring and lay under them, breathing shallow breaths, experiencing her new life in which everything ached. All this despite knowing nothing ever lasted forever. But the brain had a habit of thinking things as eternal, especially the nasty things.

The universe rarely considers anything to be as stagnant. It's made of moving, whirling parts that might or might not collapse at the end of one beautiful day, and possibly start another baby universe. No one really knows, not even the gods, and you can imagine how pissed off they are. If there are some who like certainty, it's the gods, or why else would they try to control everything and hoard all the resources while fucking others over.

But as nothing is everlasting, a hand went and yanked Sigourney up by her jacket's collar—just when she'd gotten used to her new life—making the carrots swirl off. A man with thick eyebrows, tobacco on his lips, and an angry frown on his face looked at her with confusion as he dangled her in the air.

"Look what you did," he said and shook Sigourney, who wondered how the man could see her. She went up and down like a spring toy, making her head hurt. Also, the motion made her unable to see what she was meant to see, which ruined the man's whole point. All she gathered was that everything was orange, smelled of tobacco, and her head was about to dislocate itself.

"You'll pay for this," the man yelled.

Sigourney's reflex took over when her body realized it had come out of hiding. She disappeared again, spooking the carrot vendor. He let out a scream, opened his grip, and dropped Sigourney hard against the mountain of carrots. He turned on his heel and ran away as the carrots tumbled down.

Sigourney pushed herself up and fled the scene. At the next corner, another vendor with a cartful of carrots tumbled over her and again, she got buried under the produce. This time, luckily, no one tried to use her as a spring toy. She had to rise up. The moment she became visible again, she was greeted by a man who looked both confused and concerned for her well-being. It was nice that the universe didn't solely consist of self-centered nincompoops. "I'm okay," Sigourney said as the new vendor hovered around her, trying to help.

A crowd began to gather at the scene of the accident.

"Is she okay?" someone asked.

"I think she is," someone else replied.

"No, she isn't, can't you see she is bleeding?" the vendor said.

"I'm fine," Sigourney said. But what the vendor had said was true. Blood streamed from her forehead, her jacket was torn in several places, and her trousers were cut from the right side of her knee. Under the broken fabric, her skin was sore and had several bleeding scrapes.

"You don't look that fine. Let me help you," the vendor said.

Sigourney pushed his hand away. "I'm fine."

"What the crit is going on?" an officer said with a tight, angry voice as he arrived at the scene after leaving the scene of the other upset cart. He was irritated as heck when no one replied. "And who is responsible for this one?"

"It's called aggravated luck. Whoever has it should stay inside a locked room for a couple of days or a week, or of course, they can always listen to what it's trying to tell them," a man on a cart said.

Sigourney watched as a man in a fancy outfit rode away. The man's horse snickered, and his dog cast a sympathetic look toward her. People swirled around her, trying to salvage the produce and the officer was coming at her with fast speed.

Sigourney ignored everything else and tuned in to listen to her inner voice. "He's the one," it said it over and again. She could either listen to it, obeying every word it said, or she could bang her head against a brick wall until the only sound she heard was the high-pitched scream of her brain shutting down. She chose the former, running past the officer, who was about to grab her after failing to get her attention by other means.

"Hey, wait up," Sigourney yelled after the man in the fancy outfit. The blood from her forehead continued dripping, turning her face into a red mask. She ignored a weird sense that not all was as it should be—that something else was tinkering with her flight—but luck kept guiding her and she had to trust it.

"Come back here this instant," the officer yelled after her. He began running, and so did the vendor, but they lost her at the next corner. Sigourney's tiny feet ran too fast for them, and her flickering made her impossible to follow. The vendor stopped first and panted, and then the officer gave up and returned to the scene of the accident, scratching his head. He wasn't sure how to explain this to his supervisor.

Sigourney kept running despite being chased, and despite feeling lightheaded and enduring a sharp pain in her knee. She had to get to the man in the cart. She could see him and his cart going behind the corner. She kept her eyes on him and collided again, but not with a carrot vendor like luck had intended, but with the elvish-looking woman, just like the evil woman had intended.

"Humph," the woman said and took Sigourney by her collar. She was airborne again, but at least the person who held her smelled nice this time.

Sigourney watched the horrific woman with wide eyes, listening as the sound of the fancy man's cart faded away.

"Ha, there you are," the woman said, drawing Sigourney closer and smelling her. "I know that scent anywhere. Where's our carrot eating buddy?" The elvish-looking woman squinted.

Sigourney swallowed and couldn't look away. The rabbit's words echoed in her head. She said nothing.

"Where's it?"

Sigourney blinked.

The elvish-looking woman kept Sigourney on her eye-level, but she didn't react. The woman snorted and said, "Did the rabbit get your tongue?"

Sigourney kept blinking 'SOS' with her eyes.

"Speak up or—"

Sigourney launched her right leg straight into the woman's crotch.

The woman let out a scream and let go of Sigourney, who didn't hesitate for a moment. She ran. The woman cursed her and began running as well.

"You wretched thing, what are you?" the woman yelled after Sigourney.

Sigourney kept running without stopping and without

looking behind her, but her pursuer was relentless, keeping up with her at every turn. Every now and then the elvish-looking woman glided forward when gravity was too much for her, but when she remembered where she was, she ran to blend in with the humans. The click of the woman's high heels pursued Sigourney through Leporidae Lop. They went at it for a while, Sigourney occasionally feeling a mental pull from her pursuer. She resisted it, not wanting to become a drooling idiot like Siarl. When she couldn't hear the heels behind her any longer, she stopped to draw a breath and listen. She heard nothing, but the scent of jasmine was too overpowering in the air. Sigourney made herself invisible and crept inside a building to wait for night to come.

She found her way into a cellar full of carrots. Sigourney munched away at them, letting her mind wander. She squeezed the carrots in her hands, realizing why luck had brought her here. The carrots would get the rabbit on its feet. Sigourney hid a bundle inside her jacket and stayed in the cellar until she was certain the threat had passed. She mended all she could, wiping away the cuts and bruises with a small amount of most likely unhygienic water, but it was all she could find.

When Sigourney finally dared to poke her head out, the world outside had turned quiet. She sniffed the air and stepped onto the street. When she was positive the woman was gone, she ran straight back to the rabbit and Siarl, who, thank the gods, hadn't left. Tears swelled in her eyes from sheer tiredness—and from Siarl and the rabbit still being there for her, which was darn rare.

Sigourney rushed up to the rabbit and waved her loot underneath its nose.

The rabbit stayed unconscious.

"Sorry it took me forever to get back, I… never mind. I think I saw Cornelius," she said after several attempts with the carrots, exhausting herself with all her words. She softly laid her head against the rabbit's chest. It went up and down gently, but that was all she got out of the rabbit.

She waved the carrots underneath its nose again.

No reaction.

But when Sigourney looked toward Siarl to ask for help, the carrots in her hand vanished. She was only left with stubs. She looked at them and then at the rabbit, who sniffled like nothing had happened, but its cheeks bulged out.

She could be angry, but Sigourney hugged the giant bunny instead, her eyes wet with tears. She accidentally wiped snot and blood on the rabbit's perfect fluffy white and gray fur.

For a while, the rabbit stayed frozen, but then it wrapped its huge paws around Sigourney and embraced her. That moment was the best it ever got for Sigourney. We can always entertain the thought that one day she'll find someone to share her life with[26] or find a profession or a hobby to be proud of[27], and there were more good moments to come. It's just that if you leave the good moments for later, how are you to be sure they will ever arrive? Maybe this moment is all there is, and what will follow is up for us to seize. Even more so as the whole stableness of the universe can be questioned. Maybe there's no tomorrow.

"Why?" Sigourney asked between her sobbing.

"Why what?" the rabbit asked. Its voice came from its chest because Sigourney refused to let go.

"Why did you do that? Give me all your luck," Sigourney let out between sniveling.

"Oh, that. I hoped you would sort the mess out, but you seemed to have come back," the rabbit said, twitching its nose and remembering the afterlife it had carefully planned.

Sigourney sobbed.

"There, there, all is good," the rabbit said, trying to push Sigourney away.

The small human held tighter.

"I think I saw Cornelius," she said, hoping the rabbit would

---

[26] For example, Siarl.

[27] Though if you asked Sigourney, she would no doubt end up ruining those. Insecurities and all.

stop pushing her away.

The rabbit's ears popped up. "Why didn't you say that straightaway? If they are both in the kingdom, then we are all doomed."

"I did."

"You did?"

"Yes, she did," Siarl said with a voice belonging to a man who had lost his own free will.

"Then what are we waiting for? We have to go after him," the rabbit said. It pushed Sigourney away from it with force and stood, holding its head.

"Are you all right?" Sigourney asked.

"I will be, just give me a second." The rabbit lifted its gaze to meet hers. "I think I'm the one who should be asking if you are all right," it said. The wound on Sigourney's head had dried, but it looked nasty, and her clothing was disheveled.

"I'm fine."

"You don't look fine. What the crit happened to you?"

"Just a collision." Sigourney was unsure if she should mention *her*. She made the rabbit do funny things, and Sigourney couldn't lose it for the second time.

"Come here, let me heal those," the rabbit said. It could try to fix her wounds by accelerating time around them, but it never got that far. Siarl let out of a funny sound.

"She," he gurgled out at the same instant a strong smell of jasmine floated in the air.

"What a lovely reunion..." the elvish-looking woman said as she stepped out of the shadows.

CHAPTER TWENTY-NINE
Clear Blue Water

After performing the second ritual, the ground continued trembling underneath Harriet's feet. Doing the ritual itself had been simple, but accepting the outcome was an entirely different matter. The god was there inside the cage, slithering its tongue and watching Harriet with the intent no one ever had. It was more magnificent than anything Harriet had seen. The snake god, Tamtue. The Gainsborians didn't see it, not yet. They still had their eyes shut, chanting their god's name.

The god smirked at Harriet and gave her a wink.

"Tamtue, Tamtue," the Gainsborians continued, waiting with open arms for their miracle to come, thinking, *who knew pagan rituals could be this lucrative?* If they just went on doing this, all their problems would be solved. And yes, they would schedule another one for tomorrow.

Harriet shouted over their voices to stop. "Enough!" she said. But the Gainsborians didn't stop. They were too immersed in the ritual, following each other in their pleas.

The god kept smirking at her, and the ground stopped trembling for a long second when it was the calm before the storm. The second passed and a loud rumble filled the valley, and the earth underneath them moved. The Gainsborians shut their gaping mouths and ran, barely noticing their god. Harriet squinted, trying to make the god stop what he'd started. She was welcomed only with a reptile smile.

Bethan ran past her, with Harri and Idwal not far behind. Idwal tripped, falling face flat on the ground. Harriet had no choice but to reach down and help him up. In the process, she dislocated her lower back with a loud Pop! It didn't matter. She and Idwal were swept away by a huge, wet, roaring wave. Idwal's weight kept tugging her underneath the water, her nose and mouth filling with the fresh liquid. She fought against it, trying to keep a hold on Idwal and her head above the surface. It was all too much for her, but she was unwilling to admit defeat. She kept her fingers entwined with Idwal's, refusing to let go. They sank together and everything went black.

Their deaths would have been imminent if the water had chosen malevolence over mercy. As fast as it had come, the flow of water stopped and spat them out like a rotten apple. When the living things were out of its belly, the water continued slithering onward, leaving its wet, fat tail behind. It had destroyed the backyard, knocking over statues which weren't that great to begin with, and filled the hole Leporidae Lop's treasures had made—the hole where the cage and the god was.

Next to the clear blue river, tiny green sprouts began to emerge. More and more of them came, growing at an impressive speed. They didn't care about how nature intended them to flourish, they did it at their own rate, which was their given right.

The green sprouts spread in waves onward toward the palace and the other side of the river, meeting the endless desert. Suddenly, their invasion stopped, as if someone's grand design had been filled and there was nothing else for them to do than to wait for the sun to do its magic. The sprouts waved, and they sucked moisture from of the watery soil. They were a few inches tall and had spread ten feet from the river, which was enough to promise something good to come.

Harriet missed all the excitement. She only saw black, and her head ached. She opened her eyes and shut them again, took a deep breath, and opened her eyes, unsure if she'd preferred to die or not. Like the rabbit, she knew the ultimate end took away most of one's worries. Death was good at that. But unlike in other universes, here death hadn't chosen to manifest itself and form a consciousness. Here it had left such a job for its brothers and sisters: the rabbit, Calamity, Justice, and the rest of the lot. Here it was and would ever be, everywhere at once and nowhere. Everything died. The matter was never about that, though; the question was when and sometimes how.

Harriet opened her eyes again, peering into Harri's eyes. Harriet found herself in the man's arms. She tried to stand up as fast as possible to get away from him, but she fell back into his embrace, causing her more embarrassment. She slowly counted to ten, then to twenty, to wait for her body to catch up with her mind.[28] While waiting to recover, Harriet made sure she didn't accidentally glance too long or too deeply into Harri's eyes or anywhere near his face to avoid any unwanted complications in her life. Eyes had been her doom last time. When she felt better, she nodded to Harri, who helped her stand up on her own two feet.

Harriet despised the word 'helpless.' In her opinion, it shouldn't be in any woman's vocabulary. But she despised the word 'ingratitude' almost as much, so when she'd smoothed her dress, straightened her glasses, and put all her loose wisps of hair back in their places, she gave Harri a little nod. He understood the small gesture's huge import and took it as such, but he never said a word. A man after her own heart.

She hurried to the river, and Harri followed behind her. They joined the others, who stood next to the clear blue water. Idval was safe amongst them and awake. Good. He and some others brushed their fingers against the new sprouts and let out a delighted laugh.

---

[28] Just to be clear, she didn't like being humiliated in this way, at all.

"A miracle, a miracle," the people chanted as they rushed into the river, filling their mouths with water. They splashed it over each other and played around. It was truly a happy moment. As she watched happiness spread from person to person, she watched the water ripple. She would pay a heavy price for what she'd done, that was for sure.

The payment didn't have long to come. The huge serpent god slithered out of the water in one sleek movement. The god was covered with scales, shining in metallic tones of green and silver. He drove the Gainsborians out of the river, seeking safety on the shore near Harriet. There was nothing to remind the snake god he had been imprisoned a moment ago.

The serpent moved his body in a circular motion, the part that looked like a human male—the upper half. Thank the gods. The upper half happened to be very pleasing to look at. He had long blond hair, strong facial features, and a soft and welcoming smile on his lips. Only the eyes were off.

They were the eyes of a reptile.

People next to Harriet dropped to their knees and whispered in unison, "Tamtue."

The only one still standing was Harriet. Others pressed their heads down on the sandy ground, keeping it there.

Tamtue slithered toward them, getting out of the water and stopping on the green bed the river had made. The serpent was much bigger than the rabbit god of luck. He was the size of three gorillas sitting on top of each other and riding a unicycle, the topmost of them wearing a top hat. All right, maybe not that tall, maybe only one gorilla sitting on another gorilla standing over a crushed unicycle.

The great Tamtue opened his mouth, revealing a row of sharp needle-like teeth. His jaw, which could dislocate, maim, and swallow them whole, smacked up and down, tasting the words he wanted to say. The words Tamtue said came out sounding like a hiss at first. He coughed and tried again. "My people," he said. "Stand up and be proud of who you are."

Harriet's whole body tensed as the Gainsborians followed their god's command in a trance. "Tamtue," they responded, saying the name as if it was the promise of a better future, forgetting the warnings of their murals. She knew they wouldn't. The gods were not to be trusted as they never did anything for altruistic reasons. Actually, she was wrong in that regard. Sometimes they did; to their equivalent of giving to charity, but again you could argue that there was a possibility the action was done for tax pardons, thusly the acts were done out of self-serving motives. Not that Leporidae Lop's or Gainsboro's gods had figured out the whole tax evasion thing. Partly due to the fact that they weren't sure how and who would tax them for consuming prayers and human souls. Parishes were a whole different matter. There the gods knew painfully well the cost of owning land and buildings and hiring staff. But even there they had come with a system of being freed from payments for religious grounds. And with Leporidae Lop, the whole thing wasn't an issue at all as cults were not to be seen as a congregations, just as an assembly of like-minded people who liked to chat in dark, damp cellars.

"My people," he said again, this time emphasizing the possessive, "there has been a great injustice done to you by the other nations and their gods… by Leporidae Lop. I have been fighting on your behalf, but only recently have I been able to free myself to give you strength and vitality." He spread his arms out, indicating the river, the factory, and the palace. "My work has brought you all this."

The serpent gave them a smile. *A sardonic smile*, Harriet thought.

"The chatter from the other cities and kingdoms has drowned your dying cries underneath their pleas for fame, beauty, and power. My heart aches for what has been done to you. But, finally, I'm here and able to help you, able to restore your brave, noble, and majestic nation to her full glory." Tamtue gave them a compassionate smile, and he slid his gaze through his audience. He paused to give Harriet a wink.

To her, it felt like an electric shock. She took in his gaze to the best of her ability, not turning her head away, even when it was painful. Both of them knew he had her, and most importantly, he had the Gainsborians. She couldn't argue against him. Not out right. Not without telling what she had been planning with the cage; that none of this should have happened. Harriet was sure that the god had gone into the cage to mock her, having no intention to stay there. The river had been just a theatrical way to release himself.

Harriet snorted.

Tamtue continued lulling them with his sweet words, painting the future in bright neon colors. He swayed from side to side in a slow, hypnotic rhythm.

She wasn't buying it. She looked the serpent straight in his blue reptilian eyes and saw his true intentions—and they weren't pleasant. The black narrow irises inside the bright turquoise looked at them all like they were his prey.

"With my army and with your strength, we will bring the glory back to us again!"

At those words, an army of mythical beasts rose from the river. He turned his head to face Harriet and smiled at her again, still toying with her, biding his time.

The Gainsborians gasped, but soon, the blood of injustice reflected in their eyes.

"Please, stop," Harriet said when she saw their minds had been swayed. She said it despite the army's presence, and she played right into the god's hand. "There's a better way. Bloodshed isn't beneficial to any of us. I beg you to think first before doing anything irreversible." Her words were useless. Nothing she said could match the miracle in front of them and the bright, exciting future it promised.

"No harm in waiting, right?" the serpent said. "No harm weighing your options, right? The sensible thing to do, right? It isn't like you haven't been sensible so far; it isn't like you haven't worked your hands bloody and sore, thinking finally you will succeed, and in the meantime, others have enjoyed life at your expense. They have grown fat and soft by enjoying all the pleasures you can't even imagine. Now you are to wait here until they come collecting the treasures you earned, the food you deserved—"

"Don't listen to him. It isn't—" Harriet said, fighting for reason and decency.

"It isn't, what? Tell me, great Harriet Stowe, it isn't what? Aren't you the one who ensured their suffering? Aren't you the one who saw Leporidae Lop would thrive at their expense, knowing full well what you gained was taken from them? Aren't you the true cause of their misery? Aren't you the one who planned to imprison me? The one and only god. Their guardian. And for what? So you can fool them into thinking you are their savior, not their slaver."

Tamtue paused and looked at his people. "I brought you food, prosperity, and the river of life, and what did she bring you?"

"That's a lie. I have done everything in my power to help them," Harriet said, but she cut her words short. What had she done? The beast was right; she had done this to them over the years.

Harriet looked Bethan in the eye, but she looked away.

"Just say the words and I will make all your problems disappear," Tamtue said.

Bethan, Harri, Idwal, and the rest of them looked at the serpent. Their eyes shone in the distant cold light with the heat of blood. No human should have those eyes.

Their heads nodded along with the serpent's.

"So be it," he said, and the cage emerged from the water and formed around Harriet Stowe.

Bethan and the rest of the Gainsborians looked away in shame.

"Crit," Harriet said.

CHAPTER THIRTY
I Say, Let's Skip the God Stuff

The elvish-looking woman tugged her bright blue redingote tighter around her when she emerged from the shadows and watched as the three pathetic figures trembled under the tree. She'd forgotten all about the constant draught tormenting the world above. It would be nice if humans learned how to control the weather, but she guessed that would never happen. Not if the gods didn't teach them, and without them, it would be a haphazard endeavor. Sure, they were clever food, but not very imaginative when it came to knowing how the universe worked. They thought instinct was a good source of knowledge, forgetting all the biases they had when it came to observing the world around them. Then again, they were never meant to be clever either, and somehow, they'd achieved that. Their constant evolving worried her sometimes. It might turn out to be harmful. Luckily, more often than not, they devolved to the savages they were. Maybe the gods should introduce a program that made and kept them stupid, but happy.

The elvish-looking woman stood there. Her radiant, alluring presence made Siarl's and the rabbit's breathing laborious. She took a step toward the god and smiled. Her steps wavered. She hadn't quite gotten the hang of gravity yet. She squinted, daring the others to laugh at her. None did.

One of them was frozen with fear and the two others had something else working under their skin.

"What do we have here?" she said.

"Hello, beautiful," the rabbit tried, its pink nose shaking rapidly.

The one whom she'd pursued through Leporidae Lop shot a glance toward the giant bunny. It made her smile. "Flattery won't get you far or make me forget what you did," the elvish-looking woman said. Both of them knew the rabbit had to be punished due to its breach of contract. She could feel its luck destroying her plans for the kingdom. The elvish-looking woman smelled the rabbit's fur and grimaced. A smell of urine, sweat, and wetness combined with something sweet she couldn't quite recognize. The rabbit was a pest and nothing more; she could easily deal with it. However, luck lurked somewhere behind it, and that made things tricky.

"No harm trying though," the rabbit said, pushing its ears against its head. It had been stupid of it to try flattery on her. Being afraid of her and reacting accordingly was much simpler.[29]

"No, no harm trying, but you have been busy sprinkling your luck all over the place. Should have guessed you were the one making all the racket here, on my ground," the elvish-looking woman said. "Didn't we agree that I own Leporidae Lop after the last debacle?"

"Yes..." the rabbit said. It looked around in search of an escape route, having clearly noticed that it couldn't sweet-talk its way out of this.

"Yes, is enough. You broke our contract, and that means—"

"I'm sorry," the rabbit interrupted her and lowered its ears. "Can we forget all about it and start again?" Its black eyes

---

[29] You know, for both of them.

became watery and huge, and its lower lip wavered.

"Bit too late for that, don't you think? And I don't care for such theatrics. You know that," she said.

Siarl shriek. The elvish-looking woman shot a glance toward the boy who got tucked behind the rabbit god of luck for his own protection. Or so the rabbit would have surely reasoned.

Something farther away joined in the noise and howled.

The woman smiled. "My, my, what do we have here?"

The rabbit pushed the boy farther behind its back. "Leave him be."

The elvish looking woman snorted. "I would avoid making demands, but I'm not that interested in him. I want her," she said, pointing at Sigourney, the peculiar creature who would make a nice addition to her collection.

Siarl became paralyzed, his whole body turning heavy and his earlier heartache blossoming into full-blown pain. If he had been a so-called alpha-male, he would have stepped out from hiding behind the rabbit's back, as his paralysis would have been only a minor obstacle on the path of copulation, and he would have demanded her attention, but now he preferred to stay where he was.

What the human male experienced was mildly amusing to the god, but the human female was something else. Anyone with a half of a brain would know talent when they saw one. The woman would be a terrific tool to spy other gods. Yes, she would have to teach her a thing or two about hiding, but she was sure the woman was a quick learner.

When the woman locked her gaze with Sigourney, Sigourney's instincts kicked in and she disappeared.

"Come back or I'll cut their heads off," the elvish-looking woman said softly.

Sigourney let them see her again.

"Leave them be. I'm the one you want. I'll honor my contract with you, and you can cut off my foot when they are safe and sound somewhere else," the rabbit said.

"You would do that for the mortals?"

The rabbit nodded.

"That's a new one. Still, my answer is no. I have changed my mind," she said.

"How that doesn't surprise me at all."

"You owe me. I want her and your servitude in exchange for the boy's freedom."

"That's a rotten deal."

"No, take me," Siarl said. "I'll be eternally yours and serve you the best I can."

The elvish-looking woman laughed. "Aren't they simple?" She winked and the boy let out a complex collection of noises which either needed a language expert or more likely, that very well-trained psychologist to decipher. Siarl stepped forward and began to rush toward her. The human female tried to seize his hand to save him, but he struggled against it as if it was tainted. He pretended he never ever touched or had met the girl. He gave a soft, daft smile to the elvish-looking woman. His eyes sparkled, his whole body became light, and his brain turned off its last working cells.

Sigourney tried to catch him again.[30]

Siarl evaded her reach.

The rabbit yanked the boy against its chest before he made his way to the elvish-looking woman and got himself killed. Siarl struggled, but soon submitted to its will.

"Enough with the games," the rabbit god of luck said. "Release him and I'll go on both of their behalf. My servitude is everlasting. They'll be dead in the blink of an eye. And they don't love you, worship you, Gertrude… not truly."

She snarled, but the rabbit was right. They were toys that would break, while it, on the other hand, was useful. And none of this mattered since she had more important matters to attend to. This time, she had to make sure the kingdom of Leporidae Lop bled for her. She had to avoid being a standing joke amongst the gods for another century in a row. Her heart

---

[30] To have him back, just to be clear, but she had lost him for good.

filled with hate, and she could feel it spreading all over her body. Last time Cornelius had ruined everything. She'd let her emotions get the better of her, and it had cost her dearly. The other gods didn't hold the same sentiment toward him. The elvish-looking woman crossed her arms. *Not this time.* She would stay away from him. Over the decades, she'd developed a resistance to the fat man and his charm. She tightened her grip on the glamour surrounding her as if one slip would bring back the soft girl inside her and make her life pitiful again. *Never again.*

If you look at it from another perspective. Say, like Sigourney's, never is a nice word. It's a luxury reserved for those who can decide their own destinies. Sigourney had said never when she'd left home. She'd said never when she dismantled her contract with Huxley. And she'd said never when she had let someone hurt her for the last time. She couldn't quite say never standing there under the elvish-looking woman's gaze. Sigourney could smell the electricity in the air—and it smelled like danger.

The rabbit next to her held Siarl tightly with its free paw.

Something else sensed the danger, too. The luck inside Sigourney didn't take kindly to threats made against its host. Her luck wanted to be released to prevent the inevitable death that awaited her, but there was one huge problem which made it unable to intervene to the elvish-looking woman's intentions.

Sigourney's head was full of contradicting wishes. The luck didn't know where to start.

The usual way luck worked was to send a white knight to their aid to slay the dragon—or, in this case, slay the most beautiful woman who ever lived—but it couldn't due to Sigourney's perverted ideas about knights and their uses. Luck had to find another way to help them because it didn't like going against Sigourney's wishes. It would be simpler if her wishes were about biscuits and unicorns, then luck could easily fulfil them. But the host thought simultaneously about Siarl's hand, her own freedom, and the rabbit's and Harriet's lives. And that was only the beginning of the long list of worries looping inside her head.

"I..." the rabbit stuttered.

"You still want to save them, don't you? You could just hare away and leave the small human female and male to their own devices. They are only collateral damage for you to get to keep your feet. But you can't, can you? You got too attached. The first rule of what not to do."

The luck inside Sigourney heard the death clock ticking. Sigourney took a step closer to the woman, but the rabbit grabbed her from her jacket's collar.

The woman laughed and said, "There's only one choice. All of you know it. Your time is up. You are coming with me. It's the only way to spare him."

She offered her hand to Sigourney.

"Let me go," Sigourney said.

The rabbit didn't let go. "Crit you," it said. "She's not a toy, and I won't let you break her as you have with the others."

The rabbit tensed behind Sigourney. It leaned toward her and whispered, "I can free us. You just have to duck and take the boy with you. I might be able to knock her out cold and gain time for us to get away."

"What are you whispering? Planning something, are we?" Gertrude asked.

"No, just admitting my defeat. That my mind isn't sharp enough against you. That we don't have any other option than to go with you," the rabbit said.

Siarl sighed.

"Do you think I'm a fool? You are making a huge mistake—"

"Duck!" the rabbit shouted.

Before Sigourney could duck, the elvish-looking woman waved her arm. A lightning bolt leaped from her hand, hitting the rabbit and the two humans.

"Don't you think I know what you are doing? It's always the same with you and your kind. You deities are nothing more than stupid automata," the woman said to a huge, empty, burning hole which stood in the trio's place.

"Such a shame," the woman said, then winced. "I would have had a use for your feet... after all, one can never have enough lucky charms. And the odd creature of yours would have been a nice tool. Still, now I can go back to getting Leporidae Lop. And if you are there listening to me, you and the others will pay back everything I have lost... with interest. The Leporidae Lops are mine; I invested my time and energy on them. If I lose, just pray I won't find your afterlife."

Neither the rabbit nor Sigourney were listening to the woman ravings and least of all, Siarl. What listened to her was the rabbit's luck inside Sigourney. And it had a different idea in mind. It would make the woman pay back everything she'd done, and make sure she would suffer in the process.

CHAPTER THIRTY-ONE
The Uncomfortable Noises One Makes in a Sticky Situation

The smoke from the smoldering hole made the elvish-looking woman's eyes water. She took a watch from her pocket and tapped it. "Hmm..." Getting rid of the rabbit had taken longer than Gertrude had anticipated. Luckily, there was still time to observe the kingdom before any action was needed.

She left the scene of her crime. If you asked her, the crater was just the aftermath of a failed contract and nothing else— and she had a given right to act as she did. The rabbit had known exactly what it had done when it had traded power over Leporidae Lop with her for its freedom and life. Simple as that.

Not as simple as that, the rabbit's luck still pulled strings in Leporidae Lop. She could sense it. The rabbit had tricked her. She squeezed her hand into a fist and stopped herself from lighting an aspen tree on fire as she walked back to the kingdom. It would be a pointless waste of her powers, and she needed them to regain her dominance. In the kingdom, a million little things waited for her before she could claim her victory. For starters, there was a secret society group she had to obliterate. She sensed the rabbit's luck pouring toward them. But before that, she had to observe how luck worked its magic. If she went and poked it without seeing the web built around it, everything might collapse, even the thing she'd created, and where that would leave her? It was especially important now as the rabbit's death shook the balance of power.

In the meantime, she would search for a place to lie low to observe and to feed on someone to regain her lost energy. It hadn't been easy to make sinkholes and ship the excess land to the other side of the continent for Tamtue's use. Also, all the smiting she'd done made her body feel feverish. Well, maybe not exactly feverish, as the tiny enemies of a human body had no effect on her, but she felt the same kind of strain. That meant she really had to trap some poor sucker.

Any human would do. Anyone who fell for her and worshiped every inch of her mind and body. Then that anyone had to die with her name on their lips, preferably by suicide. Murder was too much of a hassle—she might strain her back or, even worse, break a sweat. Mass suicides were even better, but wars were the tastiest treat. She preferred wars over suicides because they were bloodier and easier to advertise, not to mention, easier to achieve. One careless lie and the whole world burned. She smiled. Humans were so easy.

She glided back to the inner kingdom and seduced the first human she came across to suck them dry. The first poor sucker worked as a merchant for the royal palace of White Cuniculus's Explorer Force. She only had to whisper her name to him and he was hers.

"Gertrude Botilda Clutterbuck," she said. It wasn't the softest name, nor the most beautiful name, and it didn't roll off the tongue nor cause men's knees to wobble, but when he heard it, it stole his heart and soul. The name was honey to his ears. The sweet, soft, lustful name spread like tuberculosis in him, and then later, it spread into the entire kingdom from his lips, taking hold of every living soul—or almost every soul. Most animals didn't care about the human gods, who were too bossy, hedonistic, and full of themselves for their liking. Still, it was good to be Gertrude Botilda Clutterbuck.

Gertrude spent days with the merchant, plotting and recuperating. Then, when it was time for him to die, the stupid man refused to kill himself. He insisted on worshiping her forever and ever. She considered murdering him herself, but her nails had grown perfectly and she wasn't willing to chip them. So, she put the man to good use and made him work for her to retrieve this creature they called Otto Hobbs. Humans and their stubbornness annoyed Gertrude. Why couldn't the humans just obey when she asked them to die? It would be easier for them and for her. With one order, they would plunge into their deaths, swiftly and in an orderly fashion. Then again, they could be terrific devices for nothing and everything. One whisper here and there, and she could destroy perfectly laid plans through a meaningless grunt.

That being said, after she'd regained her strength, Gertrude watched as an old man and his companions were ushered inside the palace. A sweaty man had been carried in before them, and Gertrude smiled. A few more hours and it would be her time to enter the stage. It was about time, as Leporicae Lop had gotten restless and the right moment might pass. She knew all in life came down to the right moment—the right moment to marry, start a new adventure or business, to graduate, to happen to pass by something, anything. A right moment could determine everything in a person's life. In Gertrude's case, she had to act fast before the right moment to start a war had passed. It was annoyingly easy to change hate to understanding, and she couldn't let that happen. Wars were important and great fun.

When it was time to enter, everyone in the palace let her pass through with ease. They instantly fell under her spell. Her name had traveled there before her. Huxley, however, would turn out to be a tricky animal. He had calmly brushed her name off. To him, beauty and lust had always been alien concepts— nice bonuses to have, but far from necessary. He kept his mistress out of habit, and out of what was expected of a man of his status, but he was too self-centered to care about possessing her or being with her. Huxley was a man who had no gods but himself.

Gertrude pushed past the guards at the door and marched into Huxley's office, which was a parlor room turned into a war room. It caused an instant battle to break out between two of them, a silent war of assessing. But when it came to wars, Huxley had one huge disadvantage: he wasn't a god, not even when he saw himself being one. Gertrude easily took his measure. At first, his eyes cruised down along her perfect body and then met her blue eyes, which were as deep as the ocean. Gertrude enjoyed it. She didn't mind the hateful look Huxley had as long as she was looked at. The two seconds Huxley successfully withstood Gertrude was the only victory he was going to get. Making matters worse for him was that all the other men in the room melted to the floor solely from her smile, even his so-called 'wise brother.'

"For crit's sake," Huxley said. In his defense, it had to be said, but at least he avoided acting foolishly by crawling on the floor like a nincompoop just because a woman smiled.

"Shall we sit and begin?" Gertrude asked with a sweet and loving voice.

The other men swooned in the background, filling the room with nonsensical "Oohs" and "Aahs."

Huxley's eyebrow twitched. "Sure, sit down, as you have gotten this far." He pointed at a stool next to the doorway.

Gertrude walked past it toward the situation table.

"Who—"

Gertrude interrupted Huxley, and said to the king, "May I sit here?" She didn't wait for an answer as she ushered the king out of his seat and sat down. "Yes, now we can begin. What was I saying? Oh, yes, I'm here to make you a proposal. Something to benefit both of us... all of us."

"What—"

"Uhh, won't you be a dear and get me some sweet tea?" Gertrude asked the king. She gave Huxley a side glance and grinned when she saw pain on his face.

The king jumped up, rushed out the door, and oversaw the

whole tea making process—correcting the staff how the water should be boiled, what tea to take, and how to sweeten it. He couldn't be more proud of himself, though nothing could be further from the truth.

In the king's absence, Gertrude said, "What a sweet boy."

Huxley squeezed his knuckles red, then white. "What do you want?" he asked. He knew the king to be a simpleton, but he was *his* simpleton.

"I want what you want, the little skirmish you have been planning. Simple as that."

Huxley squinted and snorted. He had an urge to tug his sleeves, but instead he corrected his posture.

"Mr. Huxley, I'm not here to make anything uncomfortable for you. I'm here to help you and your king to get the kingdom you deserve. It saddens me to think how things have come to this point."

"Why do I find this hard to believe?" Huxley asked.

"Because you have a keen mind which doesn't let sleeping dogs lie. You know that under all the pretense there are real issues that need attention."

Huxley laughed. "Sweet words are fine in poetry, but I don't need them to boost my ego. I rather hear what you want than listen to any of your word games."

"Oh, but they are not games; I mean every word I say. You, indeed, have an astute mind. I have to say when I hand-picked you and laid your path down, I never knew you would become so… so merciless and free of constraints."

The lines around Huxley's eyes drew tighter. He fought for words to get out, but was unable to form a coherent thought. The king entered the room before Huxley answered and gave Gertrude her sweet tea. Gertrude took a sip and made a soft sigh. The king crumpled to the floor because Gertrude's sigh sounded a lot like "Bad boy!" to him.

"You," was the only thing Huxley managed to utter out while trying to figure what the crit was going on. The whole scene with the king and the woman made matters worse. Huxley looked down his nose at the king, who was about to lick Gertrude's hand. He turned his head away.

"No," Gertrude said and smacked the king, who let out a whimper. The others in the room tensed with the anticipation. They waited to see who would become Gertrude's next favorite.

"I'm a free man, not your agent. I have chosen my path and my destiny," Huxley finally said. He was still looking away, unable to meet Gertrude and the king. But then he tightened his grip on the chair and faced the god and her deep blue eyes.

"Sure you did. Your destiny is yours, and here you have a chance to decide what you are going to be next. Will you be a failed lackey or the next leader of the Leporidae Lop and who knows... the whole continent," Gertrude offered, duly ignoring what just happened. She took another sip from the tea and sighed.

The king lowered his head and whined.

The sound unnerved Huxley.

Gertrude absentmindedly scratched the king behind his ear, and again, all was good in the world. Well, not for those next in line.

Huxley narrowed his eyes, and Gertrude knew she'd gone too far with the man and his life. She should have let some moments of humility on his way. But no great leaders were made of such things. She was wrong there—something the god would never admit. And that was the thing even the gods, with all their wisdom and resources could be, fallible; unable to see and control all the moving parts with the future. They might think they weren't. They might make others think they weren't. They might make others do their bidding so that the future at least appeared to aspire to what they wanted, but the thing was... there were butterflies in the world, which had their gravitational fields and minds. Gertrude wasn't only wrong because of a butterfly effect. No, she got the whole leadership thing all skewed. It was the interpersonal skills that made a great leader. And Huxley lacked in that department, a lot.

"Spit it out. Why you are here." Huxley crossed his arms, proving yet again that Gertrude knew nothing of humans and how their minds worked. Not even about the man she'd helped create. She thought she knew; she thought greed and carrots were enough to motivate a person. What she forgot was history, emotions, and possible wrongs Huxley had endured had made him distrust her and her allure.

"If you wish. All I need you to do is continue forward with the war efforts, but rather than marching under Leporidae Lop's flag, I want you to march under my symbol and sing songs about me. That's all."

"Why would I agree to anything you say or even listen to you?" Huxley asked.

"Because I can give you anything you want. I'm your god," she said.

Huxley's eyes flashed with horror, but not for long, as his clever brain began to calculate what Gertrude had just said and how to profit from it. If she truly was a god, then she could go on and scratch and smack anyone she liked, as long as it got him something in return.

Gertrude saw the goblin-looking man was coming to terms with what she said. She insisted on thinking humans were too easy to sway, and it almost took the fun out of it. Dangle something easy like power, gold, beauty, fame, or chocolate before them, and humans were putty in her hands. Sometimes it would be nice if they tried to resist her.

"I want to fully control Leporidae Lop. I want others to do my bidding. And, I want you to get rid of an awful woman named Harriet Stowe," Huxley blurted out like a child blurting out their wishes while sitting on the lap of a soft, red, round fellow.

Yes, so easy. This time she was right. Huxley was one of those rare creatures who could push aside all his emotions in hopes of fame, fortune, and power. Gertrude watched Huxley like a prime cut of beef.

Gertrude already tasted the blood on her lips. Leporidae Lop had grown fat, soft, and selfish, not to mention bored and ignorant—just the way she wanted. Nothing could ruin this for her. She would be the god amongst her peers this time around.

She had the easiest souls on the continent. Boringly easy, but the reward was the only thing that mattered. It was just not what luck intended. It had an axe to grind, and Gertrude couldn't flash her blue eyes to get away with it. Luck sent the fat man to step in just at the right moment and time, when there was still room for reason.

"Crit," Gertrude let out. Everyone in the room turned to face the man who had entered. Behind him, a common government clerk fled, knowing when it was good to be elsewhere and fast.

"Gertrude," Cornelius replied, giving her his softest, sweetest smile.

Gertrude had to look away. She couldn't let him get her this time around. He'd lied. He'd made her life miserable. She hated him all the way to the bottom of her heart. He wanted her to be something she wasn't; he wanted her to love humans. How could she love cattle? That was their whole point: to serve and die. They were mindless. They knew nothing about what it was to be a god and control the universe, reach the stars, and alter the balance of life and death. They knew nothing of existing. All they did was dwell on their petty lives with their petty problems and waste the little amount they had doing useless things that sped their way to an early grave. Why should she love such creatures?

* * *

The clerk fled behind Cornelius as the fat man stepped into the war room. Gertrude narrowed her eyes and instantly, a real battle broke out between the two gods. This one had substance and took longer than two seconds. Gertrude gave Cornelius a smile, condescending and hateful, but wrapped with a hint of love, residue from the old days when they had been an item. If you asked her, she was naïve and easy back then, but if you asked him, she had been just perfect. Back then she didn't pretend to be anything she wasn't. But something had gone wrong, and Cornelius wasn't sure what. They had gone their separate ways, and it still made him sad and angry.

"This time you won't mess up my plans," Gertrude said, using her eyebrows. They did a rigid, hateful dance over her eyes.

"Please, won't you reconsider?" the corner of his mouth said, lowering as his message got through. He looked for a hint of the soft woman who used to live inside Gertrude before she became this, but her shell was the only thing left.

"No." She squinted, and there was no misinterpreting her squint as a yes.

"We could just walk away from here, free and happy, without blood, sacrifices, and responsibilities. Leave everything behind and be us." He gave her a shy smile, remembering her electric touch and strawberry lips. Even his eyes smiled. To him, she was perfection, but not the way other men and women saw her. He knew somewhere deep down, she saw the world the way he did. That was what he searched for and wanted to feel again.

"You are a fool if you think that. Fool to think I'd let you ruin my victory again. A fool to stand there in that fat suit of yours. Leave us, there's nothing for you here," Gertruce's frown said, then her lips curled into a snarl, causing terror in everyone but Cornelius.

"At least I gave you an opportunity, which was more than you ever gave me," his lowered head said. His heart broke again. It hurt just like the last time. The pain was deep and suffocating, slashing his insides. But she wasn't the reason he was there, and he couldn't let the feelings derail him.

"Throw him out!" Huxley interrupted them, barking at the guards, who thus far, had been nothing but wall decorations. Huxley had been watching the odd emotional roller coaster, clueless as to what was going on. He even considered throwing both of the gods out. He didn't need either of them. Like Gertrude had said, he was doing already what he was supposed to do. Of course, not according to Cornelius.

"Please," Cornelius said. The guards, who had taken their first move, stopped to their tracks as if their feet were bound to the floor.

"Take him out! Take them both out," Huxley ordered. The guards tried, but one look from Cornelius made their feet permanently stuck—all due to psychological effects and nothing magical going on... at least, if you asked Cornelius.

"I'm here to offer peace," Cornelius continued, turning his full alluring attention toward Huxley, who staggered for a while.

The jolly, peaceful appearance promising inner clarity worked better on Huxley than what Gertrude had to offer. But the man quickly recovered. "Peace? What would I need that for?" Cornelius had chosen the wrong word. Like Gertrude, he couldn't fully see the man. But unlike Gertrude, he expected Huxley to have some humanity, but Huxley didn't. His selfishness blinded his other needs.

Gertrude grinned. For a second, she had had a worried look on her face. Huxley's moment of hesitation might have been fatal, but she had chosen the right person to be helped this far. The rest should fall into place if Cornelius left to pester the other gods.

But Cornelius wasn't done. This was his only hope for a peaceful solution. Gertrude was right; Leporidae Lop was the strongest nation on the continent and their victory was given. Still, it wasn't free. There were always going to be bodies, crying mothers and fathers, daughters, wives and husbands, lost and devastated. "A peaceful solution would start a new era and you could lead humanity into it," Cornelius tried, letting his calm image wash over Huxley again.

Huxley patted the image with ease, laughing.

Cornelius glanced at Gertrude, who smiled that smile of hers. Both of their foolishness got under his skin. He seldom let anything go so deep, but he wanted them to see what a mistake they were making. He wiped the smirk off Huxley's face by saying, "I can always turn you into a chipmunk and be done with the matter."

"No one is turning anyone into a chipmunk," Gertrude warned him.

"A monkey, then? It would be a great improvement from what he's now. I can even give him a bow tie if that helps," Cornelius retorted.

Huxley turned white. There was something serious in the way Cornelius spoke. Also, because he hadn't seen nor tasted bananas, he found the thought horrifying.

"You can't do that, free will and all," Gertrude said, coming to Huxley's rescue and returning some color to his face.

Gertrude was mistaken. Free will didn't work that way, and what should gods care about free will, anyway? They themselves had all the will they and everyone else needed.

"It worked fine a moment ago, and sometimes free will is a bad excuse to do critty things to others," Cornelius said. "Still, I prefer to work this out the civilized way. I can offer you a way to solve this so it'll save lives and benefit all the nations. You'll have better control of your own destinies and it'll bring harmony. All you have to do is give up gods and the pursuit of luck, seek a bit more cooperation with your fellow humans, and you are good to go."

Gertrude snorted.

"Giving up gods and luck? And how would that benefit me?" Huxley asked.

Gertrude intervened. "It wouldn't benefit you. It would make you a poor man, an equal amongst your kind, not a legend or a god like I'm willing to make you."

"Don't listen her lies. You are nothing but a toy to her, and she can't make you a god," Cornelius said.

"I don't mind being a toy if it gives me what I want," Huxley said.

Gertrude's eyes sparkled. They seemed to say, good boy.

The king whimpered.

"You can't be serious. With me, you would be truly happy and not just another dead legend in her collection." Cornelius's words fell on deaf ears. He was a foolish man, an idealist. He assumed everyone in the world pursued happiness, harmony, and the common good. But Huxley didn't belong to that category. He would rather lose his sanity, happiness, and hairline in the pursuit of power.

Cornelius couldn't see the reason why.

"I want you to leave. You have nothing to offer me," Huxley said.

"Ha, I have everything you need, my boy," Cornelius said.

"Perhaps you want your humanity back?"

Huxley snorted.

"So, be it," Cornelius said.

He turned Huxley into a monkey.

"You can't do that," Gertrude shouted.

"Then undo it, if you want. Or come with me and you and I can ride into the sunset and be happy. Last chance, Gertrude... the last chance to be truly happy," Cornelius said, offering his hand to her.

Gertrude looked at the hand in horror, and for a fraction of a second, with love.

But Huxley screeched, and Gertrude snapped out of considering going with Cornelius. "Get your fat hands away from me," Gertrude snapped.

Cornelius sighed. A worthless wish to go back to the good old days when it had been him and her against the world. "If that's what you wish for. Be reminded that you can't win now, either. You have made Leporidae Lop too strong. You'll kill the other nations, but yours will stand. And while they sing songs about your bravery, beauty, and power, the other gods have had their massacre and your people will forget you as soon as you stop pampering their every need. You will become their slave." He left, not staying to hear her reply. There was no point. She had chosen her path.

All this meant was that he had to do this the hard way. The way of violence.

Cornelius listened as Huxley's screech echoed in the palace's hallways. It soon turned into a scream. Then the running feet of the guards came, but he was far gone by then. He was back to being the fat man without the fancy suit and mutt and old horse as a company. Perception, what a funny thing. Frame it right, frame it wrong, and people thought silly things.

CHAPTER THIRTY-TWO
I Would Like a Weapon, please? Any Weapon Will Do

After a good night's sleep in his prison cell, Edbert Pollock was hurried out to nudge the wheels of battle into motion, and all Edbert could think about was how soft and comfortable the mattress had been and where he could get one. Also, how much it would cost him. That was the important part, not a good night's sleep. He was taken out by the prison guard, and Upwood and Josh were left there to eat their caviar toast and plot their breakout. He wasn't even given time to eat his gray, gooey morning porridge—just the way his mother had done, and just as inedible.

"Where are you taking me?" Edbert asked, glancing back at the cell door and the steaming bowl was still visible from the open door.

"To Huxley," the guard answered.

Edbert frowned. "What does he want?"

"You'll have to ask him."

That was all he got out of the guard. The man escorted him through the palace toward the front doors and for a while, he entertained the thought of escaping. It was a short-lived hope as Huxley interrupted their path. He waited for Edbert at the front door, impatiently holding a paper in his hands. As soon as Edbert was near, Huxley handed him the piece of paper and said, "Read this word for word. Can you do that?"

"No, I'm leaving. You don't have any right to hold me here," he said, somehow getting his words out, but he severely lacked the extra something which made others obey, the so-called 'oomph.'

"We have every right to hold you. You have gone against the king's wishes and consorted behind his back with illegal arms traffickers. We had no choice than to confiscate the weapons, and now we are considering if we have a reason to charge you with treason. Do you know what the punishment for that is, and what the reward for cooperation is? With one—" Huxley stopped speaking to mimic hanging from a noose.

Edbert turned gray.

"And with the other," Huxley continued, "one might get a good life around books, inside or outside a prison cell, depending on how well the cooperation goes."

Huxley didn't wait for him to say anything. He shoved him outside onto the palace steps, knowing full well how weak Edbert's character was. While Edbert was good at terrorizing those who were unsure of themselves and tried to be nice to others—people like Josh and his other secret society buddies, especially Mary—he had no way to make men like Huxley yield. Not even when he suspected Huxley needed him more than he let on. Still, he kept his silence.

Edbert once again stood where he had announced his candidacy.[31] He stood there looking like a buffoon. "I don't like this. I don't want to do this," he mumbled to himself and watched with wide-eyed terror as the Leporidae Lops gathered in front of the palace to hear what was so important that they had to stop pursuing luck.

Huxley heard him and said, "The public has a right to know what happened to their husbands, relatives, and friends. You

---

[31] To be precise, where the king had announced it for him.

can't deny that from them, can you? So stop acting like a child and be their prime minister. They need you."

Huxley swung his hands in the air in an odd manner. They went from side to side, and one hand pounded his chest. None of that made sense to Edbert, but he had no clue that all this was a side effect of regaining his human form back, but the body remembering the good old times when it knew how to swing from a chandelier. So the only escape for Huxley's body was the occasional funny arm movement. Often Huxley was able to stop them as soon as he noticed what he was doing, but this time something primal had snuck out. Luckily, human gestures didn't differ that much from a monkey's, so nothing irreversible happened except Edbert now thought Huxley was a lunatic, but that notion had already been well on its way.

Huxley snarled. No one dared to speak about what had just happened, including Edbert, the king, the queen, and the rest of Huxley's secret society friends. Okay, maybe Adolf snickered, but he managed to do it out of his brother's hearing.

"But..." Edbert looked at the important men around him and then at the gathering crowd.

"There is no 'but.' They have a right to know, or you have a right not to hang." Huxley let out a very quiet screech, and he slapped his hand against his mouth.

Edbert swallowed. Whatever room he had for thinking was gone. As soon as Huxley recovered from his shift, he pushed Edbert into everyone's view. The crowd eyed him with impatience. An eager glint shone in their eyes, making it hard for him to breathe. He had no choice but to go through with it. Before saying anything, he checked if he stood there naked for all the kingdom to see. Edbert was sure he had his clothes on, but it truly didn't feel like he had.

"If you do as you're told, you'll get to be amongst your precious books," Huxley whispered.

It was meant as an encouragement, but all it did was make Edbert's mouth dry. He fought to get his words out as they were written on the piece of paper handed to him. He greeted the Leporidae Lops and said, "There has been news, I... we...

the—" He tried a few more times, but all the words got stuck inside his throat. They didn't want to come out, not when everyone eyed him. Not when he knew the truth behind them. Not when they weren't his to begin with. His hands began to shake, rustling the paper. The sound was loud to his ears. His face went red. "I…" he said again, but he managed to swallow rest of the words. His mind and body refused to let them out.

"For Lop's sake," Huxley said, stepping next to Edbert, slightly more forward than him to position himself in everyone's view. "What my friend, our hero, the prime minister, is trying to tell you, is that we know what happened. We know what caused the two sinkholes, and it's more heinous and horrible than you think."

"Huxley, don't," Edbert let out.

Huxley ignored him.

"It saddens me to tell you the two sinkholes weren't a natural event. They were a brutal attack against our home, against our beloved kingdom," Huxley said.

The audience was silent.

"It's not the only bad news I have to burden you with…"

More people poured into the square, climbing on top of the buildings, statues, and lampposts to get a better view. There was no violence, just a common understanding that this was important, and everyone had to hear and witness.

Edbert tried to pull Huxley away, but the guard came up next to him, seized Edbert, and pressed the hilt of his sword against his back. Edbert stiffened.

"Smile," the guard hissed.

Edbert tried, but he couldn't. All he got was a somber grin and that had to do.

The guard didn't complain. She just stood there and breathed into Edbert's neck.

"This news is about our beloved Harriet Stowe—" Huxley continued.

The crowd booed. There might be violence after all if he continued putting 'beloved' or anything similar in the same sentence as Harriet.

"The one and only, whom we thought we could trust. The one who promised to protect and guard us. I regret to tell you, but she's the one who betrayed us and robbed our dignity and our wealth. She's behind this all!"

The crowd moved against the palace steps like a huge thick wave. No one knew why they did. Okay, they did because, at that precise moment when Huxley had made his claim, Larissa Upwood had tried to push her way through to Edbert in search of her father and her soon-to-be husband. She'd shouted for Edbert to see her and address her, but someone next to her thought she'd mouthed a protest against Harriet's actions and that someone thought she'd charged forward to get answers. That someone and others around him went along with her and shouted, "Death to Harriet." Those next to them caught their words and in turn, moved toward the steps, shouting "Defeat Harriet!" And so the chant went on. The last one who heard the line shouted, "Meat for chariots!" and wondered why someone would shout that, but he shouted it, anyway. If everyone was shouting it, it had to make sense.

"Stop listening to him. He's lying. Stop listening to him!" Edbert cried, but his voice was muffled under the crowd's shouts. He didn't see or hear Larissa. And all everyone saw was their new prime minister in distress over the news.

Huxley lifted his hand to quiet the crowd. "The situation isn't as dire it may seem. You're right; Harriet Stowe is a disgrace, but if she thinks she can destroy our place in the world, she has another thing coming. The people of Leporidae Lop are resilient and strong. Our king and our new prime minister will do everything in their power for their people to prosper and survive. We know Edbert Pollock, the hero, has already battled head-to-head with Harriet Stowe and won. And that means we can win." Huxley let his words echo in the new silence. "We the people won't let anyone hurt us or take our luck, pride, or dignity away. Will we?"

The crowd cheered. If someone had a protest on their lips, it was oppressed with outrageous ease. The crowd went on thinking about meat chariots or something else as absurd.

"We will protect our kingdom, our way of life, and most of all, our freedom from her tyranny and evilness. We won't let her push us and take what's rightfully ours. This means we will win! We, as a nation, will walk tall and proud to the confrontation between good and evil, and we will save our way of life and our nation," Huxley said.

The crowd cheered, dampening Edbert's will to protest.

Huxley motioned to the palace guards to carry a crate to his feet. He theatrically pushed the lid off, revealing the shipment of weapons. People surged toward the box covered with cemetery soil and with Aunt Margaret's hand.

"No, no, no, no!" Huxley said. "This has to be done properly. We can't descend into anarchy just because we have been attacked. We must do this the right way, even when we face the greatest evil of all. We don't step into the darkness with Harriet Stowe; we fight with righteousness on our side. We aren't a mob; we are a proud nation with a proud enlisted army. An army collected from our brave and noble men, men like you, to fight against our spiritual enemies." Huxley straightened his back and looked the men and women straight in their eyes.

He had sold the idea of war with ease.

In the background, away from the crowd's ears, William Breheny asked the king, "Is he being serious or just plain silly?"

"I think he believes what he says," Adolf Huxley solemnly replied.

"He can't seriously believe the nonsense coming out of him," Breheny protested.

"Forget it and play along with it," Adolf Huxley said.

The king glared at both of them. "This is what she wants, and it's our duty to make it come true." He made a pining sound as he thought about her. Why couldn't she be here? He couldn't understand why they had to wait?

Others murmured.

Edbert thought his knees would give out underneath him.

Huxley let out a song, their national anthem. Everyone joined in, the king and the queen amongst them, except for

Edbert. But the words were all wrong. Where in Lop's sake had the name Gertrude Botilda Clutterbuck come from? And why did the god's name feel so natural there?

He ended up joining in the chorus, and he sang from the bottom of his heart, dreaming about the god named Gertrude and riding along with her to the battlefield.

Huxley scratched his head while singing and let out a hoot. He quickly snapped his hand back down.

"Hoot," he said again as the war finally was on its way.

* * *

Things were as dire elsewhere as in Leporidae Lop... or happy and excellent, depending on the point of view. Harriet listened to Tamtue talk the Gainsborians into attacking Leporidae Lop as easily as Huxley had talked Leporidae Lops to do the same. Harriet stood in the cage, watching the Gainsborians prepare for war. They looked more like a group of prairie dogs running around not knowing what to do while the huge serpent bossed them around. If this wasn't deadly serious, she would laugh.

She laughed.

At least the serpent god hadn't revenged for trying to trap him, though she didn't think she'd gotten away with it. The gods weren't exactly known for their forgiving nature. Still, here she sat inside the cage once again, making her reconsider that there was indeed a deity for cosmic payback, who didn't believe in lines like, for the greater good.

Harriet pushed her self-pity away. She had no room for it here in the desert. Not that it was a desert any longer. The sprouts were constantly growing and spreading, making everything green and vibrant. Even a few birds that had been alien to the landscape had landed on the riverbed and were fishing there. It was a beautiful sight. So miraculous, yet so costly. But she was the only one paying attention for the land to come alive. The Gainsborians were too busy getting familiar with the army of beasts, learning the songs Tamtue had taught them, and making weapons out of their pitchforks and shovels.

It saddened Harriet to see how easily the god had swayed the Gainsborians into a war. Wars were a tragic waste of time and effort on so many levels.

She'd attempted to summon Bethan to her, but thus far, the woman had refused every invitation. If Harriet had the capability to admit defeat, she would recognize the first signs of losing hope. But to her, her desperation might be the final hail Crit needed to save the situation. She wished the rabbit god of luck could be there with her so she could pet its soft and huge foot to prevent everything bad from happening. But 'if only' was a useless notion. And she couldn't keep relying on luck. She had to do something, but her mind kept coming up empty. It wasn't like last time she'd gotten out of the cage on her own.

There were so many things she regretted.

Harriet shut her eyes and opened them to observe with a calm demeanor all that Tamtue did. She needed to catch any misplaced word to turn it against him. It was the only way to win. Tamtue needed the Gainsborians to die—that much was obvious. All these gifts had been for a show and for motivation, for a reason to fight. If she took that away and told the Gainsborians they were sent to their slaughter, then maybe she could make sure the war never came. But whatever trust she had had was gone, especially as Tamtue had done a critting marvelous job. The Gainsborians ate out of the palm of his hand.

"Harr." Harriet beckoned. The man looked toward her but shook his head. There was a sadness to him unlike to the others, and still, he wouldn't come.

Everyone she tried refused to engage with her. So Harriet did what she could. She feverishly preached about the gods and their purposes, how they sacrificed their people once every third generation. At that precise moment in time that the last wars began to wear out from people's minds and those who'd lived through them were gone and buried six feet under. She spoke about what luck did, and how gods used it to justify the world order. How if you didn't succeed, it was your own fault as you didn't do the best you could. They left out the fact that some of your chances were determined at birth. Still, it was you and your actions alone. When that did no good, she spoke of suffering and blood. What would be left of their nation against the army Leporidae Lops had. "Will you let your god sacrifice your children? I see them training amongst you. Will you let them see the horrors the battlefield bestows upon man? Even your mythical beasts can't shield them from the Leporidae Lops and their gods and arms," Harriet said. She had doubts about the mythical beasts. If you looked at them in the right angle, they were translucent. But you had to have a very paranoid and twisted mind to unsee what was meant for you to see. She said nothing about that. Such things were a matter of belief and the Gainsborians did believe.

Still, the last remark got a rise out some, forcing Tamtue to hiss his lies to them again.

"She's trying to scare you. She's trying to protect her people again. You shouldn't listen to her lies. She wants my demise. She wants your lands for her people. She's a liar and a thief. And what do you do with such people…?" The god left the answer hang in the air. Everyone knew what he wanted them to say aloud. The god just needed someone to say it. And there was always someone who would state it a loud as was the case now.

"Hang her!" The voice rang out in the air.

Harriet winced. The last time she'd heard those words was in her forties, but she was still alive. That time the king's father had resented her chipping away his power and gradually giving it to the prime minister's position. She'd made the man change his mind, and she could do the same here. Except, this time, she had to manipulate an entire nation, along with their god, not to put a noose around her neck. No problem. They would be far easier than the king's father. He had been the quiet sort of fellow, the dangerous kind with his own opinions. Such a shame the man was dead. She'd loved their arguments. They had never been about trinkets as was the case with his son.

But she didn't have to pretend she could do that. A weak

voice asked from the crowd, "Hang her? Are you sure it's a wise thing to do?"

Finally, a voice of reason, Harriet thought. There was a greater hope for peace than she'd thought. Though, she was sure the voice sounded familiar. Someone she'd heard at Leporidae Lop. Not here. Harriet searched who'd spoken, but whoever it was got lost in the crowd.

Tamtue searched for the source of the insubordination as well but failed. So he cleared his throat and locked eyes with Harriet. "The wicked have to be punished, and she has ensured you and your loved ones endured nothing but hardship. Is she a person who should live? If we give her an opportunity to walk away alive, what'll she do? I'll tell you what; she'll see to that the Leporidae Lops have an unfair advantage over you once again. I say we hang her!" Tamtue said, trying to stare Harriet down.

Harriet withstood the stare without wincing. She'd used up all her quota of weakness for a month. There was nothing but resilience left. She stared Tamtue down. It would have been better if Harriet had even tried to pretend to be humble, but she couldn't, even when facing a god and a good or, in her case, bad hanging.

Tamtue got angry. His tongue slithered inside his mouth and a faint hissing sound filled the air.

Death and dying didn't scare Harriet. He could hiss all he wanted. Of course, she would have preferred to die on a peaceful Sunday, and not on a common Tuesday, but then again, death was death on any given day. Better to get it over with than to dwell on the matter too long.

"All right, do that," she said with a calm, almost sweet voice.

The game had begun. She refused to play the role Tamtue had given her. She would see how far the Gainsborians would go for their god. And if not that, then at least she would stall the inevitable and hope for a critting miracle.

Tamtue hissed.

One point for her.

CHAPTER THIRTY-THREE
My Doomed Life

hey say misery loves company, and they'd are right. Edbert Pollock felt miserable, and he wanted everyone around him to feel the same. More than anything, he wanted Huxley to be miserable, but that was a long shot. Edbert was back in the royal cell after he'd given his failed speech and fulfilled his part in the war effort. Edbert wanted to get his hands around Huxley's neck and squeeze the life out of him, which was unlike him. He might hate people, but never before he had seriously contemplated murder. But Huxley seemed to be the exception for everything.

"We have to get out of here," he said, massaging his hip. Not because it hurt, but because he had to give his hands something to do.

"How?" Josh asked with his mouth full of cake. He took another bite from the chocolate cake with a red cherry on top. He was the only one with an appetite. Edbert watched in disgust at how the boy's mouth moved up and down as he munched on the cake.

Edbert did his best not to snap at him. The boy was clearly doing his best in the given situation. It was just that the noise and how his mouth moved made Edbert nauseated. He said instead, "There's a way, I'm sure of it." Not that he was feeling hopeful, far from it. But it was better to think there was a possibility than to think there wasn't.

"The door is sealed and there's an army outside," Upwood said from the divan he'd occupied ever since their imprisonment. "Not to mention, the lack of windows or anything else through which to escape." This was something all of them knew, but there was always someone who liked to state the obvious. It was their moral duty.

"And we don't know where we exactly are in the palace," Josh added, going along with his father-in-law's pessimistic view of life. He'd slept badly, finding the soft mattress uncomfortable, and the two others had snored while he longed to be with Larissa. The thought of not seeing her again made his heart burn. And if Edbert had cared to ask, the boy was filling that void with the cake.

"Those are semantics. We have to do something. We can't just sit here and wait for Huxley to decide our fate. We can always dig our way out of here." Edbert would be the first one to admit he was usually the pessimist in the crowd. The one who everyone else found irritating while contemplating all the possibilities the world had to offer. He just refused to be himself today. The past couple of days had made him see that he wasn't exactly good company, he hadn't made anything out of his life, and he kept making the wrong choices. He'd let his life become lonesome without joy. He would never admit aloud that he was kind of jealous at Josh, the mouse-head boy. While he was daft and would surely be that his whole life, he still had lived and seen more than Edbert had. He had known what it meant to be part of something; Edbert had never been part of anything but the bookshop. It was his bones, his flesh, his beating heart. It was something. It was more than nothing. All the stories written were there. But there was more to life, and he wasn't going to spend his remaining few days inside a prison cell designed to pamper the rich and the powerful. He'd rather be one with the rats. At least, that would make a great story. In such stories, there would be a way out.

"It would take eons for Josh to dig his way out with a soup spoon," Upwood said. It wasn't an outright no. Upwood sounded as if he'd really considered the option and pronounced the last syllable so he left room to come back to the idea if everything else failed.

Josh looked painfully at Upwood. "We could jump one of the guards and escape," Josh said. The boy could already picture his hands full of blisters and the two old men bickering behind his back as he dug their way to freedom. And he was sure they would criticize everything he did, making him end up scooping his own brain out with the spoon.

"Or we could do a ritual," Edbert offered. He had to get out, not only to stop Huxley but also to get back to his shop. Who was he kidding? With all the other possibilities life had to offer, even the thought of unsold and unread books lying there in his shop alone was straight from those horror novels kids read these days. Being away from his precious books was starting to take its toll. He sensed the annoyed monster stirring inside him. "Josh, do you still have the mouse head with you?"

Josh's eyes lit up. "Oh yes, it's always with me," he replied, jumping at any opportunity to not have to dig his way out.

Edbert stood from the bench he had been sitting on. "Empty the table and I'll find us candles."

"I still say it's nonsense. There's no guarantee it will work or how and when it will work," Upwood said, but still, he stood.

"Oh, shut up. I'm sick and tired of your negative attitude. At least Edbert sees a way out. Larissa must be worried sick not knowing where we are." Josh took a last bite of cake. There was yet another opportunity to ask what irked the boy, but no one did. So he was left no other choice than to carry in him the fact he was afraid Larissa would find someone better if he didn't get to her fast. He would do anything to stop that, even cut his arm or leg off.

Upwood smiled and patted Josh on the back. "Don't worry, we'll get you to her." Upwood hadn't been exactly happy about his daughter's choice of a partner at first, but now he was coming around to the idea, seeing how much Josh adored her. He only hoped he would add more muscle so as to balance out his daughter's well-formed body. Maybe a few pleas to luck could change that...

Edbert gathered all the candles he found and placed them on the table. If the ritual failed to work, they had the option of burning the place down. He didn't like the sound of that, but it was better than being stuck here.

Josh laid the mouse head on the table next to the candles.

Edbert winced; he couldn't help himself. He lacked the capacity to confess the errors of his ways and to apologize for all the times he'd put Josh down for bringing the mouse head to their secret society meetings. Maybe later he would say he was sorry for tormenting the meek boy all those years and constantly pulverizing his ego. There was no time for an apology now, so later would be fine. Later happened to be always fine.

Josh began the liturgy, then Upwood joined in, and then Edbert. They skipped all the silly moves and concentrated on chanting their words with a clear, loud voice. Their words echoed from the palace walls to and through the mouse's head. Its little ghost whiskers vibrated from their voices. Josh was actually quite good leading the ritual. He had a clear and compelling voice, unlike his normal tone, which was on the squeaky side.

The rabbit's luck circling around the kingdom heard their pleas and delivered what they wanted with a loud *bang*, shaking the walls of the prison cell, to gyp Gertrude. It was the least it could do to get back at for her trying to fry its master.

Edbert, Josh, and Upwood leaped to safety behind the table and trembled. There was another loud explosion, making their ears ring, shielding the sounds of shouting and knocking coming from the prison cell door now blocked by a heavy fallen beam.

At the others side, the guards tried to get inside. They hit the door repeatedly using the pointless, ancient technique of ramming against it with their shoulders. The explosion had made the prison's outer wall and roof collapse, making the beam lodged against the door securely tight.

Dust kept falling from the ceiling, making everything look ghostly. Amidst it, a figure moved, shouting words the three men's ringing ears missed. They trembled, waiting for divine retribution for using luck so irresponsibly. The eerie figure coughed, then it stepped through the fallen rubbish into their view.

Larissa emerged from the dust, grinning. "There you are. Come with me, and hurry," she said with a soft, sweet voice. None of them really heard the sweetness in it or even anything she said. Still, they hurried after her without objection.

Lady Upwood waited outside with a carriage. "Hurry before anyone sees us," she said, motioning them to get inside.

"Ho— How?" Josh stuttered when the carriage was well on its way. He was the only one whose ears had recovered from the loud explosion.

"We figured you were kept somewhere in the palace when you didn't come home. We have been trying to find you ever since, especially after Edbert's forced speech. Your chant helped us a lot. Thanks for that," Larissa said. She held a pair of homemade earplugs composed of wool and beeswax. She twisted them between her fingers and gave her fiancé a shy look.

"But… but the—" Josh said, mimicking an explosion with his hands.

"Oh, didn't I tell you? I like to blow stuff up," Larissa said and gave her soon-to-be-husband a sweet, loving smile and a shy glance.

Josh mumbled something inaudible and rubbed his eyes. It took him the great part of a decade to get used to the idea. He would have come to terms sooner if she hadn't blown up their summer home.

Edbert missed the entire conversation. His ears rang and his head spun. He watched as mouths opened and closed without any noise coming out of them. For now, he was happy to be left out of any conversation, because even upon his escape, he felt miserable. He would never get to go home since he was a fugitive now. He missed the fact that here was an opportunity to live one of those stories from his books. It was just that in them, nothing was messy, you knew things would work out, and you didn't really have to hear explosions or taste the dust in your mouth. You didn't have to experience a headache or the high-pitched shrill that was getting louder by every second he sat there while the carriage rocked away to only the gods knew where.

* * *

It's not that easy to kill a god or in this case, a deity, especially when it was traveling with a small human female and male, to whose company it could shake to its misery. Not that it had tried that hard. Actually, not at all. So, luck delivered the rabbit, Sigourney, and Siarl through a loop in time and space to Gainsboro the moment before "Hang her" came to fruition to Tamtue's and Gertrude's disappointment. The lightning Gertrude had made had been enough energy to bend time and space for luck to transport the three figures there. You could say Gertrude had played right into its hands—not that luck had hands or a mind or wants and needs.[32] What it had was some sense of existing and understanding of there being a whole wide world out there with moving parts like cats, ants, and humans. Without the extra electricity in the air, the rabbit, Sigourney, and Siarl would have been dead. Any other form of physical harm wouldn't have given luck enough energy to experiment with teleportation.

Luck meant to get them there sooner, but it had done its calculations wrong and delivered them only in the nick of time to save Harriet from certain doom. It had accidentally invented time travel when it put a wrong symbol in its calculations as it

---

[32] Not it the normal sense at least. Though, now it had taken to its heart—which it didn't have—to be vengeful. Someone had to be, or things got a lot messier and nastier.

had intervened with the misguided force of Gertrude's smiting. Luck had a great opportunity to get rich and famous here, but a partnership with Gertrude sounded too horrible to be tried, not even for science's sake. And luck wasn't really the sort of force that went with getting rich and famous. It was more of a force that worked on the scale 'hey, I found a penny' or 'what luck that I didn't get hit by that bus I didn't see coming.' You know, the common, everyday luck of tea still being hot when you have forgotten to drink it. Some might argue that those weren't moments of luck, but they know nothing about what good fortune looks like. They think about those grand things like long-lost dead relatives leaving their whole inheritance to you. Of course, there's sort of luck that randomly gets you a job interview and you get the job of your dreams. But luck would argue that even such things turn to normalcy, unlike a tea mug that keeps the tea warm.

There was no tea at Gainsboro. There was just the new sprouting leaves amongst which Sigourney and the rabbit crept toward Harriet Stowe, past the Gainsborians and Tamtue as luck traveled inside the small human female. Siarl snuck behind them, too. He didn't get fried in the location shift, but he wasn't happy, either. Nothing made sense to him anymore. He kept obsessing over the elvish-looking woman, but still, that seemed all wrong. Yet, he couldn't get past it. He just fixated on her inside his head, making it a very uncomfortable space to be. The whole process of having a crush on someone had to be some sort of mental illness. What else came with compulsions, altered chemical state, and rewiring of the brain?

Still, neither he nor the rest of them saw Harriet's death as necessary, except maybe the rabbit, but it was willing to overlook its wants for the small human female. Yet, seeing the horrible woman inside the cage it had been trapped for so long gave the rabbit satisfaction. It was the finest poetic justice the universe could deliver. The rabbit god of luck smiled and entertained the thought of asking Harriet to stick her foot out of the cage before it agreed to save her.

They circled around to Harriet, to the side which was free

of Gainsborians and Tamtue. Harriet's cage stood outside, next
to the clear, welcoming river, which sent little waves against the
shoreline. The wavelets sounded soothing, and in a different
situation, this could have been thought as a fun holiday
adventure at the beach. Now, the rabbit god of luck wished
Sigourney's skills to hide herself and the others out of the view
kept them truly hidden, even from gods as Gertrude had
indicated. Its brother Tamtue and the rabbit weren't exactly
best buddies. You know, the whole snake and rabbit thing.
There had to be one, a myth of some sort. If there wasn't, it
was a high time it was invented. In this case, it was unclear
who would be the bad guy and who the champion, as when it
came to the rabbit god of luck, it could be a real dick.[33]
Though, you could argue that the rabbit was redeeming itself,
and fast, with all what it had done over the past couple of days.
It had to mean something for its cosmic balance.

"How are we supposed to get her out of there?" Siarl
whispered, sounding much more like himself.

"She does her thing," the rabbit said, nodding toward
Sigourney, "and then I bust her out."

"But they will notice us," Siarl said, sounding annoyingly
whiny.

"Nah, they are too occupied with their vendetta," the rabbit
replied.

"But—" Siarl said.

"Shh, before Tamtue hears us," the rabbit warned. "Do
your thing, Sigourney…" *Before I push the boy into the river.* Its
great paw rested on Sigourney's shoulder as Siarl's rested on
its, and so on went the line as a few ghosts from Siarl's past
had joined their hands with his shoulder. Not that he noticed.
But they liked to be part of the great event that might or might
not right the wrongs.

Sigourney tugged Harriet's dress, making her disappear. All
of them held their breaths, waiting for something, anything to

---

[33] It might have or might not have drunk all the booze from Tamtue while
house sitting.

happen. For Tamtue to rush in. For the Gainsborians to have an uproar. Anything that made the situation worse. All what happened was Harriet turning around to face them and say, "You are the loudest rescue party I have ever heard."

The prime minister bored her eyes at Sigourney and then at the rabbit and then gave a curious glance at Siarl. "But do go away. I don't need rescuing," she said. "I have everything under control."

The rabbit hated the horrible woman even more. Tamtue would have done everyone a great favor if he'd hanged her sooner. But it wasn't the case, and it would have to rescue her, anyway.

"But?" Sigourney said.

"I'm not afraid to die, they have a right to kill me. But that's not my intention, and it won't get that far. I'll make them come to their senses. And whatever you are thinking to do won't get us far. Tamtue has an army of beasts, and I bet he can do more than send them after us. So go away."

"You stupid mortal," the rabbit said. It saw red, knowing the small human female wouldn't leave Harriet behind and might do something drastic and get them all in Tamtue's belly in the process. There was no other option than do something it had wanted to do ever since Harriet entered its life. The rabbit punched the silly woman in her temple. The next part it hated more than anything. Before Harriet fell, the rabbit touched the cage's bars, and they crumbled to dust.

It snatched the falling woman into its lap.

During that brief moment of action, it had separated its paw from Sigourney and the rabbit stood there for all the world to see—and, more importantly, for Tamtue to see.

"You!" Tamtue hissed. The rabbit was like catnip for the giant reptile.

The rabbit's whiskers quivered and shook its pink nose. "Crit," it said, and swooped all the humans into its lap and hared away.

"Do you think you can run from me?" Tamtue roared after them. "Bring her back. Get them!"

The rabbit continued running, using its big muscles to the best of its abilities. They pulsed strength to its steps and made it ran faster than it thought possible. The three humans it carried slowed it down, but the speed it accumulated was something not many could match, not even Tamtue's mythical beasts. It easily left them behind. That might be Sigourney's and the rabbit's luck combined doing its job, or the near-death experience had lent the rabbit ways to tap the hidden potential needed to match the tortoise's speed. Too bad the tortoise wasn't there. It lay on a nice beach listening to the susurrus and the bird calls, dreaming about fruity salad bowls, not giving a crit about the eternal competition it had with the rabbit.

However slow Tamtue's army was, Harriet had been right. The god himself had other ways to hinder them. He appeared next to the rabbit. "My kin, my brother, give her back to me," he said, trying to sound soft and reasonable, but his words came out in a hiss. "I'll give whatever you want if you let me have her."

The rabbit continued running, leaving the god behind. Again, Tamtue appeared next to them, trying to stop the rabbit, who made a dive to the right, but in mid-flight, changed direction to the left and passed Tamtue with ease, leaving him behind. The rabbit had to swing Sigourney onto its shoulder because it almost lost its grip on Harriet and had to give her its full attention. Siarl, on the other hand, was latched to its back like a tiny squirrel attached to its mother. The rabbit counted twenty nails on it. Siarl whipped his metaphorical tail.

"You can't run forever," Tamtue hissed as he appeared next to them again.

"It doesn't matter," the rabbit panted. "The longer you follow me, the longer you are away from them, and someone might go there and take the souls from you. How about if I call one of your brothers to come?"

That made Tamtue stop. He shrunk to a small dot behind their dusty trail. With its big ears, the rabbit heard the god curse, "Critting rabbit, one day I'll have you." The rest of his cursing was incomprehensible, turning into hissing.

"You do that," it said and ran toward Mount Jadero without stopping. It knew no god would follow them to the place where the laws of the universe were twisted. The place where evolution governed the world. It would be their savior... and the rabbit's doom.

CHAPTER THIRTY-FOUR
Be Good or I Will Hit You with My War Hammer

So it began on Wednesday morning, the thing all feared and only a few wanted, but all prepared to do. The war of the century came faster than anyone had expected. All hurried to sharpen their weapons, their teeth, their fingernails, and even their toenails to be sure to defeat their hard-earned enemies. No nation wished to be left out of the feast, glory, and utter mayhem.

Somehow, all the other preparations needed for war got sped up. At Leporidae Lop, the weapons Huxley confiscated from Upwood had miraculously multiplied, along with all the fishes and bread and the silver left. Those little things kept the army in motion and satisfied. You could say the whole silver thing, a bullion, was invented to motivate and mobilize armies.[34] Clothing, boots, and other resources duplicated during the night from one mocked-up version to row of boots marching on the streets, a true miracle the nation needed. Now they had no excuse not to go ahead with the war. Most of them wanted to go on, anyway, not only to beat their horrible

---

[34] Or so history seemed to indicate.

neighbors, but to teach Harriet Stowe a lesson and to be free of her tyranny.

But it wasn't only them and the Gainsborians getting ready, or it wouldn't be a fun battle to watch. The uneven match between Gainsboro and Leporidae Lop wouldn't satisfy the gods. Of course, blood would flow, as the other side had an army of mythical beasts and the others' weapons made from real steel, but not enough blood for the gods' liking. The whole continent had to join the party. "The more the merrier," as the saying goes.

* * *

Somewhere at the Ferrum's boarder, a warrior stood straight up in full battle armor as he looked toward his god. A hand cannon hung from his right hip and a long sword was slung across his back. The warrior opened his mouth, and his sharpened teeth glinted from the only sunlight seeping through the clouds of doom. He stood shoulder to shoulder with other warriors. With a thunderous roar, he joined in the chant, "Ferrum, Ferrum, Ferrum..." The warriors went on with great eagerness. They banged spears against their shields, and those lucky to have firearms fired a single shot in the air, leaving rest of their bullets for their enemies to come.

In front of them stood a huge, towering figure in glinting battle armor. He charmed them with his wide shoulders, bearlike figure, and fierce face, mixed with the smell of sweat, oil, and blood. The warriors looked him in awe.

Their god had come to them, asking for devotion and respect. He had shown them how to conquer the known world and how to gain the needed resources to build a magnificent empire. The whole project was their so-called 'death project' to leave something for the next generations to come. To make them wonder and remember. What else there was to be left behind?

"For the glory!" they chanted.

"For Bhaltair," they sang.

The name made thunder crack in the ominous sky.

"Attention," Bhaltair said with a booming voice, and a murder of crows lifted from his feet. He himself had put them there, along with the ominous clouds and the choking atmosphere. Image was everything, and he knew it. There was no point to make wars willy-nilly. There was nothing like carrions, thunder, and a blackened sky to make one brave for death and destruction. At first, he had thought to make a crow feast on a beheaded soldier to give his men the right kind of mood, but then he thought better of it. It would be inconvenient to get the head's decomposition just right, and in the end. one beheaded head wouldn't really motivate his great, bloodthirsty army. Nope, he decided to do that for his own amusement later, when most of them were dead. Not all, just enough to get his blood-lust satisfied. Leaving just enough behind to keep the nation going.

As he lifted his hand, the army snapped to attention, making a metallic noise echo through the valley. Their lips wanted to speak their god's name, and he let them. His name filled the air, and it carried to the distant kingdoms.

With one wave from him, the army began its march to their destiny.

* * *

Elsewhere, at the same precise moment, a gentle song rang out in the courtyard of the royal palace of White Cuniculus. A great army wearing light gambesons covered by red tunics had gathered there. The army carried light swords and daggers on their hips, and in their hands, flags with Gertrude's symbol on them. Only the few, the elite, had pistols with them and hands free to use them.

The gentle song turned bloodier and harsher, raising anger and hate in their hearts. The Gainsborians and Harriet Stowe would pay for the injustice done to them. How dare they att? their way of life. The song lowered back to a sweet le~ make Gertrude arrive in front of them. She, their savi~

325

turn everything for the better. She would make their nation strong. She would deliver justice for them. She would make the others yield under them.

Huxley, and, of course, the king, came after her, but no one paid any attention toward them, except maybe they themselves. They marveled at their mighty soldier outfits and the dual pistols with golden finish that hung on their hips made them look. You could say they were inspirational. They were beautiful. They were the army and its soul. They were there as Gertrude had insisted.

Gertrude's name echoed from wall to wall, meeting Bhaltair's name in the thunder. Her name had a nicer ring than Bhaltair's did, if that was even possible.

She let her gaze wash over her people, her soldiers. Everyone wanted her eyes to meet theirs. Some staggered as she looked at them with her deep blue eyes. When she was finished evaluating her cattle—no, scratch that, her army—she whistled and they began their march. Nothing could go wrong for them—after all, they were the chosen people.

* * *

The serpent god, Tamtue, slithered in front of his people, ticked off by Harriet's sudden escape but concentrating on the task at hand. It badly lacked time to avenge the injustice done to him by the rabbit, going and ruining his perfectly deserved victory like that. Tamtue's teeth clenched shut.

The Gainsborians watched him with a religious passion, without seeing their god's tense mood. Their god, along with the magical creatures, would restore their glory. "Tamtue, Tamtue, Tamtue," they chanted, dressed in simple, overly large clothes and armed with pitchforks. This had to be done. Then they could go back to cultivating their reborn land and finally waste water by taking a bath. All of them looked forward to finally getting their stink off and hurried to get the war stuff over with.

At their side, manticores, gray wolves, minotaurs, and other deadly creatures stood in formation. Their victory was given. However, if you looked at the mythical beasts really close, you could see the desert sun shining through them, but you had to look really, really carefully to see what they were and ignore your bedazzled inner voice.

"Tamtue, Tamtue, Tamtue," Bethan, Harri, Idwal, and rest of the people sang.

The name got mixed with Bhaltair's and Gertrude's name, along with other gods and their smaller nations.

Hearing his name echo in the valley made Tamtue's mood better.

He smiled.

Blood would flow, and soon.

* * *

It's a sad day when the most peaceful person in the world had to take up arms, but Cornelius Rustika Inconnation This saw no other way out. Huxley's stupid behavior and Gertrude's stubbornness had forced his hand. He stood in front of a mirror, dressed in a shiny suit of armor, and marveled at the picture he made. Now even Gertrude would find him attractive.

The armor pushed his soft belly inside, making him appear majestic and strong, instead of soft and sloppy. He swirled to take one good long look at his armor. Cornelius lifted a war hammer to his shoulder and liked what he saw. The days of being the butt of a joke amongst gods and humans were gone. With one mighty swing, the war hammer would deliver blows to bring back order to the world, and hopefully, Gertrude back to his way of thinking, and maybe even back to him. A man could always hope.

"Cornelius, Cornelius, Cornelius," he chanted and looked at his reflection again. "Yeah," he added, sounding pathetic.

The horse snickered, and the dog made a sad whimperi sound.

Cornelius lowered the beautifully carved war

emblazoned with the world tree, and turned to meet his two companions. The two fell dead silent.

He wasn't angry, but the two shaggy creatures didn't fit his image anymore. He took a deep breath in, and as he let it out, he snapped his fingers and the old nag turned into a beast. *Much better.* The old horse's gray mane changed to pitch-black and its hooves to strong steel. The horse shook its body, letting out the excess stamina it had suddenly gained. It felt odd. The horse had an urge to let out a bray and dash around, maybe even rise on its hind legs and show what a magnificent creature it was. The horse liked this new feeling.

The dog whimpered when Cornelius turned his attention to it. It lowered its tail and pushed its ears against its head. Again, Cornelius snapped his fingers, and a bloodhound with three heads stood where the mutt had been. All its six eyes shone red, and its three mouths dripped thick saliva. The dog snarled, revealing a row of sharp teeth which could chew through any armor. The dog didn't quite feel like itself. It was sure it had lost its spirit somewhere during the transformation. It liked to go back to its former self, but its jaws and minds said to let out a low, menacing growl. And from somewhere, a need to taste flesh became its sole purpose, but only if Cornelius allowed it. All its three mouths whimpered as he looked at its master.

They all looked like former shadows of themselves. There was even an ugly glint in Cornelius's eyes. It was just for this occasion. It couldn't corrupt him, could it?

He mounted the horse, which almost shook him off, but soon calmed down as he whispered, "It's only me."

"Let's go," he said, and off went the three of them.

The glory of battle awaited.

* * *

All of them had a chance to die as legends or return as heroes.

CHAPTER THIRTY-FIVE
She Will Sort It Out

After the odd escape from the prison, Edbert Pollock sat comfortably in Norville's study, surrounded by sheep pictures and sculptures which stared at him. He was sure they followed his every move, that behind those painted black eyes were hidden agendas, maybe even a glint for world domination. Edbert took a deep breath in. His mind was playing tricks again. Next to him, Norville, Larissa, and Lady Upwood argued about what to do with Huxley. Josh Felis was there too, but the boy had stayed silent thus far. They had been going at it for hours, only stopping to eat and gather momentum. Nothing real had been said or done. There had been talk about fleeing the country. There had been views about assassinating Huxley. There had been so many ideas, but Edbert wasn't sure he could add any value to the conversation, so he'd stayed silent.

Edbert shut his eyes and listened to them go on. They were giving him a headache, and his ears were still ringing. For a second, he dozed off on the cursed soft, brown leather armchair of doom.

"What will we do about Huxley?" Josh asked, his sounded weary. The boy paced around the study

Edbert up, who had been snoring for a while now. Nothing good had been said during his nap, not at least in his opinion. Edbert opened his eyes and pretended to listen to their debate, but the pull of the chair was too strong. He shut his eyes again, letting his mind wander. Truly, the answer had to be there somewhere. It wasn't like this was some novel situation. His shop was full of such stories, and those stories had made the humans tick. And Edbert had seen that so many times, despite never been so into people in general. But there it was. Repeating patterns in their lives. It was silly really. So what did Huxley's story entail? Norville would know who the man had been and who he had become. But Edbert didn't need to go that far to understand the dynamics of it. Huxley needed the war to make him, him. They needed to take that away from him. And the only person who could do that was her.

Edbert grimaced and opened his eyes. He would finally have to face Harriet Stowe and he could only hope she was merciful—something she wasn't known for.

"What do you think?" Norville asked Edbert when the room fell silent and everyone watched him, puzzled by his sudden change.

"Actually, we have been overlooking the painfully simple solution. One that makes the most sense. And that is what Huxley wants the least," he said, scratching the back of his head as others tried to piece together what he was saying. "That we help Harriet Stowe. We admit our mistakes and find her to fix it all, like she always does. We need to get the documents from my bookshop to prove it all was a farce and stop the Leporidae Lops from marching to the battlefield. And I'm still technically the prime minister and some sort of hero, so that has to mean something. If I can forgive Harriet and give my position back to her, then so can the Leporidae Lops. There's nothing Huxley can do about it." He envisioned Harriet Stowe scolding Huxley into obedience, which was a glorious and scary image. "She has to be at Gainsboro, she has to." He added the last part to reassure himself. He needed to be right. He needed this small victory for himself. Edbert tensed and waited for others to respond. He shifted his gaze from Norville to the rest of them.

"I like it," Larissa said, pulling the pacing Josh closer to her to calm him down. Josh stopped right beside Larissa and took her into his arms.

"It would be the least harmful way to stop Huxley," Lady Upwood said. "I like it, too."

"There are so many things that can go wrong," Upwood said, though he muttered the latter more to himself than anyone else. "And it would mean relying on Harriet again. Then nothing really has changed, and it has all been a waste."

"That might be. What about you, Josh? What do you think?" Edbert asked, surprising the boy.

"I…" he stuttered, looking from him to his bride-to-be to his soon-to-be father-in-law with panic in his eyes.

Edbert hadn't meant to put the young man in a tough spot, but he wasn't going to take his words back, not now. And Josh had to learn how to survive in the world and through his marriage. He had to be comfortable in sticky situations, and on occasion, being stuck between his wife's and father-in-law's opinions. That was how it went.

"I…" Josh started again, turning red when he saw everyone look at him. He swallowed and gathered all his courage. "Edbert is right. The only way to stop Huxley and our entire nation is to go to the only one who has done that before. We need Harriet Stowe, whether we like it or not."

Larissa watched her father like a hawk and said, "Good. Now, you three can't go anywhere. I'll get the documents and then we can be on our way to her." She did a happy dance inside her. Her fiancé had turned out be as fantastic as she'd thought him to be. He had only needed a gentle nudge.

"But it's too dangerous," Josh protested.

Larissa gave him a menacing glance. "Who're you to say what I can and can't do?" she snapped. She expected such words from her father, but not from him. She pouted her lips.

Josh lower jaw began to shake, but still he replied with ⸢ much determination as Larissa, "I'm your husband. I may ⸜

with you, but I'm not willing to put you in jeopardy."

"No, you are not my husband yet, and we'll see if you can even be mine if you think you can just boss me around," Larissa said. She was about to stomp her foot, but she saw Josh wince, and it was clear she'd gone too far.

He gained strength and determination from somewhere and said, "It isn't like you asked me what I thought before saying you'd go there alone. Isn't that the same, commanding our lives without taking me into consideration?"

"Yes, but—"

"Josh is right, you're not going," Norville Upwood said, cutting the argument short before they would call off the wedding. He happily took the role of the bad guy. He knew Josh loved his daughter and would always do right by her.

He stepped right into a minefield.

"You two are being ridiculous. She can handle herself," Lady Upwood said, scowling at her husband.

"But—" Josh said.

"But, what?" Larissa asked.

Josh said nothing, too afraid their first fight would continue. He very much wanted to marry her, and he very much wanted to make Larissa happy.

All the arguing made Edbert's head swirl, but he felt somewhat satisfied that he had never acquired extra burdens in his life, like Mrs. Pollock.

"I guess in the meanwhile I'll get things ready for us to travel," Norville said. He looked at his daughter and wife, knowing full well there was no arguing with them when the two of them were in agreement.

"Do that," Lady Upwood said.

"I think we need a map of some sort," he mumbled as he walked out of the study, leaving a bewildered Edbert and Josh behind. "You two better come along." He stopped in the doorway, his words more as a suggestion for their own sake than as a direct command.

Edbert and Josh followed him out and began preparing themselves for the journey to come. They set the horses ready with supplies to provide for a bigger party. They planned the route to the Gainsboro and speculated where Huxley's war party would most likely attack. The whole time the atmosphere was somewhat dampened by the fear that Larissa might be harmed; that this plan was one to fail. It might fail, that was still a possibility, but luck had made sure that Larissa came back with the documents unharmed, partly due to the fact that Huxley had lost his interest toward them. The man thought there was nothing they could do to harm him.

When Larissa came back, she even brought Edbert some essentials for the ride to the battlefield. She brought his boots, a thick overcoat, and his moth-eaten hat.

"You, my girl, are a blessing." Edbert embraced Larissa, who smelled like sweet chamomile. "It never even crossed my mind to ask you to bring me anything," he said, still pressed against her.

"You are too kind," she said, trying not to wrinkle her nose at the old man's odor, which was partly composed of onions.

"Did you have any trouble?" Josh asked as he stepped between his bride and the old bookshop owner.

"No, there was no one at the shop."

Edbert frowned. "There should have been..."

"It's a good thing," Lady Upwood said. "They are too busy to be bothered by us."

"Yes, I guess so." Edbert was sure when even prison escape held no interest to the sovereign, there was something quite awful afoot.

"If we leave straight away, we might beat Huxley to Gainsboro," Norville said. "Get yourself ready, Edbert."

"You are not taking me with you?" Larissa asked after she had taken a couple of steps away from Edbert.

"No," Norville said.

She readied herself to argue back, but her mother shook her head.

Norville smiled. He was still the man of the house. In truth, Lady Upwood had asked Larissa to agree to let him go wit' Edbert. Norville had been so down lately. "Action might ' him up," her mother had said. Larissa wasn't happy about it, but her father's happiness meant more to her.

With her, Josh's, and Lady Upwood's help, they were soon on their way.

Edbert found himself mounted on a horse, but he barely stayed on it. The beast underneath him rode with the velocity of a hummingbird. The speed scared him stiff and made his old bones ache. He held on to the reins for dear life.

"This will end badly," he yelled at Norville when they left the kingdom.

"It will end badly, anyway," he yelled back.

* * *

At Mount Jadero, Harriet lay on a small ledge. Sigourney, the rabbit god of luck, and Siarl stood around her limp body. Siarl leaned against the mountain wall, feeling nauseated and panting heavily. The rabbit could hear his fast and strong heartbeat. *Poor boy*, it thought, and turned its attention back to Harriet.

"She isn't dead. Otherwise, she would be here, nagging us," the rabbit said, trying to reassure itself and those around it that its blow to Harriet's temple hadn't been too much. Its pink nose shook.

The constant wind howled around them, bringing in the smell of dried, decaying plants and bat droppings. If any of them had cared to look toward the opening view, they would have seen the armies marching to the green valley. They came from all over the continent, taking routes over the smaller mountain paths with zigzagging roads. To their left, goats climbed up the rough terrain, putting in shame even the most advantageous climber. None of that registered. They all had their eyes on Harriet.

Sigourney was on the verge of tears, but she held them back at any cost, not wanting to show any sign of weakness in front of Siarl or anyone else. Harriet couldn't die now, not when she had just got her back.

"You should touch her," the rabbit said, nudging Sigourney

forward. "Your luck might make a difference." Harriet's limp body was beginning to make it nervous.

Sigourney knelt next to Harriet and put her hand on top of the woman's chest as she was asked. Luck instantly spread from her fingers, jolting Harriet awake, just like had happened with the rabbit—though, this time, she didn't bring anyone back to life, but from a well-deserved rest. Harriet's body had decided to use the rabbit's punch as an excuse to get her to finally take a nap. The bugger refused to sleep even a single night like a normal person. When it had seen the attack coming, it chose to use the opportunity to its advantage and make Harriet shut down.

Harriet's bony fingers clutched Sigourney's wrist, making her shriek.

Harriet snapped her eyes open. "What are you screaming at?" she asked. She felt light-headed but oddly refreshed. "Who are you?"

Sigourney shifted her gaze to her wrist and then back to Harriet's eyes. She let go. Sigourney toppled over, almost falling from the ledge. The rabbit snatched Sigourney by her torn jacket collar, pulling her close. "Thank you," she said, clutching the rabbit.

"What's going on?" Harriet let out. The last couple of days had been erased from her fatigued mind, along with all the things she'd done at Gainsboro. And what the crit was the rabbit god of luck doing out of its cage? And why was Sigourney here? Harriet pushed herself up to sit and swung her head around, confused by the setting. Then she got very annoyed about feeling lost and helpless. Someone would pay for this. Her hands shook, and she clamped them together.

In the meantime, Sigourney's heart had stopped partying and was scared stiff at the lost expression on her friend's face. Everything which been locked inside her came out without her mind's agreement. She couldn't stay silent any longer. She talked about the good and the bad, using the moment to unburden her soul. She started by talking about her childhood and moved on to the current situation, taking detours at every turn. She even confessed that she hated spying for Harriet.

"Stop," Harriet said. "Please, for the love of gods' sake, stop. I get it, and I can remember now." The last couple of days had come back to her after her brain had rebooted. She had only needed time.

Sigourney breathed in and out heavily.

The rabbit glared at Harriet. The god hated her more than Tamtue, who was its mortal enemy.[35] Harriet made every fiber in its body want to push her off the ledge—and it seriously considered it. Instead, it patted the small human female to console her.

"You did good," it whispered to her.

Sigourney instantly stopped her nervous breathing.

"So the gods have already gotten Leporidae Lop?" Harriet asked, breaking the sweet moment and bringing them back to their harsh reality. It couldn't be helped.

"Yes, we think so," Sigourney replied and looked at her feet.

"I know what you are thinking, but there's nothing you can do about it. We are safe here. Better not to meddle," the rabbit said and rubbed its nose. Mount Jadero was not safe, not at least for it. It could sense the mountain's will already seeping into its body. Soon the rabbit would be just another common rabbit. So be it. It was willing to take that risk for... for her. Somehow, it had begun to care about the small human female and her worries more than its own—a reminder as to why it had stayed away from humans as long as it had. Hanging with them without a drink in its paw never amounted to anything good.

"You expect me to walk away?" Harriet asked.

"No, I don't, but you can't stop the bloodbath," the rabbit said. "It's already too late."

"Of course I can. Reason will triumph. It would have done so if you had let me stay with the Gainsborians. I could have

---

[35] If one happens to believe in such foolish things like mortal enemies and destinies and the rest of that nonsense.

reasoned them out of going to war," she said. "And that's not all I can do."

"Stupid woman. Do you think you can reason with Tamtue or any of them?" The rabbit suspected that it was playing straight into her madness. That the more it insisted, the more she would fight back. But still, the words came out.

"I might not be able to reason with them, but Gainsborians don't truly want war. Neither do the Leporidae Lops. I can reason with the people," she said.

"It isn't going to be only your two nations. It will be every single nation in Jadero and all their gods. It has been so for as long as I can remember. Every third generation has to be sacrificed for their gods, and like always, it's done down there," the rabbit said, looking down at the valley opening at the foot of Mount Jadero. "And you can't do anything about it."

For a fraction of a second, Harriet was wordless, but then a sparkle kindled in her eyes. "I still remember the last reckoning. My parents were there, and they never came back. I was still a child, no more than four. The smell of bodies and fire has never left me. I can't let that happen again. You are wrong about there's nothing I can do. You gods like to think you are invincible, but I know your weaknesses. It's the same as with humans. It might not be what..."

Before she got to finish her sentence, Siarl let out a horrible noise.

Siarl waved back and forth and barely managed to utter out a warning before the appalling feeling inside him took over. "I think I'm going to be sick." He doubled over, and his face looked ill. Before anyone managed to do or say anything, he emptied his stomach onto Sigourney's moccasins.

"Oh, Sigourney, I'm sorry," he said, wiping spit off his mouth. His words sounded sweet, and he looked straight into her eyes with a puppy dog expression.

The rabbit laughed, but it stopped abruptly when the rabbit realized it would be next. Soon Mount Jadero would make it a common rabbit.

Sigourney frowned. She didn't find the incident amusing at

all.

Siarl looked around, amazed, and then back at Sigourney's feet. "What happened?" he asked.

"If I'm correct, you were freed from Gertrude's spell," the rabbit replied. "Welcome back, boy."

It was right. Mount Jadero's will had repelled all of Gertrude's godly influence out of the small human male, but that didn't mean all got better. His destiny wasn't smooth sailing from now on. He still had a pining expression, but this time for someone else.

"Oh, crit," Sigourney said, and glared at Siarl. He had a stupid grin on his face and his eyes shone weirdly.

"Can you forgive me for how I have been a fool?" he asked.

"This is all fun, but it doesn't do any good. How about it, dear Lepus? Will you help me if I have a plan?" Harriet asked, watching Sigourney take off her shoes. Siarl rushed to her aid in spite of Sigourney's protest. They argued about her dirty moccasins and who got to clean them—an argument he won because she was still unable to say more than five words to him in spite of her couple of lapses.

The rabbit flinched. The god had thought its name wouldn't be mentioned again, and Harriet went and drew it like a rapier, and poked it through its heart. "I…" it stammered, trying to form a sentence. The wicked woman still knew how to control it, even without the horrible cage.

"I understand your hesitation, but I have a good solid plan. If we give them what they want, all the power they can have, but only for one of them, everything can be prevented," she said.

"I doubt that," the rabbit replied.

"I don't. It's our only chance. Will you help me, dear Lepus, to destroy the gods?"

CHAPTER THIRTY-SIX
You Better Know What You Are Doing!

n the morning of the battle, hot air gushed through the landscape, bringing a pleasant autumn day. Just for today, winter frost stopped to watch the upcoming spectacle. Under the gaze of Mount Jadero and its little cousins, lay a field with a numb ground and yellow grass. Soon, its serenity would be destroyed by the angry, scared, and confused soldiers of all color, size, and gender.

In truth, an hour ago, three bickering people, a rabbit and two titmice with orange sides had taken the peacefulness away. The two titmice argued if the world had gone mad.

"Yes, it has," the titmouse with a smaller tuft said.

The other titmouse, whom Mother Nature had blessed with a striking physique and chipper attitude, said, "No, it hasn't."

"Yes, it has."

"No."

"Yes." And so continued the argument, if one could even call that an argument.

It wasn't much better amongst the humans and the rabbit. They argued whether they should do as Harriet asked or not. They had descended into the middle of the valley where the armies would meet.

"This is suicide," the rabbit said, sulking over letting Harriet boss it around, again. Of course, following Harriet had meant getting out of the mountain before its animal urges took over. So, in a sense, everything was good. Still, it had to fight against the horrible woman. Someone had to say no to her and stick with the conviction to its bitter end.

"You can doubt all you want, but the fact is we'll do this," Harriet said. She was sick and tired of listening to the rabbit whining. The god had been more reasonable inside its little cage. For a short moment, she wished the cage to be there. She forced away her nastiness. If she survived all of this, the cage had to be destroyed.

In the meanwhile, Siarl had moved closer to Sigourney, who prayed for her god, it being Wednesday and all. In all fairness, her praying might have worked, if her god had heard of her, but it never had, not being the same god and all that. It just went on eating grass, ignorant of her and the world's troubles. Happy as a clam, but not a clam.

"My plan will work. You are forgetting there's another way to gain power from souls than by killing. If you want, we can wager on it. If I succeed, you'll never use your influence in Leporidae Lop ever again, not even for carrots. If I fail, you can lock me in that horrible cage I forced you to stay in. But first you have to help me succeed. Deal?" Harriet asked. If the rabbit found her half-hearted apology somewhere in her words, good, but if not, then too bad for it.

"Will you help me?" she asked again.

It wiggled its nose, did it a few times more, and replied, "All right."

"Then, dear Lepus, I need you to give me your foot one last time," she said.

It shook its head. "Oh, no. No, no, no. I promised myself never again, no."

"It's the only way," she said. "I need it more than I have ever needed it before. One last time, and I promise, I'll never ask it again."

Its ears went up and down.

"I need your luck. I know I'm in the crit already, but I'm not asking for myself. I'm asking for those people who are about to die. And for her and him," she said, nodding toward Sigourney and Siarl, who once again played 'tag, you are it,' in the weirdest way possible. When Siarl took a step toward Sigourney, she took a step away from him. They circled around the god of luck and Harriet, making her head spin.

Harriet turned her attention back to the rabbit and saw from its face that her words had done their trick.

"There's not much left... I gave most of it to Sigourney."

"I take whatever you can spare."

It reluctantly pushed its foot forward. She took it and caressed the soft fur between her fingers, feeling the luck pour in. It was as it was always. Like this slight electric tingle with a hum moving all over her body. The sensation was ecstatic, and she wanted it never to stop.

It moaned and shrieked.

Harriet let go. She had to. It was dangerous to get lost in the good moments since you never knew where it would lead you. Not, at least, in Harriet's mind. She had never been daring enough to follow the path of pure feeling. "Thank you. Now one last favor, if it isn't too much to ask," she said, getting back at the task at hand.

It looked at her angrily. There's something very frightening about an irritated rabbit, especially being the god of luck's size. One might even want to grab a weapon, or better yet, flee.

"I need you to take Sigourney and Siarl with you. What I'm about to attempt is suicide at best," she said.

"As you wish, madam," it said, its face turning back to soft and cuddly. "I appreciate what you are doing. Good luck, and I hope you succeed... but I also hope we never meet again." With those words, the rabbit scooped the two humans into its lap and hared away. At least it got to save Sigourney, Siarl, and itself.

* * *

The moment stood stagnant, pregnant with the last second before the battle. The only ones still arguing in the valley were the two titmice, but the birds fell silent when the singing and roars of defiance filled the air. The ground shook as the armies marched in from all directions, without a clue that death awaited them behind the next hill.

Now was the right time for prayers if one believed in such actions. Harriet's body shook, but she refused to give a moment of thought to useless pleas. She only needed herself and her well-refined plan, along with the rabbit's luck, to ensure her victory. The world would yield to her determination. There was no other option.

The first soldiers marched in, then more and more of them came. Armies soon noticed her. She commanded the space like a scolding mother. The only thing missing from her hand was a rolling pin or a pan. However, whichever they believed in seemed to manifest itself in her hand. A wave of worthlessness and uselessness washed over the soldiers when she lifted her right eyebrow. It was a miracle they saw the slight movement, but it was there, amplified in her—not exactly in her, but in the essence of all mothers combined in her.

"There isn't going to be war today," she said.

The gods laughed behind their soldiers, amused by her naivety.

"You all have been stupid and behaved badly. I'm disappointed in you," she continued.

In spite of the gods' doubts, all the men and women wanted to shrink away. They winced, and a few even muttered, "I'm sorry."

"I bet you are proud of yourselves. Proud of becoming murderers and fools. And with whose permission are you doing this?" Harriet scowled at them. All right, maybe she was taking this too far, but then again, maybe it was not far enough. It all depended on the results.

The soldiers looked at their feet and shuffled. Someone dared to speak. "It wasn't us... *they* asked to." His words faded into nothingness, lacking strength to protest.

The gods' amusement was gradually dying. What had seemed like a joke turned out to be a real threat. They unwisely underestimated a greater force in life than gods and their wishes; that being mothers and their wishes, or in this case, Harriet Stowe and her scolding stare sprinkled with a small amount of luck and a lot of self-assurance.

Not all humans were convinced. "Stop listening to her! She's nothing but an old crone who deserves to die," Huxley yelled. He had had enough of her and everything she did. Why couldn't she just go away?

Harriet narrowed her eyes at him. Huxley shuddered, but he lifted his golden pistols up and aimed at her with a wide, mad smile on his face. "You have to die."

He squeezed the triggers and fired.

The gods relaxed. *Good,* they thought, *the world isn't entirely twisted.* One dry old woman can't stop an army. That was unheard of.

They were gravely mistaken.

A screaming man with a beast between his legs rode onto the battlefield. The horse underneath him struggled against his reins and the man was flopping up and down. The two of them were heading between Harriet and Huxley.

The two of them arrived just in time for the bullets. The screaming man, Edbert Pollock, was struck down. The speeding objects threw him off the horse, tumbling right in front of Harriet's feet, still wailing and confused by what happened to him. Edbert had felt them, the tiny punches on his chest, but what now, what next? Maybe he should close his eyes and think. Yes, that sounded about right. His eyelids already felt heavy. Just a moment's rest and then he would give the documents for her to force the peace.

Edbert shut his eyes. All anyone else could do was look at the scene in bafflement. This was not war; this was a personal squabble, especially as Huxley's face twisted from a look of triumph to bafflement. He looked at Edbert and then back at Harriet and then at the weapons in his hands. He loaded his pistol, took his time, and again, took to aim at her, but again, he failed. This time Norville Upwood arrived. In control of his horse and holding a musket, he took aim at Huxley. He fired a shot, which knocked the pistol out of Huxley's hands, which was a mistake. He'd aimed at his head.

Huxley hooted.

Upwood cursed, jumped off from his horse, and rushed to punch him. The small goblin-like man tried to get away, but Upwood would have none of it. He launched his fist at the man's face, making him fall. His nose was bleeding, and he let out a sad screech.

"See what you all have done! You have killed an old man. Is this what you want? Death, sorrow, and madness…? I can say it isn't," Harriet cried, ignoring the personal and concentrating for the opportunity it had created. The scene with Huxley and Upwood was all nice and very cathartic, but there was no time for it, not even to marvel about how luck had once again averted her death. Luck saw it differently; it liked to hear two simple words and would be satisfied, but no, Harriet had already forgotten them.

"Say you are sorry," she said, continuing at full steam ahead.

An uncomfortable silence spread through the battlefield. *It isn't our fault*, most of them thought. *He just came out of nowhere.*

"I said… say you are sorry," she said, spicing her words with a heavy sigh of disappointment. If only luck could manage that, then maybe it would get the 'thank you' she owed it.

"I'm sorry, Miss Stowe," they all said, even the soldiers of the other nations, twisting their hands and finding their feet fascinating.

"Good, you should be," she said. "Now you have to make up what you have done."

The gods hissed and finally realized that maybe the old woman could stop the war. They had underestimated the power of well-placed words, especially when accompanied with the right tone. They'd thought that was only reserved for them.

Harriet wasn't that sure she could pull this off. Nothing had gone like she'd expected, but the right kind of pressure surrounded them. If she seized the moment, maybe then. Her heart skipped a beat. "Swear on my name, swear to give your devotion and souls to me."

The soldiers looked confused.

"I said, swear on my name, or do I have to lock you in the closet for the rest of the day?! Do I?!" It was a good thing Harriet didn't have kids.

The soldiers trembled with awe. It took one more stern look before she got them to swear by her name.

The gods' chatter grew louder. They shouted commands to their armies, who ignored them. They were more concerned with their mother who'd caught them not playing nice. There was a general wince.

"I can't hear you. Say it stronger and mean it," Harriet said, lowering her voice, making them work to hear her. Everyone knew when a mother said something slowly and quietly, all the nightmares from the other dimension have broken loose, and they can either take cover or obey.

The armies followed her command. When a neighbor said it louder, they said it louder, until they all chanted the words. The gods' possession over their subjects loosened, and they wailed with disappointment.

A weird tingling power moved inside Harriet, along with a notion that nothing could stop her now. She almost let it sweep her to the dark side with cookies, but instead, she said, "By the power of these men and women's souls I command, I relinquish their souls to the first god to kill me." She knew it would save their lives. Maybe not their souls, but really, who cared about those?

CHAPTER THIRTY-SEVEN
The Separation of Soul and Body

G eneral confusion swept over the battlefield after Harriet snatched the souls from underneath the gods' noses. Bhaltair first grasped what she offered. This was his only chance for victory, as he'd made his nation so strong that not enough of his men would die with his name on their lips. He rushed his horse forward, knocking over the empty meat sacks he'd called his people. He could already feel the power running in his veins.

"Bhaltair, stop," Gertrude yelled after him, but he refused to listen. Nothing would get in his way now. He had to win and not let Tamtue best him like last time.

The other gods soon followed behind.

"You fools! Stop it right away. You are playing right into her hand," Gertrude said, her voice high and full of venom.

No one listened to her. The gods fought with each other with punches, kicks, smiting, and even some biting.

A gang of minor gods trapped Bhaltair, dropping him off his horse. The horse left its master, fleeing from the fight. Bhaltair pushed himself up and didn't hesitate. He charged forth to attack the first god who dared approach him. He slammed his bear-like body against the jackal-headed god's torso, driving him to the ground, but soon, the others overwhelmed him. It looked like a tidal wave of gods had swallowed him whole, with Tamtue riding the crest. Gertrude pushed past them, succumbing to the situation. One of them would rise to the top, and she rather it be her. She understood why Huxley had asked her to get rid of the old woman; she was too cunning to let live. It was a wonder she hadn't been able to do more damage. But soon she wouldn't be a problem anymore. There would be no body, no mind, and no soul left when Gertrude was done with her... just pure energy to be used.

* * *

Harriet Stowe watched the onrush of gods with amusement, calmly awaiting her demise. She was ready to die. She'd accomplished everything there was to be accomplished in life. She could finally join her husband.

Any moment now.

Gertrude Botilda Clutterbuck did as she wished, reaching for her throat.

Harriet kept her eyes open, looking straight at the god and seeing only emptiness. She felt sorry for her. Gertrude pushed her hand forth and her fingers began to close. A sense of relief washed over Harriet.

But her death never came.

A low growl sounded behind her, making Gertrude freeze. Everything else stopped as well.

"Harriet Stowe?" a voice behind her back asked. The voice boomed out strong and thunderous, and the armies trembled in fear.

"Yes," she said, pushing her shoulders back and straightening her posture, annoyed by the sudden interruption of her glorious victory and self-sacrifice. The final act she would do for her people.

"Give me the souls you took, and I'll spare you and your fellow creatures' lives," the voice said.

"I'll do no such thing," she declared.

"Yes, you will. I am your god, *Cornelius Rustika Inconnation This*. I have come to deliver justice in the name of all those who have died in vain because of vanity. I am here to prevent this massacre you have only postponed," Cornelius said. "Do you think they won't die after your death? The men and women will only be collateral damage in the war you just started. That tiny war between the gods will tear the entire continent apart, and I am afraid I mean it literally. You can't tamper with their delicate balance like that. So give me the souls."

The three-headed mutt puffed warm air on her neck when she stood silent.

All eyes were upon her as everyone waited for her to say something. It was a good thing she was used to pressure. All right, this might be even more than she could handle, but she chose not to crumble. It would be so unbecoming.

"I give these souls to you my god, Cornelius Rustika Inconnation This," Harriet said with a clear, strong voice. To let everyone know she did it of her own free will and not because she was afraid or anything, she turned and kneeled before Cornelius. The mutt's heads were inches away from her face. Harriet stared past the teeth, the red eyes, and the saliva at Cornelius. "My lord."

Instantly, the tingle she'd sensed earlier was gone.

She met Cornelius's eyes and nodded.

"Thank you, my child," he said.

He shifted his attention to Gertrude and the rest of them. The elvish-looking woman trembled. There was nothing soft and funny left in him, and least of all, in his mutt. Gone were the days they and the nag looked cuddly or walked with a joyful jiggle.

"Now, let's see what you gods are made of."

He whistled and rode past the frail woman. His fierce dog rushed at the gods.

The gods disappeared, along with the rider, leaving behind a haunting tune Cornelius had let out a moment earlier.

Harriet Stowe stayed kneeling. Her ears were ringing and her breathing was laborious. She tried to push herself up, but then she lowered herself back down. All the strength in her knees had left her. They ached and reminded her she was old, and that this wasn't how things should have ended. She should have been happily married, surrounded by a string of children, and by now, a grandmother of more than a dozen. Life and luck never did what they were supposed to do. Harriet couldn't deny the good she had done for the kingdom after everything she had ever loved had been robbed from her. Her husband was gone because of the same petty rivalries nestled inside Huxley. She was tired of the minds and hearts of men repeating the same eternal logical flaw. And it was control they sought—not power, not luck—but a way to wipe off uncertainty and eat the cake every day. They just didn't know that. The same applied both to humans and their gods. The distance was the only separation, allowing the gods to be more ruthless and inconsiderate and to forget that cooperation was usually the surest way to happiness. When you didn't have to face Larry, Lana, or Lawrence, it was easy to blind one's mind and concentrate on swindling their pension funds or fooling them into wars, rather than find oneself in their hearts. Now Harriet saw she had done the same. Yes, she'd tried to stay in touch through her audiences, but that was putting into other people's life and controlling them instead of being present and helpful.

"My prime minister, may I be of any assistance?" Norville Upwood asked, offering her his hand.

"Thank you," she replied, letting him pull her up.

He smiled. "My pleasure, and if you don't mind my saying so, thank you. Thank you for saving us all!"

She nodded and let go of his hand. She looked at the lost and nervous armies, which looked small without their protectors. Even the mythical beasts had faded away. She sensed the armies' need for clarity and conclusion. What the crit was she supposed to say or do with them? Harriet hadn't thought this far. "Go home," she said weakly.

The field was silent, except for one man who screamed from the bottom of his heart. It would be too tempting to say the man jumped up and down like a spoiled child, but Udolf Huxley rarely did something so demeaning. Instead, he crawled on all fours, looking for his damaged guns or anything else he could use on Harriet Stowe, hooting all the time. There was nothing anyone could do for him.

Harriet walked up to Huxley and said, "That's enough, Mister Huxley. Stop now and I'll pardon you."

He kept going.

"Enough," she said.

He stopped to look at her. She saw his mind was broken. She offered her hand to him, but he hit it away.

"Norville, will you do me the honor?" she asked.

The man did as he was asked and seized Huxley. "We are done," he said.

Huxley didn't struggle against Upwood. He relaxed, understanding he was where he was meant to be.

Harriet moved her gaze from him and let it slide over the soldiers. When she had taken them all in, she said with a hollow voice, "You, too. This ends here and now; there's nothing for you here. Go home and forget this nonsense."

A general murmur spread amongst the men and women. "Home?" They still hungered for the conclusion that was promised.

"But… what about our enemies?" someone asked.

"There are no enemies. You made them up. Go home," she said, too tired to argue anymore. She'd used her quota of arguments.

"Daft old woman," someone said with all the defiance he managed to muster.

"Shut up. You don't know what you are talking about; she's our prime minister, and she saved your bum," someone, presumably a Leporidae Lop, said.

"Yeah? What are you going to do about it?" the other man taunted.

Gods may want blood, but unfortunately, so do men.

Things went downhill from there. The Leporidae Lop hit the man, and the fight spread from there onward. People used their fists, knees, and teeth as weapons. The brawl didn't stay between the nations, either. Men and women fought with the men and women from next door because of their well-behaved children, nice clothes, and chipper attitudes.

"Stop it. Stop it right now!" Harriet said, but her demand fell on deaf ears.

Crit it all! she thought. She had no strength to beat them back to obedience. As long as there wouldn't be any bodies, she'd let them go on.

One woman, a Leporidae Lop, who sang as she did her chores, got a well-deserved punch straight to her cheek from a sour woman who'd listened to the god awful singing for the better part of a decade. The well-aimed punch brought so much pleasure, she sought another woman who'd annoyed her with her fabulous hair, making her look bland and worn-out in the eyes of her husband. However, the sour woman had another thing coming. The woman with the fabulous hair had not only taken care of her appearance but also took self-defense-classes at the Women's Institution of Knitting—a nice, simple name with some accuracy. The woman with fabulous hair landed the first punch before the sour woman could even swing her fist. Then the fabulous-haired woman swirled and landed another punch. After the sour woman dropped to the ground unconscious, the woman with hair like honey and silk found and fought the woman who always bested her in the ring at the institute. Not only that, but her precise and beautiful stitching left her envious.

And so, the brawl continued.

Harriet turned her attention from the brawl to the still unconscious Edbert. She had a strong feeling he was the man who'd caused all the misery. Then again, he might have saved her life, so there was that. She should be thankful.

She sat next to Edbert and said, "We need to talk."

CHAPTER THIRTY-EIGHT
The End of Insanity

he great battle ended. Bruised, soulless men went back to their homes, ignorant of what had happened to their gods. What Cornelius did to them or what they did to him would stay hidden for now. Men had no time to worry. They had their hands full repairing their own lives. However, the gods would have liked humans to show a little consideration toward them, especially when Cornelius had chosen to make the most of his powers and made real changes in their order. He'd made himself their chief and was now bossing them around, demanding absurd things like no more bloodbaths. And he taught them something called 'meditation' to calm their selfish urges, or so he insisted.

They fought him at every turn.

* * *

Back in Leporidae Lop, a week after the battle, Harriet Stowe sat alone in her little office. She sat on top of a prison cell in which Udolf Huxley was locked away for an unknown duration. Many demanded Huxley be hanged, that being the common go-to after failed revolutions. Harriet found executions too barbaric. She would rather have him where she could find him—there was no telling what he would do after his death. But someone could argue locking a man inside a prison for an undefined time would be more barbaric than a quick hanging. Who knows who's right? It's a question of life versus quality of life and which one matters the most.

It wasn't only Huxley under lock and key. The rest of his revolution buddies, including the king, were left to ponder their life choices in the dungeon.

What their future would bring had to wait. She had too much to do. She waited for the morning rush of her subjects coming to seek consultations, but no one came.

She shifted her weight on the chair and began to write invitations. Her messenger bird sat on the chair's top rail, looking down at the papers.

Her position as prime minister had been renewed, but people had no use for her. Leporidae Lops were too cheerful after the beating they took and gave. People carried their bloody noses like badges of honor. Of course, some sulked, but they were the perpetual prophets of doom and gloom, and nothing satisfied them. In general, busy people lacked time to get on each other's nerves and complain about it to her. Harriet grimaced. One day they would be back, and she would welcome them with open arms. Then she remembered what she'd thought on the battlefield. Maybe it was high time for her to put more trust in people and stop the consultations. They came if they wanted her help, and if they came, she better learn to listen.

Anyway, she had no time for their petty quarrels. She was in the middle of negotiating with the Gainsborians about returning Leporidae Lop's treasures, or at least some of them. *Criting awkward.* Unsaid things stood in the middle of the negotiations like a white elk in a tutu. No one wanted to be the first to confess they saw it. All very twisted and complicated, just the way she liked it. The invitations she wrote were for the leaders of the continent of Jadero. Together they had to sort out the mess the gods had left behind. She would lead the diplomatic affair to see it went accordingly.

A knock on the broom closet's door awakened Harriet from her thoughts.

"Come in," she said.

Siarl Ellis opened the door and said, "Ma'am, you have a visitor." She had forgiven him for his betrayal. A whole lot of forgiving and a whole lot of forgetting was going on all over the continent. Siarl was a good boy, maybe not the best of assistants, but his heart was in the right place, and he didn't want to go back home, so she'd let him stay. In the same spirit, she'd pardoned Otto Hobbs, along with the rest of them. They were now busy rebuilding the bakery. All very heart-warming, but she would keep an eye on them.

"Ahem," she said. "Let them in."

Sigourney soon walked in. She went past Siarl, giving him a perplexed glance. Harriet saw their awkwardness and thought, life is wasted on the young, or so they say. More than often, she agreed with the proverb. Then again, who was she to say anything about matters of the heart? Hers was buried deep in the ground with her husband.

"So, you thought to use the door this time?" she asked.

"I came to say goodbye," Sigourney said. There was a nervous tension between the two of them. Her confession at the mountain hadn't been forgotten. After all, calling someone an evil overlord had a very everlasting ring to it.

"You are leaving?"

"Yes, with the rabbit."

Something dropped in the hallway. Harriet was sure an ear was pressed against the door, in fact, she could picture it.

Sigourney shot a glance behind her, but she turned her attention back to Harriet.

"I could still use you," Harriet said in a careful tone. "I have lots of work ahead with the diplomatic affairs and all the rest. You would be valuable for turning Leporidae Lop in the right direction. Crit, for turning the whole continent in the right direction. What do you say to us working together for the common good?" Sigourney would still do her old job, as she had always done, but this time, she made sure she would see the bigger picture. That should wipe away all her thoughts about evil deeds, along with that illogical guilty conscience of hers.

"Thank you, but no," Sigourney said, sparking a sequence of noises out in the hallway. Again, something dropped, followed by heavy breathing and then the unnerving silence when someone was trying to be indistinguishable, even when everyone could see and hear that someone.

Poor boy, Harriet thought. She almost said, "Not ever for him?" but thought better of it. She knew what the potential for real love looked like. Sigourney and Siarl would find their way to love without her help, if that was what they wanted. Instead, she said, "Won't you reconsider? I'll pay you more." She didn't want the woman to leave. Not because of the boy, but because now she knew about her talents, she could use her more efficiently. With her help, she could spy on those who plotted against her and punish their vile deeds before they struck. The woman would be a terrific tool, not some dirty trick to be deployed.

"No, I'm leaving with him," Sigourney said. She sounded almost annoyed, as if Harriet had said the wrong thing.

The tension between them grew suffocatingly heavy, but it wasn't the only tension building up in the room. Thick, tormented anxiousness seeped in from the hallway.

"Him?" Harriet asked.

"The rabbit."

"Are you sure it's a him?"

"Yes, he told me."

"A-ha, you are really letting me down if you leave," she said. She tried to stare the woman down—after all, it was the final way she could make her stay.

Sigourney didn't even flinch.

Harriet took a deep breath and said, "If your mind is made up, then there's nothing I can do. It was nice working with you. If you ever want to come back, you are always welcome." She forced a smile.

Something thumped against the wall, accompanied by cursing.

"Thank you for everything," Sigourney said.

"All the best luck for you and the rabbit," Harriet said. "Where are you heading?"

Sigourney shrugged.

"Then don't let me keep you waiting," she said.

Sigourney sighed and headed out, leaving Harriet alone into her office.

Harriet's chest felt heavy, like there was something there, but she shook the feeling off.

Out in the hallway, Siarl shouted after Sigourney, "Hey, wait up!"

If the woman said something, Harriet didn't hear it.

Siarl shouted, "I'm coming with you!"

Harriet heard the boy collect his things and run after Sigourney without even saying goodbye to her. She grimaced.

"Come, if you have to," Sigourney said.

"Thanks," Siarl replied.

Now she was truly alone. Harriet straightened a wisp of hair behind her ear, took off her glasses, and massaged her eyes. *Oh, whatever.*

She put her glasses back on and continued writing.

She hummed as her mind got busy, planning how to fill the sinkholes and all the rest. Later today she had to write a letter, which she would hand-deliver before nightfall.

* * *

It had gotten dark outside. Edbert watched as, one by one, the lamplighter placed a ladder against each streetlight, climbed up, and lit the lamp. When the man was by the bookshop, Edbert waved in greeting, but the man only gave him a quick, disinterested glance.

Edbert closed his shop's front door, keeping the cold away. The streets were covered with the first snow of winter.

Edbert took a watch from his pocket and sighed. A few

more hours until midnight, and he had no clue what to do now that his nights were free again. He resorted to his past obsession by going over his ledgers. He'd sold five books today with pennies, earning a lot more than he did yesterday, but not enough to make a living. His relocation was postponed. There were more important things to be handled in Leporidae Lop, and he was sure Harriet had forgotten about him on purpose. He knew he should be happy not to be imprisoned with Udolf Huxley, but his nature didn't allow him to be happy about simple matters.

He massaged the ache in his chest where the two bullets had hit him. *Stick to life's simple pleasures*, he reminded himself. He had everything he loved right here. Books of all sorts— read, unread, written, unwritten, fiction, and fact. And it was a miracle he'd survived to be amongst them. The two bullets had been spent, and the stack of papers in his jacket's chest pocket had stopped them. The hits still caused massive bruising and constant aching, making him relive the incident over and over.

Edbert opened an envelope which had been hand-delivered to him earlier today. He snorted. He had been sent an invitation to Josh and Larissa's wedding. He thought of ways to decline the invitation, for he hated weddings more than anything. There was something very untoward about them.

A cold breeze passed him. "Not now," he said, knowing full well either his father or grandfather had awakened. He didn't need anyone's advice right now.

"What is it?" he asked, sensing one of his father's lectures coming. At his age, they felt like a cosmic joke.

"I have to say, I find your behavior altogether—"

There was a knock on the front door.

Edbert pushed himself up and winced with the pain. He took the thick book of words with him and carefully opened the door.

All color drained from his face.

Harriet Stowe pushed her way in. "We need to talk."

* * *

In an untouched forest, where the softwood trees grow tall, two figures stood around a stone, using it as an altar. A human skull lay on the altar, but there were no candles nor any trinkets surrounding it.

The dark forest loomed around them. One figure stood on its two hind legs, and the other was on all fours. They spoke with quiet voices.

The creature standing, a brown and white mouse, said, "It has to work."

"I don't know. Are you sure a human skull works?" the other creature, a black goat, the oddball of its family, asked.

"It has to work," the mouse replied, making its whiskers quiver.

"I'm not sure. It would be better if we left the whole matter alone. This whole business with gods and luck seems too much to be bothered with."

"Uh, maybe you are right," the mouse said and pushed the skull off the stone. The skull dropped to the ground, made a few loops, and lodged itself in a pine tree's roots.

"And playing with skulls is a vile business, anyway," the goat said.

The goat began nibbling on the stone's green moss.

The mouse wiggled its tail. "Then what shall we do?"

"Watch the stars, for now. They shine bright tonight."

"Yes, they are lucky. Stars, I mean; don't you think?" the mouse asked, looking up at the stars shining amongst the treetops. The mouse sniffed, smelling the frozen air mixed with the scent of pine.

"I thought we were through pursuing luck? Shouldn't we concentrate on more meaningful things?" the goat asked.

"Oh, yes... sure," the mouse said, squinting as it looked at the starry sky. Maybe there would be a shooting star tonight...

ALSO FROM K.A. ASHCOMB

The dead don't wait.

But they do work in the factories, decide over policies, and hate to stay buried six feet under. Petula Upwood is about to find what the undead genuinely want. She follows strangers into the night to awaken a man who many would prefer to stay under. She will soon realize that being a necromancer is more about politics than perfecting the art of waking the dead. And she hates it.

Herbert Ringworm, a sculptor and a werewolf-wrestler, is willing to kill to serve his justice. Not that easy when he is forced to pair with a genteel ghoul. The only thing he wants is Ona to be alive again.

Morris Reinhardt, a banker, needs to get tonight right to save his late father's bank from the ruins by starting a conspiracy. He just isn't sure about his accomplices and should have known better than put Petula's life in danger. Everything is going haywire.

If they want to survive tonight, they'll need to cooperate.

Penny for Your Soul is an economic and political satire with humans, ghouls, and undead willing to do anything to have a win. It is full of personal stories and a few jokes about metaphysics and humanity.

Read on for an extract.

PROLOGUE

ife is not sacred. Not in Necropolis. But neither is death. Both serve a purpose, and here in Miss Wilkins' attic, death was a macabre obsession for the living. Petula Upwood, a necromancer, moved amongst the exhibitions, but she wasn't here to see the latest trends in taxidermy or the ancient ways to mummify the dead. She was here to catch a spirit let loose by a careless cleaner. Miss Wilkins had summoned her after two customers had been attacked and killed by the spirit. It had tried to possess their bodies. Without human flesh, the spirit was bound to the vessel it was trapped in and stuck here in the attic.

From its hiding place, the spirit wailed, trying to intimidate Petula. But she'd done this for too long to let the sound have any effect on her. Petula sometimes wondered at the habits of Necropolitans and their basic disregard for danger and hygiene. Tampering with the dead didn't come without a price. And this exhibition full of wonders was tempting fate. Not that this was an exception from the norm; the rest of the Necropolitans were as careless with the dead as Miss Wilkins.

All around her were not only dolls and charms containing evil spirits, but also rotting parts of some poor bastards whose families had donated them to be paraded here in the attic for a short moment of excitement.

Something crashed to Petula's right. She froze and turned around, ready to cast a protective incantation. But it wasn't the spirit. An orange tabby stared at her from the top of an empty exhibition stand. The cat had knocked down a pot, and fragments of pottery lay shattered at the foot of the stand. Around the broken pieces, white ash had spread. Petula grimaced at the bitter smell and hoped that whatever the substance was, it was tame and harmless for the living. But that was seldom the case.

"Who let you in here?" Petula asked.

The tabby tilted its head.

A black cat would have been more fitting in this environment and in Necropolis in general, but Petula had to admit the ginger cat looked cute with its big round eyes and fluffy mane.

"It's not safe," she said, not knowing if she expected the cat to reply. She hoped not. That would be a new level of bizarre even in the land of the undead.

The cat lost interest in Petula and turned its attention to licking its front paw.

"Oh, well. I guess I'd better take you out," Petula said, not understanding why she kept speaking to the cat.

She approached the tabby with caution, not wanting to spook the cat and be forced to give chase. That would be just perfect. Another reminder of what her career as a necromancer had amounted to: pest removal instead of using her full potential. But it was what it was. She had to resign herself to spirit control if she ever wanted to prove her talent. But she and the agency she worked for knew this was beneath her. She could do more. Real necromancy was about raising the dead.

The cat didn't seem to care about her approach. It sat on its post like the king of the valley, majestic and untouchable. But still, Petula crept forward with caution. It was a good thing she did, as behind the cat the air stirred. Ever so slightly. The vibration was easily missed, but Petula sensed it before seeing the disturbance. She readied herself.

It wouldn't dare, she thought.

Petula tilted her head and waited, then saw the spirit becoming more solid. It screeched and surged towards the cat. Of course, it had to be malicious. Petula had no other choice than to rush towards the cat as well. She snatched it into her arms, turning her back on the spirit. The undead lashed out, shredding the fabric of Petula's black wool coat. She let out an incantation as she held the soft cat close to her chest. Her words stunned the spirit. She slowly turned around to face it. A dark, faceless human-shaped spirit hung in the air. It flickered, but Petula's incantation held it present and in her control.

The thing had been trapped inside its vessel for so long that it had forgotten what it used to be. The only thing left was pure want.

The more recently dead usually hung on to their beliefs of what their bodies should look like and what their lives could be, but this creature didn't possess even half of that memory. Petula felt sad for it. Someone had done this to the spirit. They'd trapped it inside the vessel and prevented him or her from entering the afterlife.

The spirit screeched.

The cat clawed its way out of Petula's lap and made a run for it. She let it go.

The spirit screeched again.

It couldn't harm her, she was in control, but at least the theatrics would make anyone listening to them behind the attic door think there was a real struggle. A struggle to justify what she was about to do next. She would destroy the museum's showpiece and release the spirit from the mortal coil. It was the merciful thing to do, but Miss Wilkins wouldn't like it. But what Miss Wilkins didn't know wouldn't harm her. And if her actions ever came into the light of day, she would face the consequences from Miss Wilkins and the Necromantic Agency, her employers. What could they do? Kill her? They wouldn't dare.

1

Raising the Dead Is a Tricky Business

Amongst the thick leather-bound books scattered around him, a man worked at a pace to collect his belongings inside a doctor's bag. He pushed in stones, or, to be precise, crystals with drawn-on symbols. He worked methodically and carefully to get everything into the bag without invoking anything horrible from the darkness. His head wasn't in the right place to fight off monsters. In an ideal situation, he'd have more time to put his work-bag in order, but as it was, he was already running late. He'd forgotten tonight's appointment, and to make matters worse, his head felt groggy. Jeremiah was sure someone had slipped something into his drink at last night's poker game. He should be sober by now, but even as a new night crept in, he felt sick and thirsty. Jeremiah paused his packing.

Usually Jeremiah Black was nothing but self-confidence itself. His whole essence told him that he was the best necromancer there was. He could summon the dead back up just like that, even make them dance to his tune. His black silk shirt, long black leather jacket, and tight black trousers alone told the tale of his greatness, but now he found his gaunt legs tangled and his mind scattered.

Jeremiah flexed and squeezed his hands to stop them from shaking. A drink would help, but there was work to be done, so he shouldn't. Not with his new clients. They were the fastidious sort. But this shouldn't be that hard. He reached for the chest pocket of his jacket, where he kept his flask. He'd awoken the dead hundreds of times. So many times, in fact, he'd stopped counting. Half of the city was his to claim if he wanted it. A drink wouldn't do any harm. It would get his beat back on, quiet the whispers that chipped away his self-confidence. He took the flask out and took a sip. The first drink of tonight burned in his mouth.

One more item and he would be done with the packing.

Jeremiah put the flask back inside his jacket and plucked a small perfume bottle full of black liquid from the table. With the bottle, or vial, as he preferred to call it, he could do anything. It ensured that he was the best necromancer in the city. And tonight's job was important. He needed every piece of ammunition there was to take the edge off. He held the cold vial carefully between his fingers, moving it towards the bag. Jeremiah's shaking hands caused a tremor. He held the vial still and composed himself, wanting to take another sip from his flask.

A small creak echoed at the back of the room. Jeremiah shot a glance over his shoulder, but there was nothing out of the ordinary outside the gas lamp's circle. Just his study, full of bookshelves stacked with necromantic literature, ranging from silly fiction to the real deal, which altered the delicate balance between life and death. He swallowed and continued lowering the vial into the doctor's bag. One spill and everything would be doomed.

There was another creak; this time it came closer. It sounded like a floorboard being stepped on. He took a better hold of the perfume bottle and turned his head in the direction the noise had come from.

He saw a man standing between the bookshelves. Jeremiah bared his teeth, and said, "Come no closer, or I'll kill you."

The man made no move. Jeremiah was sure he could take him. He was no bigger than him. Even if he was, it wouldn't matter. One incantation from Jeremiah and the dead would tear the man apart.

"What do you want?" he barked.

No answer.

"There's nothing to steal here, and one spill from this and there's nothing left of you. No body, no soul, nothing." He peered at the man, not seeing far into the shadows the bookshelves cast. Anyway, Jeremiah was lying. The liquid didn't work that way. It could kill, true, but with a great effort on his part. And to be honest, it worked better for the undead. Jeremiah was sure the man in front of him was as alive as he. The man lacked the distinctive rotten smell of the dead.

"If I were you, I'd skip the wakening," the man said. He had a melancholic, melodic voice. Jeremiah was sure there was a hint of amusement in there.

"No one threatens me in my own home." Jeremiah spat the words out. The bottle between his fingers shook, but this time with rage rather than fear. The black liquid ocean shifted from side to side. A storm began to brew.

"It wasn't a threat; it was a friendly request," the man said, almost laughing out his words.

"Who do you think you are dealing with? Some common caster? I'm a certified necromancer. I'm Jeremiah Black. You made a big mistake stepping inside my home without permission."

"I know who you are, Jeremiah Black. And you look more like a poor excuse for a necromancer than the real deal with your dramatic dark clothes, charcoal-lined eyes, and cropped hair. And that top hat of yours with the skull and crossbones is a crime against fashion. I expected more from the greatest necromancer in the city, as you, Jeremiah, pronounce yourself to be," the man said.

And before Jeremiah could get a word out, the man was next to him, and he felt a punch to his left ribcage.

The stabbing sensation happened again, and again, feeling unreal and soft, as if it was happening to someone else. There was a haze, the kind of haze you get after drinking for several days straight, but the warm wetness spreading under his silk shirt felt real. Too real. Jeremiah put his hand to his side when the man stepped away from him.

He looked at his right hand, which was red. The bottle in his left hand dropped, but the man who'd attacked him caught it before it could smash against the floor. In an instant, the perfume bottle and its contents disappeared into the man's pocket.

Jeremiah collapsed to his knees and then crumpled onto the floor.

"You little fucker!" he let out, sounding winded.

Maroon-colored blood puddled all around him.

A knock sounded from the front door.

Jeremiah Black drew a deep breath in, trying to speak, but no words came out. He watched as the man walked away, unable to do anything as he slid out through a broken window.

There was another knock on the front door.

He tried to scream but couldn't.

And another knock.

Jeremiah stopped struggling and let go. He lay there motionless, frozen inside his own body, observing the world in sober alertness.

Not long after his killer slipped away, the front door was pushed open. Three men stepped in. Two of them were older gentlemen dressed in nice dark suits and top hats. The third one was similarly clothed, but he was a lot younger. He limped forward, leaning against his cane. He had been the one who contacted him.

"Morris," Jeremiah said.

"Mr. Black?" the tall and thin one asked. He had a dry, sour face and silver hair.

"I'm here," he said and stood up from his body, but he was pulled back inside.

"Oh no," another older man said when they got farther in

366

from the door. The wrinkled lines around the man's mouth made a huge "O" shape. His soft belly rose as he took a heavy breath in and looked around.

The three men stepped closer, inspecting him. The younger man, Morris, crouched to touch Jeremiah's neck, trying to find a pulse. When he found none, he shook his head. Jeremiah tried to grasp him, to pull him closer and ask for help, but his hand didn't budge.

"How unfortunate," the tall man said, the one with charismatic wrinkles and dashing hair. He'd taken his top hat off.

Morris Reinhardt stood up and said, "Dead as a doornail." He prodded Jeremiah one more time with his good leg. Morris was his age and at least half the age of the two men around him. He was a banker with a sharp wit, and he was a wiz when it came to clauses and numbers. Jeremiah knew him. They ran in the same social circles. And despite the cane, women and men alike were charmed by Morris. Even Jeremiah found his sideburns, which came down from his short-styled cut, and his somewhat dreamy, mysterious eyes convincing. Convincing enough to let them drag him into waking up their friend. Not that he had minded. The pay was good.

"What're we going to do?" the man with the soft belly asked.

"Now you wake me," Jeremiah said.

"We leave," the tall man replied.

"What about him?" Morris asked.

"Somebody else's problem," the tall man replied. "And we better leave before he attracts too much attention; we'll have to find someone else."

"What an inconvenience," Morris said.

"Yes," the tall man agreed and turned around.

Jeremiah watched Morris limp after the other men to the front door. He screamed after them, begging them not to leave him dead and alone. He begged them to send for a necromancer, but the three men didn't have his powers to see the dead. His screams went unheard. Of course, they knew he could be wakened; everyone in the city knew that. They just chose not to.

Before the front door closed behind the men, Jeremiah heard one of them, the tall one presumably, saying, "This is complete foolery. Doesn't he know we have a deadline to make?"

"It's not like he chose to die. He had quite a few stab wounds," Morris said.

"Yes, but he should know better. This is a lack of professionalism on his part."

"You can't—" the round man said.

The door closed behind them. Jeremiah was alone. He struggled free from his body, mumbling incantations he knew when alive. When he was free, he looked towards where his killer had gone and then at the door. He chose the door.

AUTHOR'S NOTE

"I write this not for the many, but for you; each of us is enough of an audience for the other."
-Seneca, Moral Letters to Lucilius, Letter VII

Hello and thank you for picking up Worth Of Luck. When I sat down to outline and write this book, I never imagined it would get into your hands. But here you are, reading it for my joy. This story was something I had to tell, and I hope you will enjoy it as much as I enjoyed writing it. The story grew from an idea of secret societies battling each other out in a kingdom of Leporidae Lop and turned more complex when I added on social issues. It is still humorous fantasy, but I'm helpless when it comes to the underdog.

Not all of us are fortunate enough to be born to a wealthy, kind, or decent enough family, or sometimes the circumstances we come across are impossible to overcome. I see no other out than empathy and compassion to our fellow creatures and a society that doesn't let its strong prey on those not so lucky.

As a writer, I know my duty is to point out those discrepancies in our lives and societies, and to add empathy. For me, there is no better way than through humor, which lets me say: "Look, the king wears no clothes." That is what I have done with Worth of Luck and continue to do with my other books in the series, and to entertain and delight you while I am at it. Without you, the reader, writing would be impossible.

Sincerely,
K.A. Ashcomb

ABOUT THE AUTHOR

K.A. Ashcomb grew up reading books by Terry Pratchett and other comical fantasy authors. After acquiring her MA in Comparative Religion, spiced with Social Psychology and Sociology, she found herself working behind a bookshop's counter. With tons of free time on her hands, she began to create stories about gods, unfortunate heroes, and other jerks to amuse herself. The stories grew bigger and bigger, and she had to put them on paper, and so *Worth Of Luck* was born.

When she isn't writing books or stories for video games, you can find her in the local forest reservation, roaming there while trying to find her way back to her keyboard, beloved books, and her two mischievous cats and her husband.

All the best,
K.A. Ashcomb

You can find me at: https://ashcombka.com